Phocaea
Sardis

Delphi
Athens
Ephesus
Miletus
Lade

Sparta

Akraia

Cyprus

Tyre

The Etruscan

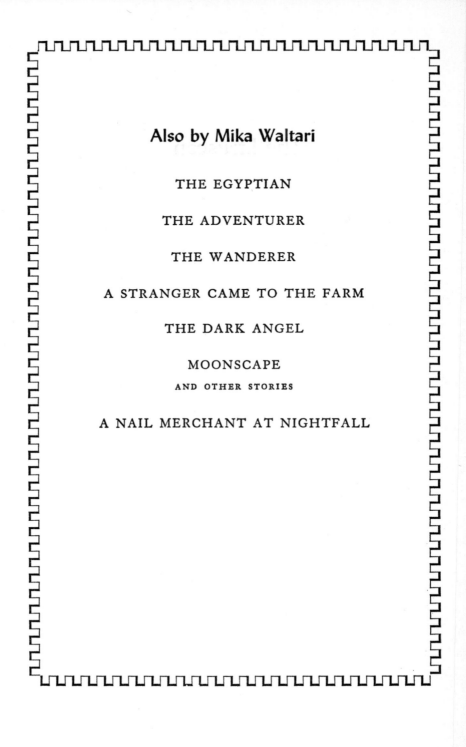

Also by Mika Waltari

THE EGYPTIAN

THE ADVENTURER

THE WANDERER

A STRANGER CAME TO THE FARM

THE DARK ANGEL

MOONSCAPE
AND OTHER STORIES

A NAIL MERCHANT AT NIGHTFALL

The Etruscan

By MIKA WALTARI

Translated by Lily Leino

G. P. Putnam's Sons
New York

Contents

The Etruscan

BOOK ONE

Delphi

I.

LARS TURMS the immortal, awakened to spring and saw that the land had once again burst into bloom.

I looked around my beautiful dwelling, saw the gold and silver, the bronze statues, the red-figured vases and the painted walls. Yet I felt no pride, for how can one who is immortal truly possess anything?

From among the myriad precious objects I took up a cheap clay vessel and for the first time in many years poured its contents into my palm and counted them. They were the stones of my life.

Then I returned the vessel with its pebbles to the feet of the goddess and struck a bronze gong. Servants entered silently, painted my face, hands and arms sacred red and clothed me in the sacred robe.

Because I did what I did for my own sake and not for my city or my people, I did not let myself be borne on the ceremonial litter but walked on my own feet through the city. When people saw my painted face and hands they stepped aside, children paused in their games, and a girl by the gate ceased playing her pipes.

I stepped out of the gate and descended into the valley along the same path that I once had followed. The sky was a radiant blue, birdsong echoed in my ears and the doves of the goddess cooed. The people toiling in the fields paused respectfully at sight of me, then turned their backs once more and continued their work.

I did not choose the easy road to the holy mountain, that which was used by the stonecutters, but the sacred stairs flanked by painted wooden pillars. They were steep stairs and I ascended them backward, looking down on my city the while, but although I stumbled many times, I did not fall. Even my attendants, who would have steadied me, were afraid,

9

for never before had anyone ascended the holy mountain in such a manner.

When I reached the sacred path the sun was at its zenith. Silently I passed the entrances to the tombs with their stone mounds, and passed also my father's tomb before I reached the summit.

Before me in every direction stretched my vast land with its fertile valleys and wooded hills. To the north gleamed the dark blue waters of my lake, from the west rose the tranquil cone that was the goddess' mountain, and opposite it the eternal dwellings of the deceased. All this had I found, all this had I known.

I looked about for an omen and saw on the ground the newly fallen feather of a dove. I picked it up, and as I did so saw beside it a small reddish pebble. This too I took into my hand. It was the last stone.

Then I stamped the ground lightly with my foot. "This is the place for my tomb," I said. "Hew it from the mountain and ornament it as befits my state."

My bedazzled eyes saw shapeless beings of light streaking through the skies as I had seen them only on rare occasions in the past. I raised my arms before me, palms down, and a moment later that indescribable sound which a man hears but once in his lifetime echoed through the cloudless sky. It was as the voice of a thousand trumpets, quivering through land and air, paralyzing the limbs but swelling the heart.

My attendants sank to the ground and covered their faces, but I touched my forehead, extended my other hand into space, and greeted the gods.

"Farewell, my era. The century of the gods has ended and another has begun, new in deeds, new in customs, new in thoughts."

To my attendants I said, "Arise and rejoice that you have been privileged to hear the divine sound of the changing era. It means that all who last heard it are dead and none among the living will hear it again. Only the yet unborn will have that privilege."

They still shook, as did I, with the trembling that comes to a person only once. Clutching the last stone of my life, I again stamped on the site of my tomb. As I did so a violent gust of wind swept over me, and I doubted no longer but knew that some day I would return. Some day I would rise from the tomb new of limb, to hear the roar of the wind under a cloudless sky, to smell the resinous fragrance of the pines in my nostrils and see the blue mound of the goddess's mountain before my eyes. If I remembered to do so, I would choose from among the treasures in my tomb only the humblest clay vessel, pour the pebbles into my palm, hold them one by one, and relive my past life.

Slowly I returned to my city and dwelling along the path over which I had come. The pebble I dropped into the black clay vessel before the goddess, then covered my face with my hands and wept. I, Turms the immortal, shed the final tears of my mortal being and yearned for the life that I had lived.

2.

It was the night of the full moon and the beginning of the spring festival. But when my attendants sought to wash the sacred color from my face and hands, to anoint me and to place a wreath of flowers around my neck, I sent them away.

"Take of my flour and bake the cakes of the gods," I said. "Choose sacrificial animals from my herd and also give gifts to the poor. Dance the sacrificial dances and play the games of the gods according to custom. But I myself shall retire to solitude." Nevertheless, I asked both augurs, both interpreters of lightning and both sacrificial priests to make certain that all was done as custom decreed.

I myself burned incense in my room until the air was heavy with the smoke of the gods. Then I stretched out on the triple mattress of my couch, crossed my arms tightly across my chest, and let the moon shine on my face. I sank into a sleep which was not sleep until my limbs became immobile. Then it was that the goddess's black dog came into my dream, but no longer barking and wild-eyed as before. It came gently, leaped into my lap, and licked my face. In my dream I spoke to it.

"I will not have you in your underworld guise, goddess. You have given me unwanted wealth and power that I have not craved. There are no earthly riches with which you could tempt me to content myself with you."

Her black dog vanished from my lap and the feeling of oppression passed. Then the arms of my lunar body, transparent in the moonlight, reached upward.

Again I rejected the goddess. "Not even in my heavenly shape will I worship you," I said.

My lunar body ceased to delude me. Instead, my guardian spirit, a winged being fairer than the fairest human, took shape before my eyes. She was more alive than any mortal as she approached and seated herself on the edge of my couch with a smile.

"Touch me with your hand," I implored, "that I may know you at last. I am tired of lusting for all that is earthly and desire only you."

"Not yet," she replied. "But some day you will know me. Whomever you have loved on earth you have loved only me in her. We two, you and I, are inseparable but always apart until that moment when I can take you in my arms and bear you away on my powerful wings."

"It is not your wings that I long for but you yourself," I said. "I want to hold you in my arms. If not in this life, then in some future life I shall compel you to assume a human shape so that I may discover you with human eyes. Only for that reason do I want to return."

Her slender fingers caressed my throat. "What a dreadful liar you are, Turms," she murmured.

I gazed on her flawless beauty, human yet flamelike. "Tell me your name that I may know you," I pleaded.

"And how domineering you are," she smiled. "Even if you knew it you could not rule me. But do not fear. When I finally take you in my arms I shall whisper my name in your ear, although you probably will have forgotten it when you awaken to the thunder of immortality."

"I don't want to forget it," I protested.

"You have done so in the past," she declared.

No longer able to resist, I extended my arms to embrace her. They closed over nothing, although I still saw her alive before me. Gradually the objects in the room became visible through her being. I sprang up with a start, my fingers clutching at moonbeams. Disconsolately I paced the room, touching the various objects, but my arms lacked strength to lift even the smallest. Again a feeling of oppression came over me and I struck the gong with my fist to summon a human companion. But no sound emanated from it.

When I awakened I was lying on the couch with my arms crossed tightly over my chest. Finding that I could move my limbs, I sat on the edge of the couch and hid my face in my hands.

Through the incense and the terrifying moonlight I tasted the metallic flavor of immortality and smelled its icy scent. Its cold flame flickered before my eyes, its thunder roared in my ears.

I rose defiantly, flung wide my arms and shouted, "I do not fear you, Chimera. I still live the life of a human. Not an immortal but a human among my own kind."

But I could not forget. I spoke again to her who ever hovered around me invisibly, protecting me with her wings.

"I confess that all I have done of my own selfish will has been wrong and harmful to myself as well as to others. Only in following your guidance, unknowingly and as one who walks in his sleep, have I unerringly done the right thing. But I must still learn for myself what I am and why I am thus."

Having clarified that, I taunted her. "It is true that you have done your utmost to make me believe, but I do not. So much a human am I still, I will believe only when I awaken in some other life to the roar of the storm and remember and know myself. When that happens I shall be your equal. Then we can better dictate our terms to each other."

I took the clay vessel from the feet of the goddess, took one pebble after another in my palm and remembered. And having remembered, I wrote down everything to the best of my ability.

3.

The majority of men never stoop to pluck a pebble from the ground and save it as a symbol of the end of one era and the beginning of another. Thus it is forgivable if relatives place in the vessel a heap of pebbles equaling in number the years and months of the deceased. In that case the pebbles reveal his age but nothing else. He has lived the ordinary life of a human and been content.

Nations also have their eras, known as the centuries of the gods. Thus we immortals know that the twelve Etruscan peoples and cities have been allotted ten cycles in which to live and die. We refer to them as lasting one thousand years because it is easy to say, but the length of a cycle may not necessarily be even one hundred years. It may be more or even less. We know only its beginning and its end from the unmistakable sign we receive.

A man seeks the certainty that cannot be had. Thus the soothsayers compare the liver of a sacrificed animal with a clay model which is divided into compartments, each bearing the name of a particular deity. Divine knowledge is lacking, therefore they are fallible.

Similarly, there are priests who have learned many rules of divining from the flight of birds. But when they are confronted by a sign with which they are not familiar they become confused and make their predictions blindly. I will not even mention the interpreters of lightning who ascend the holy mountains before a storm and confidently interpret the thunderbolts according to color and position in the vault of heaven, which they have quartered and orientated and divided into sixteen celestial regions.

But I shall say no more, for thus it must ever be. Everything grows rigid, everything ossifies, everything ages. Nothing is sadder than obsolescent and withering knowledge, fallible human knowledge instead of divine perception. A man can learn much, but learning is not knowledge. The only fountainheads of true knowledge are inward certainty and divine perception.

There are divine objects of such potency that the sick are healed by touching them. There are objects which protect their bearers and others which harm. There are sacred places which are recognized as sacred although no altar or votive stone marks their site. There are also seers who are able to view the past by holding an object. But no matter how convincingly they speak to earn their porridge and oil, it is impossible to know how much of what they say is true, how much merely dream or fabrication. Not even they themselves know. To that I can testify, for I myself have the same gift.

Nevertheless, something is retained in objects which have been used and loved by people for a long time and which are associated with good or evil. Something beyond the object itself. But all this is vague and dreamlike and fully as illusory as it is true. In the same manner a man's senses mislead him if they are fed only by his lust, the lust to see, to hear, to touch, to smell, to taste. No two persons ever see or taste the same thing in the same way. Nor does the same person hear or touch the same thing in the same way at different times. Something which is pleasing and desirable at this moment may in a short time be repulsive and worthless. Therefore a person who believes only in his senses lies to himself throughout his life.

But as I write this I know that I do so only because I am old and worn out, because life tastes bitter and the world offers nothing for which I yearn. In my earlier years I would not have written thus, although whatever I would have put down would have been equally true.

Why, then, should I write at all?

I write to conquer time and to know myself. But can I conquer time? That I will never know because I do not know whether writing which has been erased can survive. Thus I shall be content to write only that I may know myself.

But first of all I shall take in my hand a smooth black pebble and write how I had my first presentiment of what I really was, rather than that which I merely believed myself to be.

4.

It happened on the road to Delphi amidst gloomy mountains. When we had left the shore, lightning had flashed in the distant west above the mountain peaks, and upon our reaching the village the people warned the pilgrims against continuing the journey. It was autumn, they said, and a storm was about to break. Landslides might close the road or torrents sweep away the traveler.

14

But I, Turms, was on my way to be judged by the oracle at Delphi. Athenian soldiers had rescued me and granted me asylum on one of their ships when the people of Ephesus for the second time in my life had tried to stone me to death. Thus I did not stop to await the passing of the storm. The villagers lived off the pilgrims, stopping them coming and going under many pretexts. They prepared good food, offered comfortable beds and sold keepsakes of wood, bone and stone that they had made. I did not believe their warnings, for I was not afraid of storms or lightning.

Driven by guilt, I continued my journey alone. The air cooled, clouds rolled down the mountains, lightning began to flash around me. Deafening claps of thunder echoed ceaselessly through the valleys. Lightning cleft the boulders, rain and hail beat my body, squalls almost swept me into the gorges, stones scratched my elbows and knees.

But I felt no pain. While the lightning blazed around me as though to reveal its awesome strength, ecstasy gripped me for the first time in my life. Without realizing what I did I began to dance along the road to Delphi. My feet danced and my arms moved, not in a dance that I had learned from others, but in a dance that moved and lived in me. My whole body moved in joyous ecstasy.

Then it was that I knew myself for the first time. No evil could befall me, nothing could do me harm. As I danced on the road to Delphi the words of a strange language burst from my lips, words that I did not know. Even the rhythm of the song was strange, as were the steps of the dance.

Beyond the mountain wall I saw the oval valley of Delphi blackened by clouds and blurred by rain. Then the storm ended, the clouds rolled away and the sun shone upon the buildings, the monuments and the holy temple of Delphi. Alone and without guidance I found the sacred fountain, laid my pack on the ground, divested myself of my muddy garments, and dived into the purifying waters. The rain had made the round pool murky, but the water pouring from the lions' maws cleansed my hair and body. I stepped naked into the sunlight and the ecstasy still lingered, so that my limbs were like fire and I felt no cold.

Seeing the temple servants hastening toward me with fluttering robes and heads bound with sacred ribbons, I glanced upward. There, towering above everything and mightier even than the temple, was the black cliff over whose edge the guilty were flung. Black birds hovered over the gorge in the wake of the storm. I began running up the terraces toward the temple between the statues and monuments, disregarding the sacred way.

Before the temple I laid my hand on the massive altar and shouted, "I, Turms of Ephesus, evoke the protection of the deity and submit to the judgment of the oracle!"

I raised my eyes and on the frieze of the temple saw Artemis racing with her dog and Dionysus feasting. I knew then that I had farther to go. The servants tried to stop me but I pulled away and ran into the temple. Through the forecourt, by the giant silver urns, the costly statues and votive offerings I ran. In the innermost chamber I saw the eternal flame at a small altar and beside it the Omphalos, the center of the earth, black from the smoke of the centuries. On that sacred stone I laid my hand and surrendered to divine protection.

An indescribable feeling of peace emanated from the stone, and I looked around me, unafraid. I saw the holy tomb of Dionysus, the eagles of the great deity in the temple shadows above me, and knew that I was safe. The servants dared not enter. Here I would encounter only the priests, the consecrated, the interpreters of the divine word.

Alerted by the servants, the four holy men came in haste, adjusting their headbands and gathering their robes around them. Their faces were wry, their eyes swollen from sleep. They lived already on the threshold of winter, and they expected few pilgrims. That day, because of the storm, they had expected no one. Thus my arrival had disturbed them.

So long as I lay naked on the floor of the inner shrine with both arms around the Omphalos, they could not use violence on me. Nor were they anxious to lay hands on me before they had learned my identity.

They consulted one another in low tones, then asked, "Have you blood on your hands?"

I said quickly that I had not, and they were obviously relieved. Had I been guilty, they would have had to purify the temple.

"Have you sinned against the gods?" they asked then.

I deliberated for a moment and replied, "I have not sinned against the Hellenic gods. On the contrary, the sacred virgin, the sister of your deity, watches over me."

"Who are you then and what do you want?" they demanded querulously. "Why do you come dancing out of the storm and dive into the holiest waters without permission? How dare you disturb the order and customs of the temple?"

Fortunately it was not necessary for me to reply, for at that moment the Pythia entered, supported by her attendants. She was still a young woman, with a bare and direful face, dilated eyes and a swaying walk. She looked at me as though she had known me all her life, a glow suffusing her face as she began to speak.

"At last you have come, expected one! Naked you came on dancing feet, purified by the fountain. Son of the moon, the seashell, the sea horse, I know you. You come from the West."

It was in my mind to tell her that she erred badly, since I came from the East, as fast as oars and sails could travel. Nevertheless, her words moved me.

"Holy woman, do you really know me?"

She burst into wild laughter and drew still nearer. "Should I not know you! Arise and look into my face."

Under the compulsion of those eyes I released the sacred stone and stared at the woman. Before my eyes she changed into the rosy-cheeked Dione who had carved her name on an apple before tossing it to me. Then Dione faded and gave way to the black face of the statue of Artemis which had dropped from the sky at Ephesus. Again the face changed to that of a comely woman of whom I had only a dreamlike glimpse before she faded into the mists. Then I was staring into the violent eyes of the Pythia once more.

"I also know you," I said.

She would have embraced me had not the attendants restrained her. Her left hand reached toward me, touching my chest, and I felt strength flow into me from her hand.

"This youth is mine," she declared, "consecrated or not. Do not touch him. Whatever he may have done he has done in fulfillment of divine will, not his own. He is guiltless."

The priests muttered among themselves. "These are not divine words, for she is not seated on the sacred tripod. This is a false ecstasy. Take her away."

But she was stronger than her attendants and began to rage defiantly. "I see the smoke of fires beyond the sea. This man came with soot on his hands and face and with burns on his loins, but I have purified him. Hence he is pure and free to go and come as he wishes."

That much she spoke clearly and intelligently. Then she lapsed into a convulsion, foamed at the mouth and fell unconscious into the arms of her attendants, who carried her away.

The priests gathered around me, trembling and alarmed. "We must discuss this among ourselves," they said. "But fear not. The oracle has freed you, and obviously you are not an ordinary human since she went into a sacred ecstasy at the mere sight of you. However, because she was not seated on the sacred tripod, we cannot record her utterances. But we will bear them in mind."

They took laurel-wood ashes from the altar, rubbed my hands and feet with them and led me out of the temple. Servants meanwhile had brought my muddy clothes and pack from the edge of the fountain. When the priests fingered the fine wool of my robe they realized that I was not a lowly person. They were even more reassured when I handed them a purse filled with the lion-headed gold coins of Miletus and some silver stamped with the Ephesian bee. And I gave them also the two sealed wax tablets containing testimony on my behalf which they promised to read and thereafter question me.

So I spent the night in a sparsely furnished room and in the morning the servants came to me and advised me how to fast and purify myself so that my tongue and heart would be pure when I again confronted the priests.

5.

As I ascended to the deserted stadium of Delphi I saw the flash of a javelin, although the shadow of the mountain already lay heavy across the field. Again it flashed, rising into the air like an omen. Then I saw a youth, no older than myself but sturdier, running lightly to retrieve it.

I watched him as I ran around the track. His face was sullen, his body bore an ugly scar, and his muscles were knotty. Yet he exuded such an air of confidence and strength that I thought him to be the handsomest youth I had ever seen.

"Run with me!" I shouted. "I am tired of competing against myself."

He thrust the javelin into the ground and ran to join me. "Now!" he cried, and we set forth. Being lighter than he, I thought that I would win easily, but he ran effortlessly and it was all I could do to win by a hand.

We were both breathless and panting, although we tried to conceal it. "You run well," he conceded. "Now let us throw the javelin."

He had a Spartan javelin, and as I balanced it in my hand I strove not to show that I was unaccustomed to its weight. I gathered momentum and threw the javelin better than I had ever thrown before. It flew even farther than I had hoped, and as I ran to retrieve it and mark the throw I could not restrain a smile. I was still smiling when I extended the javelin to the youth, but he threw it effortlessly many lengths beyond my mark.

"What a throw that was!" I said admiringly. "But you are probably too heavy for the broad jump. Will you try?"

Even in the broad jump I surpassed him by only a hair's breadth. Silently he held out a discus. Again his toss swooped far beyond my mark like a hawk in flight. This time he smiled and said, "Wrestling will decide it."

Looking at him, I felt an odd reluctance to wrestle with him, not because I knew that his would be an easy victory, but because I had no desire to let him encircle me with his arms.

"You are better than I," I conceded. "The victory is yours."

After that we said nothing, but each pursued his own games in the empty stadium until he was sweating. When I went to the edge of the swollen brook he followed me hesitantly, and when I began washing and scouring myself with sand he did likewise.

"Will you rub my back with sand?" he asked.

I did so and he did the same for me, rubbing so hard that I pulled away and splashed water in his eyes. He smiled but did not stoop to indulge in such childish sport.

I pointed to the scar on his chest. "Are you a soldier?"

"I am a Spartan," he said proudly.

I looked at him with renewed curiosity, for he was the first Lacedaemonian I had ever seen. He did not seem brutal and unfeeling as Spartans were said to be. I knew that his city had no wall, boasting instead that the Spartan men were the only wall needed. But I also knew that they were not permitted to leave the city except in troops on their way to battle.

He read the question in my eyes and explained, "I also am a prisoner of the oracle. My uncle, King Cleomenes, had bad dreams about me and sent me away. I am a descendant of Herakles."

It was in my mind to say that, knowing the character of Herakles and his wanderings throughout the world, there were undoubtedly thousands of his descendants in various lands. But I looked at his rippling muscles and stifled the impulse.

Unasked, he began tracing his descent, then said in conclusion, "My father was Dorieus, recognized as the fairest man of his day. He likewise was disliked in his homeland and set out across the sea to win a new homeland for himself in Italy or Sicily. He fell there many years ago."

Frowning deeply, he suddenly demanded, "Why are you staring at me? Dorieus was my real father and now that I have left Sparta I have the right to use his name if I so choose. My mother used to tell me about him before I was seven and she had to give me up to the state. Because my legal father was unable to produce children, he sent Dorieus in secret to my mother, as in Sparta even husbands may meet their wives only by stealth and in secret. All this is true, and were it not for the fact that my real father was Dorieus, I would not have been banished from Sparta."

I could have told him that, since the Trojan War, Spartans had had good reason to suspect men and women of excessive beauty. But this was undoubtedly a matter of great sensitivity to him which I understood well because the circumstances of my own birth were even stranger.

We clothed ourselves in silence by the brook. The oval valley of Delphi darkened below us, the mountains gleamed violet. I was purified, I was alive, I was strong. In my heart was a glow of friendship for this stranger who had consented to compete with me without asking who or what I was.

Walking down the mountain path toward the buildings of Delphi, he glanced at me frequently from the corner of his eye and finally said, "I like you, although we Spartans usually shun strangers. But I am alone, and it is difficult to be without a companion when one has always been with other youths. Although I am no longer tied to the customs of my people, they bind me more strongly than fetters. And so I would rather be dead with my name inscribed on a gravestone than here."

"I also am alone," I said. "I came to Delphi of my own will either to be purified or to die. Life has no purpose if I am to be but a curse to my city and to all Ionia."

He looked at me skeptically under his damp, curly forelock. "Don't judge me before hearing," I pleaded. "The Pythia pronounced me innocent even though she was not chewing on the sacred bay leaf or sitting on the sacred tripod or breathing the noxious vapors from the gorge. The very sight of me sent her into a trance." Ionic skepticism made me smile and glance around cautiously. "She seemed to be a woman who is rather fond of men. Undoubtedly she is a holy person, but the priests must have great difficulties in interpreting her ravings to their satisfaction."

Dorieus raised a hand in alarm. "Don't you believe the oracle?" he demanded. "If you are blaspheming the deity I will have nothing to do with you."

"Don't be alarmed," I reassured him. "Everything has two sides, that which we see and that which we don't see. I doubt the earthly aspect of

20

the oracle, true, but that does not mean that I do not recognize her and submit to her judgment though it cost me my life. A man must believe in something."

"I don't understand you," he said in amazement.

We went our separate ways that night, but on the next day, or perhaps it was the one following, he came to me and demanded, "Was it you, man of Ephesus, who set fire to the temple of the Lydian earth goddess at Sardis and thus burned the entire city?"

"That is my crime," I confessed. "I, Turms of Ephesus, alone am guilty of the burning of Sardis."

To my surprise Dorieus' eyes began to twinkle and he clapped me on the shoulders with both hands. "How can you consider yourself a criminal, you who are the hero of the Hellenes? Don't you know that the burning of Sardis has lit the flames of revolt all over Ionia from the Hellespont to Cyprus?"

His words filled me with horror. "In that case the men of Ionia are mad! It is true that, with the arrival of the Athenian ships, we ran into Sardis in three days like a flock of sheep after a ram. But we were unable to conquer the city and its fortifications and ran right out again even faster than we had gone in. The Persian auxiliaries slaughtered many of us, and in the darkness and confusion we even killed one another. No," I said, "our expedition to Sardis was not a heroic one. To make matters worse, we became involved with some women who were holding a midnight festival outside the gates of Ephesus. The Ephesians ran out and killed even more of us. So purposeless was our expedition and so disgraceful our flight."

Dorieus shook his head. "You do not speak like a true Greek. War is war and whatever occurs must be made to reflect glory to the fatherland and honor to the dead, regardless of how they fell. I don't understand you."

"I am not a Hellene," I told him, "but a foreigner. Many years ago, near Ephesus, I found myself at the foot of an oak which had been split by lightning. When I came to my senses a ram was bucking me and dead sheep lay all around me. A thunderbolt had torn off my clothes and left a black streak on my loins. But Zeus did not succeed in killing me even though he tried."

6.

Winter was almost upon us when next the four priests summoned me. By that time I was lean from fasting, trim from exercise, and in every way so purified that I shivered. As old men are wont to do, they made me begin at the beginning and tell what I knew about the revolt of the Ionian cities and the murder or exile of the tyrants whom the Persians had installed as rulers.

I related everything that I knew about our shameful attack on the satrap city of Sardis. Then I said, "Artemis of Ephesus is a divine goddess and because she took me under her protection when I arrived in Ephesus I owe her my life. In recent years, however, the black goddess Cybele of Lydia has begun to compete for favor with the Hellenes' Artemis. The Ionians are a frivolous people, always seeking new experiences, and during the rule of the Persians many of them traveled to Sardis to sacrifice to Cybele and participate in her shameful secret rites. When I joined the Athenian expedition I was told, and had full reason to believe, that the uprising and war against the Persians was at the same time the holy virgin's war against the black goddess. So I felt that I was performing a worthy deed in setting fire to the temple of Cybele. It was not my fault that a strong wind began to blow just then, spreading the flames over the reed-thatched roofs and burning the entire city."

Once again I related our flight and skirmishes with the Persians. Then, wearying of my narration, I said, "But you have the wax tablets which I brought with me. Believe them if you do not believe me."

"We have opened and read them," they replied. "We also have determined the facts about the Ionian events and the expedition to Sardis. It is in your favor that you do not glorify them but rather regret your part in them. Although there are fools who laud this expedition as the Hellenes' most glorious exploit, the burning of a temple—even that of the Asian Cybele, whom we abhor—is a serious matter, for once temples begin to be burned, not even the gods of the Hellenes will be safe."

At my request they re-read the wax tablets and permitted me also to read them. The first of the two messages began:

Artemisia of the Ephesian temple of Artemis greets the holy council of Apollo's priests at Delphi. As the clother of the virgin goddess, I am most familiar with her manifestation and her rituals and can declare that Turms of Ephesus has gained her full approval. For that reason I confidently entrust him to the protection of our divine brother Apollo. Let the oracle free him since he did no wrong but rather good. It was the goddess herself who guided his hand when he tossed the blazing torch into that accursed temple.

22

It then described my arrival in Ephesus and my redemption by Hera-kleitos, brother of the sacrificial king, and concluded:

Live in health and do justice to the boy. He is a fair youth.

The other wax tablet began as follows:

Epenides, authorized by the Council of Elders, respectfully greets the most holy oracle at Delphi and her priests. At the request of our sacrificial king we urge you righteously to condemn the blasphemer, rebel and temple-burner Turms. The burning of Sardis was the greatest calamity that could have befallen Ionia.

The message concluded:

We live in evil times, therefore let Turms be cast off the cliff lest he bring about still greater harm to our city than he has already. When we have been informed of his death we will be glad to send a silver tripod for the inner shrine.

Having read this malicious message which purported to defend me, I said angrily, "Do they hope to appease the Persians by cowardice? No, they are in the same boat as the other Ionian cities. No matter what my origin, I am now proud that I am not a native Ephesian."

As soon as the words were out I became confused. The priests noticed it and asked, "What, then, is your origin?"

"Lightning struck me outside Ephesus and more than that I do not know. I was ill for months thereafter."

Carefully weighing my words, I told them how at the age of ten I had been sent from Sybaris in Italy to Miletus for safety. When the inhabitants of Miletus heard how the men of Croton had leveled Sybaris to the ground and diverted a river to flow over the ruins, they grieved so much they clipped their hair short. But as their hair grew again, they forgot the claims of hospitality and beat me. I had been apprenticed first to a baker and then to a shepherd, until the beatings had prompted me to flee. Then, near Ephesus, the lightning had struck me.

The priests of Delphi raised their hands in dismay. "How can we solve this troublesome problem? Turms is not even a Greek name. But he cannot be an orphan, for he would not have been sent from Sybaris to safety. The four hundred families of that city were well aware of what they did. Many barbarians lived there to acquire Greek culture, but if the boy were a barbarian, why was he sent to Miletus instead of to his home?"

My self-esteem prompted me to say, "Look closely at me. Is my face that of a barbarian?"

The four old men with the divine bands of the gods around their heads studied me. "How should we know?" they asked. "Your clothes are Ionian, your education Greek. There are as many faces as there are people. An alien is not recognized by his face but by his clothes, hair, beard and speech."

As they watched me they began to blink. Then they averted their eyes and glanced uneasily at one another, for a divine fever had permeated me after my fasting and purging, and a divine light glowed in my eyes. At that moment I saw through those four old men. So jaded were they by their knowledge that they no longer had faith in themselves. Something in me was more powerful than they. Something in me knew more.

Winter was near and soon the god would depart for the farthest north, for the land of lakes and swans, and Delphi would be left to Dionysus. Storms raged at sea, ships sought harbors, pilgrims no longer came to Delphi. The elders yearned for peace, shunned decisions, and looked forward only to the warmth of the braziers and the smoky drowsiness of winter.

"Old men," I said, "give me peace and yourselves peace as well. Let us step under the open sky and wait for an omen."

We went outside, the elders clutching their robes to them as they watched the somber sky. Suddenly the bluish feather of a dove fluttered down and I caught it in my hand.

"This is the omen!" I cried exultantly. Only later did I realize that a flock of doves had swirled to flight somewhere high above us. Still I considered the feather a sign.

The priests gathered around me. "The feather of a dove!" they marveled. "The dove is the Cythereans' bird. Behold, Aphrodite has thrown her golden veil over him. His face is radiant!"

A sudden gust of wind caught our robes and a distant flicker of lightning touched a mountain peak to the west. The rumble of thunder echoed in the valley of Delphi.

We waited for yet another moment but when nothing more happened the priests went into the temple and left me in the anteroom. I read the maxims of the seven wise men on the wall, looked at the silver vessels of Croesus and the figure of Homer. The smell of the holy bay wood burning in the eternal fire of the altar reached my nostrils.

At last the priests returned and pronounced judgment: "You are free to go where you will, Turms of Ephesus. The gods have given their signs, the Pythia has spoken. Not your will but that of the gods is fulfilled in you. Continue to worship Artemis as you have in the past and make offerings to Aphrodite who saved your life. But the god of Delphi neither condemns you nor assumes your guilt, for that is the responsibility of Artemis, who has revolted against the Asian goddess."

"Where am I to go?" I asked.

"Go to the West whence you once came. So says the Pythia and so say we."

Disappointed, I asked, "Is that the god's command?"

"Certainly not!" they cried. "Didn't you hear that the Delphic god will have nothing to do with you? It is merely good advice."

"I am not consecrated to Artemis," I said, "but at the time of the full moon she has appeared to me in dreams accompanied by a black dog. In her underworld guise of Hecate she has appeared whenever I have slept in the temple on the night of the full moon at the request of the priestess. Thus I know that I shall yet be wealthy. When that happens I shall send a votive offering to this temple."

But they rejected it, saying, "Send no offering to the Delphic god, for we will not accept it."

They even asked the keeper of the treasury to return my money, withholding only the cost of my maintenance and purifications while a prisoner of the temple. So suspicious were they of me and of everything which at that time came from the East.

7.

I was free to leave, but Dorieus had not yet received his answer from the Delphic priests. Defiantly we left the temple grounds and spent our time by the wall, carving our names into the soft stone. There on the ground, bare, lay the natural rocks which had been worshiped as the sacred rocks of the underworld deities a thousand years before the coming of Apollo to Delphi.

Dorieus lashed at the rocks impatiently with a willow switch. "I have been trained for war and for life with my own kind. Solitude and idleness merely breed foolish thoughts. I begin to doubt the oracle and her withered priests. After all, my problem is political, not divine, and as such can be better solved with the sword than by chewing on bay leaves."

"Let me be your oracle," I suggested. "We are living in a period of upheaval. Go east with me, across the sea to Ionia, where they have danced the dance of freedom. Persian reprisals threaten the insurgent cities. A trained soldier would be welcome there and might win much booty and even rise to be commander."

He said reluctantly, "We men of Sparta do not love the sea, nor do we interfere in matters beyond the sea."

"You are a free man," I insisted, "and no longer bound by the prejudices of your people. The sea is glorious even when it surges with foam, and the cities of Ionia are beautiful, neither too cold in the winter nor too hot in the summer. Be my companion and go east with me."

At that he suggested, "Let us each toss a sheep's bones to indicate the direction that we must follow."

By the rocks of the underground gods we tossed the sheep's bones three times each before we believed them. Each time they clearly pointed westward, away from Ionia.

"There is something wrong with them," said Dorieus in disgust. "They are not prophetic."

His words unconsciously revealed his desire to join me in the war against the Persians. With feigned reluctance I therefore said, "I myself have seen a replica of Hecataeus' map of the world. Undoubtedly the Great King is a formidable opponent, for he rules a thousand nations from Egypt to India."

"The stronger the opponent the more honorable the battle," retorted Dorieus.

"I have nothing to fear," I observed. "How could human weapons harm me when a thunderbolt failed to do so? I believe myself to be invulnerable. But it is different with you, so I will no longer try to persuade you to join me in an uncertain venture. The bones point west. Believe them."

"Why don't you go west with me?" he asked. "As you said, I am free, but my freedom is bleak unless I have a companion with whom to share it."

"Both the bones and the priests indicated the west, but it is precisely because of that that I shall go east. I must prove to myself that omens and divine warnings cannot prevent my doing what I will."

Dorieus laughed. "You are contradicting yourself."

"You don't understand," I said. "I want to prove to myself that I cannot escape my fate."

At that moment the temple servants came for Dorieus. He rose from the rock, his face alight, and ran toward the temple. I waited for him by the large sacrificial altar.

26

When he returned his head was bowed. "The Pythia has spoken and the priests have studied the omens. Sparta is threatened by a curse should I ever return. Therefore I must sail beyond the sea. They recommend that I go west, where any tyrant of a wealthy city would be happy to take me into his service. My grave will lie in the west, they said, and there too I will find undying fame."

"Hence we shall sail east." I smiled. "You are still young. Why should you unnecessarily hasten to your grave?"

On that very day we left for the coast, only to find that the sea was stormy and that the ships had ceased to sail. And so we undertook the journey by land, spending our nights in deserted shepherds' shelters. After we had passed Megara we had to decide how best to reach Ionia. I had friends in Athens among those who had participated in the expedition to Sardis, but because a conservative faction had gained power there the friends might not wish to be reminded of their past.

Corinth, on the other hand, was the most hospitable of Greek cities. From its two harbors ships sailed both east and west and even Phoenician vessels put in there freely. I had also heard that strangers were not shunned there.

"Let us go to Corinth," I suggested. "There we will hear the freshest news from Ionia and will be able to sail in the spring at the latest."

Dorieus became glum. "We are friends, and as an Ionian you are more familiar with travel and cities than I. But as a Spartan I cannot follow another's advice without protest."

"Then let us toss the sheep's bones once more."

I drew the cardinal points on the sand according to the sun and indicated the positions of Athens and Corinth as well as I could. Dorieus tossed the bones and they indisputably pointed west.

Morosely he said, "Let us go to Corinth. But this is my decision and not yours."

Because his will was stronger than mine, I confessed, "I am pampered by Ionian customs. My mind has been spoiled by the teachings of a sage who despised people. Whatever increases knowledge consumes the will. Hence let us obey your will and journey to Corinth."

His face brightened, he smiled, ran and threw his javelin as far as he could in the direction of Corinth. But when we reached it we saw that it had struck a rotted piece of ship's rail that had been washed up by the sea. We both felt the omen to be unfavorable although we said nothing and avoided each other's eyes. Dorieus pulled loose the javelin and we set off in the direction of Corinth without a backward glance.

8.

In Corinth a stranger is not compelled to stay with friends, for the city has inns where one can obtain food and lodgings. Nor is a stranger judged by his face, clothes or even the color of his skin, but solely by the weight of the bag in which he carries his money. I suspect that the majority of the city's residents follow no honest trade but have as their sole profession the aiding of strangers to spend their money as rapidly as possible.

Upon our arrival we found many refugees from the Ionian cities. Most of them were wealthy people who, though they feared freedom and the will of the people, feared Persian vengeance even more. They were certain that reprisals awaited all the Ionian cities which had banished their tyrants, torn down the Persian buildings and replaced the ridge-stones of their walls. Many of the refugees were waiting for spring so that they might sail on the merchant vessels to the large Greek cities in Sicily or Italy and thus be as far from the Persians as possible.

"In the west is a greater Greece with rich cities and room to breathe," they said. "The future lies in the West, while only destruction and ceaseless oppression lie in the East."

But they had to admit that the uprising had spread as far as Cyprus, that Ionian ships ruled the sea, and that all the Ionian cities were again participating in the revolt.

With the arrival of spring we sailed to Ionia on one of the first vessels.

BOOK TWO

Dionysius of Phocaea

I.

IN THE war against the Persians I won fame as a man who laughed because he did not fear death. Dorieus for his part became famous for the sense of security provided by his leadership.

But when the Persians had blockaded Miletus by land, Dorieus said, "Although Miletus still protects the Ionian cities which lie behind its back, every Ionian here fears for his native city and that fear is responsible for the confusion around us. Besides, the Persians are stronger on land than we are. Our fleet, however, is still intact behind the Lade peninsula."

Dorieus was now a bearded giant with a crest of plumes on his helmet and silver tracings on his shield. Looking around him he said, "This city with its wealth and its impregnable walls has become a trap for me. I am not accustomed to defending walls, for a Spartan's shield is his only wall. Turms, my friend, let us leave Miletus. This city already smells of death!"

"Should we forego firm ground and choose a swaying deck for our battleground?" I asked. "After all, you hate the sea and your face pales when the ship rolls."

But Dorieus was firm. "It is summer and the sea is calm. Besides, I am heavily armored and can fight on deck where the air is fresh. A vessel moves, walls do not. Let us go to Lade and look around."

We let ourselves be rowed to Lade. It was easy, since boats continually plied the waters between the city and the peninsula. Provisions, fruit and wine were regularly brought to the fleet and the sailors in turn ceaselessly visited the golden city.

At Lade we saw innumerable warships from all the Ionian cities, the largest being those from Miletus. Daily the vessels streamed out through the narrow channel to the open sea where they arranged themselves in formation, oarblades gleaming in the sunlight. Then, increasing their speed until the water foamed, they practiced ramming enemy ships with their huge underwater metallic heads.

By far the greater number of ships, however, were beached along the shores of the island where their crews had spread out sails to protect themselves from the sun. The entire island echoed with the cries of peddlers, the brawling of wine-drinkers, the arguments of the commanders, and the usual Greek chatter. But many of the men slept through the noise in sheer exhaustion.

Dorieus talked to several sailors. "Why are you lying here, drinking wine, when the Persians' fleet is approaching? They are said to have as many as three or four hundred warships."

"Let us hope that they have a thousand," replied the men, "so that this dreary war will soon be over. We are free Ionians, skilled on land and even more skilled at sea, where the Persians have never yet bested us."

But having boasted a while, the men began to complain. "We are worried only about our ambitious and war-mad commanders who compel us to row back and forth in the heat of midday and treat us more like slaves than the Persians would. Our hands are full of blisters and the skin is peeling from our faces."

They showed us their hands which were in truth blistered and torn, for these men were city dwellers who had led sheltered lives at their various trades. They felt that it was senseless to row back and forth and exhaust the crews.

"So," they said, "we have chosen new and wiser commanders. Now we are resting and gathering our strength so that we will be like lions when the Persians attack."

As the evening grew cool and the calm surface of the sea turned wine-colored, the last five vessels came towards their camp site on the island. They were only penteconters, but their fifty oars rose and fell, rowed and backed water as smoothly and rhythmically as though a single man had been at the sweeps.

Dorieus looked upon them favorably. "Let us find out from which city these vessels come and who their commander is."

When the oars had been pulled in, the rowers jumped into the water to beach the galleys. At the same time some exhausted men were tossed overboard and sufficiently revived in the water so that they could crawl to shore, where they collapsed on the sands. A few would have drowned had not their companions dragged them to safety. The galleys bore no decorations or figures of deities, but they were strong, narrow and seaworthy, and stank of tar and pitch.

We waited until the campfires had been lighted. When those still on the shore caught the smell of porridge and root vegetables, bread and oil, they dragged themselves towards the pots. Then we joined the men and asked their identity.

"We are poor and humble men from Phocaea," they replied, "and our commander is Dionysius, a brutal and merciless man whom we would kill if we dared."

But as they spoke they laughed, and the food tasted good to them even though it was not rich like that served on the ships of Miletus. They pointed out their commander who in appearance was no different from them, merely a large, bearded and very dirty man.

Dorieus went to him, clanking his leg guards, waving the plumes on his helmet and flashing his silver-ornamented shield.

"Dionysius, commander of the Phocaean ships, hire me and my friend to fight the Persians with you."

Dionysius roared with laughter. "If I had the money I would certainly hire you to be my ship's emblem, for your bold appearance would be enough to frighten the Persians. I myself have only a leather helmet and breastplate and I do not fight for money but for my city's and my own glory. It is true that, in addition to glory, I hope to seize a few Persian ships for their loot. Otherwise my men will kill me and throw me overboard, which they threaten to do daily."

"Don't anger my friend," I said. "He is slow to laughter. Nowadays a heavily armored marine is paid five and even ten drachmas a day."

Dionysius retorted, "I also am slow to laughter, perhaps even more so than your friend. But these days I have learned to laugh readily. More Persian gold is circulating in this camp than I would have believed possible. We drink and gorge ourselves, dance and sing, boast and argue, and even I, a gruff man, have learned to amuse my men. But the craziest thing I have yet heard is that you two apparently experienced warriors are volunteering to join my forces although I have neither striped sails nor bracelets on my arms."

"We are looking at the matter as soldiers," said Dorieus. "With or without wages we would rather fight on a vessel whose oars obey the wishes of the commander than serve on a ship whose crew willfully chooses its own leaders. I am not familiar with naval warfare, but on the basis of what I have seen at Lade today you are the only true sailor."

Dionysius listened and took a liking to us. Dorieus and I both had our pay and some Persian gold with which we bought several armfuls of sacrificial meat from Poseidon's altar for the crew, as well as some wine, much to Dionysius' amazement.

"We are Phocaeans," he told us that night, "and as such we live and die on the sea. Our forefathers established a colony in Massilia, far beyond the western sea. Our fathers learned the art of naval warfare while fighting the Tyrrhenians in the west, but did not return to teach us their skill. Thus we have had to learn for ourselves."

To prove his point he suddenly ordered the alert to be blown on the conchs. The men, awakened from their deep sleep, stumbled to the ships and in the darkness untied the masts, raised and wedged them into place and unfurled the sails before I had time to clamber onto the deck. Despite their speed Dionysius flailed at them with a length of rope, cursed and roared and called them snails.

The din awakened all the other camps on the island, alerts were sounded and the rumor spread that the Persians were coming. Many wept in fear and attempted to conceal themselves in the bushes. The commanders shouted orders in vain and the confusion on the island was even greater than it had been during the day. When it became known that Dionysius had blown on the conchs merely to train his men to act in the darkness, the commanders came at us with bared weapons and threats to kill us if we again disturbed their sleep. But Dionysius' men ran toward them with taut ropes over which they stumbled, losing their shields and swords. Had not the men been so sleepy, a full war might have broken out among the Ionians.

2.

Naval warfare is merciless warfare and no land battle can be compared to it. Having experienced it, I will not speak too harshly of the ships of Miletus and its allies, for they were undeniably excellent and their crews fearless. After they had grumbled a while the men rowed out to sea and exhausted themselves at the oars. Nothing is more dangerous than a sweep in the hands of an inexperienced man, for it can strike his head or snap his ribs. I know it well, for Dionysius thrust an oar into my hand and it took the skin off my palms within a day.

Miletus sent out target vessels filled with logs and twigs that kept them afloat despite the gashes in their sides. But many commanders refused to attack the targets, fearing that their bronze rams would be twisted, their oars would snap and the galleys would burst at the seams.

Dionysius however declared, "We must test the strength of our vessels and rams as well as our ability to disengage ourselves quickly once we have struck."

With the first crash I toppled off the bench, struck my head and almost lost my oar. From the deck I heard the sound of clanking from prow to stern as though a slave had dropped an armful of bronze dishes onto a paved street. But it proved to be only Dorieus who had lost his balance when we rammed the target.

When he had had evidence of my good will Dionysius released me and, because I could read and write, took me with him on deck. He taught me how to recognize the various signals and trumpet calls that were used to direct the unified movements of the galleys. Upon receiving wax tablets from the city and the fleet's council, he had me read them aloud and write replies. Previously he had tossed them overboard. After I had shown him how, he wrote a short message and as a result received, to his great surprise, a sacrificial bull, three sheep and a boat-load of fruit and root vegetables. I explained that Phocaea was obligated to contribute the same amount of provisions to the allied depot at Miletus, where there were also available flute players, oil, wine, and copper plaques decorated with lion heads to be worn as badges of rank by the helmsmen.

"This is unbelievable," muttered Dionysius. "Although I wept, cursed and stamped my foot at the depot, I wasn't given even a sack of flour for my ships. Whereas you make me rich by merely drawing letters in wax. Perhaps this war isn't as bad as I had thought."

The entire fleet had begun to suspect that the war had turned for the worse. Only the authority of Miletus kept the fleet intact, for the world's richest city, mother of a hundred colonies, could not be permitted to fall.

Then came a night when the sky over the city turned red and word spread that the Persians had robbed the Ionian temple of Apollo and set it on fire as a signal to their fleet. As I watched the glow I suddenly knew that the Persians were avenging the burning of the temple of Cybele at Sardis. It was fortunate for me that I was at the Phocaean camp, for had I remained in Miletus and been recognized I would surely had been killed by the enraged populace.

Fear and confusion gripped Lade, but during the night the men grew calmer. Many felt that the Persians had brought a curse upon themselves by destroying the oracle, others again were certain that nothing could save Ionia since the god had been unable to protect even his own temple. But all the men purified themselves, braided their hair, anointed their faces and donned their best garments in preparation for battle.

3.

When the sky lightened, a thick column of smoke was still rising from the city as a signal to the hundreds of Persian galleys which had rowed out to sea to engage us in battle. To the sound of trumpet and conch we rowed out to meet them in the battle formation determined by the council, the larger vessels in the center and the lighter on either side. The golden city of Miletus fell behind us. Progress was slow, for many oars snapped and the ships got in one another's way. The closer we came to the Persians the closer the vessels hugged one another for mutual protection.

We saw the silver and bronze glimmer of the Phoenician ships with the frightening figures of their deities. But we also saw Greek ships from Cyprus as well as other Ionian galleys in the enemy's formation. Ionian prisoners were sacrificed on the Phoenician vessels and their blood was spilled into the water under the prows.

The sea was filled with Persian ships. But the allied fleet likewise covered the sea. Mallets began beating out a quickened rhythm on the brass gongs, the song of the oarsmen became frenzied. The water churned under the prows as the two rows of vessels sped toward each other. My throat was dry, my stomach tense with fear. Then I knew only the roar and the crash, the utter confusion, the splash of water and the screams of the dying.

We were fortunate in the first attack. Our ship under Dionysius' command rowed at an angle towards the enemy's galleys as though deliberately presenting their sides, then suddenly turned and rammed into the nearest vessel. It tilted over us, its men falling into the water and onto our deck. Arrows whistled through the air. Alternately rowing and backing water, we strove to free ourselves of the sinking ship. But as we pulled loose our stern crashed into another galley and men swarmed aboard. Our deck groaned under the weight of combat.

All five of our ships were tangled in a helpless knot among the enemy galleys. Our rowers ran to the decks with their weapons but many of them fell before the Persians' arrows. In the confusion I found myself beside Dorieus on the deck of a Phoenician vessel, and before I even knew how it had happened we had taken the galley, flung the deity on its prow into the sea, and forced into the water all those who dared not fight and fall on the blood-stained deck.

But because of the meagerness of our forces we were compelled to abandon the ship and leave it drifting with broken oars. When the tumult had stilled and Dionysius had summoned his ships, all five

34

responded and we saw that we had broken the enemy's front. With the collective strength of our five galleys we surged toward the center where the magnificent vessels of Miletus were engaging the enemy.

By midday our penteconter was sinking beneath us and to save ourselves we were obliged to capture a Phoenician bireme. When Dionysius had raised his emblem he began to look around.

"What does that mean?" he demanded.

We saw sinking and drifting ships, swimmers and floating bodies, and men clutching oars and fragments of wood. Beyond them the Ionian fleet, which had remained behind to protect the strait of Lade, was rowing full speed towards our rear and before we realized what was happening it was attacking the vessels of its allies.

"They waited to see which side would be victorious," said Dionysius bitterly. "With this deed they are bargaining for clemency for their cities. The goddess of victory has abandoned Ionia."

Nevertheless we continued to fight and lost two vessels in the unequal battle. We did, however, manage to rescue the survivors so that the three remaining galleys were fully manned. Dionysius ordered the Phoenician oar-slaves, whom he did not trust, to jump into the sea, then disengaged himself from the battle and turned his vessels towards the open waters. Many Ionian ships were fleeing northward, pursued by the relentless Persians. The Ionian oarsmen now had need of the strength that they had gathered while lying under their sails for weeks.

As one of the participants I should have more to tell about the sea battle at Lade. But I was inexperienced in naval warfare and my eye could not easily distinguish one vessel from another. Most indicative of my inexperience is the fact that I was amazed to see the heaps of treasure chests, expensive weapons, sacrificial vases and urns and gold jewelry on our ships. While I had been fighting for my life, Dionysius and his men had had time to rescue the treasure in the vessels they had captured, and hastily to cut off arms and thumbs that yielded bracelets and rings.

Dionysius was pleased with the Phoenician galley that he had seized. He rapped its cedar planks, inspected its accommodations and the placement of its rowers' benches, and cried, "What a ship! If I had a hundred like it and each manned by Phocaeans, I could conquer every sea."

He did not smash the deity's figure but made it an offering. "Side with me, Phoenician god, whatever your name may be, and fight for us." He made no changes on the ship other than painting large eyes on its prow so that it would find its way even on distant seas.

By nightfall the sea around us was deserted. Dionysius made no attempt to land but had the vessels proceed within calling distance of one another, with the rowers alternating at the oars. The moans of the wounded echoed through the ship and Dionysius' only remedy was to wash the wounds with sea water and cover them with tar. Dorieus had acquired numerous bruises. He also had been struck on the head by an oar with such force that his scalp had split before he had succeeded in removing his helmet.

Seeing the misery around me in the dark of night and the frightening emptiness of the sea, I was ashamed of my own invulnerability and wept aloud, something I had not done since Herakleitos had banished me from his house, calling me ungrateful. I had danced the dance of freedom and helped the people to banish Hermadoros from Ephesus, and Herakleitos had been unable to forgive me.

4.

When I awakened the sun was high, the water was murmuring under the prow, the oarsmen were singing in time with the bronze beat, and to my surprise I saw from the sun that we were going southward instead of northward to Phocaea.

Dorieus was seated at the prow, holding a wet cloth to his head. I asked him, in the name of all the sea gods, where we were going, for there were brown hills to the left of us and shadowy blue islands to the right.

"I don't know," said Dorieus, "and I don't care. There's a swarm of bees in my head and the very sight of the sea makes me ill."

The wind had picked up and the waves were beating at our sides, occasionally splashing in through the oar ports. Dionysius was cheerfully arguing with the helmsman about shadows and landmarks.

"Where are we bound?" I demanded. "You are taking us into Persian waters."

Dionysius laughed. "The Ionian ships are fleeing northward to their respective cities, but we are behind the Persian fleet and no one would think of looking for us here."

A dolphin leaped into the air, baring its glistening loins. Dionysius pointed to it. "Can't you see that the sea nymphs are tempting us with their rounded hips? Any sign that takes us farther from the Persians and lost Ionia is a favorable one." I could see from the glint in his eyes that he was jesting and that he had already made his decision.

He indicated a large blue island before us, signaled to the helmsman, and said, "That is Cos, island of the healers. Stop talking and go below to see how many of us need a coin in our mouths to pay the ferry."

36

Leaving behind the leaping dolphin, the glorious sea breeze and the chant of the rowers, I descended to the bottom of the vessel where the wounded lay on the blood-slippery planks. A feeble light shone through the oar ports and the moaning had ceased.

"A few are dead," I told Dionysius, "others cannot lift a hand, and still others are trying to sit up and are calling for food and water."

"Throw the dead to Poseidon and his nymphs," said Dionysius. "I shall take with me only those who are able to reach the deck either on foot or on their bellies. The others we shall leave at the temple of the healer on Cos."

He shouted the same instructions to the two vessels following us. The men of Phocaea unclothed the dead, thrust a coin into the throat of each and tossed them into the sea. Most of the wounded managed to drag themselves on deck, cursing and groaning and calling upon the gods to aid them, for no one wanted to be left behind.

Not all the men reached the deck. Under the strain some of their wounds reopened, their blood bubbled forth onto the planks, their hold slackened and they fell back into the darkness.

Seeing this, I said harshly, "You are merciless, Dionysius."

He shook his head. "On the contrary, I am merciful. Who are you to talk, Turms? These wounded are my people. I have risen to be their leader, I have shared my bread and salt with them and have thrashed seamanship into them with my rope. But a man gets by in life only with his own strength. The immortals will not drag me by the hair onto the deck if I lie helpless in the dark of the ship. I am the one who must make the effort even if it means dragging myself onto the deck by my teeth. I demand no more of them than I do of myself."

Still he did not consent to say what his plans were. With the temple of Aesculapius as landmark, we rowed into the harbor of Cos. Only fishing and diving boats remained, for the Persians had seized all the larger vessels. They had not, however, destroyed the city.

Priests and physicians came to meet us at the shore and Dionysius had the badly wounded men carried off the ships. Many were unconscious, others delirious, and the priests consented to give these asylum in the temple so that they might fall into a healing slumber.

"We are not afraid of the Persians," said the priests. "A healer is not concerned with the nationality or language of the sick, or with their beard or the cut of their clothes. The Persians likewise left their wounded at the temple."

Dionysius laughed. "I respect the temple and fortunately my men are either delirious or unconscious. Otherwise they would crawl over the temple floor and with their bare hands throttle the Persians lying beside them. But even if a healer is not concerned with the language of the sick, I have always thought that he looks carefully at their purse."

The priests met his eyes frankly. "Many who have returned from the threshold of death have dedicated votive offerings to the temple. But the clay bowl of the poor is as cherished as the silver figure or the tripod sent by the wealthy. We do not heal for money but to develop the divine skill which Aesculapius has given us, his heirs. This we swear in the name of the eye, the hand and the nose, the flame, the needle and the knife."

The residents of the city hastily prepared a feast for us, but diluted the wine with five parts of water, for they had had experience with drunken sailors in the past. The day ended, the mountain peaks flamed, and splashes of purple swam in the sea, but still Dionysius delayed our departure. The priests began to glower and hint that it had not been their intention to provide asylum for warships but only for the wounded.

"I understand," said Dionysius. "Ionia's freedom has ended on sea and land and from now on you must welcome the Persians in preference to your own people. I shall leave as soon as I receive a favorable omen."

As dusk settled over the island and the fragrance of spices rose from the temple gardens, Dionysius drew me aside.

"Advise me, Turms, you who are an educated man, for I am in worse than a fix. I wouldn't for anything insult these elders and their god, but we are about to leave for dangerous waters and I can't afford to lose a single sailor. That's why I intend to carry off one of Aesculapius' heirs. He must not be too old, otherwise he won't be able to withstand the rigors of the sea, and he must be able to heal wounds, fevers and stomach complaints. In addition, it would be good if he also spoke Phoenician, as many of the priests do."

"What are you planning to do?" I asked.

He glanced at me guiltily and finally confessed. "Don't you understand, Turms? The Persians have enlisted in their service all the warships of Cyprus and Phoenicia as far as Egypt, leaving the sea open and defenseless as a cow's belly. Kairos help me, I intend to serve the god of the opportune moment."

"In the name of the immortals!" I cried in dismay. "Honest warfare for freedom is one thing, piracy on the open seas another. The life of a pirate is short, his death fearful, and his name forever disgraced. He is hunted from one end of the sea to the other, he can find no refuge, and his very name strikes terror into respectable people."

38

"Don't talk nonsense," warned Dionysius. "You, a temple-burner, accusing me!"

"Dorieus and I certainly will not follow you."

"Then remain here," he said with sarcasm. "Remain with these friendly priests and explain to the Persians who you are and whence you came. We'll meet sometime in the fields of Hades, but I swear that I'll arrive there much later than you."

His words made me hesitate. "It will soon be dark," he said urgently. "Tell me how best to snatch a physician. We'll need a good one before many days have passed."

"Learned physicians are careful of their skin," I pointed out. "That's understandable, for if a sword punctures it, all their hard-learned knowledge will ooze out together with their life. Not even the physicians of Miletus consented to board the ships although they promised to care for all the wounded gratuitously in the city after the victory. No, you will never get anyone to volunteer as physician for your pirate ships."

"We're not pirates if we continue the naval warfare in the enemy's waters after the others have given up," argued Dionysius. "I'll make the physician a rich man like all the others who follow me."

"Even if he were to survive, what pleasure would he have from his riches if he were recognized and his past discovered?" I asked. "Nobody would shield him."

"Turms," said Dionysius slowly, "I'm afraid that I shall leave you on Cos, like it or not, unless you stop chattering and do something."

With a sigh I left him and began looking around. Suddenly I noticed a short man standing apart from the others. There was something so familiar about him that I called out a greeting before I noticed that he carried a caduceus. His face was round, his eyes restless, and there was a furrow between his brows.

"Who are you?" I asked. "In the dusk I thought I recognized you."

"My name is Mikon," he said. "I am consecrated, but unless you give the sign I cannot recognize you."

"Mikon," I repeated. "On the expedition to Sardis I met an Attic pottery maker named Mikon. He went to war in the hope of winning enough loot to open his own kiln, but he returned to Athens as poor as he had left it. He was a strong man with arms like gnarled tree roots, and there was a feeling of security in fleeing by his side from the Persians. Still I never felt as close to him as I do to you."

"You came at an opportune moment, stranger," he said. "My mind is restless and smolders like ashes in a breeze. What do you want of me?"

To test his views I lauded Aesculapius, the fame of the temple and the wisdom of the physicians of Cos.

He replied, "A white beard is not always a sign of wisdom. Tradition hampers fully as much as it cures."

His words startled me. "Mikon," I said, "the world is large and knowledge does not grow only in one place. You are not yet old. Why remain here in the path of the Persians?"

He reached out a friendly hand. "Cos is not the only place I know. I have traveled through many lands, even as far as Egypt; I speak several languages and am familiar with diseases unknown here. What is it that you want of me?"

His touch was as familiar as that of an old friend. "Mikon, perhaps we all are slaves of fate. You are the kind of man needed by our commander. I am to point you out to him, whereupon his men will hit you over the head and drag you aboard our vessel."

He did not flinch but looked at me questioningly. "Why are you warning me? Your face is not that of a Greek."

As he looked at me I felt an irresistible power surging through me, raising my arms, palms downward, towards the golden thread of the new moon.

"I don't know why I am warning you," I admitted. "I don't even know who I am. I only know that the moment of departure has arrived for you as well as for me."

"Then let us go!" He laughed, tucked his hand in my arm and led me to Dionysius.

Bewildered by the suddenness of it, I asked, "Don't you want to bid farewell to anyone, or to collect your clothes and possessions?"

"If I leave, I shall leave as I am," he declared, "otherwise my departure will have little meaning. It would be helpful, of course, if I had my medicine case, but I fear that my departure would be prevented even though I have not yet given my oath."

Dionysius warned him against returning. "But if you come with me voluntarily, I shall reward you suitably."

"Voluntarily or by compulsion—they are but words," Mikon said cheerfully. "Only that will happen to me which must happen and which I cannot prevent."

We led him between us to the galley. Dionysius had the conch blown to summon the men, and our three vessels rowed out into a sea that had turned a calm amethyst. The moon of the merciless virgin goddess shone thinly in the sky as we left the harbor of Cos.

40

5.

We rowed far out into the open sea until not even a shadow of land was visible. The rowers began to pant and some of them threw up the good food that they had eaten at Cos. They cursed Dionysius and raged that there was no sense to such rowing, since the first principles of seamanship demanded that one keep in sight of land and know where one was going.

Dionysius listened laughingly to their enraged complaints and lashed at the most garrulous with his rope, not so much in anger as in benevolence. They called him ugly names but none of them stopped rowing until he ordered the galleys to be brought together and fastened for the night.

"Not that I pity you," he said, "but the intoxication of battle has probably faded, leaving your brains even more wretched than your bodies. So gather around me, for I have much to tell you."

As Dionysius spoke, he did not remind the men of their bravery at Lade. Instead he compared them to the poor peasant who has come to the city to buy a donkey but has spent his money on wine, become involved in a fight, and awakened the following morning in a strange house, his robe torn and bloody and his shoes gone. He is surrounded by riches and treasure chests and realizes that he has broken into the home of some noble. Far from pleasing him, the sight of the riches horrifies him, for he realizes that at that very moment he is being pursued and has no hope of ever returning home.

Dionysius paused and looked around. "That is the situation in which you are, my friends. But thank the immortals that you have chosen a commander who knows what he wants. I, Dionysius, son of Phocaea, will not desert you. Nor do I demand that you follow me merely because I am stronger and shrewder than any of you, and a better navigator as well. Think carefully. Is any one of you better qualified to command than I? If so, let him step forth and say so to my face."

No one came forward to question Dionysius' authority, so he finally revealed his plans.

"Because Ionia is lost we cannot return to Phocaea. But the Persian fleet is repairing its damages and is committed to blockading Miletus and its allies. Thus the sea is open and I shall sacrifice to Poseidon that he may give us a strong west wind tomorrow morning."

The men cried out in dismay, but Dionysius raised his voice triumphantly. "Yes, a west wind, so that you can rest your miserable limbs and let the wind carry us to enemy waters as far as the shores of

Phoenicia. There we will find the slow-moving merchant vessels with their bellies full of the riches of East and West, for trade must continue even in wartime. A quick voyage through enemy waters and within a month, I swear, we will be rich men, richer than we ever dreamed of being when we lived in the sooty wooden huts of Phocaea."

But the men showed little interest in the plan. The thought of dangerous waters where death lurked behind every mast and wake did not arouse cheers.

Dionysius looked at them. "One month," he pleaded. "Only one month, I ask for, no more. Then I shall summon the finest east wind in the name of the gods and we will sail directly west across the whole width of the sea to Massilia."

A few of the men observed mildly that a fair amount of booty had come their way already at Lade. The voyage to Massilia through strange waters was fearfully long, and sometimes not even an entire season sufficed for it. So if their intention was to reach Massilia, it would be best to turn the prows in that direction immediately and pray for favorable winds. But the wisest course, they said, would be to seek refuge in the Greek cities of Sicily or Italy, in that great West whose reputation for wealth and extravagant living had spread throughout the world.

Dionysius listened, furrowed his brow, and then asked with assumed meekness if someone else had advice to give him.

"Say what you have to say, then we shall know where each of us stands. Everyone has the right to speak and vote and express his opinion, so speak freely. First let us see who wish to go directly to Sicily or Italy, where the Greek cities jealously guard their respective territories and the lands have been partitioned for centuries."

A number of the men consulted hastily among themselves and declared that a partridge in the hand was better than ten on a branch. Therefore they humbly requested their share of the booty and one of the vessels with which to sail to Sicily.

"It is manly and right that you have spoken so freely," said Dionysius. "You may have your share of the loot and a generous share, but I cannot let you have a vessel. The ships are my own and all your loot would not suffice to buy one. Still, it is best for us to go our separate ways as soon as possible, so take your share and start swimming towards Sicily with the golden chains around your necks. If you hesitate I will gladly help you over the railing with the tip of my sword. The water is warm and you can determine the direction by the stars."

He took a few threatening steps and the other men laughingly began jostling the unfortunates towards the side, pretending to toss them over-board. Bitterly regretting their thoughtless words, the group pleaded loudly to be permitted to accompany Dionysius.

He shook his head and sighed. "What changeable creatures you are! One moment you want this, another moment that. But let us again be the same big family in which everyone has the right to express his thoughts freely and to vote as he wishes. Let each of us who wishes to follow me first to Phoenician waters and then to Massilia raise his hand."

All the men, including Dorieus and me, raised their hands. Only Mikon, smiling silently, did not.

Dionysius moved among the men, patting their shoulders and calling them gallant. But in front of Mikon he paused, his face darkening. "What of you, physician? Do you intend to return home on the back of a dolphin?"

Mikon met his eyes unflinchingly. "I will follow you willingly, Dionysius, and will continue to do so for as long a time as is intended. But where we will go after leaving the Phoenician waters is completely up to fate. For that reason I do not defy the immortals by raising my hand."

His manner was so docile that Dionysius could not even reproach him.

Turning back to his men, Dionysius shouted, "Tomorrow morning let us have a brisk west wind. For that I have already sacrificed to the Phoenician god on our prow and bathed his face, hands and feet with human blood according to the wishes of Phoenician deities. But to Poseidon and the gods of the sea I shall now offer this golden chain worth several houses and vineyards to prove to you how thoroughly I believe in my good luck. I sacrifice it gladly, knowing that in the near future I shall receive another even more valuable."

With those words he strode to the prow and threw his chain into the sea. The men groaned upon hearing the splash but, convinced of Dionysius' belief in his luck, they praised him and began scratching the deck to confirm the sacrifice and conjure up the wind.

Dionysius sent the men to sleep, promising to take the watch himself until daybreak. Again the men praised him, and soon the only sound over the sigh of the sea and the creak of the vessels was a heavy snoring.

I could not sleep for thinking of the unknown future. The sheep's bones had indicated the west, and whatever other methods of divination Dorieus and I had tried, they likewise had pointed westward. Stub-bornly we had set forth for the east, but winged fate would soon take us to the westernmost shore of the sea.

My throat grew dry at the realization that I had lost Ionia for all time, and I groped my way through the sleeping men to the water container. Then I climbed to the deck, looked at the silver of the sky and the darkening sea, listened to the slap of the waves and felt the slow rocking of the vessel beneath me.

I was aroused from my thoughts by a faint clanking against the side of the ship. Barefooted and silently I reached Dionysius just as he was pulling something up from the sea hand over hand.

"Are you fishing?" I asked.

Dionysius jumped so that he almost lost his balance. "Oh, it's only you, Turms," he said, trying to hide the object behind his back. But his effort was futile, for even in the darkness I recognized the golden chain that he had so ostentatiously thrown into the sea.

He was not at all abashed but laughed and said, "As a literate man you are undoubtedly unprejudiced about offerings and such. My offering to Poseidon was so to speak only allegorical, just as the Ionian sages call their fables of the gods allegories and interpret them in many ways. As a frugal man I naturally tied some string to my chain and fastened the other end firmly to the ship's prow before throwing the treasure overboard."

"But what about the west wind that you promised?" I asked.

"I sensed it already in the evening from the color of the sea and the sighs of the darkness," confessed Dionysius calmly. "Mark my words, even without the chain we will have a brisk west wind. You will see that the sun rises behind a cloud and that with the wind we will have a drenching rain."

His artlessness frightened me, for even the greatest scoffer retains in some corner of his heart a certain respect toward offerings.

"Don't you really believe in the deities?" I asked.

"I believe what I believe," he answered evasively, "but one thing I do know is that even if I had thrown a hundred chains into the sea we would not have had a west wind unless the sea had previously indicated its coming."

6.

As Dionysius had predicted, the early morning brought a wet squall that pushed us eastward with creaking masts. So violent was the churning of the sea that Dorieus, still suffering from the blow on his head, vomited time and again. Many of Dionysius' men likewise lay on the deck, clinging to the railing and unable to eat.

The west wind drove westbound merchant ships to shelter, leaving the deserted sea to Dionysius. His luck accompanied him, for when we had reached the straits between Rhodes and the mainland the wind died down. Dawn brought with it a land wind and a veritable fleet of vessels loaded to the gunwales with grain and oil for the Persian navy near Miletus. Their crews greeted us gaily, misled by the Phoenician ship and the Persian emblems which Dionysius displayed.

Presumably Dionysius had little interest in such cargo and merely sought to prove to himself and to his men that he was still waging the Ionian war. We seized the largest of the ships before its crew realized what was happening. When Dionysius learned that the vessels were Greek ships in the service of the Persians he immediately ordered both our penteconters to scuttle them. We had no need of grain or oil, nor could we have transported them.

With oars and sails we headed for Cyprus and on the way surprised a large and richly laden merchant vessel which also carried passengers. As we surrounded it and clambered up its steep sides its crew vainly attempted to ward off our attack. The passengers, recovered from their initial shock, appeared with upraised hands and in various languages promised large ransoms for themselves, their wives and their daughters. But Dionysius as a cautious man had no desire to spare anyone who might identify him or his men in the future. So he felled the male passengers himself with swift blows of his axe and left the women to his men while the ship was being plundered.

"Make haste, my clansmen," he said. "Although I cannot deny you the joys which only a woman can give, remember that I will kill with my own hands anyone who attempts to conceal a woman on one of our vessels. It would create only bickering and confusion."

The men pulled at their beards and stared with burning eyes at the weeping women.

Dionysius laughed and added, "Remember also, my gallant warriors, that every joy has its price. Whoever utilizes the short time at our disposal in gratifying childish passions instead of in sensibly collecting loot will lose his share of it."

So great was the Phocaeans' greed that only a few chose the women. The rest of us scattered over the vessel, where we found gold and silver in the form of both coins and objects, beautiful pieces of sculpture, women's jewelry and colored fabrics, even two rolls of purple cloth. We also took care of the spice supply and the wines, as well as the passengers' possessions.

The easiest way to dispose of the vessel would have been to burn it, since we were incapable of puncturing its heavy cedar sides. But

Dionysius did not wish to betray us through smoke or fire. Instead, we chopped holes in the ship's bottom and as the vessel began to sink Dionysius roused those of his men who had chosen women instead of loot and then had the throats of the women slit, thus giving them an easy death in compensation for the dishonor they had suffered.

Only Dorieus had not participated in the plundering and raping but had returned to our vessel immediately following the capture. Mikon, who had not taken part in the fighting, had inspected the ship and found an ivory-trimmed medicine case together with physician's instruments.

When Dionysius censured him for his laziness, Dorieus stated that he fought only armed men, the more skilled the better. But the killing and plundering of unarmed men was beneath his dignity. This explanation satisfied Dionysius, who promised him his share of the loot even though he had not contributed to it.

Having related this much, I have really described our entire voyage, for everything happened in the same manner. The only difference lay in the size and number of the vessels, the time of day, the stiffness of the resistance, the amount of loot, and other matters of secondary importance. We rounded Cyprus on the sea side and sank several ships from Curium and Amathus after having lured them closer with our Persian shields and emblems. But we could not prevent the escape of several fishing boats which had witnessed the attacks. In great urgency Dionysius stamped the deck and cried for a favorable wind to carry us straight toward the Phoenician coast. No one would suspect our appearance on the busiest shipping routes, for pirates had not dared venture into these safest waters of the civilized world for generations.

But the gentle breeze continued to blow toward Cyprus, just as the breeze always blows toward land in the daytime and in the morning from land to sea, unless storms or capricious gales prevail. This has been made possible by the fishermen's sea gods so that the men may sail out before dawn and return with the day winds.

The wind was not our only obstacle, for a strong current, of which the men from Salamis had warned us, made our oars powerless to carry us in the direction set by Dionysius.

As Dionysius stood on the deck, stamping his feet, rattling shields, and calling for a favorable wind, Mikon came to me.

"Why don't you summon the wind, Turms?" he suggested. "Do it if only in jest." He was smiling and there was a familiar wrinkle between his brows.

I cannot explain why I did so, but I raised my arms and summoned the wind thrice, then seven times and finally twelve times in an increasingly loud voice, until my own shouts intoxicated me and I was no longer aware of what happened around me.

When I came to my senses Mikon was holding my head on his arm and pouring wine down my throat, Dorieus was staring at me strangely, and Dionysius looked frightened, as though he didn't believe what he saw. The sky which shortly before had been cloudless had changed color, and from the west a blue-black mass of clouds was approaching with the speed of a thousand charging black horses. As Dionysius shouted for the sails we heard the thunder of hoofbeats, the sea darkened and frothed, and lightning blazed above us. Then we plunged forward with snapping sails through blinding hail and foam, unable to do anything but follow the wind to avoid being swamped by the house-high waves.

As the lightning flashed and the ship groaned we lay on deck clinging to whatever we could. Then, as the wine which Mikon had given me rose to my head, I stumbled to my feet and, clutching the mast rope, tried to dance on the rolling deck as I had once danced on the road to Delphi. The dance penetrated my limbs and from my throat burst words which I did not understand. Only when the storm began to die down did I drop in exhaustion onto the deck.

7.

Until late that night we sailed along the blue shoreline of Cyprus, striving in vain to reach the open sea. A stiff breeze forced us relentlessly northeastward and not all the shifting of sails took us from the direction in which an apparently relentless will was driving us. When darkness fell Dionysius had the sails half furled and the vessels roped together so that we would not drift apart during the night. While most of the crew slept he and several others remained on watch for possible breakers.

But nothing happened and we awakened at daybreak to the astonished shouts of the lookouts. When we reached the deck we saw that the sea had grown calm and that we were floating off the easternmost tip of Cyprus. The sun rose from the sea all red and gold, and on its mountain at the end of the promontory we saw the temple of Aphrodite of Akraia with its terraces and columns. It was so near that in the dazzling light of dawn we could distinguish every detail and hear the crowing of Aphrodite's famous black cocks over the water.

The men of Salamis cried out that this was a sign and an omen. The powerful Aphrodite of Akraia, the Aphrodite of seafarers and the

47

mightiest Aphrodite of the eastern sea, had sent a storm to lead us to her. Moreover, she was a native Cypriote, having stepped ashore there from her seashell with only her golden hair veiling her foam-white body. For all those reasons, said the men of Sardis, it was necessary that we go ashore and make a sacrifice lest we incur Aphrodite's wrath.

But Dionysius roared at the men to take to their oars since only a miracle had kept us from drifting onto the reefs between the small islands while we had stared at the temple. The men of Salamis protested that the miracle was Aphrodite's and that they would not take the responsibility of leaving without having made an offering.

"I gladly recognize the might of the golden-haired goddess," said Dionysius, "and promise to make a sacrifice at the first opportune moment. But you can see for yourselves that there are many large ships in the harbor. I would rather suffer Aphrodite's wrath than that of the god of war."

He ordered the beat of the gongs quickened to battle speed. "I'll sweat out of you the last desire to sacrifice to Aphrodite."

But despite the best efforts of the rowers, the helmsmen noticed that our speed was not what it should have been and the men themselves muttered that never before had the oars felt so heavy.

Finally, when the shadow of the temple had dropped beyond the horizon, our speed increased. The cloudless sky smiled at us, the sea breathed lightly, and everything around us seemed radiant.

Dionysius shouted triumphantly, "You see, the Cypriote has no power on the sea!"

The rowers began to sing loudly in relief, some with good voices, others cawing like ravens or screaming like gulls. The more loudly they sang the harder they pulled at the oars as though it were no longer an effort but a joy. The water frothed at the prows, the wakes bubbled, and the oars whipped up the sea at our sides.

At midday the lookouts cried out with one voice that they saw a mast and a colored sail. The vessel came directly toward us and soon we all saw the carved and painted rails, the glow of the ivory and silver deity at its prow, and the glint of the sun on the oars. It was a narrow, fast ship and lovely as a dream.

When it was sufficiently near it raised its pennants and showed its shields. The men of Salamis said, "It is one of Tyre's ships. Surely you don't intend to anger the sea goddess, Dionysius?"

But Dionysius unhesitatingly showed a Persian shield, signaled the strange ship to stop, and ordered our marines to board it. When we climbed over its side no one offered resistance, although the Phoenicians shouted in guttural voices and raised protesting hands. Among them were priests with bead-trimmed headbands, silver rattles, and bells around their necks.

"Why are they screaming?" demanded Dionysius, lowering his axe.

The men of Salamis tremblingly explained, "This is a sacred ship. It is carrying incense and votive offerings to the temple of Aphrodite at Akraia."

Dionysius glowered and scratched his head in perplexity, then inspected the ship. Its cargo was undeniably valuable, although useless for our purposes. When he sought to enter the deckhouse the priests clutched the curtain before the entrance. Dionysius tore it down, went inside, and hastily returned with a red face.

"There's nothing in there except four daughters of Astarte."

The men of Salamis talked to the priests and learned that the four girls were the gift of Astarte of Tyre to her sister, Aphrodite of Akraia, and symbolized the four corners of the world ruled by Tyre as queen of the sea.

"This is an omen!" cried the men, and insisted upon seeing the girls.

For a moment Dionysius was tempted to plunder and sink the ship, then the sight of the smiling sun, the shimmering sky and the dark blue eyes of the sea made him laugh. He ordered the girls brought forth.

They stepped out of the shelter fearlessly and gracefully, wearing only their hair ornaments, necklaces and the goddess's belt. One of them was white as snow, the second yellow as mustard, the third copper-colored, and the fourth black as pitch. We shouted in amazement, for none of us had ever seen a yellow-skinned person.

Dionysius said, "I don't deny that this is a sign and an omen. The goddess realized that we could not stop to make our offering, therefore she sent us this ship. It is ours, and as evidence of it I am burying this axe in the deck and dedicating the vessel to the goddess of Akraia."

The men were content with the decision and declared that they had no intention of warring against gods and consecrated girls. In all friendliness they took the priests' ornaments and bells as mementos, but no one touched the girls.

When they saw that we were about to leave the ship the girls began talking together in great agitation and pointing to us. The Negro girl seized Dionysius' beard, while the snow-white one ran her fingertips temptingly across the corners of my mouth.

Dionysius frowned. "What do they want?"

The priests of Tyre explained reluctantly that the girls wanted us to sacrifice to Aphrodite. Since all could not do it, the girls wished to choose those from whom they would accept the offering.

Dionysius loosened the Negro girl's fingers from his beard, waged a violent spiritual struggle with himself, and said, "He who has taken one step must also take the next. We would have to stop at any rate to eat hot food while the sea is calm. But I don't want to take advantage of my position. Let us draw lots and in that manner choose the four men to represent us."

The goddess smiled impartially, for a winning pebble—one red, one black and one yellow—was drawn by each vessel. But incredible as it was, I myself drew the white pebble from the barrel. I stared at it in alarm, remembering the touch of the slender fingers on my face. Quickly I passed the pebble to Mikon.

He looked down into his palm. "I thought the moon ruled you. Only now do I understand why the storm which you conjured up led us to the temple at Akraia."

I bid him stop chattering and hold up the pebble in his hand for all to see. Then the rowers washed and scrubbed and anointed those who had drawn the winning pebbles and ornamented them with chains and rings selected from the loot.

While the rest of us filed by the pots for our meal, the four fortunates, Mikon in the lead because of his position, stepped into the deckhouse. The priests replaced the curtain and began to chant hoarsely.

When we had eaten and drunk the wine which Dionysius had served in honor of the occasion, the sun began to drop ominously toward the west. Dionysius became impatient and finally sent for the four men.

Our hands rose involuntarily to our mouths when we saw them stagger forth with the aid of their companions. Their eyes were glazed, their tongues hung out and they could hardly stand. Even Mikon clung to the necks of two oarsmen, and when he attempted to jump aboard our vessel he fell flat on his face.

Dionysius ordered the crews to the oars and turned the prows of our ships northeastward as though our intention was to return to Ionian waters by rounding the mainland side of Cyprus. He surmised that the priests of Tyre would immediately inform the Persians of our presence and devised a daring plan. As soon as the sacrificial vessel had disappeared from view we changed to a southeasterly course. A smiling breath of wind began blowing over the sea as though Aphrodite herself were capriciously bestowing her favors on us.

Mikon raised himself shakily to his knees and vomited before he

50

had time to drag himself to the side. Then a rational look came into his eyes once more.

"I have experienced nothing like this in all my forty years," he said with a weak smile. "I thought that I knew much but actually I knew nothing. Now at last I believe in Aphrodite's invisible golden net in which even the strongest man is ensnared." He returned the smooth white pebble that I had given him. "Keep it, Turms. It was not intended for me but for you, you favorite of the goddess."

I accepted the pebble and kept it, just as I had kept the black pebble which I had found on the earth floor of the temple of Cybele in Sardis. And this white pebble also signified the end of an era in my life although I did not know it at the time.

Mikon spoke a warning. "The gods not only give, they also take away. It is apparent that Artemis is your goddess, but for some reason Aphrodite also has chosen you. This may be unfortunate, since both these powerful goddesses are jealous of each other. You must be careful not to sacrifice too much to either but try to retain the favor of both as they compete for you."

But all that was forgotten in the exhaustion of laboring at the oars as we sailed in Phoenician waters. The moon grew full and we raged over the sea like Artemis' wild dogs, murdering, plundering and sinking ships. Signal fires burned all along the Phoenician coast and in a bitter battle we succeeded in sinking two small warships which came upon us unexpectedly. We lost some men and many more were wounded. But invisible shields protected me so that I remained unscratched.

Many of the men began to complain of seeing the ghosts of our victims in the dark and of feeling the pinch of cold fingers as they were about to sleep. A convoy of vengeful spirits accompanied us, for the sea and the sky around our vessels often darkened without apparent reason.

Dionysius made several sacrifices to placate the spirits, and spat in the sea and scratched the prow with his fingernails to gain a favorable wind. But when the new moon appeared like a thread-thin silver sickle he said suddenly, "I have tested my luck sufficiently and our ships can carry no more cargo. I am not so greedy that I would sacrifice the seaworthiness of my vessels for spoils. Our expedition is now at an end and we have nothing to do but save our lives and our loot. Therefore let us turn our prows westward, and may Poseidon help us across the measureless sea."

As the Phocaeans shouted for joy Dionysius prayed to the gods of

51

Phoenicia and Ionia, smeared blood on the face, hands and feet of the deity and sacrificed several prisoners, letting their blood run into the sea. Sacrifices which would no longer be permitted on land were tolerated at sea and no one protested these barbaric offerings.

Intoxicated by the blood and the loot and our success, the oarsmen joined in calling for the wind. The sailing season was drawing to a close, flocks of birds flew restlessly above the sea, and the water changed its colors. But still the sun scorched us mercilessly, the firmament dazzled our eyes, and the wind did not appear.

Finally the rowers, palms raw from the oars and their throats hoarse, began to shout, "Turms, summon the wind for us! We would rather drown than die at the oars with this heavy cargo of loot."

With their shouts my head cleared and I saw around us the shadows of the deceased with their vindictive grimaces and hands that clutched our railings as though to prevent our escape.

An ecstasy seized me. I felt myself stronger than the spirits and began summoning the east wind. The others shouted with me, imitating the words whose meaning even I did not understand. Three times, then seven times and finally twelve times I called. Mikon covered his head in fear but made no attempt to restrain me since our lives in any event were at stake with the Phoenician and Egyptian ships at our heels.

Then the sea turned yellow in the east and a blinding storm swirled over us, carrying with it the dust of distant deserts. The last we saw of the open sea behind us was a waterspout rising from the waves to the sky. Then I collapsed onto the deck and Mikon and Dorieus carried me below, where they tied me to one of the ribs to keep me from being battered to death in the pitching ship.

BOOK THREE

Himera

I.

GREATER even than Dionysius' bravery in the battle of Lade, more notable than his raiding expeditions in Phoenician waters, was his skill as a navigator. Despite the autumn gales which sent other ships fleeing to the safety of winter ports, he succeeded in reaching the shores of Sicily in three weeks without landing once, and with the mountains of Crete as his only landmark. This incredible feat deserves full recognition.

So filthy and diseased were we, so bruised and rotted by salt water, that when we finally sighted land and knew it to be real, the men wept with joy and demanded that we put ashore no matter whose territory it was.

Our ships leaked so badly and autumn was so far advanced that not even Dionysius believed that we could continue our voyage over the wide and unknown waters that separated us from Massilia. Calling together his captains and helmsmen he said, "The gigantic smoke-capped mountain that you see tells me that we have arrived at Sicily. If you crave large cities we can continue northward to Croton or south to Syracuse, the largest of the Sicilian cities."

The helmsmen were delighted. "We are wealthy men now and it would be easiest for us to sell our loot in a large city. We could also have our vessels repaired quickly in some shipyard or even buy new ships with which to continue to Massilia in the spring. But above all we need rest and good food, music, wine and garlands to speed our recovery from these weeks at sea."

"It's true that you'll find such pleasures most readily in a large city," admitted Dionysius, "but large cities are also fortified cities. They have their walls and their mercenaries and their guarded ports, perhaps even warships. They also receive news from the outside world sooner than small cities."

He looked sharply at the men. "Our conscience is clear, for we know that we have waged legal warfare against the Persians. But we are too wealthy not to arouse suspicions no matter how we try to explain the source of our loot. And wine has caused many a man to talk his head off. We know our own talkativeness. After all, the immortals chose to make us Ionians the glibbest of all peoples.

"No," he concluded, "we must spend the winter in some secluded city and buy the friendship of its tyrant. Three warships and a trained band like ours are not to be scorned by a minor tyrant trying to preserve his independence. There are such cities on the northern coast whence we could easily set forth for Massilia in the spring. And so I must ask one final effort of you, valiant brothers. Let us sail courageously through the straits which have brought destruction to hundreds of ships, for otherwise we will lose all that we have won."

The men paled to think of the whirlpools, currents and treacherous winds of those fabled straits, but having protested for a time they grew calmer. When night fell we heard a dull roar and saw a red glow lighting the sky above the smoke-peaked mountain. Ashes began to rain onto the decks and the rowers no longer demanded to go ashore.

Dorieus alone smiled and proclaimed, "The land of my father's death greets me with thunder and pillars of fire. That sign suffices for me. I know now why the sheep's bones pointed westward."

Mikon for his part said, "Dionysius' luck has brought us thus far. Let him continue to lead us."

I also felt that the gods hardly would have protected us from the terrors of the sea only to sink our ships ignominiously in the infamous straits. So ended the conference and Dionysius was permitted to carry out his plan. In the silence of the night he sacrificed our Phoenician pilots to the pitiless god of the straits. When, the next morning, I found them gone I was sorry for I had talked to them and for all their foreignness they had shown themselves to be the same kind of people as we were.

The straits were as treacherous as they were said to be and we struggled mightily to pass through them. More dead than alive, and with the crash of the breakers still echoing in our ears, we finally reached the autumnal blue of the Tyrrhenian Sea. Now a favoring wind helped us as we sailed along the mountainous coast within sight of land. Dionysius gave offerings of thanks, poured wine into the sea, and even chopped off the feet of the Phoenician god and threw him overboard with the words, "I no longer need you, god, whoever you may be, for you don't know these waters."

But our leaking ships, damaged even more by the straits, moved with difficulty. Each of us yearned for land, for fresh water and fruit, but Dionysius pushed onward, sniffing the breeze, talking to fishermen and purchasing their catch. But as we sailed, the water inside the ship rose ever higher.

By evening the wind began to blow us toward land. We saw the mouth of a river and a city surrounded by a thick wall. Columns of steam arose from the hot springs around it, and beyond it were high mountains.

As the water reached the rowers' benches the men pulled desperately at the oars. Whether we wished to do so or not, we had to land, for the ship was sinking. Hardly had the oarsmen fled to the deck than we heard a snap and a jolt as the vessel went aground. We were saved, although waves were washing the deck and the ship rolled over on its side with a sigh. Both the penteconters landed safely and, jumping into the water, we pulled them ashore. Only then did we seize our weapons and prepare to defend ourselves, although the land swayed under our feet and we tottered from side to side.

2.

A number of ships, covered for the winter, were drawn up on either bank of the river. A motley crowd soon appeared, conversing excitedly in many languages. When the people saw our weapons they kept their distance, although a few broke off leafy twigs from the trees and waved them overhead in token of friendship.

We tossed our shields and weapons to the ground. Encouraged, the people came closer, talked to us, peered at us from every side and tugged at our clothes as the curious do in every land. Many of them spoke Greek, although in a strange dialect. Peddlers offered us grapes and fruit and gladly accepted a Persian gold coin in payment, giving us their own silver in change. They told us that the name of their city was Himera and that it had been founded by the people of Zankle who had later been joined by Syracusans wearied of the civil wars ceaselessly raging in their city. The majority of the people, however, were native Siculi whom the Greeks had married.

At sundown the city gates were closed, and we, having no desire to meet more people that evening, stretched out for the night where we were. The smell of the earth, the grass and the very touch of solid ground were a joy after the stench and hard planks that we had known at sea.

When the gates were opened again in the morning Dionysius sent for a bull and some sheep. We garlanded and sacrificed the bull and burned its leg bones as well as the fat from the sheep. Then we roasted the meat and ate our fill. More peddlers came by with their baskets to sell us bread and honey cakes and we spent freely until Dionysius put a stop to it. After all, he reminded us, we were Ionians.

The morning passed in noisy feasting and dancing that attracted all the disreputable elements of the city. Finally the Himeran tyrant, escorted by an armed guard and a number of mounted men, came to greet us and to inquire what our plans were. He was a sparsely bearded old man with stooped shoulders who walked modestly in the midst of his men in a home-loomed mantle.

Dionysius advanced, told him of the battle of Lade and of the loot that we had won from the Persians, and asked for sanctuary through the winter. He also requested ropes and oxen, a windlass and woodworkers to salvage the sunken vessel and dry-dock the penteconters.

As Dionysius spoke, the tyrant watched us shrewdly. One could see from his eyes that he was not a man of unimportance despite his modest appearance.

When Dionysius had spoken, the tyrant declared, "The will of my people made me, Krinippos, the autocrat of Himera, although ruling is distasteful to me. Hence I must discuss all important decisions with the people. But because there are matters which should not be noised about by all, I suggest that you come to my house where we may talk within four walls. Or, if you are suspicious, let us withdraw here beyond earshot of your men. The presence of too many people disturbs me because I lack eloquence and am a recluse by nature."

Dionysius acceded and the gray-haired man fearlessly accompanied him to the farther side of the field, although Dionysius was heads taller and could have snapped his frail neck with bare hands. They seated themselves on the ground and began talking earnestly.

Krinippos' warriors smiled proudly. "He is incomparable, our tyrant, and we would elevate him to the throne if he did not abhor the word king. He need fear no rival, for his house is filled with amulets of the underworld gods which he has obtained in some mysterious way. By threatening us with them he has succeeded in abolishing all destructive rivalry and has ruled us so wisely that both the Carthaginians and the Tyrrhenians are our friends, and not even Syracuse dares threaten our freedom."

56

They told us also that Krinippos had married a woman of Carthage and that he ruled all the people of his city impartially, regardless of their nationality. According to Krinippos' men, Himera was a happy city in which fear and injustice were unknown.

Finally we saw Krinippos and Dionysius rise, courteously wipe the grass off each other and return to us. When the tyrant had departed for the city with his men, Dionysius told us what had transpired.

"I have made a pact with that able ruler. From now on we are free to enter and leave the city with or without weapons. We can either rent lodgings or build houses, practice trade, worship the city's or our own gods as we wish, marry Himeran women or otherwise win their favor, for the customs here are free. We must, however, promise to guard the city's wall as though it were our own while we live in Himera."

His men said skeptically, "All that is too good to be true. Krinippos is more cunning than you think. After he has lured us into the city he will have his men kill us for our loot, or perhaps bewitch us with his magic objects or coax us to join games of chance in which we will lose everything."

Dionysius bid them keep their mouths shut, for the assurances that he had received from Krinippos could not be doubted. But even more important than the holiest oaths was the fact that their interests were identical. For that reason he had decided to store our locked and sealed loot in Krinippos' vaults as guarantee of our good behavior, and to distribute to each man only the amount needed to live through the winter. Krinippos was not anxious to have a sudden influx of money because it would raise prices and straiten the life of the residents.

Although the men suspected that Dionysius already had fallen under the spell of Krinippos, the lure of the city was so great that before long we set forth in groups, leaving the oldest to watch the ships.

The guards at the gate admitted us without demanding our weapons. As we strolled along the streets we saw the shops of the artisans, the dye-works and the weavers at their looms. We saw the market place and the stalls with teachers, scribes and merchants. We also saw the beautiful temple of Poseidon with its fluted pillars, as well as the temples of Demeter and Baal. Wherever we went the people called out greetings, children ran after us, and men and women tugged at our robes to invite us to their houses.

After their sufferings at sea the men could not resist the invitations, but gradually, in twos and threes, left us to enjoy Himeran hospitality. In that manner our group diminished until, before we realized it, only Dorieus, Mikon and I remained.

Dorieus said, "If I could find a temple of Herakles I would make a sacrifice. You perhaps noticed the figure of the cock in the frame of the city gate and the emblem of the cock on the Himeran coins. We were destined to come to this place and here to work out our fate."

I smelled the tempting fragrances of the city and asked, "Where can we find a house worthy of us? Krinippos' dwelling does not tempt me, for he is said to be frugal in his ways. But neither can we condescend to be the guests of a humble man."

Mikon said with assumed gravity, "You tell us what to do, Dorieus, you who are the descendant of Herakles."

Dorieus did not hesitate. "There is no doubt but that we should go westward as far as the city extends. That will bring us closest to the land which is my legacy."

So we walked to the westernmost end of the city where there were large houses with windowless walls facing the street and gardens surrounded by walls. The street was silent and dirty and clay had crumbled from the houses. Suddenly my head grew light and the air flickered before my eyes.

"I have walked this street in my dreams!" I cried. "I know these houses. But in my dream a chariot roared down the street, a blind poet plucked his lyre, and colored canopies protected the doors and gates. Yes, this is the street of my dreams. Or is it?" I paused and looked around, for the memory had returned only briefly, and scales were again covering my eyes.

"The street is not uninhabited," observed Mikon, "although it was formerly occupied by the wealthy and the nobility. That is apparent from the walls and the iron gates and the bronze fittings. But the days of the nobility are past now that the people have seized the power and a tyrant protects the people's rights."

I barely heard him, for my attention was caught by a newly fallen white feather. When I had picked it up I looked around and noticed that we were standing before a small door set in a large gate. Its bronze knocker pictured a satyr embracing a fleeing nymph, but it was not necessary for me to knock, for the door opened with a creak as I leaned against it. We stepped into a yard in which there were fruit trees, dark cypresses and a stone pool.

An old slave limped toward us, one knee apparently stiffened by a red-hot stone in the barbaric manner of yore. He greeted us with suspicion but we did not heed his protests. Mikon rinsed his hands in the yellow water of the pool and exclaimed that the water was quite warm. We guessed that it was the same water that we had seen bubbling forth from the hot springs surrounding the city.

Meanwhile the old slave returned indoors for help and soon we were confronted by a large woman wrapped from head to heel in a striped robe. In Himeran-accented Greek she demanded to know whether we were thieves, since we had broken into the yard of a defenseless widow.

She was not completely defenseless, however, for the old slave had seized a cudgel and a sturdy man on the steps was holding an evil-looking Phoenician bow. The woman herself gazed at us proudly and it was apparent that she had once been beautiful, although now there were wrinkles around her black eyes, her arched nose and her mocking lips.

Mikon answered humbly, "We are but refugees from Ionia who have been fighting the Persians. The sea gods brought us to the shores of Himera and your ruler Krinippos has promised us homeless men a haven for the winter."

But Dorieus rejected such humility and shouted, "You may be a homeless refugee but I am a Spartan and am here to seek a new land, not as a suppliant but as an inheritor. We stepped into your garden because all the other residents of Himera have competed with one another for the privilege of offering their friendship and hospitality to our humble seamen. We were unable to find a house worthy of us and apparently chose the wrong gate. We certainly would not expect a defenseless widow to show us hospitality."

The woman came closer, absently took from my hand the feather I was still holding, and said, "Forgive my rudeness. It was the sight of your weapons and bright shields that alarmed me. I thank whatever god brought you to my gate and bid you welcome. I shall have my servants prepare a feast worthy of you without delay. Your appearance tells me that you are far from humble men, but neither am I a humble woman. My name is Tanakil. If that means nothing to you, I can assure you that it is known to many even beyond Himera."

She led us into her house, bade us hang our weapons in the entrance hall, and showed us the banquet room with convivial couches piled high with mattresses and tasseled pillows. There were chests ornamented with oriental scenes and a Phoenician household god whose ivory face was painted lifelike and who was clothed in expensive garments. A large Corinthian mixing vessel for wine was in the center of the floor and along the walls were Attic vases, both the older black-figured vases and the new ones with red figures.

59

Tanakil said diffidently, "You can see that my banquet room is gloomy and that spiders have spun their webs in its corners. The greater, then, is my joy at having high-born guests who do not scorn the modesty of my house. If you will be patient I will put my cooks to work and the wine containers to cool and will send my slave to purchase sacrificial meat and to engage musicians."

She smiled and her black eyes flashed. "I myself am old and ugly but I know what men crave after a trying voyage and I don't think that you will be disappointed."

While the meal was being prepared she urged us to bathe in the sulphurous water of the pool. We removed our clothes and stepped in, and the hot water relaxed our limbs delightfully. Slaves came to wash us, to clean our hair and anoint our bodies with fragrant oils. Tanakil, too, came out and watched us with apparent pleasure.

When the slaves had finished we were as though reborn. Our clothes had been removed and we were given shirts of the finest wool over which we hung mantles already pleated. Having clothed ourselves, we returned to the banquet room and reclined on the couches while slaves offered us such savory bits as olives filled with salt fish and rolled smoked meat filled with a paste of oil, eggs, sweet milk and spices.

The salty food whetted our appetite and thirst so that we listened with only mild interest to the blind flute player and the three girls who sang old Himeran songs with sweet voices. Finally Tanakil reappeared, clothed in rich garments, her arms and neck bare save for a considerable fortune in gold and silver. Her hair had been combed up into a dome, she had painted her cheeks and lips red, and her eyes glowed under the black brows.

The fragrance of rosewater emanated from her as she smiled playfully and poured a sackful of wine into the mixing vessel and then added the proper amount of icy water. The singing girls hastened to fill our shallow chalices and offered them to us on bended knee.

"I can guess how thirsty you are," said Tanakil. "Quench your thirst with the wine and water. You have probably already heard the chaste song about the shepherdess who wasted away for love. Soon you will hear the tale of Daphnis and Chloe, which is sufficiently tiresome not to disturb your appetite. Let us nevertheless respect the traditions of Himera. In time you will learn why and how we honor the cock as the emblem of our city."

Covered dishes of lamb and beef as well as boned birds on a skewer were brought to us, together with root vegetables, mustard sauce and a delicious porridge. Each time we drank the girls placed in our hand a new chalice at the bottom of which was a different picture.

Finally, panting from the food, we pleaded for mercy. Tanakil then had fruit and grapes, rich cakes and other sweets brought in, and with her own hands opened a sealed jug of wine. The mint-flavored drink cooled our mouths but rose so quickly to our heads that, full as we were, it was as though we were floating on clouds. The treacherous wine made our limbs throb, and we looked with new eyes at the girls who had sung so modestly.

Tanakil noticed our looks and shifted her garment so that we might the better see her white throat and arms. In the dimness she was certainly not an ugly woman and her age was not apparent when she kept her chin up.

"The girls who have sung and served you will now dance," she said, "although they know only innocent shepherds' dances. Krinippos will not permit professional dancers to be brought to Himera."

She called out to the flute player and signaled to the girls, whereupon they began to cavort about like young foals and to doff their garments as they danced. The dance was not artistic nor would I have called it exactly innocent, for its sole purpose seemed to be to reveal the girls.

As they halted before us, breathing heavily, I said, "Tanakil, you inestimable hostess! Your meal was superb but your mint wine is dangerous and these naked girls are a seductive sight. Do not lead us to temptation, for we have promised not to harm this city's residents."

Tanakil looked enviously at the three young girls, sighed and replied, "You would certainly not harm them by laying hands on them. They are respectable girls but because of their humble birth are allowed to accept gifts from whom they please so long as it does not become a habit. Thus they can obtain a larger dowry than by working and can marry some sailor or artisan or farmer."

"Every land has its own customs," observed Mikon. "The Lydians also do this, while in Babylon a girl must sacrifice her virginity in a temple for money before she can marry. And the greatest honor that a Scythian can show a guest is to lead his own wife to the guest's bed for the night. So why should we belittle the customs of Himera, which has so graciously given us sanctuary within its walls?"

The girls ran to us, wound their arms around our necks and began kissing us. But Dorieus angrily thrust his girl away.

"By the cock which perched on Herakles' shoulder, I respect my passions too highly to lay hands on a low-born girl. It would not become

61

my position, although of course I shall give the girl the gift that she desires."

Mikon splashed a drop of wine onto the floor, kissed the girl who had brought him the chalice, and said, "The greatest crime is to insult the laws of hospitality. Time runs before me on fleet feet. In worshiping Aphrodite of Akraia I thought that I would never again wish to look at a mortal woman. But I was badly mistaken, for at this very moment Aphrodite is bewitching my eyes and causing my limbs to tingle with desire."

He carried the girl into the dusky garden. Tanakil sighed and asked that the lamps be lighted. But Dorieus caught her hand.

"Do not light the lamps, Tanakil. This lighting becomes you and softens your proud features. Your brilliant eyes and hawk nose prove that you are of noble birth. Confess that you are."

I realized that Dorieus was badly intoxicated. "Beware lest you insult our hostess," I warned him.

Tanakil's mouth dropped open in amazement. Then she hastily covered it with her hand to conceal her missing teeth.

"You have guessed correctly, Spartan. I am a daughter of Carthage and my forefathers are descended from Queen Dido who founded the city, and she in turn was of divine birth."

She became so interested that she went to one of the inner rooms and brought out a genealogical table. It was written in Phoenician letters and I could not understand it, but she read at least thirty names, each more alien than the previous.

"Now do you believe me?" she demanded in conclusion. "I can only regret my age and the wrinkles in my face for I would be only too glad to show you the hospitality that you so desire." She extended her arm to smooth Dorieus' neck and pressed her sagging breasts against his shoulder.

Dorieus exclaimed in admiration, "Truly you are a big woman and the equal of a man! Nor do your breasts seem to have shriveled. Birth and the experience of a mature woman mean more than age."

Tanakil rose at once, her face flushed from the wine, pulled Dorieus to his feet and led him to an inner room, the heavy genealogical table under her other arm. That left the three of us, the two young girls and me, and as a fourth the blind flute player blowing gentle melodies in his corner.

3.

I awakened early in the morning to the unearthly crowing of Himera's hundreds of cocks. My ears roared, my temples throbbed, and at first I didn't know where or who I was. When my eyes cleared I realized that I was lying on a couch in Tanakil's banquet room with a crushed wreath on my head and a colored woolen mantle as my only covering. The fine shirt was at my feet and I saw that it had lip coloring on it. My memory had fled and I no longer knew what had happened to me, but on another couch I saw Mikon, the physician of Cos, stretched out with his mouth open and snoring loudly.

The girls and the flute player had disappeared. I rubbed my eyes and remembered as in a dream the touch of the girls' smooth limbs against mine. There was a bad taste in my mouth and the disorder in the room was even worse. Fragments of expensive vases and cups were strewn over the floor, and in stumbling about we had overturned the Phoenician household god. The ceaseless crowing of the cocks hurt my ears and I decided never again to touch mint-flavored wine.

"Mikon," I said, "wake up. Wake up and see how we have respected the hospitality of the finest woman in Himera."

I shook him awake and he sat up, holding his head. I found a bronze mirror, glanced into it, and extended it to Mikon. He looked long at his reflection and finally asked in a thick voice, "Who is that dissolute man staring at me out of that bloated face?"

He sighed deeply. Then, suddenly overcome by realization, he cried out, "Turms, my friend, we are lost! At least I have drawn down upon myself the most fearful curse, for if I remember correctly I talked well into the night and revealed all the secrets of the consecrated to you. I remember that you tried to stop me but I clutched your arm and compelled you to listen."

"Don't worry," I reassured him. "Probably no harm has been done for I can't remember a single word you said. But if our awakening is unpleasant, brother Mikon, think of the awakening that awaits Dorieus. I'm afraid that in his drunkenness he has brought dishonor not only to our hostess and himself, but also to us and even to Dionysius who is ultimately responsible for our behavior."

"Where is he?" asked Mikon, looking around with blood-shot eyes.

"I don't know and I don't even want to know. I certainly will not search the inner rooms, for who knows what dreadful sight might confront me? The best thing we can do is to creep silently out of the house. I hardly think that Dorieus would be anxious to see any friends today."

63

Cautiously stepping over the drunken slave in the doorway, we went outside. The sun's golden rays were climbing, the cocks were crowing in every Himeran house, and the autumn air smelled fresh. We bathed in the hot waters of the pool and found our own clothes, cleaned and pleated, beside our weapons in the entrance hall. In mutual agreement we returned to the banquet room and drained the wine vessel to regain our courage before setting off across the city.

As the residents were kindling their cooking fires we met many of our unfortunate companions, groaning and holding their heads. We joined them and by the time we had stepped through the city gates there were almost a hundred of us, no one feeling himself any better than the others.

Dionysius was laboring over the ships, aided by a long row of pack donkeys and oxen. He cursed us in fury, for he and his helmsmen had spent the night at Krinippos' house and had had only water to drink and pea soup to eat. Lashing out at his ailing men with his rope, he put them to work unloading the treasure and stuffing it into sacks, barrels and chests. Mikon and I joined them in sheer humility although such work was not ours to do.

The most difficult task was the unloading of the large galley which had sunk deep into the mud. Not all the men and oxen could free it, nor did even the windlass constructed of heavy logs by Krinippos' technicians succeed in raising the heavy vessel. The only solution was to lighten it by diving for some of the cargo. The coral divers of Himera would have undertaken the dangerous task willingly but Dionysius had no desire to reveal our treasure. He said that it was only right that his own lechers and drunkards should clear their heads and cool their limbs in the refreshing sea water.

While some of us sorted and counted the booty on both penteconters, weighted baskets were lowered into the sunken ship from small boats and the best divers among us made their way down the ropes. There in the darkness they filled the baskets with the loot and came up only for air. Shivering with cold and fear they huddled in the boats until Dionysius thrashed them into the water again with his rope. On that day many an unfortunate cursed the diving skill that he had acquired in Ionia as a boy.

Mikon and I were given the task of recording the contents of the sacks and barrels on which Dionysius himself inscribed the numbers until he ran out of them. Finally he was content merely to seal the containers with a golden Persian signet without keeping account of what we wrote.

"In the name of Hermes," he declared, "I am plagued by the idea that I may be robbed but even at the risk of that I would rather keep my brain clear than be involved in lists and figures."

By evening both pentecontors had been emptied. Everyone smiled when Dionysius finally called a halt for the day and gave us permission to return to the hospitality of the Himeran homes.

But our elation soon gave way to bitter disappointment, for Dionysius ordered each of us in turn to take off his clothes. From the folds of the garments he plucked surprising amounts of jewelry, gold coins and other objects of value. A few had even hidden gold and gems in their hair, and from the mouth of one mumbling rower Dionysius produced a golden fish. The men cried out in dismay at one another's shocking dishonesty.

I relinquished a heavy golden chain voluntarily upon seeing what awaited me, and Mikon reached into an armpit for a golden winged lion. Embittered by Dionysius' greed and disillusioned by our own dishonesty, we began to demand the right to inspect Dionysius' clothes in return, for we had noticed that he had begun to move with increasing clumsiness and clanking.

Dionysius flushed. "Who is your commander?" he roared. "Who enabled you to win undying fame at Lade, made you wealthy and brought you safely to this new land? Whom can you trust if not me?"

So moved was he by his own words that his beard began to quiver and tears came into his eyes. "The cruelty and thanklessness of man! Everyone measures others, even me, by his own corrupted standards."

"Close your mouth!" we demanded bitterly. "As our commander you certainly are not the best of us but rather the worst. Indeed we wouldn't even respect you if you did not try to take advantage of us."

Bellowing and laughing, we fell upon him, pushed him to the ground and tore off his clothes. Around his waist, beneath his armpits and between his thighs he had suspended pouches from which we poured forth a stream of coins, jewelry, signets, chains and armbands equaling the collective loot of all the others.

Seeing the heap, we laughed loudly, pulled him to his feet again and slapped his broad shoulders. "What a commander you are! Truly you are the cleverest of us all and we will never give you up."

After prolonged argument it was decided that each would be permitted to retain whatever he had stolen. Only the naked divers complained.

"Must we do without anything," they cried, "although we worked the hardest?"

65

Dionysius swore at them. "No one is better than anyone else, my greedy ones. Go back and produce whatever you have hidden in the water. If someone is left with empty hands he has only himself to blame."

The divers blinked at one another and at us and then returned to the shore. They plunged into the water and began rolling aside the stones under its surface. Soon they came up with a wealth of objects, each larger and more valuable than those which we had been able to conceal in our clothes. But we did not begrudge them the loot after their efforts in the darkness of the ship among the octopi, the crabs and the stinging medusae.

"Let us offer a fair share of our loot to the Himeran gods," suggested Dionysius, "in gratitude for the peaceful and good-natured way that we have begun the division of our spoils."

That, we felt, was right and just, so we consecrated some copper tripods, copper pots and a bronze Phoenician ram to the various Himeran temples, and a Persian shield to the temple of the Carthaginian merchants.

4.

The entire day passed without our seeing Dorieus. When darkness fell and the stars were lighted in the alien sky over Himera I could no longer restrain my uneasiness.

I said to Mikon, "We must return to Tanakil's house no matter how reluctantly. Something has happened to Dorieus and I would not be surprised if that proud woman had punctured his throat with a hairpin as he slept to avenge the loss of her honor."

"As a physician I can assure you that in this condition, with his head still thick from wine and a sickening taste in his mouth, a man exaggerates his misdeeds and imagines that he will never again be able to look a decent person in the eye. What did we actually do that was so bad? I seem to remember your dancing the Phoenix dance on the table to show off your agility to the girls, but chiefs and councilors have done the same under the influence of wine and it hasn't blackened their reputation.

"Dorieus is a dangerous man," Mikon went on, "and, like most soldiers, limited to thinking that problems can best be solved by killing. He was born to create dissension and I would not grieve if we were obliged to arrange an honorable funeral. But I think that in your moonless mood you are a little premature. Therefore let us courageously find

66

out what is wrong and at the same time bring gifts to Tanakil in gratitude for her hospitality."

The plan cheered me greatly. "You are the wisest man I have met. In truth, I am not greedy and I care little for valuables. The goddess Artemis has appeared to me in the guise of Hecate and promised, with upraised poker and black dog barking at her feet, that I will never know want. So let us give Tanakil this ten-mina chain that I stole. I don't know myself why I slipped it into my robe, but it must have been for the reason that we may now placate Tanakil with it."

When we reached the market place we saw that many merchants were still at their stalls. We shared a small skin of wine and it cheered me immeasurably. We also ate some fish and some of the good Himeran ash-surfaced bread. Then we continued on our way, stumbling through the dark streets to the western end of the city. Fortunately a torch was flickering feebly at the entrance to Tanakil's house. From that we knew that she was expecting us, so we opened the creaking gate, entered the house, hung our weapons in the entrance hall and stepped into the lighted banquet room.

There on a convivial couch lounged Dorieus, fully alive although glowering, and clothed in such magnificent Phoenician garments that at first glance we did not recognize him. Opposite him, on another couch, lay Tanakil looking equally unhappy. Her cheeks were sunken and her eyes were shadowed although she had tried to improve her appearance with color. Between the couches stood a bronze-legged table with food, and the mixing vessel on the floor was half filled with a yellowish wine. The room had been cleaned, the mosaic floor washed, and the household god righted.

"Tanakil," I begged, "please forgive us our shameful behavior of last night. Your hospitality was overwhelming and we exhausted wretches, unaccustomed as we were to mint wine, could not stand it."

Tanakil looked at Mikon with her hand before her mouth and asked, "You are a Greek physician, aren't you? Tell me, can new teeth be made to replace those that a person has lost?"

Horrified, I demanded, "Has Dorieus in a drunken fit knocked out some of your teeth?"

Dorieus cursed. "Don't talk nonsense, Turms." With trembling hands he filled a cup from the mixing vessel and drank deeply, spilling some of the wine on his chin.

"Dorieus hasn't harmed me," said Tanakil defensively, "so don't insult him with your cruel insinuations. He has behaved in every way as a man of noble birth should behave toward a woman."

67

I was about to express my belief when Dorieus exclaimed, "Where in Hades have you been, you stony-hearted wretches? I don't know why I should have such friends and shield them in battle when they desert me at the very moment when I need them most."

"Yes," asked Tanakil, "where have you been hiding? I am suffering keenly because of a few missing teeth although I hadn't even thought of them until Dorieus pointed out that I have no other flaws. Tyrrhenian physicians are said to make teeth of ivory which they fasten with gold bands. I am not worried about my back teeth, for the more good food one eats the faster they wear down, so that bad teeth are actually an indication of good birth. But that doesn't console me since I lack a few front teeth as well. Now I dare not even speak before Dorieus except with my mouth covered."

Dorieus slapped his cup down so hard that it cracked. "Stop harping about your teeth, my pet! Can't you talk about anything else? I only mentioned them because I saw you lying with your mouth open when I awakened at noon. In fact, I meant only well when I said that you had no other flaws, for many a woman at your age has even fewer teeth."

Tanakil began to weep noisily, smearing the color on her sunken cheeks. "Now you are complaining about my age, although you didn't care last night."

"Silence, woman!" roared Dorieus, the veins at his temples bulging. "I can stand no more. If you continue I shall leave the house and it will be your fault if I kill every Himeran who crosses my path."

He clutched his head and moaned, "Friends, friends, why did you ever desert me! My head is on fire, my stomach aches and my limbs are helpless. I have been vomiting all day and only now have I been able to eat a few simple mouthfuls."

Mikon worriedly tried his head, rolled up his eyelids, studied his eyes and throat and pressed his stomach. While Dorieus was groaning I extended the golden chain to Tanakil with the hope that it would compensate for the damage we had done.

She accepted the chain readily and placed it around her neck. "I am not a petty woman," she said. "What good are riches if one cannot hold a banquet for one's friends? It is true that the vases you broke were valuable, but all vases break in time. I don't think that even my household god was insulted, for early this morning I gave him new clothes and burned incense before him. So I suffered no damage and accept your beautiful gift merely not to displease you. The only harm that has resulted from your visit is the fact that one of the girls who entertained you has been struck dumb."

68

Mikon and I glanced guiltily at each other, for neither of us remembered exactly what had happened. Mikon presumed that the girl had been frightened by my violent goat dance, but it turned out that the girl in question was the one Mikon had carried into the garden. Mikon declared that the girl must have slept on the dewy grass and that this had caused her throat to swell. At least, he didn't remember having done anything to hurt her.

Tanakil replied that the matter was serious and reflected unfavorably on our reputations as strangers. "Himerans are a superstitious people," she said. "Also I and my house will fall under a shadow because of this incident, for everyone knows that a person who suddenly loses his power of speech is bewitched, unless of course he has unwittingly hurt some excessively sensitive god."

Mikon became agitated like all men who are conscious of their guilt. "The only god we could have hurt was the foam-born, but by her magic belt I swear that we honored her in every way that I learned on Aphrodite's sacrificial ship, and the girl certainly did not lose her speech during that time. Indeed she used it loudly to express her joy at the completeness of my education."

"I am not blaming you," said Tanakil, "for you are a gentle and inoffensive man. I have already sent the girl some compensation on your behalf but her parents are alarmed and fear that the girl will never be married if she remains dumb."

Tanakil sent for the girl that we might see her condition for ourselves. When she finally entered with her father and mother I had difficulty in meeting the accusing looks of those simple people.

Mikon tried to hide behind us but when the girl saw him she ran to him joyously, knelt to kiss his hands and held them fondly to her cheek. With a helpless glance at her parents Mikon raised the girl to her feet, embraced her and kissed her lips.

No more was needed, for the girl drew a deep breath and burst into speech. She talked, wept, shouted and laughed until her parents, elated though they were, began to feel ashamed and told her to be quiet. Mikon gave them a handful of silver coins, whereupon they left rejoicing at their good fortune and taking their daughter with them.

When the matter had been so happily resolved I thanked Tanakil for all her goodness to us and said that we must go to seek permanent lodgings in the city.

Hastily she said, "My house is unassuming, I know, and you have probably been accustomed to the luxury of Ionia. But if you don't scorn my house, remain as my guests for as long as you wish. The longer you remain the happier I will be."

To strengthen her invitation and to prove that she did not extend it in the hope of gain, she disappeared into an inner room and reappeared with gifts for each of us. Onto Dorieus' thumb she slipped a gold ring, to Mikon she presented an ivory-framed wax tablet, and to me a moonstone suspended from a cord. The valuable gifts did much to cheer us.

Tanakil then had three beds placed in a row for us. They had copper feet and crossed iron bottoms and were made by the Tyrrhenians. On them were placed soft mattresses. We would have fallen asleep immediately had not Dorieus groaned and tossed. Finally he threw off the covers and snapped that as a soldier he was not accustomed to soft mattresses but preferred the hard ground with a shield as his cover. In the darkness he groped his way out of the room, bumping into chests and overturning objects. Then we heard no more and slept soundly through the night.

5.

So we settled in Tanakil's house, leading a carefree existence as her guests. After our treasure had been safely locked behind the iron doors of Krinippos' vaults life began to flow as evenly as a stream. Dionysius' only mishap resulted from his anxiety to salvage the large vessel. Believing that its cargo had been sufficiently lightened, he tried again to drag it to shore, but so powerful were the windlasses and so strong the ropes that the ship split in the middle.

When we had dived and scraped the mud for our remaining loot we were free to do as we pleased. But before long the people of Himera demanded that Krinippos put an end to the turmoil caused by the Phocaeans.

"The Phocaeans are upsetting our days thoroughly," they complained. "Formerly we awakened at cockcrow to practice our trades but now every house echoes with snores until midday. If we try to awaken our guests they are enraged. We are not unduly sensitive about the morals of our wives and daughters but it is annoying to see them clinging to a sailor's beard from morning to night or fondly combing the lice from his hair. As to what happens at night, we dare not even say."

Krinippos leaped to his feet from the simple wooden chair whose seat was woven of the skin of his unsuccessful predecessor.

"You came at an opportune time, citizens, for my amulets have warned me that danger threatens Himera and my spies in Syracuse have confirmed it. We will therefore put Dionysius' men to work raising the city wall by three ells, to repay our hospitality. When Syracuse hears that Himera's wall will be that much higher I hardly think that it will attack us but will choose some other city."

Dionysius had little faith in Krinippos' amulets but realized that, without discipline, the sailors would soon become an unruly herd. In their restlessness they were already picking quarrels with one another and even fighting, the men of one ship against those of another or the windward rowers against the leeward rowers.

Thus Dionysius concurred readily. "Your plan is excellent, Krinippos, and I assure you that my well-disciplined men will gladly labor to raise the wall of this friendly city. However, in specifying three ells, do you mean Greek or Phoenician ells?"

As a shrewd man Krinippos well understood what was meant and said admiringly, "You are a man after my own mind, Dionysius, but naturally I mean Phoenician ells. Simple courtesy toward my Carthaginian allies demands that I use the Phoenician measure."

Dionysius tore his shirt, pulled his beard and cried out to his men, "Did you hear, all of you, how that despicable tyrant is insulting our honor as Ionians? Naturally, we will raise Himera's wall by three Greek ells and not one finger's width more."

The men began to roar and the most rash among them even ran to their lodgings for their weapons. "A Greek ell, a Greek ell!" they howled, knowing well that a Greek ell is shorter than a Phoenician ell by three fingers.

Krinippos withdrew behind his famous seat and began bargaining with Dionysius, but he had to yield to the use of the Greek measure. Hearing that, Dionysius' men cheered and embraced one another in glee as though they had won a great victory. In that manner Dionysius achieved their voluntary submission to an entire winter's heavy labor. Dorieus, Mikon and I, however, did not have to participate since we had not been guilty of disturbing the peace.

We had not been many days in Tanakil's house before the Siculian couple returned with their daughter. The girl was pale and her glance roving.

"We are ashamed to have to disturb you again," they said, "but our daughter seems to be cursed. As soon as we reached home she became speechless again and has not been able to say a word since then. We are not blaming you, although it was peculiar how easily that Greek physician freed her tongue merely by kissing her. Let him try it again and we shall see what happens."

Mikon protested that there was a time for everything and that it was

71

not proper to kiss women while meditating on divine matters. Tanakil and Dorieus, however, felt that he had bound the girl to him either wittingly or unwittingly and thus was obliged to free her.

Obediently Mikon took the girl in his arms but nothing happened. Then he flushed and kissed her with marked enthusiasm. When he released her the girl began chattering once more and laughing and crying. It was not her fault, she said, that she had fallen under a spell. Away from Mikon her throat swelled and her tongue became immovable, therefore she begged to be allowed to remain with him.

Mikon scolded her and said that it was impossible. Her parents also protested. Nothing hindered her from occasionally singing and dancing for strangers in order to increase her dowry, but it was unthinkable that she should move to a strange house to live with an alien. A respectable girl would lose her reputation and no honorable man would wish to marry her.

The girl screamed that she could not live without Mikon, suffered a fit and sank to the floor unconscious. Her father slapped her cheeks, Tanakil poured a jugful of cold water on her face, and her mother thrust a hairpin into her thigh, and still she did not move. But when Mikon stooped to rub her limbs her eyelids flickered, the color returned to her cheeks and she sat up, demanding to know what had happened.

Reluctantly Mikon began to be interested in the matter as a physician. He urged the parents to take the girl with them and to test her once more. They returned immediately from the street with the information that the girl had become dumb as soon as they had stepped through the gate.

Mikon became serious and drew Dorieus and me aside. "I have long suspected that unseen forces are leading us," he said. "I should have mistrusted the feather that led us to this house. We have been caught in the meshes of Aphrodite and it is she who led this girl here to bind me. Having finally found the opportunity for undisturbed meditation I was just on the verge of divine comprehension, and that angered the golden-haired one for she cannot suffer any man to have thoughts other than those of her liking. If we send the girl away and she remains dumb the entire city will censure us and we will be brought before Krinippos. What shall we do?"

Dorieus and I said immediately that it was his problem, for it was he who had taken the girl into the garden and presumably done something that should not have been done to a sensitive girl.

"That is the simple reason," I said in conclusion. "No divine explanations are required."

"Don't try to roll the guilt onto my shoulders," protested Mikon. "You yourself thrust the white pebble into my hand and led me to this house. Aphrodite has flung her nets over us, as Dorieus likewise knows. Why else would he have fallen into the lap of an old hag?"

Dorieus gritted his teeth. "Tanakil is an intelligent and unprejudiced woman. You are exaggerating her age needlessly. For my part I don't understand how you—yes, and Turms, too—could stoop to touch a low-born girl. You see now what the results are. Tanakil is a refined woman and would never even dream of asking for more than she can get."

"Be that as it may," said Mikon, "you are struggling in the golden net although you may not even realize it. I also am ensnared in it. But you, Turms, you are the one I pity. She is merely playing with us to prove her might, but I dare not even think of the dreadful trap that she has set for you who are her chosen one."

"You are dreaming," I said arrogantly. "You are exaggerating the power of the goddess. I accept her gifts willingly and enjoy her friendship but I have no intention of submitting to her. There is something wrong with both of you in permitting that frivolous goddess to break your will. In that respect I am stronger than you."

As soon as the senseless words were spoken I covered my mouth in dismay, for they were a direct challenge to the foam-born.

Unable to advise Mikon, we returned to the others. The girl had become even more obstinate and was threatening to hang herself from the torch by the gate. Then we could explain that to the people and to Krinippos if we could.

Her threats placed us in an uncomfortable position. Finally, wearying of the fruitless discussion, Mikon said, "So be it. I shall take the girl and purchase her as my slave if you will be content with a reasonable price. I cannot pay exorbitantly for I am but a poor itinerant physician."

The girl's parents stared at each other in horror and then pounced on Mikon, beating him with their fists.

"Do you think we would sell our own child into slavery?" they cried. "We are free Siculi and the natives of this land!"

"Then what do you want?"

It is unlikely that the girl's parents had known exactly what they did want upon their arrival, but their thoughts had been clarified by the conversation and the girl's conduct.

"You must marry her," they declared. "You have only yourself to blame, for you have bewitched her. We will give the girl the usual

73

dowry and it is larger than you imagine, for we are not as poor as we seem."

Mikon tore his hair. "This is unbearable! It is but a trick of the goddess to keep my mind off supernatural matters. What man with a wife can think of anything but the problems of everyday life?"

The girl's parents took her hand and thrust it into Mikon's. "Her name is Ahura," they said.

As they pronounced the girl's name in their own language Mikon clutched his head.

"Aura—if that is your name—we can do nothing, for the gods are mocking us. Aura, you will remember, was a fleet-footed girl and one of Artemis' hunting companions. Dionysus loved her but she did not submit until Aphrodite touched her with madness. The name is an omen, for Dionysus and Aphrodite both had their hand in leading me into this trap."

I cannot say that the solution made us happy, but nothing else could be done. We celebrated the wedding with song and dance in the Siculian house among the cattle and goats. The dowry was on display for the neighbors to see and the parents had slaughtered, baked, cooked and roasted more than enough for everyone. After they had sacrificed a dove and smeared its blood on the clothes of the bride and groom, in accordance with the Siculian custom, music was played and wine was served. Under its influence I even danced the goat dance and won the deep admiration of those simple farmers.

Before the wedding Mikon had been depressed, saying that he probably would have to buy a house, hang his caduceus on the gate and remain in Himera to practice his profession. But Tanakil would not hear of it. During the wedding Mikon seemed considerably happier, perhaps due to the wine, and he was the first to remind us that it was time to return to Tanakil's house. Nor did he speak to me of divine matters for a long time thereafter.

6.

When we had won her confidence, Aura took us outside the city to the woods and the mountains where she showed us the sacred springs, trees and rocks of the Siculi.

A stranger would not have been able to distinguish them but Aura explained, "When I touch this sacred stone my limbs prickle; when I place my hand on this tree my hand grows numb; and when I gaze into this spring I seem to fall into a trance."

As we wandered together I realized that I likewise was beginning to sense our approach to these hallowed spots. If I held Aura's hand I would suddenly exclaim, "This is the place! That tree, that spring." How I knew it I cannot explain.

Soon it was no longer necessary for me to hold Aura's hand, but a mere indication of the direction sufficed. Far ahead of the others I would stop and say, "Here is where I feel the power. This is a sacred place."

Dionysius had asked me to make friends with the Tyrrhenians who sold iron goods and incomparably beautiful golden jewelry in their own mart. He was anxious to learn more about the sea across which we must sail in order to reach Massilia. But something made me shun those silent, odd-featured men who refused to bargain and chatter like the Greeks and instead competed with the excellence of their wares. Listening to their talk I had the feeling that I had heard the language long ago in a dream and could understand it if only I could cross some unfathomable threshold.

When I questioned the Himerans about the Tyrrhenians and their customs I was told that they were a cruel and pleasure-loving people and so licentious that at banquets even high-born women lay on the couches beside the men. On the seas the Tyrrhenians were formidable opponents and as iron-makers none could surpass them. It was also said that they had invented the anchor as well as the metallic ram on war-ships. They called themselves the Rasenna but the other peoples on the Italian mainland called them Etruscans.

Unable to explain my own reluctance, I nevertheless decided to visit the Tyrrhenian mart. But already in the yard I felt as though I had stepped into the domain of strange gods. The sky seemed to darken before me and the ground tremble underfoot. Nevertheless I seated myself on the bench which the merchants offered and began to bargain for a beautiful censer on raised legs.

While I was doing so their employer appeared from one of the inner rooms. His oval eyes, straight nose and long face seemed strangely familiar. He asked the others to leave, then smiled and said something to me in his own language. I shook my head and explained in the Himeran jargon that I didn't understand.

He replied in excellent Greek, "Don't you really understand or are you merely pretending? Even if you must appear as a Greek you surely realize that if you were to comb your hair like ours, shave your curly beard and don our clothes, you would pass for an Etruscan anywhere."

Only then did I realize why he seemed so familiar. The oval face, the eyes with a fold at the corner, the straight nose and wide mouth resembled those I had seen in a mirror.

I explained that I was an Ionian refugee from Ephesus and added playfully, "Probably his hairdress and the cut of his clothes make a man. Even the gods of the various peoples can be distinguished more readily by their clothes than by their faces. I have no reason to doubt my Ionian birth but I shall remember your remark. Tell me about the Etruscans whom I resemble and of whom so much bad is said."

"We have twelve allied cities," he began, "but each city has its own customs, laws and government. We have twelve smiling gods, twelve birds and twelve compartments in the liver which determine our lives. Our hands have twelve lines and our lives are divided into twelve eras. Will you hear more?"

There was sarcasm in my voice as I replied, "In Ionia we also had twelve cities fighting the twelve Persian satrapies, and we defeated the Persians in twelve battles. We also have twelve celestial gods as well as twelve gods of the underworld. But I am not a Pythagorean and will not argue about figures. Instead, tell me something about your customs and conditions."

"We Etruscans know more than is generally believed," he replied, "but we also know how to hold our tongue. Thus, I know more about your naval battle and your expeditions than is good for you or your commander. But you have nothing to fear since you have not violated the Etruscan naval might, at least yet. We share the western sea with our allies the Phoenicians of Carthage, and Etruscan vessels sail in Carthaginian waters as freely as the ships of Carthage in ours. But we are also friendly with the Greeks and have permitted them to settle on our shores. We gladly trade our best for the best that other peoples can offer, but our knowledge we will not barter. And speaking of trade, have you agreed on a price for that censer?"

I explained that I had not yet had time to bargain sufficiently. "I don't really enjoy bargaining," I explained, "but in trading with Greeks and Phoenicians I have noticed that bargaining is an even greater source of joy to a merchant than selling. A true merchant is deeply wounded by a ready acceptance of the price that he has set."

"You may have the censer without money or price," said the Etruscan. "I give it to you as a gift."

I looked at him suspiciously. "What reason have you to give me a gift? I don't even know whether I have anything suitable to give you in return."

The man suddenly grew grave, bowed his head, covered his eyes with his left hand, raised his right arm and declared, "I give you the gift expecting nothing in return. But I would be happy if you would drink a cup of wine with me and rest for a moment on the couch."

I misunderstood his words and said sharply, "I do not indulge in that even though I am an Ionian."

When he realized what I meant he was deeply hurt. "No, no. In that respect we Etruscans do not imitate the Greeks. I would not dare lay a hand on you, for you are who you are."

He spoke with such significance that a sudden sadness came over me. No longer reluctant to confide in this unknown man, I asked, "Who and what am I, then? How can anyone know? For each of us carries within him another and strange self which takes him by surprise and drives him to actions against his will."

The Etruscan's oval eyes looked at me knowingly and a little smile touched his lips. "Not each of us," he protested. "Far from that. For is not the majority a mere herd which is driven to the river to drink and back again to pasture?"

A deep poignancy gripped me. "The enviable and best human fate is to be content with one's lot. But he also is enviable who is not content but reaches for that which is humanly attainable. I myself, however, am probably striving for something that is not humanly attainable."

"And what is that?" he asked.

"I don't know," I admitted. "My mother I have known only in my dreams and my only father was a bitter friend of wisdom. I was born of a thunderbolt outside Ephesus and rescued by Artemis when the shepherds would have stoned me."

Again the Etruscan covered his eyes with his left hand, bowed his head and raised his right arm as though in greeting. He said nothing, however, and I began to regret having confided so much to a complete stranger. He led me to a small banquet room, produced a jug of wine, and mixed some in a vessel with cool water. The room was filled with a fragrance of violets.

He splashed a drop onto the floor and said, "I drink to the goddess whose head bears a mural crown and whose emblem is an ivy leaf. She is the goddess of walls, but the walls of the body crumble before her." He emptied his cup solemnly.

"Of whom are you speaking?" I asked.

"Of Turan."

"I know her not," I replied. But he said no more, merely smiled mysteriously as though doubting my words. Courteously I emptied my own cup. "I don't know whether I should be drinking with you. Your violet wine might go to my head. As it is, I have noticed that I no longer can drink in moderation like civilized people. Already on two occasions in this city I have become so intoxicated that I have danced the obscene goat dance and finally lost my memory."

"Thank the wine for that," he observed. "You are fortunate in finding relief from your oppression in drink. But what did you want of me? My name is Lars Alsir."

I let him refill the black wine cup and confessed, "I know what I wanted of you when I came. You could serve me best by obtaining a periplus of your sea, its shores, landmarks, winds, currents and harbors, so that we might reach Massilia safely in the spring."

"That would be a crime," he said, "for we are not friends of the Phocaeans. Several generations ago we were compelled to engage in warfare against the Phocaeans when they attempted to gain a foothold in Sardinia and Corsica where we had mines. Even were I to give you a periplus you would not reach Massilia, for Dionysius would first have to obtain a sailing permit from both the Carthaginians and the Etruscans. And that he could not buy for all his stolen treasure."

"Are you threatening me?" I demanded.

"Certainly not. How could I threaten you if you truly are a son of a thunderbolt, as you claim?"

"Lars Alsir—" I began.

"What is it that you wish of me, Lars Turms?" he asked with mock gravity.

"Why do you call me that? My name is Turms, true enough, but not Lars Turms."

"I was merely showing respect. We use the word in honoring another's birth. And because you are a Lars no harm can befall you."

I did not understand, but explained that I had bound myself to the Phocaeans and if he could not sell me a periplus perhaps he could obtain a pilot who would consent to guide us to Massilia.

Lars Alsir traced the design on the floor without looking at me. "Carthaginian merchants guard their sailing routes so closely that any captain who discovers his ship being spied upon by Greeks would rather run his vessel aground and destroy both himself and the Greek vessel rather than reveal his route. We Etruscans are not quite so secretive, but as rulers of the sea we likewise have our traditions."

He raised his head and looked into my eyes. "Understand me well, Lars Turms. Nothing would hinder me from selling you a falsified periplus at a high price, or giving you a pilot who would run you into a reef. But I could not do that to you because you are a Lars. Let

78

Dionysius reap what he has sown. Let us forget this unpleasant topic and talk instead of divine matters."

I declared with some bitterness that I could not understand why people insisted upon discussing divine matters with me after a cup of wine.

"Do I really bear the sign of a curse on my forehead?" I asked. I told him of my rescue by Artemis and declared that since then I had feared nothing. "I don't even fear you, Lars Alsir, or your smiling gods. In fact, at this very moment I seem to be sitting near the ceiling and looking down at you, and you are small indeed in my eyes."

His voice sounded distant as a whisper. "Precisely, Lars Turms. You are on a round seat, leaning against its round back. But what is that you are holding in your hands?"

Extending my hands before me, palms upward, I looked at them in surprise. "I have a pomegranate in one and a cone in the other!"

Far below me in the dimness Lars Alsir, kneeling on the floor, looked up at me. "Precisely, Lars Turms. In one hand you hold the earth, in the other the sky, and you need fear no mortal. But you still don't know our smiling gods."

His words were like a challenge. Something in me expanded to infinity, the veil of the earth was rent and I saw a shadowy goddess. She wore a mural crown and carried an ivy leaf, but her face was invisible.

"What do you see?" Lars Alsir's words carried to my ears from an unfathomable distance. "What do you see, son of the thunderbolt?"

I cried out, "I see her! For the first time I see her whom I have heretofore seen only in my dreams. But a veil covers her face and I cannot recognize her."

Suddenly I plunged from my height, the veil-like world became solid and impenetrable again, and I was aware of my body. I was lying on the couch and Lars Alsir was shaking my shoulders.

"What is wrong? You suddenly went from me into a trance."

I clutched my head with both hands, drank the wine that he offered me and then thrust the cup from me. "What poison are you giving me? I don't become intoxicated so quickly. I thought I saw a veiled woman taller than a mortal and I was like a cloud beside her."

"This is only innocent violet wine," protested Lars Alsir. "But perhaps the shape of the black cup stimulated your hand. You see, the Etruscan gods follow an Etruscan wherever he may be reborn."

"Are you claiming that I am a native Etruscan and not a Greek?"

"You may be the son of a slave or a prostitute, but you have been chosen by a divine thunderbolt. But let me advise you. Do not reveal

79

your identity or boast about your birth if you ever find yourself in our land, as I think you will. You will be recognized in time. You yourself must wander blindfold and allow the gods to lead you. More than that I cannot say."

In time we became friends, but not once did Lars Alsir again refer to my birth.

I told Dionysius that the Tyrrhenians were difficult to approach and that a stranger could not hope to bribe them into revealing their maritime secrets.

He became enraged. "The bones of Phocaeans rest on their shores, and if the Tyrrhenians choose to bite iron rather than peacefully allow us to sail to Massilia, they can blame only themselves if they cut their lips."

Dionysius had begun the construction of a new warship while supervising the elevation of Himera's wall by three Greek ells. He did not compel the men to work too hard, merely enough to maintain discipline. Many of the Phocaeans married Himeran women and planned to take them to Massilia.

The Sicilian winter was mild and gentle. I was happy to live in Himera while seeking myself. But then I met Kydippe, the granddaughter of the tyrant Krinippos.

7.

Krinippos was an ailing man who ate only vegetables even though he was not a Pythagorean. In fact, he had banished the Pythagoreans because they made the mistake of preaching oligarchy by the wise and the virtuous instead of by the aristocrats and the wealthy.

In his agony Krinippos was in the habit of expressing such bitter thoughts to his son Terillos, whose head had grown bald while vainly awaiting his father's death and the acquisition of the amulets. I had occasion to listen to Krinippos' lectures when I accompanied Mikon to his house in curiosity. Mikon's potions eased the tyrant's pain but Mikon warned him, "I cannot heal you, for the power that you have consumed has gone to your belly and is devouring you from within like a crab."

Krinippos sighed. "Ah, how willingly I would die! But I cannot think of my own pleasure for my heart is heavy with concern for Himera and I cannot understand how I can leave its government to my inexperienced son. For almost forty years I have held him by the hand and tried to teach him statesmanship, but one cannot expect much of one to whom not much has been given."

Terillos plucked at the gold-leafed wreath that he wore to conceal his baldness and whined, "Dear father, I have at least learned that Himera's peace and freedom depend on its friendship with Carthage. The goddess of Eryx gave me a wife from Segesta whom I have suffered all these years merely to assure us of an ally should Syracuse threaten us. But the only child she gave me was Kydippe. Because of your statesmanship I have not even a son to whom I can bequeath your amulets."

Mikon tried Krinippos' pulse as he lay groaning on a dirty sheepskin. "Don't agitate yourself, ruler Krinippos, for anger and vexation will merely increase your discomfort."

"My entire life has consisted of anger and vexation," said Krinippos morosely. "I would feel uncomfortable if something were not constantly troubling me. But you, Terillos, do not concern yourself with your successor, for I greatly fear that you will have little power to bequeath. Marry off Kydippe in time to some trustworthy city and ruler so that when you have lost Himera you can gnaw her bread of charity."

Terillos, who was a sensitive man, burst into tears at his father's unkind words. Krinippos relented and patted his knee with a veined hand.

"I am not blaming you, my son. I myself sired you and must bear the consequences. You were born into a worse period than I and I doubt whether even with my amulets I could persuade the present Himera to make me its tyrant. People are no longer as superstitious as in the good old days. But I am glad, my son, for you will be relieved of the responsibility of power and will live out your days in Kydippe's care." Then he said, "Bring Kydippe here to kiss her grandfather. I want to show her to these men. It will do no harm to have the fame of her beauty spread beyond the city."

I did not expect much of her, for grandfathers are easily blinded by love, but when Terillos escorted her in it was as though dawn had burst upon the bleak room. She was only fifteen, but her golden eyes shone, her skin was as white as milk, and when she smiled her little teeth gleamed like pearls.

After she had greeted us shyly Kydippe ran to kiss her grandfather and to stroke his sparse beard. Krinippos turned her from side to side like a heifer being offered for sale, tilted her chin and asked proudly, "Have you ever seen a more desirable maiden?"

Mikon said firmly that it was not wise to make a young girl aware of her beauty.

Krinippos cackled. "If it were a question of a more stupid girl you would be right, but Kydippe is not only fair but intelligent. I myself have taught her. Don't believe in the gentleness of her eyes and the shyness of her smile, for she has already weighed you and decided how best to benefit by you. Haven't you, Kydippe?"

Kydippe placed a rosy palm before his toothless mouth, blushed and said, "Oh, grandfather, why are you always so cruel? I couldn't be calculating if I tried. I probably am not even beautiful in their opinion. You make me ashamed."

Mikon and I cried out with one voice that she was the fairest maiden we had ever seen, and Mikon expressed his gratitude that he was already married and so could not be tempted to yearn for the moon in the sky.

"Not the moon," I corrected him, "but the brightest, most dazzling sunrise. Seeing you, Kydippe, I wish that I were a king so that I might win you for my own."

She tilted her head and looked at me through long lashes. "I am not yet of an age to think of men. But if I should think of someone, it would be of a handsome man whose hearth I would tend and for whom I would weave cloth from the wool of my own sheep. But I am sure that you are mocking me. My clothes are probably pleated in an old-fashioned manner and my shoes ridiculous."

She was wearing a pair of soft leather shoes dyed red and bound with purple ribbons to her knees.

Krinippos said proudly, "I myself have walked half my life with bare feet and even yet I often take off my shoes lest they be worn needlessly. But this vain girl makes me poor with her demands. As she strokes my beard she whispers softly, 'Grandfather, buy me some Etruscan shoes.' As she kisses my forehead she murmurs, 'Grandfather, today I saw a Phoenician comb that would look well in my hair.' But if I become angry at her vanity she explains that she is not ornamenting herself for her own sake but for the sake of my position."

Kydippe scolded him. "Oh, grandfather, how can you tease me so in the presence of strangers? You know well that I am not vain or demanding. But not everyone is like you. Even in a ragged robe and bare feet you are the autocrat of Himera. But my father must wear a golden wreath to distinguish himself from the people and I must ornament myself for sacrificial ceremonies and processions lest some drover or sailor mistakenly pinch me in passing."

When we left Krinippos' house Mikon said warningly, "That Kydippe is a heartless girl and just at the age when she wants to test her power over men. Don't try to win her. In the first place you would not succeed, for her ambition is boundless. But even if you did, she would only cause you suffering, and finally Krinippos would have you killed like an annoying fly."

But I could not think unkindly of such a wondrously fair maiden, and her innocent vanity was to me merely a childlike desire to charm. When I thought of her it was as though the sun shone on me and soon I ceased to think of anything else. I began to circle Krinippos' house on the edge of the market place in the hope of catching a glimpse of her.

My only hope of meeting Kydippe was when she went to the marts with her servants and two scar-faced guards. She walked chastely with her eyes down, but she had a wreath on her head, rings in her ears, bracelets on her arms, and soft sandals on her feet.

When nothing else availed I turned to Lars Alsir. He consented to help me but said scornfully, "Are you really content with such worthless pastimes, Turms, when the miraculous games of the gods could be available to you? If you lust for that hard-hearted girl, why not use your powers over her? You will not win her heart with bribes."

I told him that the very sight of Kydippe drained all my strength.

When she came to look at the Etruscan jewelry she admired a necklace of golden grains which Lars Alsir held against a black cloth so that the light from a hole in the ceiling fell on it. She asked its price.

Lars Alsir shook his head in regret. "I have already sold it." And when Kydippe asked the purchaser he mentioned my name, as we had agreed.

"Turms of Ephesus!" cried Kydippe. "I know him. What does he want with such jewelry? I thought he was a single man."

Lars Alsir ventured to suppose that I had some friend to whom I wished to present it. He sent for me nevertheless, and of course I was not far away.

Kydippe smiled her most radiant smile, greeted me shyly and said, "Oh, Turms, I am so enchanted with this necklace. Won't you give it up for my sake?"

I pretended to be embarrassed and said that I had already promised it to another. She laid her hand on my arm and breathed into my face. "I believed you to be a serious man," she said. "It was that which attracted me to you so that I have been unable to forget your oval eyes. I am truly disappointed in you."

I whispered that such matters could not be discussed before curious servant girls. Quickly she sent them into the yard and then we were three, she, Lars Alsir and I.

"Sell it to me," pleaded Kydippe. "Otherwise I must consider you

83

a frivolous man who pursues notorious women, for only a bad woman would accept such an expensive gift from a strange man."

I pretended to hesitate. "How much will you pay for it?"

Lars Alsir considerately turned his back. Kydippe fingered her pouch and said unhappily, "Alas, I have perhaps only ten coins and grandfather already accuses me of wastefulness. Won't you sell it to me cheaply?"

"That I will, Kydippe," I said. "I will sell it to you for one silver coin if you will also allow me to kiss your mouth."

She pretended to be deeply shocked. "You don't know what you are asking. No man has yet kissed my mouth except my father and grandfather. Grandfather has warned me and said that a girl who allows a man to kiss her is lost. Don't even suggest it, Turms."

"It is true that I intended to give that necklace to a certain frivolous woman, but it would be easier for me to forget her if I could but kiss your innocent mouth."

Kydippe hesitated. "Will you promise not to tell anyone? I want those beautiful golden beads so badly, but even more I would desire to rescue you from evil temptation if I could only believe that thereafter you would think only of me."

I swore secrecy. Kydippe ascertained that Lars Alsir's back was still turned, parted her lips for my kiss and even pushed her gown aside. Then suddenly she drew back, straightened her gown, took a silver coin from her purse and reached for the necklace.

"Take your drachma," she said coldly. "Grandfather was right. But you did not affect me in any way, and, frankly, it was as though I had kissed the wet nose of a calf."

She was shrewder than I and I had gained nothing with the kiss. Instead, I owed Lars Alsir for the expensive necklace. That should have served as a lesson, but I saved the silver coin and trembled each time I handled it.

I prayed in vain to Aphrodite. I was certain that she had rejected me but in truth the goddess was preparing an entirely different snare for me in which Kydippe was merely the bait.

When the spring winds began to blow Dorieus called me aside and said, "Turms, I have thought much during these months and my decision has been made. I intend to travel to Eryx, by land so that I may acquaint myself with the entire western region. Tanakil will accompany me, for the goldsmiths of Eryx know how to make teeth of ivory and gold. People will believe her if she says that she is on her way to sacrifice to Aphrodite because of her widowhood. Mikon and Aura likewise are going, and naturally I would want you also to see the grain city of Segesta and the land of Eryx."

I barely noticed his grimness, for I was thinking of Kydippe. "Your plan is excellent," I said eagerly. "I also have matters for Aphrodite of Eryx. After all, she is the most famous Aphrodite of the western sea. Let us leave immediately."

On the following day we departed for Eryx by horse, donkey and litter. We left our shields at Tanakil's house and took with us only the traveler's necessary weapons to defend ourselves against robbers and wild beasts. With my senses inflamed by Kydippe I was prepared for the journey and thought that my wish would be fulfilled with the aid of Aphrodite of Eryx. But the goddess was more cunning than I.

BOOK FOUR

The Goddess of Eryx

I.

I, THE TURMS who journeyed from Himera to Eryx, was a differ-ent being from the man who danced in the storm on the road to Delphi. A man changes slowly during every phase of his life until he realizes with a start that it is difficult for him to remember and recognize his former self. Thus life is a series of rebirths, and the beginning of each new phase is like a sudden leap over a chasm which stretches insurmountably behind one so that there is no return to the past.

The soft mist of the spring clouds wreathed the Sicilian crags, and the gentle spring rains fell on the thick Sicilian forests and flooded the dried rivers as we wandered from Himera westward toward Eryx. Because of Tanakil's comfortable beds and banquet table we had grown flabby during the winter months and it was a pleasure for Dorieus and me and even Mikon to exert ourselves and feel our muscles again swelling with strength.

We followed the road taken by the pilgrims, and the Siccani who lived in the woods did not molest us. They respected the goddess while retaining their primitive customs and called themselves the first inhabitants of the land.

After we had journeyed through the almost impossible mountains and the endless woods and were approaching the smiling valleys of Segesta, we saw a pack of sinewy hunting dogs pursuing game. The highborn hunters were dressed in the Greek manner and claimed that their dogs were descended directly from Krimisos, the canine deity who had married the nymph Segesta.

When they had continued on their way Mikon looked at the fields around us and remarked, "The blood of many peoples has made these

86

fields fertile. Phocaeans also are buried here. Let us follow Dionysius' suggestion and make an offering."

Nor was it necessary for us to do so secretly, for the Segestans themselves had erected altars to the men who had attempted to conquer their land. Pointing to the monuments at the edge of the grain fields they said proudly, "Many have attempted to come here but few have returned."

Their fathers and forefathers had been in the habit of burying the bodies of the vanquished in the fields, but they said reassuringly, "We are living in civilized times and no longer have to go to war for Eryx. If someone were to attack us, Carthage would consider it reason for war, and certainly no one would be bold enough to seek a quarrel with Carthage deliberately."

When we had made our sacrifice at the altar of the Phocaeans, Dorieus began to look around inquiringly. "If they erect altars to heroes, where then is the altar to my father? He should have the most splendid altar of all, for did he not come here to conquer the land as the descendant of Herakles?"

Fortunately the Segestans did not understand his dialect. When I asked them about a monument to Dorieus of Sparta, they shook their heads.

"It is true that we conquered a great number of Spartans but they were hardly worth remembering and we did not note their names. However, with them came Philip of Croton, a many-time winner of the Olympic games and the fairest of his contemporaries. Even dead he was so beautiful that we erected a temple to him and every fourth year honor his memory by holding games."

They indicated the large monument and the stadium before it. At first Dorieus could not say a word, then his face darkened and his shoulder straps snapped in rage.

"That is nonsense!" he shrieked. "My father Dorieus was the winner of laurel wreaths at Olympia and the fairest of his contemporaries. How could any Crotonian have competed with him?"

The Segestans fled his rage and Mikon and I had difficulty in calming him.

When he could again breathe easily Dorieus said, "Now I realize why my father's spirit did not give me peace and why the sheep's bones so unfailingly pointed westward. The earth is trembling beneath my feet, for these hills, these valleys and fields are the legacy of Herakles and thus my father's and my land. But I no longer covet it merely to rule. My deepest desire from now on is the righting of that dreadful wrong so that my father's spirit may rest in peace."

I began to fear that he would cause disturbances which would delay our journey. "The less you talk about your father and your legacy in this city the better for us all," I warned him. "Remember that we are on our way to Eryx and not attempting to have monuments erected to our memory in the fields of Segesta."

Tanakil also spoke soothingly to him. "Your thoughts are regal, Dorieus, but permit me to be your councilor, as we have agreed. I have already buried three husbands and I am experienced in these matters. You will receive an answer to everything in Eryx."

Mikon likewise had advice for him. "You are a greater threat to yourself than are the Segestans," he warned. "If you permit your passions to rise, your veins will burst before you realize it. Perhaps the oarstroke that you received at Lade affected you more than we thought. Your forefather Herakles also suffered outbursts of rage after his head had been struck and he heard the imaginary weeping of an infant."

Dorieus protested angrily that it had not been an oarstroke but an honest swordstroke. Besides, it had not injured his head but merely crushed his helmet. Thus we returned to normal conversation and he no longer alarmed the Segestans with his threats.

Segesta was a civilized and pleasant city with its temples, market places and baths, and more Greek in its habits than Himera. Its people claimed to be of Trojan origin and declared that their progenitress was a Trojan woman to whom Krimisos, the canine god of the river, had taken a liking.

While in Segesta we enjoyed the hospitality of Tanakil's sons by her second marriage. Theirs was a prosperous house with several yards, many sheds and large granaries. We were received with the greatest honor but Tanakil forbade her sons to appear until they had shaved their beards and recombed their hair. The demand probably aroused some bitterness, for both of them were elderly men and that fact could not be concealed by a shaven chin and youthful curls. In deference to their mother's wishes, however, they obeyed her and for the duration of our visit sent away their full-grown children lest their presence remind Tanakil of her age.

We were permitted to acquaint ourselves freely with the city and its sights. In the pen of the river god Krimisos' temple we saw the holy dog to which the city's fairest maiden was wed each year in secret rites. Dorieus, however, chose to walk atop the city wall which the people had permitted to crumble and watched the games, the wrestling and the boxing performed for the enjoyment of the nobles by paid athletes. But he kept his mouth shut and did not criticize the barbaric customs of the city.

On the morning before our departure Dorieus arose with a sigh, shook his head and complained, "Throughout the night I have been expecting my father's spirit to appear in a dream with an omen. But I had no dream and I don't know what to think of my father."

Upon our arrival we had been given new clothes to wear while the servants washed the garments that had been soiled during the journey. As we prepared for our departure Dorieus missed his heavy woolen mantle. We searched for it everywhere and Tanakil scolded her sons until we noticed that it had been left on a pole to dry. Because of its thickness it had dried more slowly than the other clothes and had been forgotten by the servants.

Tanakil observed tartly that such a thing could never have happened in her house and Dorieus remarked that as an exile far from home he was accustomed to such humiliating treatment. A full quarrel was rapidly ripening in gratitude for the hospitality that we had enjoyed.

Pushing aside the alarmed servants, Dorieus snatched the mantle from the pole. As he did so a little bird flitted from the folds and began to circle Dorieus with fluttering wings. Soon it was joined by another bird, chirping in angry protest.

Dorieus shook the mantle in amazement. A nest dropped from its folds and from the nest rolled two small eggs which smashed on the ground.

But Dorieus was not angry. Instead, he smiled and said, "See, there is the omen that I craved. My mantle wished to remain here although I myself am departing. I could not hope for a better omen."

Mikon and I glanced uneasily at each other, for to us the broken nest and eggs seemed an ill omen. But Tanakil likewise began to smile and covered her mouth shyly. "I shall remember this omen, Dorieus, and in Eryx I shall remind you of it."

On the following day we saw from a distance the high cone of the holy mountain of Eryx. Its peak was concealed by soft clouds, but when they parted we saw the ancient temple of Aphrodite of Eryx.

The land of Eryx was bursting into spring, flowers dotted the fields and doves cooed in the thickets although the sea still was restless. Unwilling to wait we began to ascend the deserted pilgrims' road that circled the bleak mountain. We reached the small city at its peak just as the darkness of the sea and the entire land of Eryx glowed red in the sunset. The guards had noticed our approach and had delayed the closing of the gate to permit us to enter the city before night.

At the gate we were met by a crowd of noisy men who sought to outdo one another in tugging at our robes and offering their hospitality. But Tanakil was familiar with the city and its habits, dispersed the importuners with sharp words and led us through the city toward the temple area to a house surrounded by a garden in which we were graciously received. Our horses and donkeys were led to a stable and a crackling fire of resinous wood was lighted for us since the air of the holy mountain grew bitterly cold after sunset in the early spring.

The dark-faced innkeeper bade us welcome in fluent Greek. "There is still time to the festival of spring, the sea is uneasy and the goddess has not yet arrived from beyond the waters. Therefore my house is still in its winter condition and I know not whether I can arrange banquets worthy of you. But if you will content yourselves with my chilly rooms, uncomfortable beds and poor food, you may consider my house your home so long as you remain in Eryx."

He made no attempt to pry into our affairs but departed with dignity and sent his slaves and servants to care for us. His behavior made a deep impression on me and I asked Tanakil whether he was by any chance a highborn man.

Tanakil laughed sarcastically. "He is the greediest and most unscrupulous extortioner in the entire city and weighs with gold every mouthful that he offers. But his house is the only one worthy of us and while we live here he will protect us from all the other vermin in this holy city."

"But must we wait before an empty temple until the spring festival?" I asked in disappointment. "We have no time for that."

Tanakil smiled slyly. "Aphrodite of Eryx has her mysteries just like the other deities. At the beginning of the sailing season she arrives from Africa with her retinue in a ship with purple sails. But still the temple is not empty during the winter to one who is familiar with it. On the contrary, the most important state visits are paid and the most expensive offerings made during the quiet season when large crowds, sailors and peddlers do not disturb the mysteries. The time-honored fountain of the goddess stands both winter and summer and the goddess may manifest herself within the temple although she does not bathe in the fountain until the spring festival."

Her words filled me with doubt. I looked at her painted cheeks and cunning eyes and asked, "Do you really believe in the goddess?"

She stared long at me. "Turms of Ephesus," she said at last, "you don't know what you ask. The goddess's fountain in Eryx is ancient. It is older than the Greek fountains, older than the Etruscan, older even than the Phoenician. It was a sacred fountain even before the goddess appeared to the Phoenicians as Astarte and to the Greeks as Aphrodite. What could I believe if I didn't believe in the goddess?"

The heat of the embers sent me outside to breathe the sharp air of the mountain peak. The sky glittered with the small stars of spring and in the thin air I smelled the fragrance of earth and of pines. The sturdy temple reached upward from its terrace against the night sky, and I was overcome by a presentiment that the goddess in her capriciousness was a more formidable enigma than I had believed.

2.

But when I awakened to a new dawn everything was different. When one arrives in a strange city at dusk it seems larger and more mysterious than by the light of day. In looking around with rested eyes I saw that the holy city of Eryx was really quite insignificant with its log hovels and stone huts. After all, I had seen Delphi, I had lived in Ephesus, and in Miletus I had seen a large modern city the like of which was nowhere in the world. This tiny alien city with its screaming inhabitants and peddlers seemed pitifully unimportant compared to what I had seen before, and its insignificance grew as I looked about me from atop the wall which had been heaped together of earth and stones. The vastness of the sea surrounded it. This was the westernmost tip of the civilized world, and beyond it lay only unknown Phoenician waters extending to the Pillars of Herakles and beyond them to the sea of the world. On the landward side stretched the plain with its chestnut forests, olive trees and cultivated fields, and behind them rose the steep mountains of the land of Eryx.

With my ears humming from the wind and my eyes dazzled by the infinite sea, I looked at the temple walls and the barbarically clumsy colonnades. What could I hope to find in that insignificant temple? I was overcome by a sudden feeling that I had been born into the world alone and that I no longer believed in gods.

After Tanakil had made arrangements for us to enter the temple we bathed and dressed in spotless clothes, cut a tuft of hair from our heads and burned it in a flame. Then we took our votive offerings and went to the temple.

We were allowed to enter the temple freely and to view the votive offerings in the entrance hall as well as the empty pedestal in the goddess's chamber. Several irritable priests guided us and accepted our offerings without a word of thanks. Save for several large silver urns we saw few expensive offerings, but the priests explained that the goddess's clothes and jewels were kept in a treasure vault. When she had doffed her winter garments and bathed in the ancient fountain she would again be dressed in her incomparable clothes, pearls and gems.

In fact, it was as though we were visiting any other public building. Only when we approached the fountain and the goddess's doves took flight did I feel the proximity of power. The fountain was large and deep and its concave walls curved unseen into the mountain beneath its opening. It was half filled with water and the dark unrippled surface reflected our faces. Surrounding it inside the modern peristyle was a row of ancient conical rocks, and the priests assured us that a man who had lost his virility had only to lay a hand on one of those stones to recover it immediately.

I saw none of the customary temple maidens, the priests explaining that they arrived with the goddess to participate in the spring festival and to serve the more demanding visitors, but departed with her in the autumn. Besides, Aphrodite of Eryx did not favor such sacrifices within the walls of her temple. The city was for that purpose. Harlots from everywhere came to Eryx for the summer and erected their leaf shelters outside the walls and along the mountain slopes.

One of the priests asked derisively whether I had no other problems for Aphrodite of Eryx. "Little do you Greeks understand Aphrodite," he said scornfully. "Her power is not founded only in proficiency. Sensual ecstasy and erotic pleasures are merely her disguises, just as she ornaments herself with nine strings of pearls for the sole purpose of contrasting the gleam of her living skin to the lifelessness of the pearls."

Tanakil spoke to him placatingly. "Don't you remember me? Twice already the goddess has appeared to me and shown me my future husband. First she married me to Segesta, then to Himera, and on each occasion I made an offering, first upon receiving a husband and then again having buried him. Now I am hopeful that the goddess will appear yet a third time to me."

The priest looked first at her and then at Dorieus and said with a grimace, "Of course I remember you, Tanakil, you incorrigible one. The goddess favors you, but even her power is limited."

He turned to us and Mikon hastened to explain, "I am consecrated and as a physician am striving to familiarize myself with divine matters. Because of the goddess's whim I had to marry this Siculian girl. When I first touched her she lost her power of speech but now that we are wedded she talks even too much, especially when I want to contemplate supernatural affairs. As a consequence, I became increasingly weak and now am completely impotent. We therefore hope that the goddess will appear to us and aid us so that our marital relations will be more harmonious."

For my part I said, "Aphrodite once favored me in clothing my nakedness in her sacred woolen bonds. One single name rings through my mind night and day, but I dare mention it only to the goddess herself if she appears to me." I looked around at the dove-spattered courtyard, the unhewn rocks and eroded bull's-heads in the wall, saw how cheap and insignificant everything was and added, "I don't think, however, that she will appear."

The priest disregarded my words and invited us to his lodgings, mixed some inferior wine for us and told us what to eat and how to purge ourselves while awaiting the appearance of the goddess. As he gave his advice he looked at each of us in turn and waved his arms in the air.

Resting his hand on my shoulder the priest said, "Do not doubt and fall into despair. I believe that the goddess will appear to you and free you from your trouble."

His touch dispelled my sluggishness, my limbs felt light and the priest no longer seemed an angry old man but a mentor worthy of all confidence.

Words came to my lips. "I have met the Delphic oracle. She said that she recognized me, but she was a restless and violent woman. You I trust."

He allowed the others to go ahead, held me by the shoulders, looked into my eyes and said, "You have come far."

"I have," I replied. "I shall go perhaps even farther."

"Have you already bound yourself?" he asked.

"I don't know what you mean," I said, "but a certain name binds me and forces me to seek the goddess."

"Such was the purpose. Apparently the goddess wished to have you here. Set your mind at ease for she will surely appear to you. Whoever binds you can also relax the bonds."

That same evening Dorieus and Tanakil went to the temple together to spend the night by the empty pedestal awaiting the goddess's appearance, while Mikon and I sat drinking wine together.

Later we drank more wine with the learned artisan who earlier that evening had taken an impression of Tanakil's missing teeth in soft wax. He told us of his skill which he said he had acquired in Carthage.

The new teeth were carved from ivory and fastened with gold bands to the remaining teeth.

"But after that," he said, "one can eat only food that has already been cut. The Etruscans claim that they can fasten teeth even more securely than the natural teeth, but that is probably just boasting."

He was a well-traveled man who said that with his own eyes he had seen in the temple of Baal in Carthage the skins of three completely hairy men which a Phoenician expedition had brought back from a voyage southward from the Pillars of Herakles. Of all the people, he declared, only the Phoenicians knew the secrets of the ocean. They had sailed so far north in it that the waters had turned to ice and so far west that the ships had been caught in a sea of seaweed.

He told us many other unbelievable things about the Phoenicians of Carthage and we drank so much that the host sent his servant to lead the tooth carver back to his lodgings and Aura tearfully took Mikon to bed with her. I don't know whether the wine made us more receptive to the goddess but I do know that on the following day all the foods I was permitted to eat tasted like pitch in my mouth.

When Dorieus and Tanakil returned from the temple in the morning they clung to each other, looked at no one else and did not answer our questions. They went to sleep immediately and slept until evening, when Mikon and Aura in turn went to the temple.

Dorieus arose and confided to me that he intended to marry Tanakil, whom he called the dove of Aphrodite.

"In the first place," he declared, "Tanakil is the most beautiful woman in the world. I have always respected her, but when Aphrodite entered into her in the temple her face began to shine like the sun, her body became as consuming as a pyre and I realized that from now on she would be the only woman in the world for me. Secondly, she is infinitely wealthy. Thirdly, through her earlier marriages and her own birth she has excellent connections with most of the land of Eryx. Heretofore she has not used them to political advantage because she is a woman. But I have succeeded in arousing her ambition."

"In the name of the goddess," I cried, "are you really going to bind yourself to a Phoenician hag who could be your grandmother?"

But Dorieus was not even angered by my words. With a pitying shake of his head he replied, "You are the one who is crazy, not I. Some witchcraft has blinded your eyes so that you fail to see how fine-featured Tanakil's face is, how her eyes shine and how full-blown her figure is."

His eyes began to gleam like a bull's; he rose and said, "Why am I

94

wasting time in chattering with you? My dove, my Aphrodite, is undoubtedly waiting for me impatiently after having tried her new teeth."

Later that night when the house had grown still Tanakil crept out of her bedchamber, came to me and asked joyously, "Has Dorieus confided our great secret to you? You must have noticed already in Himera that he took advantage of my widowhood. Now, because of the goddess, he has promised to make me an honorable woman once more."

I said sharply that Dorieus as a Spartan was inexperienced in matters of the heart. She, Tanakil, as a three-time widow should have known better than to seduce a susceptible man.

But Tanakil replied accusingly, "Dorieus is the one who has been the seducer. When you came to my house I would never even have thought of tempting him, for I am an old woman. Even last night I repulsed him three times but three times he weakened me."

She spoke so convincingly that I was compelled to believe. I do not know whether the witchery of the goddess was responsible or whether it was just the wine that dimmed my eyes, but in the light of the torch Tanakil's features appeared beautiful and her black eyes gleamed compellingly. Dorieus' behavior suddenly became understandable.

Noticing that my heart had melted, Tanakil sat beside me, placed her hand on my knee and explained, "Dorieus' liking for me is not nearly so unnatural as you think. He has hinted at many things that not even he understands, but I who have buried three husbands can read a man's mind from half a word. He told me that that forefather of his, Herakles, dressed in a woman's clothes for a year during which he wove cloth and did other womanly tasks although he was usually a most quarrelsome man. Once a part of the herd that he had stolen fled to Sicily by swimming across the straits from Italy. A valuable bull named Europa was among them, and Herakles left his other cattle to search for the escaped animals. In pursuing them he reached Eryx and killed its king but restored the land to the Elymi. Before leaving he said that one of his descendants would some day return to claim the land as his legacy."

Tanakil raised her hands to her face in confusion. "Forgive me for prattling so in my joy. But as I understand it Dorieus, as Herakles' heir, considers himself the only legal king of Eryx and hence also of Segesta. As a woman I am not nearly so interested in this matter as he is. A man has to engage in all kinds of political activities and it helps to pass his time. But I noticed how approvingly Dorieus told me time and again about Herakles' dressing like a woman. He has also told

95

me that Spartan boys are separated from their mothers at the age of seven to live only among men. It is obvious that poor Dorieus secretly yearns for the motherly care and tenderness that he never enjoyed. This explains his inclination for a woman as old as I. I understand his secret desires better than any other woman could."

"But we are bound to our commander Dionysius. As soon as the sailing season begins we must follow him across the sea to Massilia."

Into my mind came the senseless thought that with the aid of Aphrodite I could abduct Kydippe and take her with me on the voyage.

But Tanakil shook her head and said firmly, "Dorieus will remain obediently at home and will no longer sail the uncertain seas. After all, he has been trained for land war. Why should he go to some barbaric country when his legacy matter must be pursued here?"

"Are you really going to encourage Dorieus in his wild dreams?" I demanded. "Haven't those altars and monuments to the invaders warned you sufficiently? You have already buried three husbands. Why let the Segestans bury a fourth?"

Tanakil pondered a moment, chin in hand. "Men have their own pursuits," she said finally. "In all honesty, I really don't know what I'll do. Physically Dorieus is, without a doubt, a regal man and the dog crown of Segesta would become him. But I fear that he is entirely too stupid to be a king in Sicily's complicated political situation. The rattling of shields and the cleaving of skulls with a sword does not suffice as statesmanship. But if he wants to make me a queen as well as an honorable woman, I must bow to his will."

3.

Mikon and Aura returned from the temple in the morning, both deadly pale and with dark shadows under their eyes from being awake all night. Mikon put Aura to bed, covered her and kissed her forehead. Then he came to me with trembling knees.

"I promised to tell you about the goddess's appearance so that you might be prepared," he said, wiping his forehead, "but it is so bewildering that I can find no words to describe it. I suppose she appears in different ways to different people and to each according to his needs. Besides, I had to swear that I would never reveal the manner of her appearance. You probably noticed that Aura was completely silent upon our return. All this may be similar to the tranquilizing of the sick in Aesculapius' temple, but I have only to touch Aura with my hand to silence her so that I may contemplate supernatural matters."

Late that afternoon Aura awakened and began to call Mikon. He winked at me, sat on the edge of her bed, pulled down the cover and with his fingertip touched the tip of the girl's breast. A deep sigh escaped her, her face grew even paler, her eyes stared into blankness, her body twitched and became still.

"You see, Turms," said Mikon proudly, "what powers Aphrodite has given me. But the person on whom the goddess lavishes such gifts will die young. I don't mean myself but Aura. I feel no physical enjoyment whatsoever; merely spiritual satisfaction in knowing that I have control over her body."

"But how do you know that you and only you affect her like that?" I asked. "Perhaps any other man could do the same; in which case I truly don't envy you."

Mikon stared at me. "I am the one she has pursued ever since I initiated her into the embrace of Aphrodite of Akraia. Now Aphrodite of Eryx has shown her power by making Aura so susceptible that the mere touch of a finger induces an erotic exaltation. It saves me much trouble and time which I can utilize in the meditation of divine matters. But I can't understand how anyone else could produce the same effect."

Blinded by the goddess, I suggested, "It would be wisest to make sure, if only for scientific reasons. I don't know why you should be any different from other men if Aura is once so sensitive."

Mikon smiled a superior smile. "You don't know what you are saying, Turms. You are younger than I and less experienced in these matters. But why don't you test it if you wish? Then we shall see."

I assured him that I did not mean myself and suggested that we let someone else, for example the innkeeper, make the experiment. But Mikon said that he was reluctant to let a stranger's hand touch his wife's breasts.

The more I protested, the more anxious he was that I try, swelling like a frog in sheer smugness. Thus, when Aura's lids began to flicker and she sat up in bed, asking in a weak voice what had happened, Mikon thrust me to her side. I extended my forefinger and hesitantly touched the tip of her breast.

The result of the unhappy experiment exceeded all expectations. A spark flashed from my finger and I felt the flick of an invisible whip on my arm. Aura's body twitched, her mouth opened, her face darkened as the blood rushed to her head, and she fell back in the bed, her limbs jerking convulsively. A rattle sounded in her throat as the air was ejected from her lungs. Her eyes became lifeless and then her already weakened heart failed and she passed away before we even realized what had happened.

97

But even in death the glassy eyes and open mouth were touched with a smile of such an agonizing ecstasy that I can never forget the sight. Mikon hastened to chafe her hands but soon realized the futility of his effort.

Our cries of distress brought Tanakil and Dorieus, and the servants fetched the innkeeper. At first he wrung his hands and shouted and cursed, but then came to his senses, indicated Aura's face and admitted, "No one could hope for a happier death. Her face shows of what she died."

While Mikon sat with his head between his hands, crushed by sorrow, Tanakil arranged with the innkeeper to have the body washed and removed and the bed cleaned. Dorieus was so shocked by the event that he again cut a tuft of hair from his head and burned it. He patted Mikon's shoulder and spoke words of comfort.

The same night we gathered in the yard of the temple where Aura, clothed in beautiful garments, with her cheeks and lips colored and hair ornamented with pearl combs, lay on the pyre of white poplars fairer than she had ever been in life. The temple sacrificed incense and perfumes for the pyre and Mikon lighted it saying, "To the goddess."

At the suggestion of the priests we did not engage wailing women but instead young girls to dance the goddess's dances around the pyre and to sing her praises with Elymian hymns. So moving was the sight that, as the flames shot up against the limpid sky and the smell of burning flesh was lost in the fragrance of the incense, we wept tears of joy for Aura and wished one another as beautiful and quick a death in as sacred a place.

"A long life is by no means a desirable gift from the gods," said Mikon pensively. "Rather does it indicate that a person is slow and stubborn and needs a longer time to fulfill his mission than some faster person. A long life is usually also accompanied by a dimming of the eyes and a tendency to believe former times were better than the present. If I were wiser, I would perhaps throw myself on Aura's pyre and follow her on her journey, but a binding omen would be needed for that. In all that has happened, however, I can see no other binding sign but that this marriage was a mistake. That realization enables me to bear my deep sorrow manfully."

But all the time my mind was troubled by the unresolved question of Aura's death. Would she really have died from the touch of any other man or was I unwittingly the sole cause of her death? I looked at my nails and assured myself that as a person I was like everyone else. But the diet of the goddess and the wine that I had been drinking for three days at the request of the priests were dulling my powers of reasoning. I was haunted by the memory of the storm on the road to Delphi and the sea which had foamed at my call. I had also recognized the sacred places of the Siculi and with the black Etruscan cup in my hand I had soared to the ceiling. Perhaps that was why Aura had died of my touch when I had thoughtlessly and in sheer curiosity extended my finger to touch her.

With the setting of the sun the funeral pyre crumbled and the sea turned amethyst. Mikon was inviting the people to the funerary feast when one of the priests came to me and said, "The time has come for you to prepare for the goddess."

I had thought that the unexpected death would postpone my turn in the temple. But as the priest touched me I realized that this was how it should be. With the heat of the funeral pyre, the smell of the incense in my nostrils, the darkening sea and the lighting of the first star, I was overcome by a conviction that at some time in the past I had lived that same moment. So buoyant did I feel myself that my feet barely touched the ground as I followed the priest to his lodging.

There he asked me to take off my clothes, after which he studied me, looked at the whites of my eyes, blew into my mouth and asked what had caused the white blemishes on my arms. I explained truthfully that they were burns, but did not consider it necessary to say that they had been caused by the burning reeds blown off the roofs at Sardis. When he had examined me, he anointed my armpits, chest and groin with a pungent salve and extended a handful of fragrant grass with which I was to rub my palms and the soles of my feet. With his every touch I felt increasingly buoyant until my body was like air. Joy bubbled within me and I felt that at any moment I could have burst into laughter.

Finally he helped me don a woolen mantle decorated with a design of doves and myrtle leaves. Then he conducted me indifferently to the steps of the temple and said, "Enter."

"What must I do?" I asked.

"That is your own affair," he replied. "Do what you wish, but after a moment you will feel drowsy and then ever more drowsy. The drowsiness will creep into your limbs, your eyelids will close and you will be unable to open them. You will rest more deeply than you ever have, but you will not sleep. Then something will happen, you will open your eyes and meet the goddess."

He pushed me on my way and returned to his lodging. I walked into the silent darkness of the temple and waited until my eyes became accustomed to the glimmer of night that shone faintly through an opening in the roof. Then I distinguished the empty pedestal of the goddess and before it a lion-legged couch, the very sight of which made me sleepy. As soon as I had stretched out on it I began to feel so heavy that I marveled how a light couch could support my weight and why I did not plunge through the stone floor to the depths of the earth. My eyes closed. I knew that I did not sleep, but I felt myself sinking, endlessly sinking.

Suddenly I opened my eyes to bright sunlight and saw that I was seated on a stone bench in a market place. The shadows of passing people glided over the worn flagstones. When I raised my head I did not recognize the place. People were busy selling their wares, peasants led donkeys laden with baskets of vegetables, and beside me a wrinkled old woman had placed a few cheeses on display.

I roamed through the city and knew then that I had, after all, once walked those same streets. The houses were ornamented with painted tiles, the paving was worn from much use and as I turned a corner I saw before me a temple with its colonnade. I entered and a sleepy door-keeper sprinkled a few drops of holy water on me. At that moment I heard a tiny sound, a tinkle.

I opened my eyes to the darkness of the temple of Aphrodite of Eryx and knew that my vision had been only a dream although I had not slept.

Another tinkle brought me to my feet. Never before had I felt so rested, so alert and so sensitive. In the dim light I saw that a veiled woman had seated herself on the edge of the goddess's pedestal. From neck to heels she was swathed in a glittering robe heavy with embroidery. A gleaming wreath on her head held in place the veil that concealed her face. She moved, and again I heard the same tinkle of her bracelets. She moved, she lived and was real.

"If you are the goddess," I said tremblingly, "show me your face."

I heard a laugh behind the veil. The woman assumed a more comfortable position and said in understandable Greek, "The goddess has no face of her own. Whose face do you wish to see, Turms, you temple-burner?"

Suspicion seized me, for her laugh was a human laugh, her voice a human voice, and no one in Eryx could know that I had once set fire to the temple of Cybele at Sardis. Only Dorieus or Mikon could have gossiped about it to this unknown person.

I said sharply, "Be your face what it may, it is too dark here to see it."

"You skeptic!" she laughed. "Do you think that the goddess fears light?" Her bracelets tinkled as she struck a flame and lighted the lamp beside her. Blinking after the darkness, I was able to distinguish the pearl design on her robe and smelled the faint fragrance of amber.

"You are a mortal like me," I said in disappointment. "You are a woman like other women. I expected to meet the goddess."

"Isn't the goddess a woman?" she asked. "More a woman than any mortal woman. What do you want of me?"

"Show me your face," I demanded and took a step toward her.

She stiffened and her voice changed. "Don't touch me. It isn't permitted."

"Would I turn to ashes?" I asked mockingly. "Would I drop lifeless to the ground if I were to touch you?"

Her voice was warning. "Don't jest about such a thing. Remember what happened to you today when you sacrificed a human to the goddess."

I remembered Aura and no longer felt like jesting. "Show me your face," I asked again, "that I may know you."

"As you wish," she said. "But remember that the goddess has no face of her own." She took the shining wreath from her head and removed the veil. Lifting her face to the light she cried out, "Turms, Turms, don't you remember me?"

Shaken to the bottom of my heart I recognized the merry voice, the laughing eyes and the round youthful chin.

"Dione!" I exclaimed. "How have you come here?" For a moment I actually thought that Dione had fled westward to escape the Persians threatening Ionia, and that some miraculous whim of fate had led her to the temple of Aphrodite of Eryx. Then I realized that unreturnable years had passed since Dione had tossed me the apple. She could no longer be the same young girl nor was I the same dazzled youth.

The woman covered her face with the veil and said, "So you recognized me, Turms."

I replied petulantly, "The shadows and the flickering light of the lamp blurred my eyes. I thought I recognized in you a girl whom I knew in my youth in Ephesus. But you are not she. You are not a young girl."

"The goddess has no age. She is ageless and timeless, and her face changes with the beholder. What do you want of me?"

"If you were the goddess," I said in disappointment, "you would know without my saying why I came here."

She swung the shining wreath in her hand so that my eyes were compelled to follow it. Holding the veil over her face with her other hand she urged, "Lie down again. You are drowsy. Rest."

Lightly she stepped to the foot of the couch, still swinging the wreath. My alertness disappeared and a feeling of drowsy security came over me.

Suddenly she straightened, revealed her face and demanded, "Turms, where are you?"

Her face grew black and shiny before my eyes, her mantle was ornamented with the breasts of Amazons, the moon was her headdress, and lions lay at her feet. I felt the sacred woolen bonds of Artemis binding my limbs. Artemis herself stood before me, no longer a statue toppled from the sky, but alive and threatening and with a merciless smile on her face.

"Where are you?" repeated the voice.

With a tremendous effort I could move my tongue. "Artemis, Artemis!" I cried.

A merciful hand was laid over my eyes, my whole body sighed and I was freed of the oppression. The moon no longer had me in its power.

"I will liberate you from the hold of the strange goddess if you wish and promise to serve only me. Reject the melancholy of the moon and I will give you joy and sunshine."

I whispered, or at least think I did, "You foam-born, I consecrated myself to you long before Artemis had me in her power. Never again forsake me."

I heard a roaring in my ears, the couch swayed beneath me and a voice repeated over and over again, "Where are you, Turms? Awaken. Open your eyes."

I opened my eyes and said in amazement, "I see a lovely valley above which rise snowcapped mountains. I smell the fragrance of herbs, and the slope of the valley is warm to lie upon. I have never seen a more beautiful valley, but I am alone. I see no houses, no path, not a single person."

From a vast distance I heard a voice whisper, "Return, Turms. Come back. Where are you?"

Once again I opened my eyes. It was night and I stood in a strange room. With a catch of my breath I recognized Kydippe lying in bed. She was sleeping with her lips parted, and she sighed as she slept. Suddenly she awakened, saw me and attempted to cover her nakedness. But upon recognizing my face she began to smile and her hand paused. I ran to her and embraced her. She started to scream, then relaxed in my arms and let me do as I wished. But her girl's lips were cold under my mouth, her heart did not pound against my own, and when I released her and she covered her eyes in shame I knew that I had nothing in common with her.

A groan of disappointment escaped me, and when I opened my eyes again I was lying on the couch in the temple of Aphrodite of Eryx with my arms stiffly upraised. On the edge of the couch sat that strange woman who had talked to me and who was trying to hold my arms down.

"What has happened, Turms?" she asked and bowed her head to look at my face in the lamplight.

I saw that she had removed the stiffly-embroidered robe, the necklace and the armbands. They lay on the floor, as did the veil and the wreath. She was wearing only a thin shift and her fair hair was combed to the top of her head. The shape of her high, thin brows made her eyes appear slanting. As she leaned toward me I knew that I had never before seen her, yet I felt that she was familiar.

My arms slackened and fell to my sides. My limbs were exhausted as after hard labor. She touched my brows, chest and mouth with her fingertips and absently began to draw a circle on my bare chest. Her face suddenly paled and I noticed to my surprise that she was weeping.

Frightened, I asked, "What has happened?"

"Nothing," she snapped and abruptly withdrew her hand.

"Why are you weeping?"

She shook her head so sharply that a tear dropped onto my chest. "I am not weeping." Then she slapped my cheek and demanded angrily, "Who is that Kydippe whose name you repeated so ecstatically?"

"Kydippe? It was because of her that I came here. She is the grand-daughter of the tyrant of Himera. But I no longer have any desire for her. I took what I wanted and the goddess freed me of her."

"That is good," she said capriciously. "That is very good. Why don't you go your way if you got what you wanted?" She raised her hand as though to strike me once more, but I caught her wrist. It was narrow and beautiful in my hand.

"Why do you strike me?" I asked. "I have not harmed you."

"Haven't you! No man has hurt me as you have. Why don't you leave and never return to Eryx?"

"I can't, for you are sitting on me. Besides, you are clutching my robe."

She had in truth wrapped a corner of my robe around her knees as though she were cold.

"Who are you?" I asked, touching her white neck.

She started and cried out, "Don't touch me! I hate those hands of yours!"

When I tried to rise she pushed me back, bent over me and hotly kissed my mouth. She did it so unexpectedly that I did not realize what had happened until she had straightened again and was sitting on the edge of the couch with chin haughtily upraised.

I caught her hand. "Let us talk sensibly like human beings, for you are a human and my kind. What has happened? Why have you wept and struck me?"

She curled her hand into a fist but permitted me to hold it. "It was useless for you to come here for aid, for you know more about the goddess than I. I am but the body in which the goddess manifests herself, but your power has entered into me and I can do nothing. I don't understand what has happened. I should have taken my clothes and left, and upon awakening you would have considered your vision the answer to your problem. I don't know why I remained here. Tell me, are you really awake?"

I felt my head and body. "I think so. Yet a moment ago I could have sworn that I also was awake. I have never experienced anything like this."

"Probably not. And I suppose that women have never cared for you since you have to seek the goddess's aid."

Holding her little fist in my hand I stared at her. "Your lips are beautiful. I know the curve of your brows and also your eyes and cheeks. Are you one of the returned? I seem to recognize you."

"The returned?" she asked. "I don't know what you mean."

I wound my arm around her shoulders and drew her to me. Her body was stiff but she did not resist.

"Your arms are cold," I said. "Permit me to warm you with my body. Or is it already morning?"

She glanced at the sky through the opening. "Not yet. But why are you still interested in me? Why should you warm me with your body? You have already had what you wanted." Suddenly she buried her face in my neck and began to weep bitterly. "Don't be angry with me if I am troublesome. The dark of the moon always makes me capricious. Usually I do humbly what is requested, but you make me obstinate."

Through the thin cloth I felt the softness of her limbs and shivers passed over my body. I seemed to be standing hesitantly on a threshold over which there would be no return once I passed it.

"Tell me your name," I pleaded, "so that I may know you and talk to you."

She shook her head stubbornly. Her hair escaped the combs and tumbled onto my chest. As she pressed her face against my neck she embraced me with both arms.

"If you knew my name you would have me in your power. Don't you understand?—I belong to the goddess. I cannot and must not be dominated by any man."

"You cannot escape me," I told her. "In starting a new life a person chooses a new name. At this very moment I am giving you a new name. It will be yours and through it I will hold you—Arsinoe."

"Arsinoe," she repeated slowly. "How did you invent that? Have you known an Arsinoe?"

"Never," I assured her. "The name just came to my mind. It came from somewhere or was in me, for a person does not invent names by himself."

"Arsinoe," she said again, as though savoring the name. "What if I don't accept the name you have given me? What right have you to re-name me?"

"Arsinoe," I whispered, "when I warm you like this in my lap and wrap the woolen mantle of the goddess around you, you are the most familiar of all persons to me although I don't know you." I thought for a moment. "You are not a Greek, that I can hear from your speech. Nor can you be a Phoenician for your face is not copper-colored. You are white as foam. Could you be a descendant of Trojan refugees?"

"Why concern yourself with my nationality? The goddess does not distinguish between nationalities or clans, languages or colors of skin. She chooses people at random, makes the fair still fairer and beautifies even the ugly. But tell me, Turms, do you now see my face as it really is?"

She turned to me and I studied her. "Never have I seen a face as vivid and changing as yours, Arsinoe. Your every thought is reflected in it. Now I understand that the goddess gives you an infinite number of faces and each man sleeping the sleep of the goddess thinks that he sees in you the face of someone he loves or has loved. But when you lean against me thus as a human I believe that I do see your real face."

Drawing back she touched the corners of my eyes and mouth and pleaded, "Turms, swear that you are only a human."

"In the name of the goddess I swear that I experience hunger and thirst, exhaustion and sleep, lust and longing like a human. But what I am I cannot say for I myself do not know. Will you swear that you will not suddenly disappear from my lap or change your face? To me it is the most beautiful face I have ever seen."

She spoke the oath and then said, "At times the goddess appears in

105

me and I no longer know myself. At other times again my task feels tedious and I know that I am only deceiving the people who in their dream think that I am the goddess. Turms, sometimes I don't even believe in the goddess but crave to be free to lead the life of an ordinary human. Now my only world is the mountain of Eryx, and the goddess's fountain will be my grave when I am worn out and another steps into my place to serve the goddess."

She touched the clothes on the floor with her foot, shook her head and said, "It is shocking that I speak like this to you, a stranger. Tell me, have you the power to bewitch people, since I did not leave in time?"

But an odd thought had begun to perplex me. "In my dream, if it was merely a dream, I was in Himera, in Kydippe's room. I embraced her as a man embraces a woman and she permitted it to happen. I took my fill of her and knew that only my lust had blinded me and that actually I had nothing in common with her. But that which happened was real. I know it and feel it in my body. Whom, therefore, did I embrace if my body remained here and was not in Himera?"

She evaded the question and snapped angrily, "Don't talk to me about that Kydippe. I have already heard too much about her." Then she continued triumphantly, "At any rate, she is not for you. Her father has already received the goddess's prophecy. Kydippe will be sent with a mule team to her wedding chamber and a rabbit will run before her. The rabbit is the emblem of Rhegion, and Rhegion rules the straits on the Italian side as Zankle rules them on the Sicilian side. Because the goddess of Eryx also fulfills political plans in the visions and prophecies I cannot always believe in her.

"In fact," she continued, "the temple of Eryx is the marriage mart for the entire western sea. The wise ones only half believe in the goddess and instead negotiate directly with the priests for the most advantageous marriage. Many an unsuspecting man and woman has received an omen to visit Eryx and there seen his future spouse in a vision although he has not even heard of her before. The goddess can persuade the reluctant."

"And what of me?" I asked. "Am I also the victim of someone's calculations?"

She became serious. "Don't misunderstand my words. The goddess is more powerful than we think, and sometimes she confuses the most careful calculations with her own will. Why else would I have been compelled to remain here and reveal myself to you?"

She touched my mouth in fear. "No, Turms, I feel alternately hot and cold when I look at your oval eyes and broad mouth. Something stronger than me binds me to you and makes my knees so weak that I cannot stoop to gather up my clothes from the floor. Something terrible must happen." She glanced up at the opening in the roof. "The sky is growing light," she exclaimed. "How short this night has been! I must go, never to meet you again."

I caught her hand. "Arsinoe, don't go yet. We must meet again, but how? Tell me what I must do."

"You don't know what you are saying," she protested. "Wasn't it enough that one woman died from your touch? There has been much talk of that in the temple. Do you want me also to die?"

At that moment we heard the flap of wings. Someone had walked in the temple courtyard and a frightened flock of doves had taken wing. Something fluttered down from the opening and fell within the circle of light at our feet. I picked up a small feather.

"The goddess has given us a sign!" I cried elatedly. "She herself is on our side. If I had not believed in her before, I do now, for this is a miracle and an omen."

Her body quivered in my lap. "Someone moved in the courtyard," she whispered. "But already innumerable lies are darting about in my head like lizards. Perhaps the goddess is bestowing her own ingenuity on me. Turms, why did you do this to me?"

I kissed her protesting mouth until she submitted and breathed her own passion into me.

"Turms," she said at last with tear-filled eyes, "I am horribly afraid. Would you recognize my face if you were to see me in the light of day? Lamplight is treacherous. Perhaps I am uglier and older than you think and you would be disappointed in me."

"What of my own face?" I asked.

"You have nothing to fear, Turms," she laughed. "You have the face of a god."

At that moment I trembled from head to foot and in the grip of a deep ecstasy I felt myself to be more than myself. There was nothing that I could not conquer.

"Arsinoe," I said, "You were born for me and not for the goddess, just as I was born for you. That was why I had to come to Eryx, to meet you. I am here, I am free, I am strong. Go, therefore, and do not be afraid. If we do not meet in the day we will meet at night—that I know, and no power in the world can prevent it."

I helped her gather her clothes and jewelry from the floor. She blew out the lamp, took it with her and left the temple through a narrow door behind the goddess's empty pedestal. I lay down on the couch, pulled the myrrh-odored woolen mantle over me, patted the embroidered doves on it and stared at the lightening sky above me.

4.

The sun was already high when I was awakened by the touch of one of the priests who had come into the temple with a beautifully decorated drinking vessel in his hand. When I saw him I did not at first know which of my experiences had been merely a dream. But when memory returned I was filled with such supreme joy that I laughed aloud.

"Oh, priest, the goddess has freed me of the pangs of love!" I exclaimed. "Last night I saw the girl whom I thought I loved and even embraced her, although she is far away in Himera. But she turned into a rabbit and fled from my arms and I no longer craved her."

"Drink this," he said, extending the cup to me. "I see from your face that you are still in a state of excitement. This drink will calm you."

"I don't want to be calmed," I protested. "On the contrary, this condition is delightful and I would gladly prolong it. But you know the goddess's secrets. Why should I conceal from you that I, an alien, hoped for the impossible and fell in love with Kydippe, the granddaughter of the tyrant of Himera? Fortunately, however, the goddess liberated me from my yearning." As I babbled, I drank the mixture of honey and wine that he offered.

He looked at me shrewdly and frowned. "Did you really say that Kydippe turned into a rabbit and fled from you?" he asked suspiciously. "If that is so, the goddess has truly favored you, for this omen confirms other previous omens we have had about that Kydippe."

"Kydippe," I repeated slowly. "But yesterday that name made my whole body tremble. Now I do not care if I ever see her again."

"What else did you see?" the priest asked curiously. "Try to remember."

I covered my eyes with my hand and pretended to think. "I think I saw a team of mules and a chariot ornamented with silver. The mules walked through the water across the straits, but how that was possible I do not know. Only a moment ago the visions were still clear but the drink that you gave me has blurred them. No, I can no longer see or remember anything. But that is of no significance. Kydippe at least will no longer trouble my mind."

"Undoubtedly you have some talent as a seer," he said.

I left the temple and returned to the inn, where the remains of the funerary feast, broken dishes and puddles of wine were on the floor.

Mikon was sleeping off his sorrow so soundly that I could not arouse him. Tanakil, however, was up and having her teeth fitted by the tooth-maker. Blood streamed from her gums but she drank wine to fortify herself and uncomplainingly allowed the tooth-maker to pinch her with his pliers and to thrust the golden bands securely in place. The tooth-maker lauded her bravery and was himself amazed by the beauty of the teeth he had made. When they were in place at last, he rubbed the bloody gums with an herb salve and collected the fee for his work. It was not small, but in order to increase his gains he thrust upon Tanakil tooth cleansers, face ointments, eyebrow darkeners and Carthaginian cheek coloring which made wrinkles invisible.

When he had finally left I seized Tanakil by both hands and said, "We are mature people, both of us. You are familiar with the goddess's secret rites here in Eryx, but I also have powers that you don't suspect. Remember what happened to Aura when I touched her. Who is the woman in whom the goddess appears to the suppliants at the temple?"

Tanakil drew back in alarm, glanced about her and said, "Speak softly, although I don't know what you mean."

I said firmly, "She is a woman, made of flesh and blood like me. Remember that it is in my power to reveal many things to Dorieus that might turn him from you despite your new teeth. So be frank with me and tell me what you know."

She pondered the matter for a moment. "What exactly do you want?" she asked. "Let us be friends. Of course I shall help you if I can."

"I want to meet that woman of the temple again," I demanded. "As soon as possible and preferably in daylight and by ourselves."

"That is forbidden," insisted Tanakil. "Besides, she is but a cheap vessel whom the goddess fills with wine if she so chooses. The vessels change, but the wine of the goddess remains the same. The power is not hers. She is but a slave who has been trained in the goddess's school."

"That may be," I said, "but it is precisely that cheap vessel that I desire, preferably empty and without wine, for I intend to fill her with my own wine."

Tanakil looked at me thoughtfully, touched her new teeth and admitted, "I am consecrated, as you guessed. I will confess that I have many times helped that woman play pranks on men as they sleep the sleep of the goddess. It was she who helped Dorieus to see me fairer than Helen of Troy and to enjoy unsuspected delights in my embrace."

"Who is she?" I asked.

"How should I know?" Tanakil shrugged her shoulders. "Such women are bought when they are young girls and are trained in the temple. This one, I think, has been trained in Carthage and has traveled in other lands as well to develop the necessary talents. The temples frequently exchange gifted women, but one who has risen to Eryx can go no farther. She can live like a goddess and experience all the pleasures of such a life until she becomes insane or useless. Don't think of her, Turms. You are only wasting your time."

"Tanakil," I said, "once you told me that you believe in the goddess. I also believe in her, as I must after the many indications she has given to me of herself. She has the power to confuse the selfish calculations of humans, including even her own priests. Her whim brought me to Eryx. Her whim revealed that woman to me, and it is her whim that forces me to meet that woman again. How could I resist her whim? Help me, Tanakil. For your own sake, for my sake and also for the sake of that woman."

Irritably Tanakil replied, "Why don't you entrust your problem to the priest? He could prove to you better than I how wrong you are."

"Why don't you go to the priest yourself?" I pleaded. "Tell him that you still need the kind of advice that only a woman can give. Surely the woman is not a prisoner. Surely she can leave the temple with a trustworthy companion. After all, she appears to suppliants in many different guises and probably no one but the priests and you and naturally the temple servants even know her true face. Surely she can move as a woman among women even though she serves the goddess by night."

"Of course she has her own amusements," conceded Tanakil. "In fact, she is the worst slut I know. In the summer she even appears to the sailors, drovers and shepherds on the mountain slopes. No, Turms, turn your thoughts away from her. If I am an experienced and even a treacherous old woman, she is immeasurably more experienced and treacherous."

Her cruel words alarmed me but I was sure that she was deliberately speaking unkindly of Arsinoe to lead me astray and to free herself from the predicament. I saw before me those high slanting brows, the vivid face, the beautiful mouth and the white neck. I still felt her womanly warmth on my limbs and everything within me cried out that there could be nothing evil in her.

"Tanakil," I said, "look me in the eyes. You must obey me. Since it is so easy, go and bring her to me. In the name of the goddess I demand that you fulfill my request. Otherwise she will abandon you."

The words made Tanakil hesitate. As a woman she knew better than I the capriciousness of the goddess and feared that the goddess really would forsake her.

"Let it happen as you wish," she said with a sigh. "But only on condition that the woman herself consents to meet you as a person among people and in daylight. It is difficult for me to believe that, for there is not much to see in her face."

When she had combed her hair, painted her face and donned her jewels she actually left for the temple. With the new teeth in her mouth she walked erect and with her chin up.

Nor did she remain long. Soon she reappeared with a woman dressed from head to feet in Phoenician garb and shielding her face from the sun with a fringe-bordered parasol. They came through the house to the terrace and the orchard under the flowering fruit trees. Hot waves beat through my body at sight of them. Tanakil left the woman sitting on a stone bench and said that she would bring food and drink.

"Turms," she called, "come and make sure that none of the lowly servants disturb this goddess of the temple. I want to serve her with my own hands."

As I took those few steps toward Arsinoe my limbs were like water and my lips trembled. Blossoms fell to my feet and the sea at the foot of the mountain was restless. She closed her parasol, raised her head and looked me in the face.

I recognized the high slanting brows but not the eyes or the cruel painted mouth.

"Arsinoe," I whispered and extended my hand. But I did not dare to touch her.

The woman wrinkled her arched forehead impatiently. "The sunlight makes my temples throb and I have not slept enough. If I did not respect Tanakil so highly I certainly would not have awakened so early and come here to visit her. But I don't know you. Were you speaking to me? What do you wish?"

The paint made her face look hard. In talking she narrowed her eyes to mere slits, and there were wrinkles at their corners. Her face was more experienced than I had believed in the lamplight, but the longer I looked at her the more clearly I began to discern her other face through the paint.

"Arsinoe," I repeated in a whisper, "don't you really remember me?"

The corners of her mouth began to tremble. She opened her eyes and they were no longer furtive but shining with joy.

"Turms, oh Turms!" she cried. "Do you really recognize my face in

III

the daylight and as I am? Do you really fear me, like a little boy at a forbidden gate? Oh, Turms, if you only knew how afraid I myself was."

She sprang to her feet and ran into my arms. I felt the quivering of her body through her garment as I wound my arms around her.

"Arsinoe, Arsinoe!" I whispered. "Of course I recognize you."

Her face began to glow as though I were holding the goddess herself in my arms. The sky above us swelled to a mighty blue and my own blood roared in my ears.

"Arsinoe," I said, "for this I was born, for this I lived, for this I saw my restless dreams. The veil no longer covers your face. You have shown me your face and this moment I am ready to die."

She placed her palms against my chest. "An arrow has pierced my heart," she said, "and my blood runs dry whenever you look at me, Turms. Whenever you smile your godlike smile I turn powerless. How strong and beautiful are your manly limbs! Hold me tightly lest I fall. And I thought that I was an invulnerable servant of the goddess!"

She pressed her mouth against my neck, bit my chest and writhed in my lap until the brooch at her shoulder opened and her robe fell to the ground. The wind began to whine and fallen petals blew over us but no power on earth could have separated us. Anyone could have pierced us with the same spear and we would not even have been aware of it. Then her lips turned cold, her eyelids quivered, a cry burst from her throat and she grew completely limp.

Only then did I come to my senses and look around. The wind was tearing at the fruit trees and Tanakil stood beside us with billowing robe, staring at us in horror.

"Are you out of your mind, both of you!" she cried in a voice shrill with fear. "Haven't you sense enough even to seek the shelter of the bushes like decent people?"

With shaking hands she helped Arsinoe to don her robe. Flowers and broken branches were flying through the air and reeds from the city's roofs darkened the day. Far below us the sea foamed and mountains of clouds rolled from the horizon toward Eryx.

"You have aroused the wrath of the immortals with your obscene behavior," Tanakil scolded us, her dark eyes gleaming with envy. "But the goddess had mercy on you and threw her veil over you. She even dimmed my eyes so that you seemed to be covered with mist. How could you have done that?"

"A storm is breaking," I said, still panting, "a storm from the west. I don't wonder. The storm in me and my body sweeps over all Eryx."

Arsinoe looked down like a girl who has been found in mischief, caught Tanakil's hand and pleaded, "Forgive us, you most blessed of all women. Help me again, for I must wash myself."

"Let us all go in and seek the shelter of stone walls," Tanakil suggested.

She led Arsinoe to her room where everything was ready, for that cunning and experienced woman had provided towels and warm water so that when Arsinoe had cleaned herself I also went there to wash. While I did so the three of us began to laugh without further embarrassment.

Tanakil wiped tears of laughter from her eyes and said, "Didn't I tell you, Turms, that she is the worst slut I know! I actually envied her when I heard her squeal in your embrace just now, although she might have been pretending in order to flatter you and to draw you more easily into her power. Never believe a woman, Turms, for a woman's body lies as cunningly as her eyes and her tongue."

Arsinoe smiled radiantly. "Don't believe this jealous woman, Turms. You yourself felt the mountain beneath us split and the earth tremble."

She spoke over her shoulder as she peered into Tanakil's bronze mirror and deftly wiped clean her cheeks and lips. The face which but a moment before had been swollen with passion was again small and childlike, but her eyes still glowed darkly and the blue of the high brows emphasized their gleam.

"Again you have a new face, Arsinoe," I said. "But to me this is your truest face. Don't ever mask it from me again."

She shook her head and her hair, the traditionally fair hair of the foamborn, tumbled down her bare back. As she studied her reflection she wrinkled her nose, every thought rippling visibly across her capriciously changing face. Jealous of the mirror, I put my hand on her bare shoulder to turn her to me. She dropped the mirror and covered her face with both hands.

"In the name of the goddess!" cried Tanakil in honest amazement. "She is blushing at your very touch. Surely you are not seriously in love with each other? This is what your mysterious smiles predicted, Turms. The goddess of Eryx has bewitched you."

"Tanakil," I requested, "do go and bring us the refreshments that you promised, for I am unable to understand what you are saying."

She bobbed her head like a bird pecking at the ground, laughed to herself and said, "At least bolt the door so that I'll know enough to knock when I return."

After she had gone we stood staring at each other. Arsinoe paled slowly and the pupils of her eyes dilated until I was looking into black pools. I extended my arms but she raised a repelling hand.

"Don't come," she pleaded.

But my strength rejoiced in me and I did not heed her protests. On the contrary, they stimulated my joy, for I realized that she was compelled to bow to my will. The violence of the storm increased and rattled the shutter as though alien forces were attempting to enter the room. The roof creaked and the wind whistled through the door cracks. The spirits of the air tumbled about us in tumultuous joy while we seemed to sway on a cloud in the midst of the storm.

When we finally lay exhausted on the bed she pressed her cheek against my shoulder and said, "No man has ever made love to me in such a rapturous and fearful way."

"Arsinoe," I said, "to me you are fresh and untouched. No matter how many times I lay hands on you, you will always be new and untouched."

The storm whistled through the cracks and shook the shutters. We heard the cries of people, the weeping of children and the lowing of cattle. But we were completely unmoved by any of it. I held her hands in mine as we stared into each other's eyes.

"It is as though I had drunk poison," she said. "I see black shadows before me and my limbs are growing cold. I seem to be slowly dying when you look at me."

"Arsinoe, never before have I been afraid of the future. I have rushed toward it greedily and impatiently. But now I am afraid. Not for myself but for you."

"The goddess is in me and of me," she said. "Otherwise nothing like this could have happened. I listen to myself. Waves of fire ripple through my body and I feel within myself the bliss of the immortals. The goddess must protect us, otherwise I will no longer believe in her."

At that moment we heard a knock on the door.

When I had unbolted it Tanakil entered with a small wineskin under her arm and some cups.

"Aren't you even afraid of the storm?" she demanded. "Roofs have blown away, walls have crumbled and many people have been hurt. Poseidon is shaking the mountain and the sea is foaming with rage. I at least must drink some wine for courage."

She raised the wineskin and aimed a stream into her mouth. When she had swallowed enough she filled the cups and offered them to us, talking the while.

"My hero Dorieus is tossing in bed with his head covered and moaning that the earth is swaying beneath him. Mikon is clutching his head and imagining that he is in the underworld. The day is dark and no one remembers such a sudden and violent storm, although the spring weather in Eryx is always unpredictable. But you two are frolicking mouth to mouth as though intoxicated even without wine."

Scornfully exultant, I looked at the trembling woman and at Arsinoe whose head was bowed submissively. Some power within me raised my arms and moved my limbs in a dance as though the dance were within me. Around the room I moved in the storm dance, stamping the floor and lifting my arms as though to snatch the clouds. The storm responded to my dance with drums, trumpets and whistles.

I paused to listen, and something made my mouth shout, "Hush, wind; subside, storm, for I no longer need you!"

After only a moment the screaming of the wind through the cracks lowered to an inquisitive whine, the crash and the turmoil receded, the room lightened and everything grew calm. The storm had obeyed me.

My ecstasy vanished and I looked around. Reason assured me that it could not be true. Something in me had merely sensed that the peak of the storm had passed and had prompted my outburst.

But Tanakil stared at me with round eyes and asked fearfully, "Is it you, Turms, or did the storm-subduer enter your body?"

"I am Turms, born of a thunderbolt, and lord of the storm," I said. "The spirits of the air obey me. Sometimes," reason forced me to add, "if the power is in me."

Tanakil pointed accusingly at Arsinoe. "Already yesterday you killed an innocent girl with a touch of your finger. Today even more people have suffered because of you. If you will not think of human lives, at least consider the economic damage you have caused this innocent city."

We went outside and saw that the storm was receding along the plain toward Segesta, felling the trees in its path. But above Eryx the sun was already shining, although the sea still seethed and the waves were beating at the cliffs so that the mountain quivered. Roofs had blown away, walls had collapsed and fowl had been killed. The ground was white with petals from fruit trees. But fortunately the people had had time to extinguish their fires so that no flames had spread.

Mikon came toward us on uncertain feet. Tears were streaming down his kindly face as he clutched at us. "Are you also dead and in the underworld? I fear that I have mistakenly drunk from the stream of forgetfulness for I can remember nothing that has occurred. Is that Kore with you, and where is the shade of my unfortunate wife Aura?

115

But if she is here and still as talkative as in life I don't want to meet her for the time being."

Only after he had felt me sufficiently and pulled at Arsinoe's hair was he convinced.

"So you are still alive and are flesh and blood! Therefore I also am still alive. Be merciful, Turms; take a stone, break open my skull and release this swarm of angry bees that is disturbing my contemplation with its buzzing."

He tore out a tuft of hair, stamped on it and cursed. "Behold the pig, which is the gentlest of all animals. But when it rages it bares its fangs. I, a gentle man, am no better than a pig and have no defense other than that I drank in sorrow rather than in joy."

We calmed him after a time and then Dorieus came out with a wrinkled cloth around his shoulders.

"What has happened?" he demanded. "I distinctly dreamed that I was on a ship. It swayed beneath me and the waves crashed against its sides so violently that I thought it best to lie on my belly and grip the sides of my bed."

Upon looking around his interest was aroused. "I see that a war has broken out without my knowledge!" he exclaimed. "Why did I leave my shield in Himera? But at least bring me my sword and show me whom to smite and I in turn will show you how a Spartan fights."

Seeing the confused state of both Mikon and Dorieus, I knew that it was not caused by wine alone, and I began to suspect myself. Perhaps my senses were so disturbed by my dreams in the temple that I had no conception of reality and exaggerated my experiences.

But at least the confusion in the city was real. People were fleeing into the temple, carrying the wounded and dragging weeping children by the hand. No one paid any attention to us. Rich and poor, merchants and shepherds, masters and slaves mingled together in a noisy conglomeration.

Tanakil said, "If we are wise, we will quietly gather my servants, the donkeys and the horses, leave farewell gifts for the innkeeper to distribute, and depart from Eryx. I know and you know best, Turms, why this catastrophe has struck the city. The people and the priests may also soon realize it."

Her words held wisdom, but when I glanced at Arsinoe's face, her soft mouth and shining eyes, I knew that I could not relinquish her.

"Yes," I said boldly, "let us leave. But you, Arsinoe, must accompany us."

As my companions stared incredulously from Arsinoe to me, I

116

suggested, "Clothe yourself in Aura's garments and assume her countenance just as you change your face at the will of the goddess. Everything has happened for a purpose. Aura's ashes will remain in Eryx in your stead. We can easily leave the city in this confusion."

But my words horrified Arsinoe. "You don't know what you are saying, Turms. How could I trust you who are a man and a stranger? What could you offer me? As the priestess of Aphrodite of Eryx I have attained the highest position possible for a woman. Would I abandon a life of luxury and the jewels and beautiful clothes of the goddess merely because I happened to take a liking to you during the boredom of winter? On the contrary, I should fear you and flee from you because of the very power that you exert over me and my body."

She touched my hand pleadingly. "Don't look at me with such reproach, Turms. You know well that I weep and long for you. But soon the goddess will arrive from beyond the sea. The processions and secret rites, the joy, the variety and the crowds will soon dispel my yearning. Be sensible and do not tempt me with the impossible."

The muscles in my cheeks tightened in anger. "But a moment ago, weeping with joy, you swore in the name of the goddess that you could not live without me."

Arsinoe looked vexed, moved her foot and studied the ground. "A moment ago was a moment ago, but now is now. I spoke the truth when I said that I could not imagine myself loving any man as I love you. But I would not even dare try to recapture that moment. Now my head is aching, my eyes are smarting and my breasts pain me. Your very suggestion makes me ill with fear."

Tanakil broke into the conversation. "Don't you realize, you foolish man, that she is a slave to the goddess? If you abduct her from the temple you will have the entire land of Eryx in pursuit."

I bade her be quiet and asked Arsinoe sharply, "Are you a slave or free?"

She avoided my eyes and retorted, "What then? Would you despise me if I were a slave?"

My heart sank but I said, "It depends on whether you are a slave by birth or whether you were sold into slavery as a child. Besides, even a born slave who is permitted to dedicate himself to some deity is considered free."

Tanakil became angry and shouted, "Dorieus, hit Turms over the head to silence him and you, woman, return as quickly to the shelter of the temple as though you were already there."

Arsinoe made haste to leave, then stopped and returned. "Where is my parasol? I left it in the orchard."

I told her that the storm probably had blown it into the sea and she burst into tears, saying that it had cost dearly. So I went to look for it and finally found it wedged so tightly in the crotch of a fruit tree that the gayly colored cloth tore when I pulled it free.

She began to weep once more and said accusingly, "See what misfortune you bring me! The round cloth is torn and the ivory handle broken."

Enraged by her pettiness when more important matters were in question, I asked Tanakil to lend me a few gold coins that I might buy Arsinoe a new and even finer parasol. Tanakil complained that she had already spent far too much money but nevertheless, at Dorieus' request, went to her coffer and counted out the money. Whereupon Arsinoe smiled, clapped her hands in glee and said that she knew of a Phoenician merchant who sold both round and square parasols, with fringes or tassels.

I looked at her incredulously and asked, "Arsinoe, how can you think of parasols when the city lies in ruins around us and you yourself are a matter of life and death to me?"

She fluttered her eyelashes playfully at me. "But, Turms, I am a woman. Haven't you realized that yet? You still have much to learn."

And so it happened that she led us all to the shop of the Phoenician merchant, skipping happily over the broken timbers and stones in the street. The Phoenician's shop was strongly built and had not suffered much damage. At our approach he lit the incense before the Baal on his wall, rubbed his hands and prepared for a profitable sale.

While Tanakil and Arsinoe were looking at parasols as well as other wares, Mikon said, "Turms and Dorieus, my friends, this is a city of folly. Watching those two women I foresee that we will be here until evening. In the meantime, the only sensible thing we three can do is to drink ourselves intoxicated."

Watching Arsinoe's quick fingers feeling the cloth and fringe of the parasols and listening to her light laugh as she bartered with the Phoenician, I clutched my head in my hands to see whether it was still in place.

"Why in truth should we worry about tomorrow?" I asked. "At least the wine can make nothing worse, for matters are already as bad as they can be."

The Phoenician sent his slave to fetch some wine. The smell of the incense and the wares made us so queasy that we moved outside and seated ourselves on the backs of the stone lions framing the door. Before many blinks of an eye we had emptied a jug of expensive sweet wine.

"We are behaving like barbarians," I said, "for we haven't even a mixing vessel and I for one have never drunk wine from the edge of a jar."

Dorieus said then, "This wine has a musty taste. It is preserved with flavorings that make the belly loose. Let us have honest resinous wine instead."

We drank a wineskin of it and sprayed it on one another in lieu of an offering. Arsinoe came to the doorway to try a delicate nose ring in her nostrils and to ask us how we liked it.

Mikon covered his face with his hands and groaned, "I thought my wife Aura had died, but there she is again as large as life!"

"Don't begin to see visions again as you did last night," Dorieus said contemptuously. "She is only the goddess who appears in the temple. I recognize her by her ears. But she is nothing compared to Tanakil. She is as though one dipped a finger in honey and licked it clean. But when I enfold Tanakil in my embrace it is as though I were falling head first into a well. Soon we will be man and wife according to both Phoenician and Dorian laws, and then you can both try her if you wish. A Spartan refuses his friends nothing." He thought for a moment, eyes dull from the wine, and then added, "But if you do I shall kill you. That would be best, for once having embraced Tanakil you would crave death more than life. It is difficult to rise from the bottom of a well."

He buried his face in his hands and wept with heaving shoulders.

Mikon also shed tears. "All three of us are alone in the world. Alone we have come here and alone we shall return. Let us not quarrel among ourselves but drink wine moderately and with deliberation, just like this. Have I already told you that last night I descended to the underworld to accompany my wife Aura, or at least to see her on her way?"

Just then Arsinoe came out of the shop and showed us the parasol she had chosen. It was no more than the width of several hands, square and edged with fringe, undeniably a fine thing; but it would not have shielded even a frog from the sun.

"Oh, Turms, I am so pleased with this parasol!" she exclaimed. "The merchant also promised to repair my old one, so that now I have two. But I must leave now. I will surely remember you, Turms, especially when I look at this enchanting parasol. Have a good journey, and do not forget me immediately, either."

"Arsinoe," I said threateningly, "remember that I gave you a new name. With it I control you whether you wish it or not."

She patted my cheek and laughed giddily. "Of course, dear Turms, just as you wish. But at this moment you are just drunk enough not to be able to answer for your words."

She turned and went down the street, holding the new parasol daintily on her shoulder and lifting the hem of her robe with the other hand as she jumped lightly over the obstacles heaped by the storm. As I tried to run after her I stumbled over the first timber, crashed onto my face and was unable to rise until Dorieus and Mikon helped me to my feet. Holding onto one another we started back to the inn, Tanakil behind us with a large parasol over her shoulder.

5.

I awakened in the middle of the night to a paralyzing agony, as though the venom of a snake were spreading through my veins. At the moment of awakening I knew and remembered everything that had happened, and I knew that the goddess had seized me in her power. She had made me love a frivolous woman whose words I could not believe and whose very body lay in my embrace.

But even as I thought the worst of her I saw distinctly her changing face and slanting brows, and her eyes grew dark before me. Perhaps she had experienced a thousand men. Perhaps she was a slut, as Tanakil claimed. But at the very thought of her my mind was torn by desire, tenderness and longing, and I knew that every moment apart from her was mortally dreadful.

I staggered to the courtyard and drank some cold water from a clay container hanging by the door. The sounds had stilled and the lamps had been extinguished in the city. The firmament was full of stars and the new moon, a cruel sickle, threatened me from the edge of the sky.

I went into the stable and in a basket found the pegs belonging to Tanakil's travel tent. Then I crept through the night to the gate of the temple. It was closed, but the guard was not on the wall and no sound came from within. I circled the wall until I found a suitable place, thrust one tent peg between the stones, rose onto it and then thrust in another. In that manner I built steps for myself and reached the top of the wall. Crawling on my belly I finally found the guard's stairs and descended into the inner courtyard.

Heaps of rubble left by the storm were still there. Dimly I saw the gleam of the marble peristyle around the fountain and groped my way to it.

I prostrated myself by the fountain and prayed, "You foam-born, by your eternal fountain, heal me of the agony of my love. You kindled it and only you can extinguish it."

By leaning over the edge I managed to touch the surface of the water with a willow twig and thus got a few drops into my mouth. Carefully I tossed a silver coin into the fountain. The light of the new moon brightened and the goddess Artemis watched me ominously from the sky. But I had no regret. I was not afraid of her fatal arrows, and around my neck was the moonstone which shielded me from madness.

"Come," I called, "appear before me, you most glorious of deities—without a priest, without the mediation of a mortal woman, though I burn to ashes at sight of you."

From the depths of the fountain I heard a gurgle as though someone had replied to me. Looking into the water I thought I saw ripples. I began to feel dizzy and had to sit up and rub my eyes to remain conscious.

For a long time nothing happened. Then a shadowy body of light began to assume shape before me. It was winged and naked but so immaterial that I could see the columns through it. She was fairer than all mortal women and even Arsinoe's living beauty was but the shadow of this body of light in mortal clay.

"Aphrodite, Aphrodite!" I whispered. "Is it you, goddess?"

She shook her head sadly and looked at me with reproachful eyes. "Do you not know me? No, I see that you do not. But some day I will enfold you in my arms and bear you away on powerful wings."

"Who are you then, that I may know you?" I asked.

She smiled a radiant smile that pierced my heart. "I am your guardian spirit," she said. "I know you and am bound to you. Pray not to earthly gods nor surrender yourself to their power. You yourself are immortal if you but dare admit it."

She shook her beautiful head forlornly. "Images of you will be sculptured," she said, "and offerings made to you. I am within you and of you until that final moment when you recognize me and I kiss the mortal breath from your mouth. Oh, Turms, bind not yourself to earthly deities. Both Artemis and Aphrodite are but jealous, capricious and malevolent spirits of the earth and air. They have their power and their sorcery and they are both competing for you. But neither the moon nor sun will give you immortality, merely the seat of oblivion. And again you must return, again you will bind me to the pain of your birth and to your living, greedy human body."

My mortal eyes reveled in her radiance. Then doubt crept into my

121

mind. "You are only a vision," I said, "like other visions. Why should you appear to me just at this moment if you have accompanied me all my life?"

"You are in danger of binding yourself," she explained. "Never before have you wanted to do that. Now you are ready to do so for the sake of a mortal woman, for foam and sensual pleasure. You came here to bind yourself to Aphrodite although you are the son of the storm. If you only had sufficient faith in yourself, Turms, you would know better."

I replied stubbornly, "That woman, Arsinoe, is blood of my blood. Without her I cannot and will not live. Never before have I yearned for anything so terribly, and I am ready to bind myself to whichever goddess will give her to me for the duration of this life. I do not even ask for another life. So tempt me not, you unknown one, as fair as you are."

"Do you really think I am beautiful?" she asked and her wings trembled. Then, angered by her own vanity, she rebuked me sharply. "Do not try to confuse me, Turms. I wish I were like those exasperating earth deities so that I might assume a woman's body if only for a moment to box your ears. You are so wicked and so difficult to protect."

"Then why don't you disappear?" I demanded. "I called the goddess, not you. You are free to abandon me if you wish. I have no need of you."

The body of light quivered with rage. Then mournfully she bowed her head and said submissively, "Let it be as you wish, Turms, but for the sake of your immortality swear that you will not bind yourself. Even without it you will get whatever you want. You will get it through your own power if you but believe in yourself. You will even get that detestable bitch Arsinoe. But do not imagine that I want to be with you when you embrace that hateful body of clay. Artemis also has appeared to you and promised you earthly riches. Let them bribe you if you wish but under no circumstances bind yourself to them. You will not be indebted to them for their gifts. Accept whatever is given to you on earth, for sacrifices are made to immortals. Remember that always."

Her speech quickened, her wings flashed. "Turms, you are more than a human if only you will believe it. Fear nothing either here or beyond. Turms, the greatest courage is in believing oneself to be more than just a human. However tired, however dejected you are, never succumb to the temptation to bind yourself to the earth deities. Rejoice in your wicked body if you wish. It does not concern me. But do not bind yourself."

As I listened to her convincing words I was filled with courage. I must win Arsinoe through my own strength, and the strength was in me. I had been consecrated by the thunderbolt and that consecration sufficed for my lifetime.

She read my thoughts, her body grew dazzling and her face radiant. "I must go, Turms, my own. But remember me sometimes, if only for a moment. Yearn for me even a little. You must realize why I long to enfold you in my arms when you die."

She faded before my eyes until the marble columns were again visible through her body. But I no longer doubted her reality.

An inexpressible joy swelled through me. I raised my hand in farewell and cried, "I thank you, guardian spirit! I believe you. And I will yearn for you as I will never yearn for any mortal woman. The longer I live, the more deeply I will yearn for you. You probably are my only true love, and if you are, try to understand me. Then, in my moment of greatest longing, as I embrace a mortal woman, I will perhaps be embracing you a little, too."

She disappeared, and I was alone again by Aphrodite's fountain in Eryx. I laid my hand on the marble floor. It was cold to my touch and I breathed deeply. I knew that I lived and existed and that I had not merely dreamed. In the silence of the night, under the starry sky, in the threatening light of the moon's sickle, I sat by the ancient fountain of the goddess and felt a void within me.

At that moment a door creaked, I saw a light, and a priest came toward me across the courtyard, a Phoenician lamp in his hand. He threw its beams on me, recognized my face and demanded angrily, "How have you come here and why did you awaken me in the midst of my dream, accursed stranger?"

With his arrival the poison of the goddess again crept into my blood and my passion inflamed me as though glowing threads were searing my skin.

"I came to meet her," I said, "that priestess who appears in the temple and makes the foolish imagine that they have met the goddess."

"What do you want of her?" the priest asked, frowning deeply.

But the frown did not frighten me. "I want her," I declared. "The poison of the goddess came from her into my body and I cannot free myself of her."

After he had glared at me lethally for a time the priest became disconcerted and the lamp began to tremble in his hand.

"That is blasphemy, stranger. Shall I summon the guards? I have the right to have you killed as a profaner of the temple."

123

"Call the guards if you wish," I said cheerfully. "Let them kill me. I am sure that it would add to the reputation of your temple."

He looked at me suspiciously. "Who are you?"

"You should know that," I replied arrogantly. "Didn't the funeral pyre in the temple yard offer evidence? Didn't you recognize me from the storm which wiped the roofs from the houses and deposited rubble before your temple? But you may examine me still more if you wish."

He laughed hollowly, tossed something into the fountain with a splash and commanded, "Look into the fountain, stranger, that I may examine you."

As he raised the lamp I leaned over the edge of the fountain. I saw expanding and contracting ripples and the reflection of the lamp in the black water. I stared into the fountain until the water grew calm, rose and wiped my kness and asked, "What now?"

He stared at me in disbelief. "Did you really look into the fountain or were your eyes closed?"

"I saw the ripples in the water and the reflection of your lamp, that is all."

He swung the lamp slowly back and forth. Then at last he said, "Come with me to the temple."

I thanked him and he walked before me, lamp in hand. The air was so still that the flame did not even flicker. As I followed him I felt the chill of the night on my skin but my body was so hot with desire that I did not shiver. We entered the temple, he placed the lamp on the empty pedestal of the goddess and lowered himself onto a copper-legged seat.

"What do you want?" he asked.

"That woman, whatever her name is," I replied with equal patience. "The one with the changing face. I myself call her Arsinoe because it amuses me to do so."

"You have had a Scythian drink," he said. "Sleep your head clear and then come back and seek forgiveness."

"Babble as you will, old man. I want her and I shall have her. With or without the assistance of the goddess."

The furrow between his brows deepened until it almost split his head. In the light of the Phoenician lamp he leered at me with evil eyes.

"For tonight?" he asked. "Perhaps it can be arranged if you are sufficiently rich and keep the matter to yourself. Let us agree on it. I am an old man and would avoid wrangling. Probably the goddess has touched you with madness since you can no longer answer for your deeds. How much do you offer?"

"For one night? Nothing. That I can have whenever I wish. No, old man, you don't understand. I want her completely. I intend to take her with me and live with her until either she dies or I die."

Convulsed with rage, he leaped to his feet. "You don't know what you are saying! You may die sooner than you think."

"Don't waste your declining strength," I laughed. "Examine me instead, so that you may realize that I am in earnest."

He raised his hand in a gesture of conjuration and his eyes widened to the size of drinking cups. I would have feared them had not my power remained in me. I withstood his stare smilingly, until he suddenly pointed to the floor and exclaimed, "Behold the serpent!"

I looked down and involuntarily retreated, for a gigantic snake took shape before my eyes. It was the length of many men and the thickness of a thigh, and as it wriggled its skin glistened in a checkered design. It shaped itself into supple coils and raised its flat head toward me.

"Aye," I said, "you are more powerful than I thought, old man. I have heard that such a serpent once lived in the gorge at Delphi and guarded the Omphalos."

"Beware!" cried the priest threateningly.

Like lightning the snake rose upright and wound itself around my limbs until I was completely enveloped in its coils and its head swayed menacingly before my face. I felt its cold skin. Its weight was unbearable. Panic swept over me.

Then I laughed. "I will gladly play with you if you wish, priest. But I am not afraid. Not of subterranean, not of earthly, not even of celestial things. Least of all do I fear what is not even real. But I am willing to play these childish games with you through the night, if you are amused. Perhaps I myself could show you something amusing if I were to try."

"Don't," he said, breathing heavily. He passed a hand before his eyes and the snake disappeared, although I still felt its heavy coils on my skin. I shook myself, rubbed my limbs and smiled. ·

"You are a powerful old man," I admitted. "But don't tire yourself because of me. Sit down while I show you something that you perhaps would not want to see."

"Don't," he repeated. Trembling, he sank onto the seat. Again he was but an old man with sharp eyes and a furrow between his brows. After many deep breaths he asked in a completely changed voice, "Who are you, stranger?"

"If you don't want to recognize me, I will gladly remain unknown," I said.

"But you must realize that you are asking the impossible. Your very request blasphemes the goddess. Surely you don't want to enrage her even though you dare provoke me, a powerless man."

"I don't want to enrage or provoke anyone," I said amiably. "I am certainly not blaspheming the goddess. On the contrary. Don't you realize, old man, that I am honoring the goddess by requesting her priestess for myself?"

Suddenly he began to weep. Covering his face with his hand he swayed back and forth. "The goddess has abandoned me," he moaned. Wiping the tears from his beard he continued in a shrill voice, "You cannot be a human, although you are in a human guise! A human could not have resisted the spell of the snake. That gigantic serpent is the symbol of the earth, its weight and power. Whomever it fails to subdue cannot be a mortal."

I took advantage of the situation and said, "To return to my request, it was a friendly request and certainly not a demand. I likewise try to avoid quarrels and because of it hope that this matter may be resolved through mutual understanding. But I am also ready to make demands. Then I, in turn, will be compelled to resort to strength."

Again his voice became shrill. "Even if you are not mortal your request is unprecedented. How do you know whether that woman even wants to follow you?"

"She doesn't," I admitted cheerfully. "But this is a question of my will, not hers or yours."

I raised my hand to rub my tired eyes but he misunderstood the gesture and retreated with upraised hands.

"Don't," he pleaded once again. "Permit me to think." Then he said in despair, "She is an exceptional woman. There are not many like her and she is worth more than her weight in gold."

"I know that." The memory of Arsinoe sent tremors through my body. "After all, I have embraced her."

"Her body answers the requirements of the goddess and that is not unusual. She has been trained in the skills of the goddess and they can be learned. But the mobility of her face is a wonder. She is whatever I want and however I want it for any purpose whatsoever. Nor is she a stupid woman. That is the greatest wonder of all."

"I care little about her intelligence," I said, not realizing what I was saying. "But everything else is true enough. She is the equal of her goddess."

The priest extended his veined hands pleadingly to me. "In the temple of Eryx she serves the entire western sea, Carthage, Sicily, the Tyrrhenians, the Greeks. Through her body peace is built upon conflicting interests. There is not a councilor or tyrant whom she cannot persuade to believe the goddess."

I gritted my teeth in thinking of the men who had believed themselves to be meeting the goddess while in Arsinoe's arms.

"Enough," I said. "I don't intend to remember her past but will accept her as she is. I have even given her a new name."

The old man began tearing at his beard, then opened his mouth to cry out.

"Stop!" I ordered him. "What do you think the guard could do to me? And don't anger me."

His mouth remained open, his tongue twitched but not a sound came nor could he close his mouth. I stared at him in bewilderment until I realized that my power had affected him just as his disciplined power had enslaved me earlier. I laughed once more.

"You may close your mouth," I said, "and let your power of speech return."

He closed his jaws with a snap and wet his lips. "If I permit you to take her with you, I myself will suffer," he declared stubbornly. "No matter what tale I devise, it will not be believed. After all, we are living in civilized times and among priests the goddess no longer manifests her will but rather it is manifested in her behalf by the priests."

He deliberated for a time and then a sly expression came over his face. "The only way is for you to abduct her and take her with you as naked as when she was born into this world. She must not have with her a single object belonging to the goddess. I will close my eyes while you seize her and only after several days have elapsed will I reveal her disappearance. No one need even know who has abducted her, although naturally all strangers will be suspected. When she returns she may defend herself by saying that you stole her by force."

"She will not return," I said firmly.

"When she returns," he continued with equal firmness, "she may once again don the goddess's jewels, and with greater wisdom than before. Perhaps that was precisely the goddess's purpose. Why else would you have come here?"

A look of malicious delight came over his face. "But you," he said, "you will not have a peaceful day the rest of your life. I don't mean merely that you will be pursued by Carthage and all the native cities of Sicily. No, I mean that she herself will be a thorn in your flesh. Even if you are not a mortal, you still have a body and she will be its greatest affliction." He stroked his beard and tittered maliciously. "Truly, you don't know what you are asking. The goddess has bound you in her skein and the threads will scorch your flesh unto your heart until you wish that you were dead."

But his words only excited me and once again I felt the glorious sting of the goddess's threads and was filled with impatience.

"Arsinoe," I whispered. "Arsinoe."

"Her name is Istafra," said the old man petulantly. "Why shouldn't you know that also? I must die either now or later and I would rather do so later. That is really the only problem. But some day I must die anyway, and compared to that, what happens to her or you is unimportant. I wasted my powers in vain, and in vain rose from my soft bed. Do what you will, it does not concern me."

We quarreled no more. He took the lamp and led me behind the empty pedestal of the goddess, opened a narrow door and descended before me down stone steps into the earth. The passage was so narrow that I had to turn my shoulders sideways. He led me past the treasure chamber of the goddess into Arsinoe's room and awakened her.

Arsinoe had been sleeping with only a thin woolen cover over her, the new parasol in her hand. But when she awakened and saw us she flew into a rage.

"How have you been reared, Turms, that you don't allow a woman to sleep in peace? You must be mad to force yourself into the goddess's secret chambers in search of me."

Angry, naked, and with the parasol in her hand she was so enchanting that I was overcome by an irresistible desire to push the priest out of the room and take her in my arms. But since I knew that it would have lasted until morning I controlled my impatience.

"Arsinoe," I said, "rejoice. The goddess is giving you to me but we must leave immediately and in all secrecy and you must go as you are."

The priest nodded. "That is so, Istafra. The power of this stranger is greater than mine, therefore it is best that you leave with him. When you are rid of him you can return and I will testify that he abducted you by force. But before that, to please me, make his life as difficult as you can and let him suffer the results of his madness."

Arsinoe protested sleepily, "I don't want to go with him and have never promised that I would. Besides, I don't even know what to wear."

Impatiently I told her that she had to come as she was because of my promise that we would take nothing belonging to the goddess. I did not wish to rob the goddess, I said, and for my part Arsinoe's white skin was her most beautiful garment until such a time as I could buy her new clothes.

My words seemed to appease her and she said that she would at least take the parasol since it was my gift to her. But under no circumstances did she intend to follow me and throw herself like some stupid girl at the first stranger.

"So be it," I said in fury. "I shall hit you over the head and carry you over my shoulder if you prefer that, although I may injure your lovely skin."

She grew calmer at that and turned her back on us as though in contemplation.

The priest extended a round bowl and a stone knife to me and said, "Now consecrate yourself."

"Consecrate," I repeated. "What do you mean?"

"Bind yourself eternally to Aphrodite. It is the least I can expect of you whether you are mortal or not."

When I remained silent he thought that I hesitated for lack of knowledge. Irritably he explained, "Scratch a wound in your thigh with the goddess's knife, which is as old as the goddess's fountain. Shed your blood into the bowl which is made of the goddess's wood. Drop by drop repeat after me the words of consecration. That is all."

"Nay," I protested, "I have not the slightest intention of consecrating myself to Aphrodite. I am what I am. Let that suffice for the goddess from whom I accept this woman as a gift."

The priest stared at me, not believing his ears. Then his temples and lips swelled with anger, words failed him and he fell to the floor, the goddess's bowl and knife rolling from his hand. I feared that he had suffered a stroke, but there was no time to revive him.

Arsinoe watched, her lips tightly closed, as I felt her hair to make certain that she had nothing belonging to the goddess. Then I seized her hand, flung my mantle over her and led her out of the chamber. She followed me submissively up to the temple without saying a word.

We crossed the dark courtyard, stumbling over storm-torn branches, and climbed the wall where I had come down. I descended ahead of her, placing her foot on each tent peg so that she was able to reach the ground with but a few scratches. Then I climbed up again and removed the pegs so that no one would know how I had entered the temple. I put my arm around Arsinoe and with pounding heart led her to the inn. Still she had not said a word.

6.

But we were barely within four clay walls when her behavior changed completely. Wrathfully she spat out of her mouth a handful of golden jewelry, hairpins and rings and then fell upon me, beating and kicking and scratching. All the while she poured forth the most horrible words, but fortunately for me her knowledge of Greek was soon exhausted and she had to curse me in Phoenician which I did not fully understand. I had no opportunity to reproach her for having stolen despite her promise, so occupied was I in holding her kicking limbs and in pressing my palm against her mouth lest she awaken the entire inn.

Afterwards I realized that she did not actually scream very loudly but rather guardedly as though unwilling to awaken my sleeping comrades and the people of the inn. At the time, however, in the silence of the night, her voice sounded louder in my ears than warning drums. But soon the touch of her aroused the fire of Aphrodite in my body, I closed her mouth with my own, and in a moment we were lying breast to breast. I felt her heart beating against me as violently as my own, until her body softened, her arms wound themselves around my neck, and with a backward toss of her head she exhaled her hot breath in my face.

"Oh, Turms!" she whispered finally. "Why do you do this to me? I didn't want to. I resisted with all my strength, but you are stronger than I. I will follow you even to the ends of the earth."

She hugged my loins fiercely, kissed my face and shoulders, caressed the scratches she had made and murmured, "I didn't hurt you, did I, beloved? I didn't mean to. Oh, Turms, no man has been to me what you are. I am yours, solely and completely yours."

She raised herself on her elbow, touched my face and looked at me lovingly.

"I will follow you to the ends of the earth," she swore. "I will forsake the goddess and my life of luxury and all other men for your sake. Even if you were the poorest beggar I would gladly share your pauper's porridge and be content with water to drink because you are what you are. I love you madly, Turms, and you must love me a little, too, since you risked such danger to abduct me from the temple."

Sapless like a crushed plum, I assured her of my love. She listened contentedly, then began walking to and fro, describing with animation the clothes she intended to obtain. Suddenly she noticed the moonstone that hung around my neck on a cord.

"That is beautiful," she said, fingering it absently. "May I try it?"

She slipped it off my neck and around her own. Twisting her body this way and that to see it, she asked, "Isn't it beautiful against my skin? But I must get a thin golden chain for it, like those made by the Etruscans."

I remarked that the simple fiber cord was made of Artemis' fibers and thus belonged to the moonstone. "But keep it if you wish," I smiled. "It didn't shield me from madness since I so madly fell in love with you."

She stared at me and then demanded, "What do you mean? Is it madness to love me? In that case let us end the matter right now and I will return to the temple. Keep your stupid stone since you are so miserly about it."

She tore the cord, flung the stone in my face and began to weep bitterly. I bounded from the bed to console her, pressed the stone into her palm and promised to buy her a golden chain as soon as we reached Himera.

"I really don't need it," I assured her. "The stone is quite worthless to me."

Looking at me through her tears she said accusingly, "So now you are forcing worthless gifts on me! You certainly are not considerate. Yes, I know, you intend to keep me as your dog. Oh, why did you kindle my heart?"

Tiring of her talk, I said, "The stone is beautiful, but for my part you may throw it out the window. Only a moment ago it gleamed against your bosom, but I would rather look at your lovely breasts on either side of it. They are your finest jewels and suffice to make you the most beautiful woman wherever you may be."

"Surely you don't expect me to follow you naked to the ends of the earth to share the lot of a poor man?" she asked in a tight voice.

"Listen, Arsinoe or Istafra, whichever you are," I said. "At this moment we have more important things to do than to argue. After all, we have the rest of our lives for that. Even if I had the means to purchase all the clothing that you mentioned, they would fill at least ten baskets and we would need more donkeys and drovers to transport them. We must leave as quickly and inconspicuously as possible. For the time being you will wear Aura's clothes and assume her countenance until we reach Himera. Once there, I will see what I can do for you."

"How can I wear the coarse clothes of a lowly Sicilian girl?" she demanded. "How could I appear before the people without ornamenting my hair? No, no, you don't realize what you are asking of me, Turms. I am ready for any sacrifice in your behalf, but I could not imagine that you would expect such humiliating sacrifices of me."

Her face was pale in the lamplight because I had abducted her from bed as she was. A tear dropped from her eyes and rolled down her cheeks. I tried to explain that Aura, after all, had been the wife of a Greek physician and that Mikon had been able to provide a moderate wardrobe for her. True, Aura had been so young that she had not found it necessary to redden her lips and color her eyes, but she, Arsinoe, could use Tanakil's paints to make herself seem younger.

That I should have left unsaid, and my only defense is that at that time I did not understand women.

"So you consider me decrepit!" she began, and our argument was sharper than any previous exchange. To my horror the gray dawn began to creep into the room and the first cock crowed somewhere in the city before I succeeded in calming her.

Without daring to open my mouth again since I seemed always to say the wrong thing, I hastened to awaken Dorieus and Mikon and then ran to explain everything to Tanakil.

As an experienced woman she immediately understood the inevitable and did not waste time in fruitless accusations. Quickly she clothed Arsinoe in Aura's best garments, gave her her own bead-embroidered shoes because Aura's shoes were too large, and helped her to paint her face to resemble Aura.

Then she lashed awake her servants, packed her goods and settled her account with the innkeeper. As the sun was coloring the peaks of Eryx a rosy red, we were already hurrying across the city and reached the wall just as the sleepy guards were opening the gate. We left the city without being stopped, and as we started down the circling pilgrims' road our horses whinnied and donkeys brayed with joy.

Tanakil had made room for Arsinoe in her own litter. When we were halfway down the mountain the sun was up, the sky smiled with twinkling blue eyes, and the calm sea called to the ships with playful waves to begin the sailing season. The barren mountain cone had turned green, in the valley black and white oxen were plowing the fields, farmers were spitting seeds into the earth and the land was gay with flowers.

Mikon was still so confused from his wine-drinking that he followed us involuntarily, swaying like a sack on the back of a donkey. When he saw Arsinoe he sighed heavily, addressed her as Aura and asked how she was. He apparently had either forgotten Aura's death or considered it but a drunken hallucination. Presumably he thought that everything was as it should be, although he did not appear as contented as he had during the previous days.

I myself did not dare to talk to Arsinoe during our entire descent down the mountain. But when we had reached the valley and were watering our animals before turning onto the road to Segesta, she drew aside the curtain and called to me softly.

"Oh, Turms! Is the air really so delightful to breathe, and is it possible that ash-smeared bread can be so delicious? Oh, Turms, never have I been so happy! I believe I really love you. You will never again be as cruel to me as you were this morning, will you?"

We turned onto the road to Segesta and finally reached Himera safely. True, the trying journey had made us irritable, but at least we were alive and no one had pursued us. Immediately upon our arrival in the city, at Dorieus' suggestion, we sacrificed the largest cock in Himera to Herakles.

BOOK FIVE

Voyage to Eryx

I.

OUR return to Himera attracted no attention. Five we had been
when we set forth and five returned. So consummately had
Arsinoe assumed the countenance and demeanor of Aura that Mikon,
his perception dulled from days of drinking in Eryx, actually believed
her his wife. It was with difficulty that I banished him from Arsinoe's
resting place whenever he sought to exercise his conjugal prerogatives
during the journey.

More important matters than our return occupied the people of
Himera. A courier ship had braved the spring storms to bring news to
Sicily of the fall of Miletus. The Persians, after a long siege, had taken
the city by storm, plundered and burned it, and killed or enslaved its
people. At the King's express command Miletus had been leveled to
the ground for its part in the rebellion. It had not been easy to destroy
a city populated by hundreds of thousands, but the army had managed
to do so, aided by engines of war and thousands of Greek slaves.

So ended the dance of freedom. Other Ionian cities suffered somewhat
less. True, Greek tyrants again ruled, but the conquered cities experienced no worse than the usual slaughter, arson, raping and looting.
But when the revolt had been quelled, the natives were, as always, more
merciless than the strangers, and the reinstated tyrants so effectively
purged the dancers of freedom that those who had been wise enough
to flee to the west with their families and property could be counted
fortunate indeed.

Such were the tales told of Ionia. I, who felt that I had already discharged my duty in the rebellion, was not greatly moved by the fate of
Miletus. But it must be said that much that was luxurious, refined and

pleasurable in life disappeared forever with the destruction of Miletus. We drank a toast to its memory in Tanakil's best wine, Dorieus and I, but we did not go so far as to cut our hair in mourning. That, we felt, would have been hypocrisy.

From Dionysius we obtained more dependable information, for as one who was himself well versed in the art of exaggeration he could easily strip senseless rumors to their core.

"Athens is not yet in ruins," he said reassuringly, "although many swear that the Persian king himself has sailed to undertake retaliation for the Athenians' raid on Sardis. But that will take many years. The Persian must first strengthen his hold on the islands, and launching an attack on the mainland of Greece requires lengthy preparations. It is said, however—and this I well believe—that he has instructed his favorite slave to whisper frequently into his ear, 'My lord, forget not the Athenians.'

"That is how matters stand," concluded Dionysius. "With the fall of Miletus the eastern sea is now the Phoenicians', and the unnumbered ships of Ionia are now Persian. Should the mainland fall there would remain only this Western Greece caught between Carthage and the Tyrrhenians. For that reason it would be wisest for us to retrieve our treasure from Krinippos' vaults with all haste and sail for Massilia as though we had already arrived. Perhaps during our lifetime the clutch of the Persian may extend even to there."

Mikon raised his hands in horror. "Surely you exaggerate, Dionysius! I know from history that no one, not even Egypt or Babylon, has yet ruled the entire world. For that matter, no one could conceive of Egypt's fall. I was perhaps twelve when the rumor swept the islands that the great King Kambyses had conquered Egypt. My father, who was a learned man, refused at first to believe it, but when the truth could no longer be denied, he said that he had no desire to live in such times. And so he swathed his head in a cloth, lay down on his bed and died. Then they began to make jars ornamented in red in Attica as a sign that the world had turned upside down. But not even Darius could vanquish the Scythians."

Dorieus became indignant. "Keep your mouth closed, physician, since you know nothing about warfare. No one can vanquish the Scythians because they wander with their herds from place to place. They have no true kingdom, and a victory of the Scythians would not bring honor to a soldier. I myself understand well the idea of world conquest. The Greeks who have become mercenaries in the forces of the Persian ruler have perhaps chosen the best lot. But my fate ordained otherwise and I must look to my inheritance while there is yet time."

He grew silent, bit his lip, and studied Dionysius moodily. "I respect you at sea," he said finally, "for in matters maritime there is none shrewder than you. But I was born to fight on land and so am troubled with things that are happening at home. The fate of Greece hangs in the balance. Should not this Western Greece strengthen itself while time permits? The first task would be to free Segesta and all Eryx and sweep the Carthaginian bridgeheads in Sicily into the sea."

"Your plan is a good one, Spartan," said Dionysius soothingly, "but many others have already attempted it. The bones of Phocaeans are rotting in Segesta's fields, and you no doubt had the opportunity during your pilgrimage to pay homage to your late father's spirit in the same region." He scratched his head. "But why are we wasting time on trifles? Our task is to sail speedily to Massilia and there found a new colony to vex the Carthaginians."

Dorieus lost all patience. "You may sail to Hades for all I care! I have heard so much talk about Massilia that my head aches!"

"It is that oarstroke you received at Lade," nodded Dionysius sympathetically.

"Swordstroke, by Herakles!" corrected Dorieus angrily. "And do not tempt me to violate the laws of hospitality by killing you on the spot. I have no intention of sailing to Massilia, but will take possession of Segesta and Eryx to which I have a legal right as a descendant of Herakles. For that I shall need your ships and men, Dionysius, and our treasure. The venture looks promising, for my wife's sons by her second husband are already preparing for a revolt in Segesta, and with Tanakil's wealth we will buy allies from among the Siccani who dwell in the forest."

He warmed to his story. "The conquest of Segesta will not even be difficult, for the nobles are interested only in breeding hunting dogs, and pay professional athletes to compete in their stead. Mount Eryx may be unconquerable, but I have a woman—" He stopped, glanced at me, flushed and corrected himself. "We have a woman, a priestess of Aphrodite, who is familiar with the subterranean passages of Eryx. With her aid we can seize the temple and its votive offerings."

Now it was my turn to spring to my feet and demand, in a voice quivering with rage, "How and when have you had time to devise such schemes with Arsinoe behind my back? Why hasn't she breathed one word to me?"

Dorieus averted his eyes. "Presumably you have other matters to discuss," he said lamely. "We did not wish to disturb you. Arsinoe is quite willing to think for you, too."

Mikon blinked, shook his head and asked, "Forgive me, but who is Arsinoe?"

"The woman whom you believe to be Aura is not Aura but a priestess of Aphrodite whom I abducted from Eryx," I explained. "She merely assumed the guise of Aura to enable us to escape without detection." When Mikon hid his face in his hands I continued encouragingly, "Don't you remember that Aura died because of your unwarranted curiosity? You yourself heaped the white poplar into a funeral pyre and anointed her body."

Mikon suddenly raised his head. His eyes began to shine and he cried gleefully, "So it was true, the goddess be thanked! And I thought that it was just the wine. Blessed be Aura's bones!" In sheer joy he leaped from the couch and began to skip around the table, laughing and clapping his hands. "No wonder I was skeptical when I saw how Aura had changed, but I thought that it was the goddess's doing. Now I know why I have lately experienced such rapture in her embrace."

As the full significance of his words came over me my jaw dropped. Then my fingers curled to clutch his throat.

But Dorieus was faster. Face purple with anger, he shattered a drinking cup and roared, "You wretched charlatan! Have you dared to touch Arsinoe?" He would have pounced on Mikon but my cry arrested him.

"Mikon's error is understandable," I said slowly, my fingers twitching, "but why are you so anxious to defend Arsinoe's chastity and honor? And once again, when have you enticed her to conspire with you about Eryx?"

Dorieus cleared his throat. "In no way have I enticed her, Turms, that I swear in the name of the goddess. It's merely that Mikon's vulgar talk about such a sensitive and noble woman distresses me."

I wanted to scream, weep and break clay bowls, but Dorieus said hastily, "Control yourself, Turms. Why speak of such matters in the presence of a stranger?"

He glanced at Dionysius, who retorted, "I listened with curiosity to your political plans, but in all honesty I admit to even greater curiosity about the woman who has aroused such emotions in three so gifted men."

Hardly had he spoken than Arsinoe entered, followed by Tanakil in her finest garments and jewelry which jangled and clattered as she walked. Arsinoe in contrast was simply clothed, even more simply than I would have wished, for she wore only a sheer gown fastened at one shoulder with a large gold brooch. The result was revealing rather than concealing. She had combed her golden hair upward in the manner of the goddess and fastened it with jewels that she had stolen from the temple. Between her breasts was suspended, like an evil eye, the large moonstone I had given her. The golden Etruscan chain on which it hung was not my gift, since I had forgotten all about the matter during our busy days in Himera.

"Dionysius, mighty warrior of the sea," she said in greeting. "I am happy indeed to see you after having heard so much about your exploits and, in all confidence, also about the treasures which you have stored in the vaults of the tyrant Krinippos."

Dionysius looked her up and down, then cursed. "Are you mad, the three of you, or has a rabid dog bitten you, that you should reveal our secrets to a woman?"

Arsinoe bowed her head humbly. "I am but a weak woman," she conceded, "but believe me, fair Dionysius, the deepest secrets of men are safer in my heart than are your treasures in the vaults of the greedy Krinippos." She smiled, a new, wistful smile that I had never seen before.

Dionysius rubbed his eyes and shook his massive head. "The only thing which my slave mother could teach me was not to trust sailors. I myself have learned that no woman's word is to be trusted. But when you look at me with those sad eyes, you priestess, I am overcome by a great temptation to believe that you among all women might be an exception."

"Arsinoe," I cried, "I forbid you to look at any man in that manner!"

But I might as well have spoken to a wall. Arsinoe did not even notice me, but seated herself lightly on the edge of Dionysius' couch. Tanakil brought forth another pitcher of wine and Arsinoe offered Dionysius a goblet filled to the brim.

Absently he splashed the first drop on the floor and said, "I no longer remember just what I said, but your words amazed me. Strong I have been called by both men and women, but no one has yet dared call me fair, not even my own mother. Why did you use that word?"

Arsinoe rested her chin in her palm and with tilted head studied Dionysius. "Do not distract me with your glances, man of the sea, for you make me blush. Perhaps it isn't proper for a woman to speak in this manner to a man, but when I entered and saw you there with those massive gold rings in your ears I was overcome with trembling. It was as though I saw a terrifyingly big and beautiful black-bearded god." Rapturously, she continued, "Manly beauty is so rare. So rare and so dissimilar. Some may admire a slender youth—I, never. No, give me a man with limbs hard as logs, a curly beard from which a woman may hang with her full weight, and eyes bigger than those of the fairest ox. Ah, Dionysius," she breathed, "I respect your fame, but most of all I admire you because you are the fairest man I have ever seen." She raised her hand and touched the golden ring in his ear with slender fingers.

Dionysius recoiled as at the blow of a whip. "By Poseidon," he muttered. He reached toward her cheek as though to smooth it, then recovered himself, swung to the other side of the couch and leaped to his feet. He cursed loudly twice, three times.

"Slut!" he roared. "Slut and once again slut, not one word of it do I believe."

Cursing, he rushed from the room. We heard him snatch his shield from the entrance hall and stumble down the stairs, but before we could reach him he had recovered himself, plunged out of the house and into the street, slamming the gate behind him.

We returned to the room, glancing helplessly at one another. Arsinoe recovered herself first. "Dear Turms," she coaxed playfully, "come with me. You are unnecessarily agitated. I have matters to discuss with you."

As we left I saw Dorieus strike Mikon across the face so hard that he fell against the wall and slid to the floor with one hand holding his cheek.

2.

When we were alone I stared at Arsinoe as at a stranger. Seeking the proper words with which to begin I impulsively spoke the wrong ones. "Aren't you ashamed to step half naked into the presence of a strange man?"

"But you want me to dress simply," she protested. "Hundreds of times you have said that you cannot satisfy my small wants and that within these few days I have plunged you into debt for years to come with my excessive demands. Could I have dressed more simply than this?"

As I opened my mouth to reply, she laid a restraining hand on my arm, bit her lip and said beseechingly, "No, Turms, don't speak before you have considered your words well, for I can stand no more."

"You can stand no more!" I cried in amazement.

"Precisely. Even the patience of a woman in love has its limits. During these days in Himera I have all too clearly realized that I cannot please you, try as I may. Ah, Turms, how could this have happened to us!"

She flung herself onto the bed, buried her face in her arms and began to weep. Each sob wrenched my heart so that at length I began to wonder whether I was not, after all, the cause of all her misdeeds. Then, remembering Dorieus' averted gaze and Mikon's guilty face, I forgot Dionysius. The blood rushed to my head and I raised my hand to strike her. But the hand remained aloft, for I suddenly noticed the tempting helplessness of her beautiful body as it quivered under the sheer fabric. The natural result was that, with her arms around my neck, I again experienced one of those moments when all else faded and I seemed to be resting on a cloud with Arsinoe.

Soon she roused herself and touched my damp forehead with cool fingers. "Why are you always so cruel to me, Turms, when I love you so madly?"

Nor did her face belie her words. She spoke in all sincerity. "How can you say that?" I reproached her. "Aren't you ashamed to look at me with those clear eyes when I have just learned that you have been deceiving me with my two best friends."

"That is not so," she protested, but her glance evaded mine.

"If you really loved me—" I began and could go no farther, for anger and humiliation throttled the words.

Arsinoe grew serious and in an entirely different tone continued, "I am a vacillating person, I know. After all, I am a woman. Perhaps you cannot always be sure of me for I am not always sure of myself. The one thing of which you may be certain, now and forever, is that I love you and only you. Would I otherwise have abandoned my old life?"

She spoke with such sincerity that I felt her words to be true. My bitterness faded into regret. "Mikon's words revealed—"

She pressed her soft palm against my lips. "Don't go on. I admit it, but it was not to my liking. It was only for your sake that I consented, Turms. You yourself said that your life was in danger if it came out too soon that I was not Aura."

"But Mikon said—" I began again.

"Of course," she admitted. "But you must realize that a woman's pride in such matters must also be considered. When I was compelled to yield for your sake I could not behave like a lowly Sicilian girl."

"Silence!" I begged. "How dare you boast? But what of Dorieus?"

"Naturally I talked to him," Arsinoe conceded, "after Tanakil told me of his plans. He is a handsome man and would tempt any woman.

Perhaps he misinterpreted my interest, and it is not my fault that I am beautiful."

"He, too!" I groaned and reached for my sword.

Arsinoe calmed me. "Nothing has happened. I explained to Dorieus that it could not. He asked my forgiveness and we agreed to be merely friends." She stared into the distance thoughtfully. "You see, Turms, I may be of assistance to him in his political plans. He is not so stupid as to antagonize one who can help him."

Hope and doubt struggled within me. "Do you swear that Dorieus has not touched you?"

"Touched me—touched me—stop repeating that! Perhaps he has touched me a little. But he does not tempt me as a man, that I will swear by any god's name you wish."

"Do you swear it by our love?"

"By our love," she repeated after only a moment's hesitation.

But I saw the doubt in her eyes and rose. "Good. I shall find out for myself."

"Don't!" she pleaded in alarm, then shrugged. "Or go if you wish, since you don't believe me. It is best so. But I would not have expected such treatment from you, Turms."

Her tearful, accusing eyes haunted me, but I had to learn the truth from Dorieus' own lips. Only then would I be free of doubts. How childish I was! As though my heart could ever be at peace for a single moment with Arsinoe.

I found Dorieus in the garden, lolling in the warm pool. The yellowish water smelled of sulphur and his strong body gleamed larger than life through it. To calm my mind I sat on the edge of the pool, dangling my feet in it.

"Dorieus," I began, "remember the stadium at Delphi. Remember the sheep's bones we tossed to divine the direction of our travels. Remember Corinth and the war in Ionia. Surely our friendship is above all else. I will not be angry if you but tell the truth. In the name of our friendship, have you lain with Arsinoe?"

His glance wavered. Finally he said, "Well, once or twice. I meant no harm. Her enticements are irresistible."

Dorieus' honest confession proved him to be as childish as I in such matters although I did not realize it at the time. Cold shivers sped up my back. "Did you compel her to submit?"

"I, compel?" Dorieus stared at me in wonder. "In the name of Herakles, little do you know her! Haven't I already explained that I could not withstand her?" Thus launched on his tale he was anxious to unburden himself. "Don't tell Tanakil, I pray you. I would not want her to worry. You see, it was Arsinoe who started it all by admiring my muscles. She said that you were not much of a man compared to me."

"Did she really?" I said in a hoarse voice.

"Yes. It seems that Tanakil had so boasted of my strength that Arsinoe grew envious. You yourself know what happens when she strokes a man's loins a few times. In all honesty I could not think of friendship, honor or anything else. Shall I continue?"

"No. I understand." But I did not. "Dorieus, why did she claim that you do not attract her?"

He burst into laughter and began flexing his muscles in the water. "Don't I? Perhaps she said so out of pity, but you should have been there to see and hear for yourself."

I rose so suddenly that I almost toppled into the pool. "So be it, Dorieus. I do not hate you for it nor will I brood over the matter. But don't ever do it again."

Eyes brimming with hot tears, I fled into the house. I knew then that I could no longer trust anyone, least of all Arsinoe. This bitter truth must come to each one of us sooner or later. It is as inescapable a part of life as ashen bread or a cold. Then a feeling of relief swept over me as I knew that I was under no obligation to Dorieus. Our friendship no longer bound me to him since he himself had violated that friendship.

When I returned to our room Arsinoe raised herself eagerly from the couch. "Well, Turms, have you spoken to Dorieus and are you not ashamed of your cruel suspicions?"

"How brazen can you be, Arsinoe? Dorieus confessed."

"Confessed what?" she demanded.

"To having lain with you, as you well know." I sank onto the couch in despair. "Why did you lie and falsely swear by our love? Never again will I be able to trust you, Arsinoe."

She wound her arms around my neck. "But, Turms, what nonsense is this? Dorieus could not have confessed. Do you think that Spartan is trying to alienate us by sowing seeds of doubt in your mind? I can think of no other reason."

Reluctantly I looked at her with hungry, hopeful eyes. She read my longing to believe, and hastened to explain. "Now I understand, Turms. Naturally I wounded his masculine pride in rejecting his advances and, knowing how credulous you are, he is retaliating by speaking falsely of me."

"Don't, Arsinoe," I pleaded. "I am already heartsick unto death. Dorieus did not lie, for I know him better than you."

She took my head between her palms. For a moment she studied me, then thrust me aside. "So be it. I no longer have the strength to fight for our love. All is at an end, Turms. Farewell. Tomorrow I shall return to Eryx."

What could I have said? What could I have done but fling myself on the floor and beg forgiveness for my ugly suspicions? She was in my blood and I could not lose her. Again we climbed a dazzling cloud, and viewed from there everything on earth seemed insignificant, even lies and deception.

3.

The sailing season was upon us and, after a winter of laboring to raise Himera's walls, the men of Phocaea were restless, sniffing the winds and studying the heavenly portents. Dionysius had launched a new ship and both the penteconters had been caulked and tarred tighter than ever. There was not an oar, a rope or a knothole that Dionysius had not inspected with his own eyes. In the evening the sailors were already sharpening their light weapons and the marines, grown fat over the winter, were struggling to don their breastplates and cuirasses of bronze scales and piercing new holes in their straps. The oarsmen were singing rowdy songs of farewell, while the men who had married Himeran women in the autumn were beginning to wonder whether it would, after all, be wise to subject a frail woman to the dangers of the sea. And so the women, despite their tears and pleading, were to remain behind in Himera.

But Krinippos decreed that every wedded man must provide his wife with funds in accordance with his position on the ship, thirty drachmas for an oar and one hundred drachmas for a sword. In addition, every Himeran woman, whether single or wedded, who had become pregnant during the winter was to receive ten silver drachmas from Dionysius' treasure.

Enraged by such extortionate demands, the sailors gathered in the market place to scream that Krinippos was the most thankless tyrant and the greediest human they had ever known.

"Are we the only men in Himera?" they wailed. "After all, your own symbol is the cock, and it is not our fault if we were contaminated by your city's whoredom. All winter we have labored like slaves for you, and by night were so exhausted that we could only fall into bed. It is surely not our fault if the city's maidens—yes, and matrons too—crept in beside us."

143

But Krinippos was merciless. "The law is the law, and my word is the law in Himera. But willingly I grant you permission to take your wives with you and also those maidens whom you have made pregnant. The choice is yours."

During the confusion Dionysius stood apart and made no attempt to defend his men. He still had to obtain water and supplies for the ships and above all the treasure from Krinippos' stone vaults. As the men stormed about the market place, tearing their clothes in rage, he studied each shrewdly.

Suddenly he clutched the arm of the noisiest rower. "What is that mark on your back?"

The man glanced over his shoulder and explained eagerly, "It is a holy mark that will protect me in battle and cost only one drachma."

A group of men clustered around Dionysius, each anxious to show his own holy crescent. Angrily Dionysius asked, "How many of you have such a mark and who made them?"

More than half the men had hastened to obtain the charm and the wounds had not yet healed, for the seer had but recently arrived in Himera. With a sharp knife he had shaped the crescent on the edge of the left shoulder blade, painted it with holy indigo, covered it with holy ashes and finally spat holy spittle on it.

"Bring forth the seer that I may study his own shoulder blade," commanded Dionysius. But the seer who but a few minutes earlier had been drawing holy symbols on his tablet in a corner of the market place had suddenly disappeared, nor could he be found anywhere in the city.

That evening Dionysius came to see us with the chief helmsman of his large ship. "We are in grave danger because of that blue mark," he said. "Krinippos will come here tonight to discuss the matter. Let us say nothing of our own affairs and merely listen to him."

Dorieus explained eagerly, "My plans are now ready. I am glad that you, Dionysius, have decided to join forces with me so that we no longer have to compete for leadership."

Dionysius sighed patiently. "That is so. But do not breathe a word about Segesta in Krinippos' presence or he will not permit us to sail. Can't we agree that I will have command at sea and you on land?"

"That may be best," conceded Dorieus after a moment. "But when we go ashore we will have no further use for the ships, so I will have them burned."

Dionysius nodded but with averted head. Mikon asked curiously,

"Why are we so concerned about that blue mark and a charlatan who earns his living by deceiving susceptible sailors?"

Dionysius sent the helmsman to watch that no women crept behind the drapes to listen, then explained, "A Carthaginian ship has been sighted outside Himera. Presumably it is a courier ship whose task is to inform the Carthaginian fleet of our departure."

"But Himera is not at war with the Phoenicians," I protested. "On the contrary, Krinippos is a friend of Carthage. What has that to do with the seer or the mark?"

Dionysius touched the lower edge of my left shoulder blade with his thick forefinger and smiled a twisted smile. "Just there is the spot where the Carthaginian sacrificial priest begins skinning a pirate alive. The head, hands and feet he leaves untouched so that the victim may live for days. That is how Carthage punishes piracy.

"Yes," he continued, "we have been discovered. The Carthaginians know that our loot is not from the battle at Lade, and for that reason we are no longer safe anywhere at sea. They have probably told their allies the Etruscans about us, too, although that does not matter much since we already know that they will not allow us to sail through their sea."

Mikon, who had been drinking wine since morning, began to tremble. "I am not a coward," he said, "but I am weary of the sea and with your permission, Dionysius, I shall remain behind in Himera."

Dionysius roared with laughter and clapped him on the shoulder. "Stay if you wish. Nothing worse will happen than that some day Krinippos will be compelled to surrender you to the Phoenicians who will nail your skin to the sea gate at Carthage. Their spy has most certainly memorized our faces as well as those of our ablest helmsmen, for the Phoenicians are not thinking only of today but ten years hence in the event that we succeed in reaching Massilia."

"But we are not sailing for Massilia," interrupted Dorieus.

"Naturally not," agreed Dionysius readily. "They merely think so because such a rumor has circulated. It is for that reason that they have marked even the lowliest of our sailors, so that they may recognize us anywhere and under whatever circumstances." He laughed at our horrified expressions. "A man who thrusts his fist into a bee's nest for honey knows what he is doing. You well knew what faced you when you joined our forces."

That was not strictly true, but we had no desire to argue the matter. In the eyes of the Phoenicians, at least, we were bound skin and hair to him.

At that moment the helmsman appeared at the doorway wringing his hands and saying that the lady of the house and her friend sought entrance. Arsinoe brushed by him, holding in her arms a glossy-coated animal which she thrust toward me.

"See what I have bought, Turms!"

I looked at the spitting, gleaming-eyed animal and recognized it as a cat. The Egyptians consider it holy but one rarely encounters it in other lands. I had, however, seen one in Miletus, where women of the nobility kept cats in their homes, although they should have known better.

"It is a cat!" I cried. "Put down that dangerous animal instantly. Don't you know that it conceals sharp claws in those soft paws?" I was shocked, not the least because I knew that cats are expensive and I never was quite sure how Arsinoe obtained the money for her purchases.

She laughed merrily. "Turms, don't be unkind. Take it in your lap and pat it. You will find it enchanting." She tossed the cat at me, whereupon it dug its claws into my chest, climbed onto my head, and from there leaped onto the shoulder of the Phoenician household god.

"All my life I have yearned for such an enchanting animal," prattled Arsinoe. "Believe me, it is entirely tame. It was you who frightened it, Turms, with your cry of alarm. Think of its softness as it lies in bed guarding my sleep, with eyes glowing in the darkness like protecting lanterns. You cannot deny me that great joy."

Feeling the pitying glances of the three men I flushed and protested, "I did not cry out nor do I fear the creature. But it is a useless animal and we cannot take it on board the ship when we shortly put to sea."

"Say rather to Hades," observed Dionysius sarcastically. "Well, Turms, I did not think that you would prove to be the most loose-tongued of us all."

"But the entire city already knows that you are about to sail," said Arsinoe innocently. "The council of Carthage demands that Krinippos either detain or deport you. Even the merchant who sold me this beautiful animal knew that and for that reason sold it to me cheaply, so that it would bring us luck at sea."

Dionysius raised his arms. "May the gods have mercy on us!" he prayed.

"It is obviously a Phoenician scheme," I said. "They have thrust the cat on Arsinoe so that it will bring us misfortune. The merchant must have been a Phoenician."

Arsinoe hugged the cat to her. "On the contrary, he was Etruscan and a friend of yours, Turms. His name is Lars Alsir. That is why he gave me the cat on credit."

146

That relieved my mind, for Lars Alsir would hardly wish me ill. Dionysius burst into laughter, extended a hand cautiously toward the cat and began rubbing its chin with a heavy forefinger.

Arsinoe looked at him gratefully. "You understand me best of all, Dionysius," she murmured. "Isn't Turms childish not to see what takes place before his very nose? No Phoenician merchant could have sold me anything because they have all discontinued trading and have hired men armed with battle-axes to stand guard over their shops. Moreover, they have forbidden all other merchants to trade with us under threat of banning all Carthaginian goods in the future. That I think is silly, for the task of a merchant is to trade and not to prevent trade."

Still absently scratching the cat, Dionysius called his helmsman and ordered, "Go immediately and arouse the priests of Poseidon and have them sacrifice ten bulls for us, cost what it may. If necessary have some trustworthy resident purchase them in his own name. The thighbones and fat may remain at the altar, but the meat must be stored in the vessels tonight." He turned back to Arsinoe. "I apologize for interrupting you, but watching you and the cat I was suddenly overcome by an irresistible desire to sacrifice ten bulls to Poseidon."

Arsinoe narrowed her eyes playfully. "Lars Alsir would hardly have dared sell me the cat if people knew that I am Turms' companion. But of course no one does know, although I arouse great curiosity when I walk through the city with a boy holding my parasol."

I held my head in dismay, for I had sharply forbidden her to leave the house or to attract attention in any way. But she looked at me sharply. "That reminds me. Lars Alsir said something about you and Krinippos' granddaughter. What has taken place between you and that girl?"

At that moment, of course, Krinippos' faithful runner arrived to inform us that his master was on his way, and a minute later Krinippos himself pushed into the chamber, sandals in hand and panting heavily. He was followed by a trembling Terillos, his bald head covered with a golden wreath, and—as though summoned by evil spirits—Kydippe.

When Arsinoe saw her she thrust the cat from her lap and rose threateningly. "Since when have girls taken to pursuing men? I can believe almost anything about Himera, but that a father accompanies his daughter to stalk a man who is not interested—" She took a step toward Kydippe and laughed. "Why, she has not even breasts! And her eyes are too far apart and her feet are huge."

All I could do to silence Arsinoe was to snatch her in my arms and carry her, kicking violently, to our room. The cat shot by us and was already on the bed when I tossed Arsinoe there so hard that she had difficulty in recovering her breath.

Finally she spoke. "Turms, how can you treat me so cruelly? Is it because you love that spoiled girl? It was for her sake that you went to Eryx. Why then did you entice me to follow you, when you consider me only your plaything?"

"Save your strength," I said. "This very night we may sail, so pack your possessions and pray to the goddess."

She clutched at my robe and shouted, "Don't evade me, you traitor! Confess at once what that girl has been to you so that I may kill her."

"You are wrong, all wrong," I assured her. "I was even more surprised than you to see Kydippe, and cannot understand why her witless grandfather should have brought her to a secret conference. Nor do I understand why Lars Alsir, whom I believed to be my friend, should have gossiped to you about such a trivial matter."

Arsinoe smiled in apparent satisfaction, then spoke again. "Now I remember. Lars Alsir sent you a message, but what it was I cannot say at the moment for you have driven it from my mind. I am glad that we are going where there will be no foolish girls to distract you, which seems incredibly easy to do."

Only then did I realize that there would be only men on board the ship, and that a woman like Arsinoe, even without a cat, could drive a crew to destruction.

Suddenly she reached into her bosom. "Now I remember Lars Alsir's message." She brought forth a tiny sea horse the size of my thumb and carved of black stone. "He sent you this as a memento. He said as a joke that you could settle your debts with him another time when you come into your kingdom, so I selected a few small pieces of jewelry in addition to the cat. He also gave me a golden sea horse to make sure that I gave you the stone one."

"What was the message?" I asked impatiently.

"Don't hurry me." She wrinkled her brow in thought. "He said that presumably nothing bad would happen to you, but that you have bound yourself to the earth. Then he said—and this he impressed on me—that two Carthaginian warships are hidden on a beach west of Himera, and that outside the city walls, by the altar of Iacchus, there is a pyre which will be lighted as a signal if you should sail at night. More warships are on their way, he said, so it would be wisest to escape in time."

She stretched out on the bed temptingly, but I dared not look at her. The news she had given me was of greater importance.

"I must go," I said hastily. "The conference has begun and Dionysius needs me."

"Won't you even kiss me good-bye?" she asked faintly.

With closed lids I bent over her. She held my head to her breast only long enough to make it difficult for me to leave, then thrust me from her. As she lay back on the bed and reached for the cat her eyes shone in triumph.

4.

Had he dared, Krinippos in his greed would certainly have kept our treasure and killed Dionysius and his crew. But being a cunning man, he felt a healthy respect for Dionysius' shrewdness and was aware that all precautions had been taken against a surprise attack.

An old and sickly man who knew that death was gnawing at his belly like a crab, he clung to the vows by which he had sworn to govern Himera. And so I found him arguing with Dionysius about his share of the treasure, demanding a tithe in addition to the fines already decreed.

Kydippe looked from one to the other of us with ingratiating smiles but when I met her cold virginal eyes, I hastened to recount what I had just learned from Arsinoe. At the same moment the helmsman entered to announce that the sacrificial fires were already burning. Dionysius then sent him to destroy the signal pyre outside the city and to assemble the crews with all haste.

Faced by reality, Krinippos ceased his muttering and outlined a plan of action. Dionysius' most trustworthy men were to force their way into his home during the early hours of the morning, beat the guards and break into the vault. The farewell gift could be scattered over the floor as though fallen from a torn sack.

Krinippos tittered and stroked his sparse beard. "I don't know whether the Phoenicians will believe the story of your escape, but the council of Carthage is experienced. It enjoys peace and trade more than foolish discord and will quickly realize that it is to its advantage to believe what I say. Thus my reputation will remain unsullied although I have provided a haven for pirates all winter."

We bade farewell to Krinippos, thanked him for his hospitality and wished him a long life.

The plan was executed swiftly and easily. Krinippos' guards relinquished their weapons after only slight protests, after which Dionysius' men tied them and happily kicked them full of bruises to provide evidence of a struggle. Frugal Krinippos had left the key to the vault in evidence to render unnecessary our breaking the complicated lock. We found our treasure much diminished but despite this there was more than enough for our sailors to carry through the city gates and to the shore, while the guards laughed at our exertion. The sacrificial meat was placed on board, the stores of oil and dried peas replenished, and the men even found time during their last moments on shore to steal some wineskins. Some also must have found time for other things, too, for we heard feminine wailings and shrieks from various houses.

The spring night enveloped us as we clambered over the wet stones to the trireme already floating free. Both smaller galleys slid ahead of us with a splash of oars and disappeared into the darkness so that we heard merely the muffled rhythmic beat of the gong across the water. Then Dionysius ordered our own vessel into action. The three rows of oars dipped into the water, tangling with one another. From below the deck we heard yelps of pain as the rowers, unaccustomed to the new galley, caught their thumbs between the oars. We lurched ahead uncertainly, saved from the reefs by a land wind that helped us until the men gained control of the oars and the vessel began to obey the tiller.

So we left Himera, and the sadness of departure filled my eyes with hot tears. Yet it was not so much for Himera that I wept as for my own enslavement. Only when Dionysius called on me for wind did I understand what Lars Alsir had meant in telling Arsinoe that I was bound to the earth. It was Arsinoe who drew me to the earth, confused my thoughts and made trivial matters seem important. The very thought of conjuring the wind made me realize the dreadful heaviness of my body. My power had been drained out of me by Arsinoe.

Dionysius heard my tortured breathing, patted my shoulder and said, "Do not exert yourself unnecessarily. It is better that we use the oars until we are accustomed to the vessel and know how it responds to the waves. A storm might snap the mast and sink us."

"What is our direction?" I asked.

"Leave that to Poseidon," he replied amiably. "But make certain that your sword has not rusted in its scabbard during the winter. You see, we are on our way to greet those two Carthaginian warships for the very reason that no one expects us to do so. I have passed a little time fishing along these shores and watched the schools of round dolphin. That is how I know the landmarks to the west and can guess the inlet in which the Carthaginians have beached their galleys if they are able mariners."

"I thought you were planning to elude them under cover of darkness. Water was poured on their bonfire so that by dawn we would be out of sight."

"But they would pursue us like a pair of hounds," Dionysius pointed out. "No, their purpose is not to wage battle but to drive us straight into the lap of the fleet that is on its way here. Why shouldn't I take advantage of the situation? Besides, the oarsmen will familiarize themselves with the new vessel more quickly if they realize that they must elude the murderous blow of a bronze ram. But if you are so opposed to fighting, Turms, you can go lie with your Arsinoe below deck."

Sailing through the darkness and feeling the ship roll with the waves, I was overcome by despair. I knew nothing about currents and tides, I was unable to read the clouds like Dionysius, and the wind no longer obeyed me. I was merely earth and body. Everything around me happened merely by chance, nor was I consoled by the thought that Arsinoe awaited me in safety below. The certainty of all the sorrows and pleasures that she held in store for me was my bitterest knowledge.

With the break of day all three of our galleys were together and heading straight for an inlet. Seeing us appear like spirits from the shadowy sea, the Carthaginian lookouts no doubt could hardly believe their eyes. Immediately horns and drums began to sound their warning, and before we were in the shelter of the inlet both the warships were launched and their men armed. However, in the confusion born of surprise, contradictory orders were shouted, the beat of the gong faltered and the oars became tangled.

Dionysius roared encouragement to his men, and his amazing fortune enabled our vessel to pursue one of the fleeing Phoenicians and crush it against the rocky shore. Cries of terror arose from beneath us as the heavily armed marines of Carthage fell into the sea and the rowers sought to swim to safety. Only two archers attempted to cause trouble, but one of them Dionysius pinned to the deck with his spear while the other was swept into the water by the rowers.

Recognizing certain disaster, the second Phoenician galley made for the shore and its crew fled to the safety of the woods. Those of their companions who had managed to escape from the first vessel followed, and soon arrows began to rain on us from the shore. Some of them penetrated the oar ports, wounding several rowers and giving a thankful Mikon reason to go below. The arrows became so thick that Dionysius hastily gave the order to retreat.

"In the Phoenician manner they have more archers than swordsmen," he said. "It is not from cowardice that I am pulling away, but because I do not wish to endanger our vessel on the rocks."

All this time the Carthaginians were dragging their wounded to land, shouting encouragement to one another, shaking their fists at us and cursing in many languages.

Dorieus angrily held up his shield. "Let us go ashore and kill them," he suggested. "It is shameful to tolerate such insults when we have vanquished them."

"If we go ashore they will lead us into the woods where they will kill us one by one," replied Dionysius. Then he continued thoughtfully, "The overturned vessel will never again be seaworthy, but the other must be burned even if the smoke betrays us. I will not have it nosing in our rear."

"Permit me to add to my fame by going ashore and holding these Carthaginians at a distance until someone has set fire to their vessel," suggested Dorieus.

Dionysius stared at him open-mouthed, then hastened to agree. "I ask for nothing better. I would have suggested it myself had I not feared that you might consider the task too humble for yourself."

Dorieus then called to the men around him asking who of them wished to gain everlasting fame at his side, but the men of Phocaea suddenly found other matters of interest. Only when Dionysius observed that the Carthaginian galley might contain objects worth stealing did one of the penteconters approach, pick up Dorieus and take him ashore. Two men with tinder boxes and pitchers of oil hastily climbed aboard the Carthaginian vessel but Dorieus called out calmly to them not to hurry.

Seeing Dorieus standing there alone defiantly waving his shield, a bundle of spears under his arm, the Carthaginians momentarily ceased their howling. Then, when they noticed a wisp of smoke rising from their red-and-black galley, the commander and ten of his marines finally plunged in rage from the woods. They ran straight for Dorieus, who tossed his deadly spears with accuracy, felling four of the men. Then, baring his sword, he called upon his forefather Herakles to witness his deed and rushed toward the survivors. Several escaped but the others, including the commander, he killed.

Dionysius cursed in admiration as he watched the exploit. "What a fighter! Why did he have to take that blow on the head at Lade?"

During a lull Dorieus stooped over the Carthaginian commander. He had time to tear off the golden earrings and the heavy chain with its lion medallion before the spears and arrows again began flying from the woods. His shield drooped with the weight of the spears it bore and we heard the snap of the arrows as they struck his breastplates. Soon he plucked an arrow from his thigh, and a moment later another entered his open mouth, piercing the cheek.

With a shout of joy the Phoenicians ran out of the woods but he limped toward them, so tall and threatening that they suddenly spun around and fled, calling on their god for help as they ran.

Dionysius wept bitterly at the sight. "I cannot allow such a brave man to fall, although it would be for the good of us all."

At that moment I knew that I also had secretly hoped for the worst. Guiltily I had watched the unequal battle without even attempting to go to his aid, and now it was too late. Dionysius called out to one of the penteconters to steer to the shore and fetch Dorieus, who waded out to meet it, staining the water red with the blood from his wounds.

So breathlessly had I followed Dorieus' exploit that only after he was once more on the deck of the trireme did I notice that Arsinoe stood behind me, gazing in wide-eyed admiration at Dorieus. She was wearing only a short robe fastened with a wide silver belt which accentuated her slender waist.

Dionysius and the helmsmen stared at her and forgot Dorieus. Even the oars became tangled as some of the oarsmen caught sight of her through an aperture in the deck. But Dionysius quickly recovered himself and began to swear and roar and lay about him with his rope-end until the men returned to their tasks. The water again rushed past the bows and the burning hulk on shore soon lay far behind us.

Having divested Dorieus of his armor and watched Mikon apply healing salves to his wounds, I turned to Arsinoe in anger. "What do you mean by showing yourself to the sailors in that garment? Your place is below deck and see that you remain there. You might have been wounded by an arrow."

Without taking any notice of me, she went over to Dorieus, looked at him admiringly and said, "Ah, Dorieus, what a hero you are! I thought I beheld the god of war himself and not a mere mortal. How crimson your blood is as it streams down your neck! I would heal that wounded cheek with a kiss if I could."

His limbs stopped trembling and his lips grew calm. Recognition came into his eyes. He looked at her with desire, at me with disdain.

"Gladly would I have had Turms at my side as in the past," he said. "I expected him but he never came. Had I known that you were watching I would have killed even more Carthaginians in honor of your beauty."

Arsinoe glanced at me, her lips curved scornfully, and knelt on the

153

rough planks beside Dorieus. "What an unforgettable battle! Would that I could have taken from the shore even a handful of sand or a shell in memory of your heroism."

Dorieus laughed exultantly. "I would be worthless indeed if I were satisfied with sand and shells as battle trophies. Take these as a remembrance of this occasion." He held out the golden earrings of the Carthaginian commander with his ragged lobes still sticking to them.

Arsinoe clapped her hands with joy, accepted the bloody gift with no revulsion, and began admiring the gleaming rings. "I cannot refuse since you insist. Naturally you know that I shall treasure them, not for their weight in gold, but because they remind me of your courage." She waited expectantly for a moment but when Dorieus remained silent she shook her head. "No, I cannot take them after all for you yourself have nothing to show for your heroism."

To disprove that Dorieus pulled out the chain and medallion and showed them to her. Arsinoe took the chain and studied it closely. "I know what it is," she exclaimed, "it is the emblem of a naval commander. At school one of the girls was given such a chain and lion medallion by a satisfied guest. I remember well how I wept in envy, knowing that no one would ever give me such a gift."

Dorieus gritted his teeth, for Spartans are not prodigal by nature, and said, "Take this also if it pleases you. It means little to me and I doubt whether Turms will ever be able to give you one."

Pretending amazement, Arsinoe refused the offer many times and declared, "No, no, I cannot accept, nor would I if I were not anxious to erase my youthful humiliation at the temple school. Only because Turms and you are such good friends can I accept the gift. But how can I ever repay your goodness?"

Friendship was far from my mind as I watched that unworthy spectacle. But when she realized that Dorieus had nothing else to offer, Arsinoe rose, rubbed her bare knees and said that she would no longer disturb him since he was undoubtedly suffering from his wounds.

By that time Dionysius had the vessels in a column and the oar-strokes quickened to overcome the pull of the shore currents. Having watched us from the corner of his eye, he now approached, thoughtfully fingering the large gold rings in his ears.

"Arsinoe," he said respectfully, "the men believe they have a goddess on board. But in watching you they forget to row and in time they may have even more dangerous thoughts. It would be better also for Turms if you were to go below and not show yourself too frequently."

Seeing a stubborn look on Arsinoe's face I said hastily, "I know that no one can compel you to do so, but it would be a pity if the burning sun were to scorch your milk-white skin."

She screamed in dismay and attempted to cover as much of her bareness as she could. "Why didn't you say so immediately?" she reproached me and hastily went below to the compartment which the helmsmen had made comfortable for her. I was left to trail behind like a pet dog.

5.

For three days we rowed through the open sea and no winds awoke to help us on our way. At night we roped the vessels together and Arsinoe's cat crept surreptitiously along the rails with flaming eyes, arousing the superstitious awe of the sailors. Nor did they grumble, but rowed willingly, believing every stroke took them farther from the dreaded Carthaginian galleys.

But on the fourth night Dorieus girded himself, began talking to his sword, sang war songs to rouse his spirit and finally confronted Dionysius.

"What are your real intentions, Dionysius of Phocaea?" he demanded. "We have long ago eluded the vessels of Carthage. Yet from the sun and stars I see that we have sailed northward day after day. We will never reach Eryx this way."

Dionysius agreed good-naturedly, then gestured with his thumb. Instantly the crew seized and bound Dorieus so quickly that he had not even time to touch his sword. He roared at the outrage, then remembered his honor and grew silent, contenting himself with murderous looks.

Dionysius began to speak soothingly. "We respect you as a hero, and by birth you are far above any of us, but you must admit that the blow on the head you suffered at Lade still troubles you at times. When I heard you talking to your sword, when you spoke of the stars and the sun and seafaring, of which you know nothing, I realized that for your own good I would have to imprison you in the hold until our arrival in Massilia."

Even the men patted him kindly on the shoulder and said, "Don't be angry with us, for it was for your own good that we did this. The vastness of the sea easily affects a mind unaccustomed to it. Even the sly Odysseus had himself bound to the mast when he heard the sirens' song in his ears."

Dorieus quivered with rage. "We are not going to Massilia! Instead of a dangerous voyage I offer you a good battle on land, and when I have won the crown of Segesta I will divide the land of Eryx among you and allow you to build houses where you can raise your sons to be soldiers. I will give you slaves for your fields and you can amuse yourselves by hunting the Siccanians and taking their women. Of all this pleasure Dionysius would treacherously deprive you."

To silence him Dionysius burst into long laughter, slapped his thighs and shouted, "Listen to his confused babble! Would we, men of Phocaea, leave the sea to dig in the earth? I have heard nothing more ridiculous."

But his men began to shift from one foot to the other and glance at one another. Rowers left their benches and the crews of the penteconters climbed to the stern the better to hear.

Dionysius then grew grave. "We are sailing north straight to Massilia and already we are in Tyrrhenian waters. But the sea is wide and my good luck still holds. If necessary, we will overcome the Etruscan vessels also and break through to Massilia. There they make red wine, there even a slave dips his bread in honey, and milk-white slave girls are sold for a few drachmas."

"Listen, you men!" shouted Dorieus. "Instead of unknown dangers and strange gods I offer you a familiar land whose temples are built in the Greek manner and whose natives pride themselves on speaking the language of Greece. I offer you a short voyage and an easy war. You have seen me fight. I now offer you a life of ease under the protection of my crown."

Dionysius tried to kick his head, but his own men intervened. "There is much truth in Dorieus' words," they conceded, "for we do not even know how our kinsmen in Massilia will greet us. The Etruscans easily sank the hundred ships of our forefathers and we have only three, with a total of but three hundred men. They would not suffice when the sea before us turns red and black with Etruscan vessels."

"Three hundred brave men behind my shield is an army!" cried Dorieus. "I do not even ask you to lead the way but only to follow me. You are out of your wits unless you believe me rather than Dionysius, that breaker of vows."

Dionysius raised his hand for silence. "Permit me to speak. It is true that I have negotiated with Dorieus. It is also true that we would lose nothing in warring in Eryx since Carthage will not pardon us in any case. But all this I have planned only in the event that the gods do not favor our reaching Massilia. Only as a last resort will we strike somewhere on the coast of Eryx."

At sea Dionysius was mightier than Dorieus, and after lengthy argument the men decided to try for Massilia. It was, after all, their original objective.

But the strange sea was pitiless and the winds fickle. In time our drinking water became foul and many fell ill and saw fevered visions. Nor did Dorieus' occasional outbursts from the prow make matters easier. Arsinoe grew paler, complained of continual nausea and wished herself dead. Each night she begged me to free Dorieus so that he might start a mutiny since any fate would be preferable to aimless drifting with only maggoty flour and rancid oil to eat.

Then at last we sighted land. Dionysius smelled and tasted the water, sounded the bottom and inspected the mud clinging to the wax plummet. But he had to admit, "I do not recognize this land. It stretches north and south as far as the eye can carry, and is, I fear, the Etruscan mainland. We have drifted too far to the east."

Soon we met two Greek cargo vessels and from them learned that the shore in front of us was indeed Etruscan territory. We asked them for fresh water and oil but the crew, looking dubiously at our matted beards and scorched faces, refused and urged us to go ashore. The fishermen, they said, would help us.

Since they were Greeks, Dionysius did not wish to rob them, but allowed them to sail away and bravely turned our own vessels toward the land. Soon we found the mouth of a stream and a cluster of reed-roofed huts. It was evidently civilized country, for the people did not flee from us. The houses were timbered, there were iron kettles and clay images of gods, and the women wore jewelry.

The very sight of that smiling land with its blue mountains was so delightful that not even the rowers had any desire to do violence. We took on a supply of drinking water slowly, for no one was anxious to return to the sea, not even Dionysius.

Suddenly a chariot appeared and an armed man spoke to us sternly. Though his language was strange, we understood just enough to know that he demanded to see our sailing papers. We pretended not to understand, whereupon he looked searchingly at our weapons, warned us not to leave and drove away in a cloud of dust. A little later a panting troop of spearmen approached and settled down to stand guard nearby.

They did not stop us from boarding our ships, but as we thrust our vessels into the water they shouted threateningly and flung spears after us. By the time we were safely offshore a row of signal fires was burning along the coast and a fleet of fast war vessels, narrow and light in build, was bearing down on us from the north. Again we headed for the open sea, but our rowers were so exhausted that the galleys soon overtook us. When we failed to respond to their signals, an arrow with a bloodstained clump of feathers plunged into the deck of our vessel.

Dionysius wrenched it free and looked at it. "I know what this means," he said, "but I am a patient man and will not engage in battle unless I am attacked."

The sails pursued us relentlessly until nightfall, when they fanned out and suddenly attacked. We heard the crack of snapping oars, the sound of metal rams smashing the sides of our penteconters, and the death screams of our oarsmen as arrows and spears whistled in through the oar ports. Our galleys listed and came to a halt at the very moment that an Etruscan vessel crashed into the trireme, severing both its steering oars. Enraged, Dionysius seized a grappling hook and chain and tossed them so cleverly at the Etruscan vessel that they caught in its stern and with a sudden jerk the ship came to a standstill. From our high deck it was easy to kill the rowers who ran to free the hook. An enemy attack from our rear was unsuccessful, for try as it might the frail Etruscan galley could not pierce the heavy oaken planks with its feeble ram.

Although the entire battle lasted only a few minutes, it caused great damage especially to our smaller vessels. We managed to repair the steering oars of the trireme, and the penteconters stuffed their leaks with sheepskins, but it was late that night before we had succeeded in bailing out the sea water which already had spoiled our recently acquired drinking water and provisions.

What was worse, we had not escaped the Etruscan galleys. Although most of them had fled toward shore, two remained nearby and when darkness fell they lit the pitch pots on their after decks as signal fires.

"I can almost hear the excitement in the shore cities as each chief hastens to be the first to reach us," said Dionysius bitterly. "True, I have not heard that Etruscans skin pirates alive, since they themselves once practiced piracy, but they are a cruel people and fond of earthy pleasures."

Arsinoe's cat appeared silently out of the darkness on its nightly round, stopping to rub Dionysius' leg and then stretched out to scratch its claws on the deck.

Dionysius gasped. "That sacred animal is wiser than we are! As you can see, it has turned its head toward the east and is clawing the deck to conjure up an east wind. Let us all scratch together, whistle like the wind and summon a storm."

He ordered the men to scratch the deck. A few even tried to perform a Phocaean rain dance, but in vain. Even the slight breeze that we had felt died down and the sea became calm. Finally Dionysius gave up and ordered the vessels to be roped together so that the men could rest and pray, comb their hair and wash and anoint their bodies and be ready to die at dawn.

The Tyrrhenian fires disappeared and in the darkness I exclaimed to Dionysius, "Your luck is still with us. The Etruscans fear the black sea and are returning to shore."

He stared out over the water and thus lost a precious moment. From the stern we heard a crash and, lighting the torches, saw that all the steering oars had been chopped off by the stealthy Etruscans, who had approached under cover of the dark. In the distance they again set fire to their pitchpots.

A feeling of guilt came over me as I thought of Arsinoe. She would still be in the safety of the temple if I had not abducted her and led her to certain death. I descended to her compartment where she lay, thin and wan, her eyes darker than ever in the flicker of the tallow lamp.

"Arsinoe," I said, "the Etruscans are upon us. Our steering oars are broken, and when dawn comes the heavy Etruscan galleys will arrive to stave in our sides. Nothing can save us."

Arsinoe merely sighed and said, "I have been counting the days on my fingers and am amazed. And I have developed a terrifying longing to eat crushed snail shells such as are given to hens."

I thought her mind was muddled from fear and felt her forehead, but she had no fever. Softly I said, "I did wrong in abducting you from the temple, but all is not yet lost. We can signal the Etruscans and hand you to them before the battle. When you tell them that you are a priestess of Eryx they will not harm you, for the Etruscans are a god-fearing people."

She stared at me in disbelief and began to weep. "I cannot live without you, Turms! Even though I am a little frivolous I love you more than I believed it possible to love any man. Besides, I greatly fear that I am pregnant by you. It must have happened that first time when I forgot my mystic silver ring in the temple."

"In the name of the goddess," I cried, "that is impossible!"

"Why should it be," she retorted, "although it is a disgrace since I am a priestess. But in your arms that time I forgot everything. I had never experienced anything so wonderful as I did that time with you."

I pressed her close to my breast. "Ah, Arsinoe, I too never experienced anything like that. How happy I am!"

"Happy!" she repeated and wrinkled her nose. "I myself am anything but happy. I feel so wretched that I actually hate you. If you in-

159

tended to bind yourself to me, Turms, you have succeeded, and see that you answer for your deed."

Holding her in my arms, so frail and helpless and bitter, I felt a greater tenderness toward her than ever before. Whatever was her guilt with Dorieus and Mikon, it had nothing to do with us and I forgave her. Such was my faith in her.

Then I remembered where we were and what was happening, and knew that only my own strength could save Arsinoe and our unborn child. Despite hunger, exhaustion and lack of sleep I suddenly felt myself freed of earthly clay. My power was kindled within me like a flame in a lamp, and I was no longer mortal. I released Arsinoe, rose and ran to the deck. It was as though I walked on air.

Exultantly, head high and arms upraised, I turned in every direction and shouted, "Come, wind; wake, storm, for I, Turms, call you!"

So loud was my cry over the black sea that Dionysius hurried to me. "Are you calling the wind, Turms? If you are, you might as well ask that it be the east wind. That would best answer our purpose."

My feet were already moving uncontrollably in the steps of the sacred dance. "Silence, Dionysius, shame not the gods. Let them determine the direction. I merely summon the storm."

At that moment the sea already sighed, our vessels swayed, the ropes creaked, the air grew damp and a puff of wind blew over us. Dionysius called for the torches to be extinguished. Quickly it was done, but the Etruscans, who were caught unaware, saw the wind whip the flames from their pitchpots onto the deck of the nearer galley. In a few minutes the vessel was ablaze. Over the howl of the wind we heard the mast of the second Etruscan vessel crack in two.

My dance grew wilder, my calls to the wind louder until Dionysius, to silence me, struck me a blow that sent me to the deck. As the storm raged Dionysius himself cut the ropes that tied the vessels together. From one of the penteconters came cries that the sheepskins had loosened and water was rushing in through the holes. In anger and disappointment Dionysius commanded the men to abandon the sinking vessel and clamber onto the trireme, which itself was listing badly. The second penteconter disappeared into the thundering darkness.

Somehow Dionysius righted our vessel, raised the mast and part of the sail, and the trireme began to obey its temporary steering oars.

With the sunrise the sea brightened and the storm calmed to a brisk breeze that bulged the sail. We raced with the giant waves toward the west, the vessel leaping under us like a snorting mount. The men began to laugh and shout and Dionysius gave them all a measure of wine. He

160

sacrificed some to Poseidon also, although many felt that to be unnecessary.

A sail was sighted far ahead. The sharpest-eyed sailor climbed the mast and cried out joyously that it was the striped sail of our lost penteconter. By midday we had reached it and saw that it was not badly damaged.

The east wind continued to blow and on the third day we sighted blue mountains rising like clouds against the sky. During the night the currents carried us with them, and at dawn we sighted the outline of a hump-necked mountain.

Dionysius cried out in surprise, "By all the gods of the sea, I recognize that mountain, so often have I heard it described! How the gods must be laughing, for we are back almost to our starting point. That mountain is on Sicily's coast, the shore is a part of Eryx and behind the mountain is the town and harbor of Panormos. At last I see that the gods did not intend to lead us to Massilia. I can only regret it though, for they could have piloted us to Massilia with far less trouble. Now Dorieus may assume command, since that seems to be the will of the gods. I will stand down."

He sent his men to see whether Dorieus was still alive and, if so, to untie him and bring him on deck. But, to tell the truth, Mikon and I had long since cut away his fetters, in such bad condition was he.

At last Dorieus appeared, hair matted by the salt water, face lined and eyes narrowed like a bat blinded by the sudden light. He seemed to have aged ten years during that month of imprisonment. Faintly he called for his sword and shield. I brought him the sword but had to confess that his shield had been tossed into the sea as an offering to the gods. He nodded and said that he well understood how such a noble offering had saved the vessel.

"So thank my shield for your lives, you wretched men of Phocaea," he said. "I myself would have sacrificed it to the sea goddess Thetis, who is well disposed toward me. I have had strange experiences the while you have thought that I lay in the hold. But I will not speak of them."

His eyes were the color of gray salt as he turned to Dionysius and tested the edge of his sword. "I should kill you, Dionysius of Phocaea, but seeing your foolish head finally bowed before me, I forgive you. I will even admit that the oarstroke which I received at Lade still troubles me at times." He laughed and nudged Dionysius with his elbow. "Yes, oarstroke, not swordstroke. I don't understand why I should have been ashamed to call it an oarstroke. Only when the goddess Thetis and I met as equals in the depths of the sea did I come to realize that nothing

161

shameful can happen to me, but that everything I experience is godly in its way. For that reason, Dionysius, I thank you for what you did to me."

Suddenly he straightened himself and shouted, "But enough of foolish prattle! To arms, men! We will go ashore and conquer Panormos as was intended."

The men ran for their spears, arrows and shields. When we had numbered our ranks we found that, in addition to Arsinoe and the cat, one hundred and fifty of us had survived. Three hundred had sailed from Himera, and the fact that exactly one half remained was considered by the men to be a good omen.

But Dorieus commanded them to be silent about things of which they knew nothing. "Three hundred we were, three hundred we still are, and three hundred we shall always be no matter how many fall. But you will not fall, for from now on you are Dorieus' three hundred. Let three hundred be our battle cry, and three hundred years from now people will still talk of our exploits."

"Three hundred, three hundred!" shouted the men and beat their shields with their swords. Light-headed from hunger and thirst, we forgot our past miseries and impatiently ran to and fro on the deck.

The water murmured under our leaking prow and when we had passed the hump-necked mountain, there before us lay the harbor of Panormos with a few galleys and boats, a miserable wall and beyond, a fertile plain with fields and woods. But behind the plain rose the mountains of Eryx, steep and of a wondrous blue.

BOOK SIX

Dorieus

I.

SURPRISE is the mother of victory. I doubt whether a single Carthaginian in Panormos could have believed it possible that the battered galley entering the harbor in bright daylight was the pirate ship which had fled Himera a month earlier. Lars Tular's silver Gorgon head which dangled from our prow misled the patrols into believing us Etruscan, while the peaceful gestures of our men and the meaningless jargon they shouted in greeting contributed to the uncertainty. And so the patrols merely stared at us in wonder without sounding an alarm on their brass drums.

From a large round cargo vessel tied to the shore we heard cries of warning and injunctions not to row so rapidly. And when the men, peacefully dangling their feet over the water, saw our split sides and sagging rails they laughed heartily. Curious townspeople began to gather at the shore.

Even after our ram had crashed into their vessel with such force as to thrust it onto land, snap its mast and send the men toppling backward onto the deck, the sailors thought it all an accident. Their commander ran toward us, shaking his fist, cursing loudly and demanding compensation for the damage wrought by our carelessness.

But the men of Phocaea, led by Dorieus, leaped onto the vessel with their weapons, struck down everyone in their path and raced to shore. Cutting through the throng that hastened toward them, they climbed the hill and pushed through the gate into the city before the guards quite realized what had happened. While the vanguard was overcoming the resistance in the puny city and killing the fear-stunned men, Dionysius with his rearguard was seizing the ships on shore merely by lashing out with his rope. Having seen what happened to the first ship, the crews of the remaining cargo vessels did not even attempt to resist but begged on their knees for mercy. Only a few sought escape, but when Dionysius ordered his men to stone them, they halted in their flight and returned.

Dionysius opened the large shed on the shore in which the residents of Panormos housed the slaves used in unloading the ships. Into it he thrust the prisoners he had just seized, while the liberated slaves, among them a number of Greeks, prostrated themselves before us, hailing us as saviors. Dionysius asked them to prepare food, which they did gladly, lighting fires on the shore and slaughtering some of the neighborhood cattle. But before the meat was roasted, most of us satisfied our deepest pangs of hunger with raw flour mixed with oil.

So sudden and successful was the conquest of Panormos that a wave of audacity swept over the men of Phocaea and they recklessly swore to follow Dorieus wherever he led them. Naturally, some of this courage was born of the wine they had stolen from the houses after killing the able-bodied men of the city.

In truth, the entire garrison in the city and harbor consisted of barely fifty armed men, for the people of Panormos, with their long history of peace, did not consider weapons necessary. Since the only men in that seafaring city were artisans and hence not difficult to kill, the ease of Dorieus' victory was not surprising. The men of Phocaea, however, considered it a miracle that none of them had received even the smallest wound and, heady from the wine, began to consider themselves invulnerable. In the evening, when they again counted their ranks and numbered three hundred—but only because they saw double—they considered that also a miracle.

To the credit of the Phocaean men be it said that, having overcome their own fear, they did not unnecessarily annoy the peaceful residents of the city. True, they went from house to house in search of loot, but they seized nothing by violence, merely pointing to that which they desired. Beholding their sea-lined faces and bloody hands, the trembling occupants willingly relinquished whatever was wanted. If someone demurred, the men laughingly moved on to the next house. That is how pleased they were with their victory, the food and the wine, and the future which Dorieus held out to them as the rulers of Eryx.

Having set up a watch, Dorieus installed himself in the timbered building occupied by the city council. When he saw that the only treasures it contained were the city charter and the sacred reeds of the river god, he angrily summoned the council before him. The quivering patriarchs in their long Carthaginian robes, their hair bound with colored bands, swore that Panormos was a wretched, poverty-stricken city whose available funds all went to Segesta as taxes. Indeed, they lamented, whenever they held feasts for the gods or welcomed state visitors, each lent his own dishes for the occasion.

Dorieus inquired ominously whether they did not consider him, a descendant of Herakles, worthy of a banquet. After shrill consultation, the old men assured him with one voice that their wives and servants had already undertaken the necessary preparations and that slaves were polishing the scanty silverware in his honor. But a satisfactory banquet could not be arranged without security of person and property.

Dorieus smiled sadly. "Have you scales over your eyes, old men, that you do not recognize me? At least feel the hot wind of my presence. My power is not founded solely on my incontestable hereditary rights or on the weapons of my men, but on the sanctification bestowed on my sovereignty by the sea goddess Thetis. Perhaps you do not recognize her by her Greek name, but you must worship her in one form or another since you engage in fishing and trading by sea."

The men fearfully covered their eyes with a corner of their robes and explained, "We have our Baal and the ancient goddess of Eryx, but the sea gods of Carthage can be mentioned only in whispers."

"For my part," said Dorieus, "I can speak openly. I have entered into an eternal pact with the sea goddess Thetis, just as I have in the earthly manner married a highborn woman descended from the founders of Carthage. But since you know so little about sea gods, it is useless for me to describe my matrimonial adventures."

The members of the council had fine foods prepared in their houses and brought their silver dishes to the council building. Nor did Dorieus steal them but instead presented to the council a large Phoenician silver beaker from among Dionysius' treasure.

To Dionysius' protest Dorieus replied, "I have learned many bitter lessons in my life, perhaps the bitterest of which has been that a man's heart is where his treasures are. Because of my divine ancestry I have always been something more than just a human and thus have difficulty in comprehending that fact. I can only say that where my sword is, there am I. I do not desire your treasure, Dionysius, but you must admit that you and your ship would both be at the bottom of the sea had I not saved you all by allying myself with the sea goddess Thetis."

"I have already heard enough about Thetis and your voyages at the bottom of the sea," retorted Dionysius angrily. "I do not intend to let you deal with the treasure as though it were your own."

Dorieus replied with a pitying smile, "Tomorrow morning we march on Segesta, and there is nothing better than a brisk journey on foot for recovering from the trials of the sea. The treasure we must take with us since it cannot be left on the vessel. At any moment the warships of Carthage may sail into the harbor. On that fertile plain we can obtain donkeys, horses and other beasts of burden for transporting the treasure. I have already given orders for them to be assembled, and their owners may follow us to care for the animals since sailors fear horses."

Now it was Dionysius' turn to gnash his teeth, but he had to admit that Dorieus' decision was the only possible one. The dry-docking of the trireme and its repair would take weeks, during which time we would be vulnerable to attack by the Phoenician warships. Our only possibility was to push inland, the faster the better. Having the treasure with them, the men of Phocaea were bound to fight for it on land despite their annoyance at the rigors of an overland journey.

"So be it," said Dionysius grimly. "Tomorrow morning we leave for Segesta with the treasure. But it is as though I were abandoning my own child to leave my trireme defenseless in Panormos."

Dorieus snapped at him, "You probably have left children behind at every port you have ever visited. Let us burn your vessel and all the others in Panormos so that no one will be tempted to flee."

Dionysius scowled at the very thought.

"Have the trireme dry-docked and let the city council attend to the repairs," I suggested. "The silver shield of Gorgon will be its protector. Should Phoenician warships sail into the harbor the council can give assurance that the trireme is the property of the new king of Segesta. The Carthaginian commanders will not dare to interfere in the internal affairs of Panormos without returning to Carthage for consultation. If we do this, we will lose nothing."

Dorieus scratched his head. "Let Dionysius have charge of maritime matters. If he accedes, I will not insist that the vessels be burned. Besides, it would be wasteful to destroy something which must later be built again, and I will need ships to protect the interests of Eryx at sea."

Dorieus entrusted the welfare of Panormos to its former council, promising to return as king of Segesta to punish or reward as he saw fit.

2.

The following day Dorieus organized the men of Phocaea for a refreshing march, as he put it, to help them recover from the trials of the sea. The men had spread his fame throughout the city and when he made his offering before their departure, the market place grew still and the people of Panormos stared at him in awe. He was a head taller than humans, they said to one another, invulnerable and godlike.

"Let us be on our way," he said, and without a backward glance headed out of the city dressed in full armor despite the heat. We three hundred, as he called us, followed him, Dionysius at the rear with a length of rope in his hand. We had unloaded the treasure from the trireme and piled it on the backs of the animals without much difficulty since a goodly part of it had gone down with our penteconters.

Having reached the plain we looked behind and to our amazement saw that many of the men of Panormos were following us. By the time we had begun ascending the slope of the mountain at dusk our rearguard had been joined by hundreds of shepherds and plowmen, each armed to the best of his ability. When we made camp for the night the entire mountain slope was dotted with small fires. It seemed as though all of the backwoods people were eager to rise in revolt against Segesta.

On the third day of our exhausting march the men of Phocaea, unaccustomed to land travel, began to grumble and show their blisters. Then Dorieus spoke to them. "I myself march ahead of you and enjoy marching despite my full armor. As you can see, I am not even sweating. And you have only your weapons to carry."

"It is easy for you to talk," they retorted, "for you are not like us." At the first spring they threw themselves on the ground, doused their heads in the water and wept in misery. Dorieus' words did not help the situation, but they had to believe Dionysius' rope and continue the journey.

Dorieus then spoke to Dionysius. "You are not stupid," he admitted, "and apparently are beginning to understand a commander's responsibilities on land. We are approaching Segesta and before a battle a responsible commander must march his men to such exhaustion that they no longer have the strength to flee. The distance from Panormos to Segesta is precisely right, as though measured by the gods for our purpose. We will go directly to Segesta and spread ourselves in battle formation before it."

Dionysius replied somberly, "You know best what you are saying, but we are sailors and not soldiers. For that reason we will most certainly not spread out in a battle line but will remain supporting one another in a body, side to side and back to back. But if you go ahead, we will follow."

But Dorieus bristled in anger and said that he would wage the battle in accordance with the rules of war so that future generations might learn from it. In the midst of the argument a group of Siccanians crept from the woods with their slings, bows and spears. They wore animal skins and had stained their faces and bodies red, black and yellow. Their chief, who had a fearsome wooden mask over his head, danced before Dorieus, after which the Siccanians placed at Dorieus' feet the decayed and foul-smelling heads of several Segestan nobles.

They explained that seers had sought them out in the forests and mountains, had given them salt and presaged the coming of a new king. Encouraged by the predictions, they had begun to raid Segestan fields, and when the nobles had pursued them with horses and dogs they had led them into an ambush and killed them.

Now, however, they were afraid of revenge and so placed themselves under Dorieus' protection. For as long as they could remember, they said, a tale had passed from father to son of a powerful stranger who had once come to their land, vanquished the king in a duel and given the land to the natives, promising some day to claim his inheritance. They called Dorieus "Erkle" and expressed the wish that he would banish the Elymi and restore the land to the Siccani.

Dorieus accepted their homage as his due. He attempted to teach them to say "Herakles" but when their mouths could not shape it he shook his head. Little joy would he have of such barbarians.

Barbarians they were, indeed. The only metallic weapons they had were a few spears, knives and the chief's sword, for the Segestans stringently forbade itinerant merchants to sell them weapons. Instead, they had other skills. Never did they fell a tree wherein dwelled a nymph, or drink from the spring of a malevolent deity. Their priest, they explained, had swallowed a divining potion the previous night and had seen the coming of Dorieus while in a trance.

When Dorieus asked them to join in open battle against the Segestans they refused. They were too afraid of the horses and angry dogs to venture beyond the woods, but they would be happy to encourage Dorieus by beating on drums made of hollow logs.

As we continued the march, more and more Siccanians appeared to stare at us and to shout, "Erkle! Erkle!" The peasants of Panormos were amazed at the sight of these usually shy natives who did not reveal themselves even when trading, but placed their goods on display in certain locations and accepted whatever was left in return.

Now the fertile fields of Segesta with their altars and monuments lay before us. But we saw no people, for they had all withdrawn into the city. At the memorial to the spurious Philip of Croton, Dorieus halted and said, "Here we will fight, so that my father's spirit may be appeased for the humiliation it suffered."

We could see people moving restlessly on the city wall, and Dorieus ordered the men of Phocaea to beat their shields as proof that he had no intention of taking the city by surprise. Then he sent a herald to proclaim to the Segestans his hereditary right to the throne and to challenge the king to a duel. Thereafter we made camp around the memorial and ate, drank and rested. Despite Dorieus' warning not to trample the grain we could not avoid doing so, for there must have been several thousand of us if one includes the Siccanians at our rear.

I believe the trampling of the grain annoyed the Segestans even more than Dorieus' demands. Having noticed that the grain would in any case be ruined and that a battle was inescapable, their ruler assembled his athletes and noble youths and hitched his horses to the war chariots which for decades had been used only in races. Although the king had no more power than the sacrificial king in Ionian cities, the dog crown imposed certain obligations. Afterward we heard that he was not especially anxious to retain it and while harnessing the horses had taken the crown from his head and offered it to those around him. But at that moment no one else was anxious to wear the crown either.

They summoned up one another's courage by retelling tales of the battles that their forefathers had waged against invaders and recalling the bones which fertilized their fields. Meanwhile the king's heralds went from door to door to summon able-bodied men to arms, but the citizens said openly that a political controversy over the dog crown was no concern of theirs. And so the nobles and landowners drank wine and made their offering to the gods of the underworld to gain courage to die honorably if that was ordained. They also spent much time in oiling and combing their hair.

Having fetched the holy dog and led it to its place among the pack, the Segestans, finally ready for battle, flung open the gates and sent the chariots thundering toward us. The chariots were an imposing sight, the like of which had hardly been seen in battle for a generation. We counted twenty-eight spread out in a phalanx to protect the gates. The horses were magnificent with their plumed heads and their harnesses gilded with silver.

Behind the chariots were spread the armored warriors, the nobles, the mercenaries and the athletes. Dorieus forbade us to count the shields lest we grow alarmed. The warriors were followed by the dogs and their trainers and they in turn by the stone-throwers and the archers.

We could hear the charioteers urge on the horses. Seeing the flaring nostrils and the flashing hoofs approach, the men of Phocaea began to tremble so that their shields rattled against one another. Calmly Dorieus stood before them and urged them to aim their spears manfully at the horses' bellies. But as the chariots rumbled toward them, flattening the grain field, the men of Phocaea withdrew behind the memorial and the altars and declared that, for their part, Dorieus could handle the problem of the chariots alone since they were unaccustomed to such matters. Whereupon the remaining forces likewise withdrew beyond the wide irrigation ditch.

Dorieus threw two spears, wounding one of a quadriga's four horses and killing the charioteer whose body was dragged along the ground. I wasted one of my spears but, as a horse before me reared, I hurled a second with all my might at his belly. Whatever happened I was determined not to leave Dorieus' side but to prove myself at least as brave as he, even though I was not his equal in strength or use of weapons.

Seeing me advance those few steps toward the horses, Dorieus became infuriated and flung himself, sword in hand, at the nearest team, bringing it sprawling to the ground. An archer's arrow struck the eye of another horse. The wounded animal reared and fell backward, overturning the chariot and disrupting the entire front.

When the king of Segesta saw that a number of his peerless horses were wounded or killed, he lost his courage and shouted for the chariots to return. The unharmed chariots circled back and the charioteer who had been overturned forgot the battle. Clasping the dying animals to him, he kissed their muzzles and eyes and tried to call them back to life with endearing words.

The charioteers who had circled back, right and left, jumped to the ground and began calming their trembling and sweating horses while spitting curses and shaking their fists at us. The men of Phocaea ventured out from behind the memorial and the altars and gathered around Dorieus, shield touching shield, the rear forces physically supporting those in front. The mud-stained rebels of Eryx likewise recrossed the irrigation ditch, bravely brandishing their clubs and axes, and emitting fierce battle cries.

Now the heavily armed warriors of Segesta made way for the dogs and their trainers who set the animals on us. Hugging the ground, they sped toward us with bared fangs. I wore my cuirass and leg guards as did Dorieus, and the men of Phocaea succeeded in warding off the dogs with their shields. Indeed Dorieus did not even trouble to kill the animals but as they leaped for his throat struck their muzzles a blow that dropped them whining to the ground. Over the growls and the din we heard the Siccanians' squeals of terror as they fled into the safety of the woods. The Siccanians' flight so amused Dorieus that he burst into laughter and that heartened the men of Phocaea perhaps more than anything else.

The bloodthirsty pack now were by us, and made for the rebels of Eryx. They tore open unprotected throats, mutilated thighs and crushed bare arms between their jaws. But the peasants staunchly withstood the attacks of the hated dogs and shouted in triumph upon discovering that they could club them to death. The killing of pedigreed dogs was a serious offense in the land of Eryx and the peasants and their wives had many times helplessly felt their fangs and seen them mangle sheep and frighten children.

I doubt whether the releasing of the Segestans' holy dog Krimisos was deliberate. Probably it had broken its leash, or the trainer had accidentally loosened his hold on it. At any rate, that gray-muzzled, gentle animal which had lived peacefully in its pen for years trotted stiffly behind the other dogs. Fat and gigantic in size, it looked around in bewilderment, not realizing what was happening. The barking and growling of its own kind annoyed it, and its sensitive muzzle was offended by the stench of blood rising from the ground.

Dorieus called the dog to him and it came, sniffed amiably at his knees and raised its head to look at Dorieus' face while he patted its head and spoke to it softly, promising it an even fairer maiden as its wife each year once he wore the dog crown. Slowly the holy dog, panting from its short trot, stretched itself out at his feet. From there it glowered at the shining front of heavy-armored warriors, wrinkled its muzzle and bared its yellow fangs in a growl.

Cries of amazement arose from the Segestan ranks and the king himself, seeing his power slip from his fingers with the loss of the holy dog, condescended to whistle to it, but in vain. The dog only looked lovingly at Dorieus and licked his iron shoe.

Dorieus spoke to the holy dog, asking it to guard his father's memorial. Actually it was a memorial to Philip of Croton, but Dorieus probably did not remember that. The dog dropped its gray muzzle between its paws and remained lying on the ground.

Dorieus then glanced at the men of Phocaea, struck his shield with his sword and set forth to meet the wavering row of heavily armed Segestan warriors. I marched beside him, and when Dionysius realized that the moment of decision was at hand he thrust the length of rope under his belt, seized his shield and sword and took his place at Dorieus' right.

Dorieus did not glance back, nor did Dionysius. As we marched abreast our steps necessarily quickened since none of us was willing to let any other gain the lead—Dorieus for reasons of rank, Dionysius because of honor and I from sheer vanity. In this manner our march soon quickened to a trot. Behind us we heard the battle cries of the men of Phocaea and the thud of their feet as they sought to overtake us. At the same moment the lowly rebels of Eryx stirred in the rear, while from the distance we heard the throb of hollow logs and guessed that the Siccanians were returning from the woods.

The distance was but several hundred paces, yet it seemed to be the longest journey of my life. Vanity kept my eyes on our advancing feet and I did not look up until Dorieus' roar raised my shield in line with his to receive the spears that were angrily thrown at us. My shield arm drooped with the weight of the spears and one spear had penetrated the shield, wounding me, but at the moment I did not notice it. In vain I tried to shake the spears from the shield. Suddenly, as once before, Dorieus' sword flashed at my side and with a single stroke cut the shafts in time for me to raise the shield as we clashed head on with the column of heavily armed Segestans.

I doubt whether anyone who has been in an actual battle knows much about its progress, so absorbed is he in saving his own life. The first line of Segestans had linked their shields together by means of hooks, and when the shock of our attack downed some of the men, they dragged down the entire line so that it rippled like a wave. We passed over the shields to the next line, and that is when the real fighting began, sword against sword and man against man.

Although the Segestans were effete, their anger over their wounded animals made them formidable opponents. The nobles fought for their property and hereditary power without which life held no meaning. But even more formidable were the athletes whose only function was the development of their strength and skill as wrestlers and boxers for the amusement of their masters. In our hand-to-hand fighting in such close quarters that it was difficult to raise a sword, the athletes abandoned the shields and swords to which they were unaccustomed and began wielding iron fists and breaking necks.

Emaciated from our voyage and exhausted by the long march, we were in no condition to endure a prolonged battle. Our only hope lay in suddenness and speed. For that reason Dorieus had hoped to break through the middle of the Segestan line. But the battle was not so easily won, for both wings of the front began to bend as we pressed ahead. Now the Segestans shouted in elation as they ran to encircle our dwindling forces. Sweat and blood blinded me, my body was numb and my arms so tired that I did not know how I had the strength to strike and thrust over and over again.

Dionysius called out encouraging words: "Men of Phocaea, our fore-fathers fought in these fields. So let us be at home and fight for our lives." To the hesitant and exhausted he cried, "Remember that you fight for your treasure! The rabble of Eryx think we are lost and are all ready to pillage it."

A concerted roar of rage rose from the throats of the weary men. For a moment the Segestans lowered their swords and it was then that Dorieus glanced at the sky.

"Listen!" he cried. "Listen to the wings of the goddess of victory!"

He spoke in one of those breath-long periods of silence that some-times occur in a battle. I do not know whether it was merely the blood throbbing at my temples, but I seemed to hear clearly the rustle of heavy wings above us. The men of Phocaea also heard it, or so they afterward declared.

At that moment an unnatural exaltation came over Dorieus, multiply-ing his strength so that no one in his path could withstand him. Beside him charged Dionysius, head down like a bull, clearing the way with his axe. They were followed by the men of Phocaea in a blind rage, and so it was that, with the strength born of desperation, we managed to break through the lines of heavily armed Segestans. Behind them their lightly armed companions fled in chaos.

The violence of the unexpected attack took the king of Segesta by surprise and he had no time for escape. Dorieus killed him so swiftly that he barely could raise his sword in defense. The dog crown rolled on the ground and Dorieus snatched it, holding it up for all to see.

Actually it meant little since the Segestans did not hold the king and the crown in great esteem. In fact, the holy dog's surrender at Dorieus' feet shocked them more than the king's death and the loss of the dog crown. But the men of Phocaea did not know that. They cried out in victory although the Segestans' line closed behind us and the way to the city was still blocked with horses and warriors.

Suddenly shouts of alarm came from the city gates. The charioteers, who were attempting to drive their valuable horses to safety, swerved back, shouting that all was lost. The people of the city, following the events from atop the wall, had thought the battle over when they saw the chariots turn back to the city and had surprised and disarmed the few guards, locked the gates and taken the power into their own hands.

At the gate we paused to wipe the blood from our wounds and to gasp for air. Dorieus hammered at the gate with his shield, demanding entrance and holding up the dog crown that the people might see it. It was too small for him, since Segestan nobles had narrower heads than the Greeks and even bred their dogs narrow-headed.

To our surprise the gate creaked open and out came Tanakil's two sons in their capacity as leaders of the people. They greeted Dorieus glumly, admitted us, and quickly closed the gate behind the barely forty survivors of the men of Phocaea. From all sides the people cheered Dorieus and extolled his brilliance in battle.

Soon we saw Tanakil coming along the street clothed in rich robes and wearing a Carthaginian headdress while a female slave held a parasol over her head to indicate her descent from Carthaginian gods. How valid Tanakil's genealogical table was in Carthage I do not know, but in Segesta the people made way for her with respect.

She bowed her head before Dorieus and raised both hands in greeting. Dorieus extended the dog crown to her in order to free his hands and looked around somewhat stupidly.

To me it seemed that he could have greeted his earthly wife with greater warmth despite his union at sea with the white-limbed Thetis. And so I said quickly, "Tanakil, I greet you with all my heart. At this moment you are fairer in my eyes than the sun, but Arsinoe is still by the memorial together with our goods and we must save her from the Segestan nobles."

Dionysius also spoke up, "There is a time for everything, and I would not willingly disturb you at such a solmen moment, Dorieus. But our treasure is still at the memorial and I greatly fear that the peasants who accompanied us will steal it."

Quickly Dorieus recovered himself. "So it is. I was about to forget that," he admitted. "I have atoned for my father's bones and brought peace to his spirit. The name of the spurious Philip is to be cut away from the memorial immediately and in its stead must be the words: *To Dorieus, father of Segesta's king Dorieus, Spartan, fairest of his contemporaries and thrice winner in the Olympic games.* In addition, his lineage beginning with Herakles, as well as I can remember it."

We explained the matter to Tanakil's sons, who sighed in relief and said that they had nothing against the rectification of an error. On the contrary, they declared themselves to be greatly relieved that Dorieus demanded no more.

Dorieus said then, "I do not need the treasure and Arsinoe is able to take care of herself, for she is surrounded by men. But I left the holy dog Krimisos to await me by my father's memorial and it should be brought back to the city. Is anyone willing to fetch it? I myself am exhausted from the battle and wouldn't care to walk that distance."

No one among the Segestans was willing to go, and the men of Phocaea shook their heads and declared that they themselves were so battered and covered with wounds that they could hardly stand.

Dorieus sighed. "The burden of kingship is heavy. I already feel myself a lonely being among mortals and can trust no one. A king is the servant of his people and as such his own first servant. So I suppose nothing will do but that I myself must fetch the dog. After all, I can't forsake it when it surrendered to me and licked my foot."

Tanakil burst into tears and begged him not to go; the men of Phocaea stared at him with round eyes and Dionysius declared that he was insane. But Dorieus had the gate opened and walked alone out of the city, his arms drooping in exhaustion.

We climbed the wall to watch his progress. The Segestan nobles had formed a protective circle around the horses; some distance away the lightly armed troops were arguing among themselves and the rebels of Eryx had withdrawn to safety beyond the irrigation ditch. At the edge of the woods, barely visible, were the Siccanians who now and then sounded their hollow logs inquiringly.

Dorieus strode through the deserted battlefield with its bloody corpses and its wounded crying for water and mother. He greeted by name every fallen man of Phocaea and lauded his heroism. "You are not dead," he proclaimed loudly to each one. "You are invulnerable and we are still the three hundred, as we will be for eternity."

As he moved among the fallen, all other voices were silenced. The Segestans watched him incredulously and it did not occur to anyone to attack him. The heavy clouds which always cover the sky during a battle began to break, and the sun shone on Dorieus' blood-stained figure with dazzling brightness.

The men of Phocaea whispered among themselves. "He's truly a god and not a human, although we only half believed it."

To this Dionysius added, "True, he is not a human, at least not a sane human."

Having reached the memorial, Dorieus called the holy dog by name. It rose immediately, trotted to him with wagging tail and looked at him lovingly.

Dorieus then called to his father's spirit in a loud voice. "Are you content, my father Dorieus? Will you now rest in peace and not torment me?"

Afterwards it was said that a hollow voice from within the memorial responded, "I am content, my son, and will go to my rest."

I myself did not hear the voice nor do I believe that it spoke, since the Segestans had erected the memorial to Philip of Croton several decades earlier and had buried Dorieus' father in their fields with the other fallen. On the other hand, Dorieus might well have heard the voice within him. This I admit lest it be thought that I accuse Dorieus of lying.

The beasts of burden had been driven to the irrigation ditch, their owners happy in the belief that they were about to make off with our treasure. But the bridges had fallen and the men dared not drive the animals into the ditch lest they be drowned in the mire. Dorieus called out to them cheerfully, ordering them to return.

Upon hearing his voice, Arsinoe greeted him from the back of a donkey, accusing the wretches of not obeying her but of attempting to steal both her and the treasure. Mikon she had had stuffed into an empty feed basket after he had drunk himself into a stupor at the height of the battle.

A few threatening gestures from Dorieus hastily brought back the drovers and their animals. But as Arsinoe approached with the cat in its cage, the holy dog of Segesta raised its hackles and growled, with the result that Dorieus decided to return to the city well ahead of Arsinoe. This time the Segestan nobles urged one another to fall upon Dorieus and kill him, but the sight of the bare-fanged, growling Krimisos sent them retreating into their fortress of shields.

The shepherds and field workers of Eryx now attempted to enter the city, but the gate was shut relentlessly before them. Dorieus was at first annoyed, but when Tanakil's sons explained that poor and undisciplined peasants would only create a disturbance in the city, he conceded that he owed the men nothing.

Meanwhile the wounded began to complain. "Why have we brought a learned physician with us? Have we fattened him and paid him a salary only to have him lie in a drunken stupor when we need him the most?"

Because of our friendship I hastily spilled Mikon out of the feed basket and revived him. He managed to stay on his feet although he knew little of what went on around him, but so experienced was he that he performed his duties as well as—and in the opinion of some even better than—when he was sober.

Of myself I shall say only that my knees were skinned, my arm had a spear wound, and my neck just above the collarbone had been pierced by an arrow. Mikon had to cut open my neck to remove the arrow-head. He said, however, that my wounds were merely of a kind to remind me of my body's mortality. I mention the wounds only because Dorieus began to assemble and count those of his men who still could stand or raise an arm.

"I wouldn't want to trouble you," he said, "but the Segestan nobles are still lingering on the plain behind their shields. It may be necessary to go out and continue the battle."

But that was too much for the men of Phocaea. They shouted in protest and demanded that he be content with the dog crown that now was his.

Dionysius counted his men and cried bitterly, "We were three hundred, but now there are not even enough Phocaeans to man a penteconter. Spirits cannot move oars and raise sails."

At length Dorieus consented to take off his helmet. "Perhaps I have completed my task," he conceded with a sigh.

Tanakil's sons also declared that enough blood had been shed, and that Segesta needed its heavily armed forces to maintain its power in the land of Eryx. They promised to conduct all necessary negotiations so that Dorieus would be spared the trouble.

"My sons are right," said Tanakil. "It is time for you to rest. Your most important task at this moment is to lead the holy dog back to its pen, after which we may retire to discuss all that has happened."

Dorieus' glance strayed restlessly. He said in a weak voice, "You seem so distant, Tanakil. I feel as though years have elapsed since our meeting in Himera."

Tanakil tried to smile. "I have grown thin worrying about you. But I will surely regain my strength after we are alone, and you will look at me with different eyes when you have rested."

Tanakil's sons hastily declared that, with the grain fields trampled and the land otherwise damaged, it was not a propitious time for erecting a new temple. Besides, omens had to be studied and the years calculated by seers.

At that Dorieus drooped, permitted himself to be divested of his armor and dressed in a Phoenician robe decorated with the moon and the stars, the nymph of Segesta and the holy dog. The people led him in a festive procession to the temple but the holy dog was unwilling to enter its pen. It looked beseechingly at Dorieus, who had to drag it forcibly into the pen. There the dog immediately sat down and began to howl ominously. Nor did it consent to eat or drink anything that the people offered it.

Dorieus nervously adjusted the dog crown that was tied to his head. "The howling of that dog hurts my ears and brings dismal thoughts," he snapped. "Unless you can silence it I shall whip the animal."

Fortunately, the people did not understand his threat. But the ominous howling depressed me also. Turning to Tanakil I asked, "If I remember correctly, the custom here is to marry the city's fairest maiden each year to the holy dog. Why isn't she here to attend to her spouse?"

"It is merely a tradition and no longer involves any responsibilities," explained Tanakil. "In fact, the maiden merely shares the wedding cake with the dog and then leaves. But in honor of Dorieus we could find another maiden to comfort the dog."

We could tell by Dorieus' face that there was no time for delay. Tanakil called out to the people and immediately a little girl ran into the pen, wound her arms around the dog's neck and began whispering in its ear. The dog looked at her in surprise and tried to free itself, but the little girl was insistent. Finally the dog ceased its howling and submitted to the girl's caresses. The envious people then declared that a beggar girl was not good enough for the dog, but Tanakil retorted firmly that many another old custom had been violated that day. If the holy dog Krimisos accepted and was satisfied, its decision could not be questioned.

The pen was attached to the king's residence, in which Tanakil had already prepared food and a bath. The building had been unoccupied and, because of its collection of holy objects, many of them obtained from animals, had a foul odor. The previous king had visited it only in connection with his official duties, but Dorieus was content with it, billeted the men of Phocaea at a nearby house, and asked that the wounded be cared for by Segestan residents.

Tanakil bustled about making Dorieus as comfortable as possible. After he had been bathed, anointed and massaged as thoroughly as his wounds permitted, he was carried by servants to the convivial couch. He tried to eat, but could not hold the food. Sighing he turned to Tanakil and said, "Earthly food apparently does not please my body which Thetis made invulnerable in her undersea chambers."

"What do you mean, noble husband?" demanded Tanakil, glancing suspiciously at us. "Does your head ache? Undoubtedly it is exhaustion that makes you vomit and rave. Formerly my food was more than good enough for you."

Dorieus smiled dejectedly and vomited once more. "I don't understand what is wrong with me," he said shamefacedly. "Ever since I achieved my goal I have felt weak, for I no longer know what I want.

Take away this accursed dog crown for it smells vile! Everything in this house smells of dog. It must be that which nauseates me."

"Breathe my fragrance, my husband," urged Tanakil. "In preparing to receive you, I let my body be anointed and had a scent cup tied to my forehead."

Dorieus hopefully sniffed her forehead, then drew back, wrinkling his brows. "You also smell of dog, Tanakil."

He held his stomach and complained, "It is as though I were on the vessel again. I am swaying on the couch just as I swayed in the arms of my beloved. Ah, Thetis, Thetis, I shall always long for you while I am on land!"

Tanakil looked at us glumly. I hastened to explain what had happened during the voyage while Mikon whispered into her other ear in his capacity as physician.

She glanced at Arsinoe suspiciously but nodded. Then, patting Dorieus' cheeks, she said soothingly, "I understand and do not mind your union with that Thetis since I am not jealous by nature. But it would be best for you to remain indoors for a few days. The more a king remains aloof from trivial matters the more respected he is. I have already provided you with the garment of a maiden so that, like your holy forefather Herakles, you may perform a woman's tasks in order to placate the gods."

The men of Phocaea listened with open mouths but no one laughed. Dionysius agreed that Dorieus had shown such incomparable virility that it undoubtedly would be wisest for him to wear woman's garments for a few days to allay the gods' envy.

Tanakil's promise and Dionysius' understanding calmed Dorieus. His eyes closed and he fell face down onto the couch. We carried him into the bedchamber and left him there, his head at Tanakil's breast.

3.

Dorieus remained out of sight for twelve days, and in that period Segestan affairs worked out for the best. The nobles suddenly attacked the rebels of Eryx, compelling them to give up their weapons and return to their masters. To the Siccani the people of Segesta gave gifts of salt and clay pots with the injunction to return to the forest.

The people also made peace with the nobles, permitting them to return to the city with their horses, dogs and athletes, and convincing them that the assumption of the heavy burden of government by the people was to the nobles' advantage. Not only could they retain the outward symbols of their rank but, having been relieved of the responsibility of government, they would have more time to devote to horse breeding, dog training and watching athletic competitions. However, they must henceforth permit wealthy merchants and skilled artisans to marry their daughters and inherit land, and also permit certain leading city officials to keep dogs even though they were not of noble birth.

Dorieus was anxious to send emissaries to the large Greek cities in Sicily to herald his acquisition of the crown, but Tanakil protested vehemently. "You cannot do that, for the council of Carthage would suspect you of harboring plans for an alliance with the Greeks. Much happened while you were at sea. Anaxilaos of Rhegion conquered Zankle with the aid of some refugees fleeing from the Persians. When Krinippos of Himera heard that, he hastily married off his grand-daughter Kydippe to Anaxilaos, who changed the name of Zankle to Messina, signed a treaty of friendship with Carthage, and now rules both shores of the strait. So, through marriage, actually the entire north shore of Sicily is under the influence of Carthage. My sons will have much explaining to do before Carthage recognizes your legal right to the dog crown."

After the harvest, two emissaries arrived from Carthage by way of Eryx to investigate Segestan affairs. They were two because the council of Carthage did not willingly entrust important matters to only one man, and three again would have been too many. But naturally, the two were accompanied by servants, bookkeepers, surveyors, and military experts.

Dorieus let Tanakil arrange a banquet in their honor. She brought forth her genealogical table for the guests to see and assured them that Dorieus would soon learn the Elymian language and habits. Dorieus for his part took the guests to see the holy dog. He had little else to show them.

After lengthy negotiations, which Dorieus permitted the city council to conduct on his behalf, the Carthaginian emissaries recognized Dorieus as the king of Segesta and all Eryx. But they bade him make reparation for the damage he had caused Panormos. Actually, the Carthaginians had already confiscated the trireme. Other demands were the recognition of Eryx as a Carthaginian city, the right of Carthage, as the winter residence of the goddess, to continue drawing the revenue derived from the pilgrimages to Eryx, and the right of approval by Carthage of all trade agreements with the Sicilian Greek cities as well as of all matters pertaining to war and peace. And finally, Dionysius and the other men of Phocaea must be turned over to Carthage for judgment for their piracy on the eastern sea.

To all else Dorieus yielded since the demands meant merely the recognition of existing conditions, but the men of Phocaea he refused to surrender. He resisted staunchly, although Tanakil tried to prove that he owed nothing to Dionysius but on the contrary had suffered an injustice at his hands.

"What happened on the sea was a matter unto itself," said Dorieus. "I cannot violate the brotherhood that we sealed on land with our blood."

But when Dionysius heard that the negotiations threatened to run aground because of him, he came voluntarily to Dorieus. "I don't want to endanger the kingship which I unselfishly helped you to obtain, and so we will step out of your way and return to sea."

Dorieus brightened at the suggestion. "That may be the best thing to do, although I had hoped to fulfill my promise and make you lord of the land. But what can I do when Carthage does not agree to it?"

For some reason the Carthaginians did not demand Arsinoe, Mikon or myself, and we lived in Dorieus' residence enjoying Tanakil's hospitality as we had in Himera. Meanwhile the men of Phocaea were not having a pleasant time in Segesta. They were compelled to shut themselves in their lodgings and even pay for their own maintenance while the Carthaginian emissaries ordered them guarded day and night lest they repeat their escape from Himera. But there we had been on the shore of the sea and the ships had been ready for sailing.

With the approach of autumn the Phocaeans felt as though a noose were being tightened around their throats. They began to rub the indelible blue marks on their backs and to wonder how it would feel to be skinned alive. Every day the Carthaginian emissaries with their coppery faces and gold-threaded beards strolled by the Phocaeans' lodgings while their retinue shouted threats. At Dionysius' order the Phocaeans bore the insults in silence.

Dorieus understandably grew tired of them since they were in his way. The Carthaginian emissaries became impatient and demanded the surrender of the Phocaeans before the end of the sailing season. When I talked with them they pretended tolerance, assuring me the tales of their skinning people alive were sheer slander. The Carthaginian maritime law was severe, true, but not senseless. They had mines in Iberia which were constantly in need of labor. Ill-tempered slaves might be blinded or disjointed at the knee to prevent escape, but nothing worse happened to them.

I explained this to Dionysius, who stroked his beard and replied that the Phocaeans had no desire to work in the poisonous mines of Iberia or to turn millstones in Carthage merely to please Dorieus.

Dionysius no longer entrusted his plans to me, although we continued to be friends. One day, seeing thick smoke pouring forth from their courtyard, I hastened there and saw that they had dug pits and battered their beautiful silver vessels which they were melting down with a bellows. They were also prying loose the precious stones from the jewel caskets and breaking the ivory carvings.

I watched their activities with suspicion and saw that they broke the hardened silver into chunks which they then weighed and divided among themselves.

"My eyes cannot bear the sight of such senseless destruction of art treasures," I said indignantly. "But I do notice that you are sharing them according to weight and deciding with a toss of the knucklebones who gets the pearls and the precious stones. I believe that I also am due a share in that treasure, as is Mikon. Dorieus, too, would be offended if he were not to receive the share won by his sword."

Dionysius showed his white teeth in a smile. "Ah, Turms, you spent more than your share in Himera. Don't you remember borrowing from me before you left for your pilgrimage to Eryx? And upon your return you borrowed still more to satisfy the whims of that woman whom you brought with you. Dorieus for his part owes us more than we owe him. But Mikon we will gladly grant his physician's share if he will accompany us to the tribunal at Carthage. Perhaps he will be able to stitch together our skin after it has been stripped from our backs."

The men of Phocaea laughed through their sweat and grime. "Yes, Turms, and Mikon, and above all Dorieus, come and get your share of the loot," they cried, "but don't forget your swords! There may be a difference of opinion."

In view of their threatening behavior I thought it best to tell Dorieus only that they were sacrificing to the gods prior to surrender. Dorieus sighed in relief. "What fine fellows they are! This is the best service they could do for me. Now at last I will be able to attend to the political affairs of Segesta in peace."

Joy spread throughout the city when it appeared that the unpleasant matter was about to be resolved without difficulties. Because a person willingly believes what he desires to believe, the Segestans were sure that Dionysius and his men had finally regained their senses. That night the Segestan leaders listened to the noises issuing from the Phocaeans' house as the men drank wine and feasted to fortify their courage. The Carthaginian emissaries nodded contentedly. "It is high time, for our ship has waited far too long in Eryx. Those pirates are more foolish than we imagined in thus trusting in Carthaginian laws."

In gratitude they made sacrifices to Baal and to other gods and brought fetters and ropes with which to take the Phocaeans to Eryx. On the following day they again walked by the house and paused before it expectantly. Soon Dionysius came out of the gate with his men and, quicker than I can relate it, slew the members of the retinue and seized the amazed emissaries. They did not kill the Segestans and merely warned the guards not to interfere in a matter which did not concern them.

Dionysius came into the street, axe in his hand, to meet Dorieus and the Segestan leaders. "We have surrendered to the sacred emissaries from Carthage and have humbly requested them to conduct us to Eryx and their ship," he explained coolly. "We can only regret the unfortunate incident caused by the retinue's shameless assault on us as we attempted to negotiate with the emissaries. In doing so they stumbled over their own swords and swung at one another with their spears. Possibly we also, as men quick to anger, were guilty of striking some of them too hard, unaccustomed as we are to using metallic weapons. But the Carthaginian emissaries have already forgiven us and have promised that we need not surrender our weapons until we board the vessel. If you do not believe my words, step inside the house and ask them yourselves."

But the Segestan leaders were not anxious to enter the Phocaeans' house and Dorieus maintained that the matter no longer concerned him since Dionysius had surrendered to the Carthaginians.

Dionysius continued, "You have only your own hostility to blame for our actions. The holy Carthaginians agree with us and greatly fear that you will attack us along the way and thus prevent their taking us alive to Carthage. If you attack us, they promise to take their own lives. Thus their blood will be on your heads and Carthage will never forgive you."

While the Segestan leaders were digesting his words he smiled cheerfully and announced, "We Phocaeans would rather sail to Carthage by way of Panormos, since we know that route, but the Carthaginian leaders insist upon Eryx, and we must obey. As prisoners we Phocaeans are willing to go humbly on foot, but such honorable men cannot be expected to walk such a long distance. Thus you must find us mules and a guide as well so that we will surely find our way to Eryx."

The Segestan leaders, realizing their hopelessness, could only pretend to believe that all would happen according to Dionysius' promise. In a procession of honor they conducted the Carthaginian emissaries behind

183

their wall of Phocaean shields through the city to the west gate. They saw that the emissaries were gagged and roped to the mules but pretended not to notice it.

Mikon and I accompanied the Phocaeans to the gate. There, with infinite arrogance, Dionysius paused and said, "I almost forgot that the holy emissaries' money bags, documents and writing tablets are still at their lodgings. Fetch them quickly, you officials, and bring also fresh meat and wine, as well as two maidens to warm them through the cold night."

When the emissaries' goods were brought, Dionysius taunted the Segestan leaders by donning a Carthaginian ceremonial robe. Unable to read the scrolls of parchment and the tablets, he glanced at them disdainfully and tossed them to his men, who drew ribald pictures, showed them to one another and cackled in glee.

Finally Dionysius saw fit to depart after one of the Segestan leaders suffered a stroke from sheer rage and died before our very eyes. The Phocaeans, considering that a bad omen, urged on their mules and set off on the road to Eryx.

Nor did they delay. Having rested only during the darkest hours of night, they arrived in the harbor of Eryx the following evening, swarmed onto the ship that had been awaiting the emissaries, tossed its crew into the sea, threw torches onto the other vessels and brought chaos to the entire port.

When they made for the sea they had the emissaries with them. One they fastened to the prow for luck in ramming the first ship they would meet, the second they jokingly sacrificed to Baal after they had robbed several treasure ships near the African coast. Dionysius no longer made any attempt to reach Massilia but devoted himself to piracy, in accordance with the apparent wishes of the gods. Because he did not rob Greek ships, the Greek cities in Sicily soon secretly began to shield him and the fleet which he had assembled. Indeed, during the succeeding years, Dionysius' daring activity at sea did much to bring about further deterioration of the already bad relations between Carthage and the Sicilian Greek cities.

I have related all this about Dionysius and his men for he was a man worth remembering. The thirty-three who were with him I would list by name, but I no longer remember them.

4.

During that winter in Segesta a strange oppression came over me. There was no apparent reason for it, since I was highly respected as Dorieus' companion and Arsinoe for her part had forgotten her capriciousness and withdrawn from the public eye to await our child. She grew fatter and calmer and sometimes in her moments of fear turned to me with greater tenderness than ever before. But she did not speak much and it seemed at times as though I were living with a strange woman. Whenever I thought of our coming child, it, too, seemed a stranger.

But if I suffered, Dorieus did likewise. He had reached his goal and in reaching it had lost it, so that he no longer knew what he wanted. His experiences at sea had so unsettled him that during his spells of melancholy his eyes stared vacantly as though everything in him were but gray salt. He had lost all interest in Tanakil and often spoke to her sharply.

Dog breeding and horse racing did not appeal to him. Instead, he tried to interest the Segestan youths in developing their bodies in the Greek manner. They watched his skillful performances in the stadium with respect, but observed that there was nothing admirable in exhausting oneself when professional athletes could obtain better results than any amateur.

Dorieus did succeed in calling together all able-bodied men regardless of rank or trade for military exercises on certain days. Many of them complained of aches and reported themselves ill time and again, but the people realized the necessity for learning to use arms if they intended to retain their power. Dorieus pointed out that a well-armed city is more respected at negotiations than a weak one and the people knew that with the coming of spring the council of Carthage would hold them responsible for the fate of its emissaries. Although the Segestans intended to blame Dionysius for everything, a feeling of guilt induced the people to run themselves to a sweat and to strain their limbs at the exercises which they heartily despised.

After a time they gladly acceded to Dorieus' suggestion that the city install as a permanent garrison one thousand youths from among those who had indicated aptitude and who had no desire to follow other trades. Dorieus divided the youths into groups of one hundred, lodged them in various houses and himself often slept among them to avoid sharing the marriage bed with Tanakil. He maintained strict discipline and each had to obey the leaders selected by him, but despite this the robberies and outrages increased. The only difference was that the guilty were not discovered as readily as before. If one of Dorieus' wreath-crowned youths was found guilty of a crime, Dorieus had him severely whipped.

"I am not punishing you for the crime," Dorieus would explain, "but for the fact that you were discovered." That appealed greatly to his men who admired him more than the city council which paid their wages.

Dorieus managed to pass his time, but whenever a melancholy mood came upon him he retired to his room for many days and did not consent to talk even to Tanakil. Through the walls we heard him cry out to his forefather Herakles and endeavor to conjure up again the white-limbed Thetis.

When he had recovered, he called Mikon and me to him, drank wine with us and explained, "You cannot know how difficult it is to be a king, and bear the responsibility for an entire city's welfare. My divine heritage likewise complicates my position and makes me lonely." He turned his head painfully. "Although I have appeased my father's spirit and attained my legacy, my head aches to think that I shall leave behind nothing but enduring fame. I should have an heir to give purpose to all that has happened. But Tanakil can no longer give birth to one, and I have not the slightest desire to adopt her sons, as she suggests."

I admitted that such a problem was enough to make one's head ache. "Yet of us three, you should look to the future with the greatest confidence," I said consolingly, "for the gods have charted your path with such clarity that you could hardly have done other than what you did. In your position I would not worry about an heir, for in time you will surely have one if it is so ordained."

I thought the moment propitious for announcing Arsinoe's condition since it could no longer be concealed. It was surprising that Mikon's experienced physician's eye had not already noticed it.

"Not all are equally favored by fortune, Dorieus. I have gained nothing from our expeditions, I am still your companion and have not even my own hearth, although poor Arsinoe is awaiting my child. It can no longer be concealed, for she should give birth in but a few months, at the darkest time of the year."

Enthusiastically I babbled on. "You, Dorieus, naturally know little about women's affairs, but you, Mikon, should have noticed it long ago. Therefore congratulate me and let us shake hands. You have everything else, Dorieus, but I shall have what you never will have unless the situation unexpectedly changes."

186

Dorieus jumped to his feet, knocked over a valuable bowl and demanded, "Is that the truth? How can a priestess have a child?"

Mikon evaded my look and muttered, "Are you sure that you are not mistaken? I would not have wished that to happen to you."

In my joy I failed to understand, and hastened to fetch Arsinoe to confirm the fact. Tanakil followed us suspiciously.

Arsinoe stood before us, already awkward and with a dreamy look in her eyes. "It is true," she admitted humbly. "I am expecting a child which will be born at the most dismal time of the year. But I assure you that I am still under the protection of the goddess. My dreams and omens have clearly indicated that."

Tanakil's face darkened in envy. Glaring alternately at Arsinoe and Dorieus, she screamed, "I suspected it but could not believe my own eyes. You have brought shame upon my house. Don't drag the goddess into this affair, either. It is the fruit of your own cunning in trying to outdo me in shrewdness."

Dorieus stared at Arsinoe and raised a hand to silence Tanakil. "Shut your mouth, you Phoenician hag, or you will become still uglier in my eyes than you already are. This is not your house but the king's residence which I won with my sword. And don't envy Arsinoe. Instead, look upon her condition as an omen, although I must think hard to determine just how it is to be interpreted."

He covered his eyes for a moment, then his face softened and he smiled. "Don't be afraid, Arsinoe. I shall take you under my protection and all will be well. The child will not bring you shame but rather glory. Tell me, do you think that it will be a boy or a girl?"

Arsinoe said shyly that one could not know in advance, but that she felt almost certain it was to be a boy.

I remember little about the birth except that it happened on the rawest night of the year and that the boy came into the world at dawn while a cold rain poured down on the land. Arsinoe nursed the child herself, for despite her apparent frailness the goddess blessed her with an abundance of milk. The boy himself was strong and cried lustily from the very beginning. I was so relieved that I wanted to name him immediately, but Dorieus said, "There is no hurry. Let us wait for the right omen."

Arsinoe agreed. "Don't hurt Dorieus by choosing a name hastily. It will be better for us and for the boy also if Dorieus names him."

I was not happy to have Dorieus interfere in matters that were not his concern. He seemed as bemused as I, watched the child with interest and even gave an offering of thanks in the temple which he had robbed from the Phoenicians' god of fire and dedicated to Herakles.

As spring came, with its bright rains and violent storms that felled trees in the forests, Dorieus became increasingly gloomy. He began to stare at me peculiarly, and frequently I would come upon him watching the child and talking with Arsinoe. As soon as I entered they would stop and Arsinoe would begin chattering about something foolish.

With the approach of the full moon I grew restless, had bad dreams and began to walk in my sleep, something which had never happened to me before. I felt that Artemis was haunting me and tried many ways to avoid leaving the room at night, but nothing helped. Most alarming was the fact that Arsinoe's cat always followed me, slipping out of the door behind me. I would awaken in the middle of the street when it rubbed its head against my bare leg.

Once again I awakened in the middle of the night with the moon shining on my face. I saw that I was standing by the pen of the holy dog Krimisos and that on the stone step sat the beggar girl whom Tanakil had called from the crowd to care for the dog. Chin in hand she stared at the moon as though under its spell. I was touched to think that someone else was awake because of the moon, even though that someone was but a little girl. During the yearly celebration she had been legally married to the holy dog in accordance with tradition, had baked a wedding cake and had shared it with the dog. Since then she had lived around the pen and, like the slaves and servants, had been fed from the king's kettles. She had nowhere else to go, for she was a lowborn girl and had lost her parents.

"Why are you awake, litle girl?" I asked, sitting beside her on the stone step.

"I am not a little girl," she replied. "I am ten years old. Besides, I am the wife of the dog Krimisos and a holy woman."

"What is your name, holy woman?"

"Egesta," she said proudly. "You should know that, Turms. But my real name is Hanna. That is why people throw stones at me on the street and shout insults."

"Why are you awake?" I asked again.

She looked at me in distress. "Krimisos is ill. He just lies still and breathes heavily and doesn't eat anything. I think he's too old and doesn't want to live any longer. If he dies, the people will blame me." She showed me the bites on her thin arms, sobbed and said, "He doesn't even want me to touch him any more, although we were such good friends. I think that his ears are sore, for he often shakes his head. But if I touch him he bites."

The girl opened the door and showed me the holy old dog panting heavily on its straw, an untouched bowl of water by its muzzle. It opened its eyes but did not even have the strength to bare its fangs when Arsinoe's cat slipped like a shadow into the pen and began to circle the holy dog. The cat thereupon lapped at the water, was reassured, rubbed its side against the dog's neck and gently began to lick its ear. The dog permitted it to do so.

"This is a miracle!" I cried. "It must be that holy animals recognize each other. The cat is so holy that in Egypt any person who harms one is instantly killed. Why it is holy I do not know."

The girl said in amazement, "My husband is ill and suffering and I cannot comfort him but a cat can. Is it your cat?"

"No," I replied, "it belongs to my wife, Arsinoe."

"You mean Istafra," corrected the girl, "the priestess who fled from Eryx. Is she supposed to be your wife?"

"Of course she is. We even have a son. You must have seen him."

The girl stifled a titter with her palm, then became serious again. "Is he really your son? It is Dorieus who carries him in his lap while the woman follows, holding onto the king's robe. But she is a beautiful woman, that I do not deny."

I laughed. "Dorieus is our friend and fond of the boy since he has not an heir of his own. But both the boy and the wife are mine."

The girl shook her head in disbelief, then looked at me. "If I were more beautiful, would you take me in your lap and hold me close? I feel like crying."

Her thin girl's face moved me. I touched her cheek and said, "Of course I will take you in my lap and comfort you. I myself am often unhappy even though I have a wife and son, or perhaps because of that."

I lifted her onto my lap, she pressed her tearstained cheek against my chest, wound her arms around my neck and sighed deeply. "It feels so good. No one has held me like this since my mother died. I like you more than Dorieus or that bloated Mikon. When I asked him to look at the dog he said he took care only of people and wanted to know who would pay him. Yes," she repeated, "I like you very much because you are good to me. Doesn't this make you think of anything?"

"No," I said absently.

Suddenly she squeezed me hard. "Turms, I am hard-working and willing to learn, I can stand beatings and I eat little. If the dog dies, won't you take me under your protection, if only to care for your son?"

I looked at her in surprise. "I can talk to Arsinoe about it," I promised finally. "Do you know how to take care of children?"

"I have even taken care of a prematurely born boy and kept him alive on goat's milk when his own mother spurned him," she said. "I can spin and weave, wash clothes, prepare food, and prophesy from chicken bones. I could be very useful to you but I would rather be beautiful."

I looked at her dark face and bright girl's eyes and explained gently, "Every young woman is beautiful if she wants to be. You should learn to bathe like the Greeks, to keep your clothes clean and comb your hair."

She drew back. "I don't even have a comb," she confessed, "and this is my only dress. For the festivities I was washed and combed, anointed and clothed, but the festive garments were taken away as soon as the wedding cake had been eaten. I cannot go naked to the well to wash this."

"Tomorrow I shall bring you a comb and one of my wife's old garments," I promised. But I forgot.

The next day was oppressively hot, as though it were midsummer, the sun was scorching and the air still. The dogs howled restlessly in their pens and many broke loose, fleeing from the city. Flocks of birds swirled up from the forest and flew toward the blue mountains. Tanakil's sons came to consult their mother, withdrawing with her inside four walls.

Then, before the hour of rest, Dorieus summoned Arsinoe and had her bring the boy.

"It is time for the goddess to appear," he said harshly. "I have listened to excuses too long. Prove that you are still a priestess and show your skill. You must decide whether or not I launch a military expedition against Eryx tomorrow."

I tried to discourage him. "Are you mad or just drunk, Dorieus? Surely you wouldn't deliberately start a war with Carthage?"

Arsinoe whispered to me, "Don't say anything rash that might excite him. I'll try to calm him for he trusts me."

Body dripping with sweat from the heat, I waited behind the door. Their voices came to me in a confused mumble as though they were arguing.

Finally the door creaked and Arsinoe appeared, crushing our sleeping boy to her. Her face was wet with tears.

"Turms," she whispered in agony, "Dorieus is stark mad. He thinks that he is a god and that I am the sea goddess Thetis. I finally succeeded in putting him to sleep. He is snoring now, but as soon as he awakens he will kill both you and Tanakil."

I stared at her in disbelief. "You are the one who is mad, Arsinoe. The heat has unbalanced your mind. What reason has he to kill me, even if he is tired of Tanakil?"

Arsinoe groaned and covered her eyes. "The fault is mine," she confessed, "although I meant it for the best and didn't think that he would go so far. You see, for one reason or another, Dorieus believes the boy to be his and because of that wants Tanakil and you out of the way so that he can marry me. But I never intended this. My plan was entirely different."

I shook her arm. "What had you planned and whatever gave Dorieus the idea that our son is his?"

"Don't shout," begged Arsinoe. "It is just like you to seize on trivial details when your life is at stake. You know how stubborn Dorieus is when he gets an idea. He himself noticed that the boy supposedly resembles him, whereupon in jest I painted a mark on the boy's thigh to resemble the birthmark which true descendants of Herakles are said to bear. But I didn't think that Dorieus would turn against you. I did it only so that he would make the boy his heir."

Seeing my face, she pulled herself free and said, "If you hit me I shall awaken Dorieus. I thought he had sense enough to conceal his feelings, but he covets me and hates you so since the birth of the boy that he no longer wants to breathe the same air with you."

My thoughts were like a swarm of angry wasps. I should have guessed that behind her apparent docility Arsinoe had been scheming a more dangerous plot than one involving merely clothes and jewels. In my heart I knew that she spoke the truth and that Dorieus planned to kill me. A sudden chill came over me.

"I suppose you hope that I will slit his throat while he sleeps. But first tell me how you succeeded in quieting him."

Arsinoe opened her eyes and said innocently, "I merely held his hand and assured him that he would meet the goddess in his dreams. What is it that you suspect, Turms?" Then she paled. "If you have ever doubted my love for you, you can do so no longer, for it would have been more advantageous for me to remain silent and let him kill you. But I could not bear to lose you. Neither do I want harm to come to Tanakil although she has so often hurt me."

That last sentence she added presumably because she noticed Tanakil's approach.

"I can thank you, Istafra, for my marriage but also for my misfortune. You have tried to bite off more than you can swallow, and I hope that you choke on it. I suspect also that you used your wiles at sea, for why else should Dorieus have begun to rave about that white-limbed Thetis?"

191

"Tanakil," I warned her, "don't talk nonsense even though you hate Arsinoe. During the voyage Arsinoe was sick and smelled vile, she was wet from the brine and unable to care for her beauty. She could have had nothing to do with Dorieus' visions."

My words wounded her vanity. "What do you know about the goddess's miracles, Turms?" she demanded angrily. "Tanakil is much wiser. I assure you that everything happened as was meant, for the goddess has always yearned to assume a sea guise."

Tanakil looked at me shrewdly and advised, "You would be wise to take that candlestick and smash Arsinoe's head. Thereby you would spare yourself much grief. But it is useless for us to chatter. What do you intend to do, Turms?"

"Yes," demanded Arsinoe, "what do you intend to do?"

I became even more confused. "Is it my duty to solve the problem that you have created? So be it. I will fetch my sword and run it through his throat, although not gladly, for he has been my friend."

"Yes, do that," urged Arsinoe eagerly, "and while you are about it, seize the dog crown, win the soldiers to your side, pacify the council of Carthage and make me the priestess of Eryx by peaceful means. I could not ask for more than that."

Tanakil shook her head in pity. "It would not go well with you, Turms, if Dorieus were to be found with his throat slit. But have no fear. I have seen three husbands to the grave and I dare say I have the strength to bury yet a fourth. It is my duty to perform this last service for him before he takes my life and plunges all Eryx into disaster. Go your way, both of you, take the accursed bastard with you and pretend that you are aware of nothing."

She sent us to our room, where we sat silently with folded hands. I stared at our son and tried to find something in his infant face that might have given Dorieus reason to believe the boy his. But look as I might, I could see only that his mouth was mine and his nose Arsinoe's.

Suddenly the earth rumbled with a noise more terrifying than any I had ever heard. The ground beneath us shook, the floor cracked, and the sound of crumbling walls reached our ears. Arsinoe snatched the boy into her arms while I shielded her with my body as we rushed into the street through the twisted gate. Arsinoe's cat swished by us in terror.

Again the ground shook and walls cracked. Then the sky darkened, the wind began to blow and the air suddenly cooled.

"Dorieus is dead," I said slowly. "This land was his, and it quivered at his passing. Perhaps he really was descended from the gods, although it was difficult to believe that when he smelled of human sweat and shed human blood."

"Dorieus is dead," Arsinoe repeated, then asked quickly, "What will become of us now, Turms?"

Frightened people were carrying things out of their houses, while beasts of burden ran wildly through the streets. But as the wind blew the air freshened and it was as though I were once again free.

Tanakil came out of the king's residence. She had torn her clothes as a sign of grief, and in her hair was some rubble from the housetop. Her sons followed her, arguing loudly as always.

Arsinoe and I went with them to Dorieus' room where Mikon with his physician's case was studying the body in amazement. Dorieus lay on the couch, his face black, tongue swollen and lips blistered.

Mikon said slowly, "If it were summer and the time for wasps I would swear that a wasp had bitten his tongue. That happens to a drunkard who falls asleep with his mouth open or to a child who crams a wasp into his mouth with berries. But whatever the reason, Dorieus' tongue has swelled and choked him."

Tanakil's sons cried out with one voice, "This is fate and a singular coincidence! We remember well that our father died in almost exactly the same manner. His tongue also swelled and his face blackened."

Tanakil stared at Dorieus' blackened face and body that was divinely tall even in death. "Nothing matters to me any more, but don't you dare touch Turms." She turned her aged, sorrow-lined face toward Arsinoe. "Turms may leave in peace, but we will send that goddess's harlot back to the temple to pay the penalty for her flight. She is a temple slave and her son also is a slave and as such the property of the temple. Let them castrate the boy and train him to be a priest or a dancer. But first they must punish the woman as befits an escaped slave."

I looked at Tanakil standing there with dirt in her dyed and coronet-wound hair, her clothes torn and her ancient face set in fury. She seemed like the embodiment of an alien god.

She smiled grimly and flicked away the flies that were beginning to hover about Dorieus' eyes and mouth. "I have already felt the goddess's wrath through your presence. Having lost Dorieus, whom I loved most dearly of my husbands, I no longer fear anything, divine or mortal."

Suddenly her restraint crumbled. She struck her mouth with her fist so that the ivory teeth broke and blood began to trickle from her thin lips. Digging her nails into her breasts, she wailed, "You don't know how deeply an old woman can love! I wanted him dead rather than despising me."

I put my arm around Arsinoe and said firmly, "I am bound to Arsinoe and will take her and the boy with me regardless of your laws. Try to prevent me, Tanakil, and you will see what happens." Once more I was ready, sword in hand, to abduct. Arsinoe and to die rather than be separated from her and the boy.

Mikon, plump and bloated from the wine though he was, collected the remnants of his wits and said decisively, "I also am a stranger in the city and an undesirable person if I have to testify as to the cause of Dorieus' death. For the sake of our friendship, Turms, I feel it my responsibility to prevent Arsinoe and the boy from falling into the hands of evil priests."

Tanakil's sons glanced at her uncertainly. "Shall we call the guards and have them killed, Mother? That would be the easiest way of ridding ourselves of them. You may determine what happens to the woman."

Tanakil pointed an accusing finger at Arsinoe. "Look at that too beautiful face!" she cried. "Look at that face that changes with her every whim. If I send her back to the temple she will surely win over the priests. I know her too well. No, the best punishment for her is to follow Turms as a fugitive, taking the boy with her. Let the sun darken her white face, let her limbs wither from want. Not a single garment, not a jewel or a silver coin will you take from my house, Istafra."

Arsinoe realized from Tanakil's stony face that it was her final decision. For a brief moment she seemed to weigh the chances of regaining her old position in the temple, then raised her chin.

"Clothes and jewels I can always get, but I can never win back Turms if I now leave him. You should be grateful to me, Tanakil. But for me you yourself would be lying there, your ugly face black and the mark of Dorieus' fingers around your throat. Had I remained silent and let Dorieus fulfill his threat, everything would be different. But I didn't want to lose Turms, nor do I hesitate to follow him now even if you should rob me of all I own."

At that moment it was as though I stepped out of myself to watch everything from the side. I smiled. Irresistibly my glance was drawn to a pebble on the floor. I bent down to pick it up, hardly realizing what I was doing. It was an ordinary pebble that had been brought into the house by someone's feet, and why I was compelled to pick it up I cannot explain, for I had no way of knowing that it again signified the end of one period in my life and the beginning of another.

I plucked the pebble from the floor, undisturbed by the fact that Tanakil was stamping her foot and demanding, "Go! Go quickly lest I regret it. Go as you are, for not one piece of bread, not one garment will you take from my house."

Thus she banished us but did not dare to touch us or to set the guards upon us. Arsinoe managed to snatch up a child's sheepskin and I took Dorieus' heavy woolen mantle from the wall in addition to my sword and shield. Mikon had his caduceus and medicine case and at the doorway laid hands on a half-filled wineskin.

Because of the confusion wrought by the earthquake our flight attracted no attention. Crowds were pushing their way out of the city with their possessions to the open fields. The earthquake was, in fact, slight and caused little damage. Probably the land of Eryx sighed in relief at the death of Dorieus, descendant of Herakles, for had he lived he would surely have plunged it to destruction.

As we hurried toward the north gate in the midst of the moaning mass, the orphan girl Hanna, wife of the holy dog Krimisos, ran after us. Pulling at my robe, she said tearfully, "The dog Krimisos is dead. This morning it crept into the darkest corner of its pen, and when the earth began to shake and I wanted to lead it outside, it did not move. But your cat came to me and leaped into my lap in fright."

She had wrapped the cat in her dress and held it to her so that her lower body was bare. I could not shake her loose for I had enough to do in running toward the gate with the crying boy in my arms. Arsinoe clung to my arm, Mikon panted behind us and the girl clutched tightly at my robe. Our departure from Segesta was not dignified.

No one stopped us. We crossed the open fields as quickly as possible and turned from the road toward the mountains into the evergreen forest. We spent the night under the trees pressed close to one another for warmth. We did not dare to build a fire until we met some Siccanians by their sacred rock. They welcomed us and we lived among them for five years. During that time Mikon disappeared, Arsinoe gave birth to a daughter, and Hanna grew into a maiden.

But before telling of that I must describe Tanakil's fate. After Dorieus' death Tanakil's sons strengthened their power in the city and bribed the leaders of Dorieus' forces to support them so that the city officials had little to say. For the sake of appearances they built a magnificent funeral pyre of oaken logs for Dorieus and before lighting it told their mother that they were tired of her lust for power and would send her back to Himera. Whereupon Tanakil said that life without Dorieus held little meaning and that she would rather share the funeral pyre with him in the faint hope of accompanying him to the underworld.

Her sons did not protest so Tanakil, garbed in her best, climbed the pyre, embraced Dorieus' body a final time and with her own hands set fire to the logs. Her body burned with that of Dorieus.

All that I learned later from the Siccani and that is all I have to say about Tanakil and Dorieus.

BOOK SEVEN

The Siccani

I.

THUS it was that we met the Siccanians by their sacred rock. As was their custom, they explained that they had expected us and had known in advance of our coming. A skeptic might think that their young men had secretly followed our progress, since the Siccani were able to move unseen in their forests and mountains until such a time as they wished to appear.

But the Siccani did, in truth, possess the power to know who and how many people were on their way. They knew where their tribesmen were located at a given time and even what a specific chief happened to be doing at a given moment. In this respect they were like an oracle. Nor were their priests the only possessors of this ability. Most of the people had it, some keenly, others less distinctly, and could not themselves explain it. They erred only seldom, as even an oracle can err, or at least as the inspired words of the oracle can be misinterpreted. Nor did they consider their ability in any way remarkable, but thought that other people had the same ability.

They had anointed their sacred rock with oil and as they awaited our arrival they danced sacred dances around it. Their priest had donned a mask of carved wood as well as a sacred tail and horns. A fire was burning and on the fire were clay pots ready for the donkey which they sacrificed and cooked upon our arrival. They considered the donkey a sacred animal and respected us because we arrived in their midst under the protection of a donkey. Being skilled hunters they did not lack meat but believed that the donkey's tough flesh gave them strength and patience. Above all they wanted a donkey's head to put atop a pole so that they might worship it in their secret rites. The donkey's skull, they believed, shielded them from lightning. Nor did the donkey resist but meekly submitted to the sacrifice. That also they considered a good omen.

But they feared the cat, found no name for it and would probably have killed it had not Arsinoe taken it in her lap and indicated its tameness. They respected her because she had arrived on a donkey with a male child in her arms. After the sacrifice their priest performed triumphal leaps before the boy, indicated that he was to be placed on the anointed rock and sprinkled donkey blood on him. Then they all shouted in one voice, "Erkle, Erkle!"

Mikon had hoarded a few drops at the bottom of the wineskin, and I doubt whether he would have withstood the rigors of the journey without the wine. He offered some to the Siccanians to win their friendship but after tasting it they shook their heads. Some even spat out the wine. Their priest laughed and offered Mikon a drink from a hollowed tree knot. When he had tasted it he said that it was not the equal of wine. A moment later, however, his eyes widened and he claimed that his limbs were numb, that the roots of his hair were tingling and that he could see through tree trunks to the very depths of the earth.

The Siccanian priests and chieftains brewed their sacred potion at secret rites, using poisonous berries, mushrooms and roots that they gathered in certain cycles of the moon during various seasons. They drank it at such times as they wished to come in contact with the spirits of the underworld and obtain their advice. I suspect they drank it also to become intoxicated since they had no wine. At least Mikon gradually began to drink it and became fond of it while we lived with the Siccani.

As the sacrificial rites continued, the exhaustion induced by our journey, the proximity of the sacred rock and the feeling of relief at finding sanctuary with the Siccani, who had shown us friendliness instead of hostility, combined to transport me beyond myself. In the silence, as everyone waited for a sign, the hoot of an owl sounded in the dark of the forest, time and time again.

"Arsinoe," I said, "our son has no name. Let his name be Hiuls after the cry of the owl."

Mikon burst into laughter, struck his knees and declared, "Just so, Turms. Who are you to give him a name? Let the forest owl give him a name, and as for his father's name, it is useless to mention it."

Arsinoe was so exhausted that she could not protest. After we had eaten the tough donkey meat she tried to nurse the boy but the exertion of our dangerous journey and the shock of Dorieus' death had dried her breasts. Hanna took the boy in her lap, fed him hot broth from the horn of a buck, wrapped him in a sheepskin and hummed him to sleep. When they saw that the boy was slumbering, the Siccanians led us along a secret path to a cave hidden in a thicket of brambles. Reeds had been spread on the stone floor for a bed.

Upon awakening in the gray of dawn and realizing where we were and what had happened, my first thought was of our next move. But as I stepped out of the cave I stumbled over a hedgehog which curled up into a ball at the touch of my foot. I knew the animal was a warning and realized that we must remain among the Siccani. That would also be the safest course, for it would be useless to wander so long as I did not know where to go.

After I had reached the decision an indescribable feeling of relief came over me, as though I had at long last found myself again. I went to the stream to drink and the water tasted glorious. I was still young and strong and full of the joy of living.

But Arsinoe, when she awakened, was not pleased to see the sooty ceiling of the cave, the hearthstones, and the misshapen clay dishes. She reproached me bitterly, saying, "So this is what you have made me, Turms, a pauper and an outlaw. At this moment, with the reeds pricking my body, I again don't know whether I love you or hate you."

Joyous laughter bubbled within me despite her words. "Arsinoe, my dearest, you have always asked for security and your own hearth. Here you are surrounded by strong walls. A hearth is a hearth though it consist of only a few sooty stones. You even have a servant, as well as a physician to care for the health of our son. With the aid of the Siccani I will soon learn to obtain food for you and the boy. For the first time in my life I am completely happy."

Realizing that I spoke in earnest, she fell upon me, scratching and spitting and screaming that I must take her to some Greek city in Sicily to a life worthy of her. Nor do I care to relate how long her fury lasted since all that was unpleasant has vanished from my memory of those times. But by the end of the summer, when she saw how big and robust her son had grown despite the primitive existence, she began to reconcile herself to her fate and to look upon matters in a more favorable light.

Until that time she kept her head tightly swathed in a cloth night and day to conceal her hair. She claimed that she did so in grief for the good life that I had destroyed, but I myself believed that she did so to annoy me, knowing how I loved her fair tresses. Finally, during a moment of ardor, she flung off the cloth to show me that her fair

199

curls had become straight black hair during our life with the Siccani.

"See for yourself what you have done to me," she said accusingly. "Do you finally realize my suffering? Formerly I had the fair hair of the goddess. Now the surroundings to which you have subjected me have shaped me to them, and my beautiful hair is like the black, coarse mane of the Siccanian women."

I touched her hair in disbelief. It was still as soft as before, but black it was. At first this seemed a miracle to me. I remembered her amazing skill in transforming herself and thought that the darkness of the gloomy forest and the terrifying nights had in truth blackened her hair. But reason triumphed and I began to laugh. "How vain you are, Arsinoe! As a priestess you naturally had to dye your hair, since the goddess's tresses are like the sun. No wonder you have mourned the loss of your beauty case. This is your real hair, and I love it just as I love everything about you, even your vanity, for it proves that you wish to be more beautiful in my eyes than you are. Of course miracles do happen, that I cannot deny, but how could even the most capricious deity have thought of turning your fair hair black?"

Eyes shining with anger, she said, "I am a woman of the goddess, and the goddess is the most capricious of all deities. You should know that, Turms, and believe her. This is evidence of your cruelty toward me. If I succeed in propitiating the goddess, perhaps she will yet restore my hair to its fairness."

"Precisely," I mocked her. "If we ever reach a civilized city and you have sufficient money with which to buy the necessary dyes. You cannot deceive me in this matter and make me believe the impossible."

Her slender fingers gripped my shoulders and her eyes turned to dark pools as in our moments of passion. "Turms, in the name of the goddess and in the name of our son, I swear that it is the truth. Of course I am a woman and as such lie to you in insignificant matters because you are a man and unable to understand everything. I admit that. But why should I lie about something that changes my whole appearance and life and makes me a completely different woman? You must believe me."

Looking into her eyes and hearing her oath, I began to tremble. If she had sworn only in the name of the goddess I would not have believed her, for that she had done also in the past and lied. Aphrodite, after all, is the most deceptive of goddesses and still one is compelled to love her. But I could not believe that she would lie in the name of our son.

Little Hiuls was crawling on the floor of the cave beyond the reach of Hanna's eye. I took him into my lap and gave him a greasy bone to suck.

To Arsinoe I said, "Lay your hand on our son's head and repeat your oath. Then I will believe you even though I cannot understand."

Without a moment's hesitation Arsinoe placed her hand, brown from the sun, on Hiul's head, rubbed his sprouting hair and repeated the oath. I had to believe her. Age grays a man's hair, so why couldn't displeasure blacken the hair of a capricious woman? It is not an ordinary occurrence but Arsinoe was not an ordinary woman.

When she had finally convinced me she began to smile, wiped the tears from her eyes, wound her arms around my neck and scolded me.

"How could you hurt me so, Turms, when just a few moments ago we were swaying on a cloud? I thought I had lost you when you doubted my words. Now I know that you are all mine just as you should be." She touched her hair and asked shyly, "Am I much uglier now than before?"

I looked at her. With her bare shoulders and black hair which emphasized their whiteness she was more beautiful than ever. She had strung a necklace for herself out of red berries, and the moonstone gleamed between her breasts. My heart swelled at the sight of her.

"Arsinoe, you are fairer than ever before. There is no one like you. Each time I take you in my arms you are like a new woman. I love you."

After that Arsinoe conformed to Siccanian life and ornamented herself with colored stones, coral, feathers and soft pelts. From the women she learned how to color her brows slantingly and to widen her mouth. The Siccani valued circles on their cheeks and serpentine streaks on their bodies, but such marks were irremovable and Arsinoe did not wish to have her skin slashed. I realized then that she had no intention of spending her entire life among the Siccani.

2.

Mikon remained with us for a year, and the Siccanians brought their sick from near and far to be healed. But he practiced his profession carelessly and declared that the Siccanian priests were fully as capable as he of healing wounds, putting broken bones in splints and submerging the sick into a curative sleep with the sound of a small drum.

"I have nothing to learn from them," he said, "nor they from me. Nothing makes any difference. Perhaps it is proper to relieve the pains of the body, but who will heal the suffering spirit, when not even one who is consecrated can find peace in his heart?"

I could not cheer him in his depression. One morning, having awakened late, Mikon looked at the blue mountains and radiant sunshine, touched the grass, breathed the warm fragrance of the forest and took my hand in his own trembling hands.

"This is my moment of clarity," he said. "I am enough of a physician to know that I am either ill or slowly being poisoned by the Siccanian potion. I am living in a haze and can no longer distinguish the real from the unreal. But perhaps the worlds are passing one another or are within one another so that at times I can live in two worlds simultaneously."

He gave me one of his rare smiles. "My moment of clarity must have little significance since I see you supernaturally tall, and your body glows like fire through your clothes. But ever since I first began to think, I have pondered the meaning of everything. For that reason I became consecrated and learned much that was beyond this reality. But even such secret knowledge is limited. Only the Siccanians' poisonous potion has provided me with the answer to why I was born and what the purpose of life is."

He released my hand, again touched the grass and looked at the blue mountains and said, "I should rejoice at my knowledge, but nothing gladdens me. It is as though I had run too long a distance. I am not consoled by the thought that some day I will awaken again, that the earth will be green and beautiful and that it will be a joy to live."

I looked at him pityingly, but as I looked I saw death behind his swollen face. I wanted to be kind to him because he was my friend, but he was angered by my look.

"You don't have to pity me," he said sharply. "You don't have to pity anyone, because you are what you are. Showing me pity is an affront, for I have served as a herald for you if nothing more. I ask only that you recognize me again when next we meet. That will suffice."

At that moment his swollen face was ugly in my eyes, and the envy that shone from it darkened the radiant dawn. Realizing it himself, he covered his eyes, rose, and walked away with uncertain steps.

When I tried to restrain him he said, "My throat is dry. I am going to the stream to drink."

I wanted to lead him there but he repulsed me angrily and did not look back. Nor did he return from the stream. We sought him in vain and the Siccanians looked for him in the thickets and gorges until I realized that he had meant another stream.

I did not condemn his action but as a friend granted him the choice of continuing this life or of ending it like a task that has grown too

202

heavy. After we had mourned him we made a sacrifice to his memory, and thereafter I felt greatly unburdened, for his melancholy had long thrown a shadow over our lives. But Hiuls missed him greatly, for he had taught the boy to walk, listened to his first words, and whittled playthings with his sharp physician's knife.

When she realized what had happened, Arsinoe became indignant and blamed me for not keeping an eye on Mikon.

"I don't care about his death," she said, "but at least he could have waited until I had given birth to the child and could have helped me. He knew well that I am pregnant again and I would have wanted to give birth in a civilized manner without depending on these Siccanian hags."

I did not reproach Arsinoe for her unkind words, for pregnancy made her capricious, and Mikon could in truth have waited yet a few months for the sake of our friendship. In due time Arsinoe gave birth effortlessly to a daughter without the aid of the experienced Siccanian women, although she succeeded in disrupting the entire tribe for the period of the birth. She refused to use a chair with a hole, as the Siccanian women urged her to do, but like a civilized person insisted on giving birth to her child in bed.

3.

I laud the endless forests of the Siccani, the eternal oaks, the blue mountains, the swift-flowing streams. But throughout the time I lived with the Siccani I knew that their land was not mine. It remained strange to me, just as the Siccani themselves remained strangers.

For five years I lived among the Siccani, learning their language and their strange and often amazing customs, and Arsinoe was content to share the life because of our love, although she often threatened to leave with some merchant who had ventured into the forest. Most of the merchants who came there with their wares were from Eryx, but some were from the Greek cities of Sicily, even from as far as Selinus and Agrigentum. Occasionally an Etruscan would bring a few sacks of salt for the Siccani, concealing iron knives and axe blades in them in expectation of great gains. The Siccani for their part displayed pelts, bright feathers, the bark of dyewood, wild honey and wax. They themselves remained hidden, but after I joined them I often talked for them with the merchants who frequently did not see a single Siccanian during their entire journey.

In this manner I heard news of the world and realized that times were restless and that the Greeks were spreading inland with increasing

203

tenacity into the Siculian region. The Segestans too were beginning to thrust ever more deeply into the forests with their dogs and horses. On several occasions we were compelled to flee to the mountaintop to escape from the path of such an expedition. But the Siccani laid traps for their pursuers and frightened them with their terrifying drums. I did not reveal my identity, and the merchants believed me to be a Siccanian who somehow had learned languages. Although they were uncivilized men whose tales one did not have to believe, they nevertheless related that the Persians had conquered the Greek islands, even sacred Delos, through their foothold in Ionia. They had imprisoned the islanders, sent the most beautiful maidens to the Great King, and castrated the finest youths as servants. They had even robbed and burned the temples to avenge the burning of the temple of Cybele at Sardis.

My deed haunted me in the depths of the Sicilian forests and made me uneasy. Holding Arsinoe's moonstone in my hand, I called to Artemis.

"You fleet virgin, holy and eternal, for you the Amazons sacrificed their right breast, for you I burned the temple of Cybele at Sardis. Remember me if the other gods begin to persecute me because of the destruction of their temples."

My uneasiness compelled me to propitiate the gods. The Siccani worshiped the underworld gods and thus also Demeter, for she is much more than the goddess of wheat sheaves. And since our daughter was born among the Siccani, I thought it best to name her Misme after the woman who had given water to Demeter as the goddess was searching for her lost daughter.

Only a few days had elapsed when the Siccanian priest came to me and said, "Somewhere a mighty battle is raging and many are dying." He looked and listened in every direction, finally pointed eastward and said, "It is far away, beyond the sea."

"How do you know?" I asked skeptically.

He stared at me in amazement. "Can't you hear the thunder of fighting and the groans of the dying? It is a big battle since it carries this far."

Other Siccanians gathered around us to listen and look toward the east. I also listened but heard only the murmur of the forest. They confirmed the words of their priest and quickly went to their sacrificial rock to propitiate the underworld gods lest the spirits of the numerous fallen enter the Siccanian newborn or the forest animals. Patiently they tried to explain to me that when so many men fell at one time their spirits would spread around the world and there was a possibility that the strange spirits might even enter the Siccanian forests in search of a resting place. The Siccanians were, however, unable to tell me who was fighting whom.

The Siccanian priest was drinking the sacred potion and in the grip of my restlessness I asked for some also. I knew that it was poisonous, but hoped that it would give me the Siccanians' power to hear what was happening afar. Although the priest's eyes were already inverted and he fell with twitching limbs to the ground, I swallowed the bitter potion greedily. But I did not hear the crash of battle. Instead, everything around me became transparent and the trees and rocks were like veils through which I could have thrust my hand. Finally I sank into the bowels of the earth among the voracious tree roots and in my trance saw the glitter of gold and silver under the sacred rock.

Upon awakening I vomited time and again until morning, and for several days thereafter felt more benumbed than I ever had after drinking wine. In my somber state of mind I no longer believed the Siccanians' story of a battle, but considered it sheer delirium. Nothing made any difference to me and I could well understand why Mikon had wanted to die after drinking that poisonous potion.

But that same autumn brought with it a Greek merchant from Agrigentum whom I had met once before by the river. He boasted that the Athenians had vanquished the Persian army on the field of Marathon near Athens and called it the greatest and most glorious battle of all times, since the Athenians had defeated the Persians alone without waiting for the promised Spartan reinforcements.

To me his story seemed incredible when I remembered how the Athenians had fled with us from Sardis to Ephesus, where they had sought shelter on their ships. Perhaps the Persians had suffered a defeat in attempting to land in Attica. But the Persians could not have transported many cavalrymen across the sea, and the use of ships in itself limited the size of an army. Such a defeat hardly weakened the King's military reserves but on the contrary would provoke him to launch a real expedition into Greece at some opportune time.

The destruction of the free states of Greece was therefore but a matter of time. Instead of joy, the news of Marathon aroused evil forebodings in me. For me, the burner of the temple of Cybele at Sardis, Sicily was no longer a safe refuge.

One morning, as I bent over the spring to drink, a willow leaf fell onto the surface of the water before me. As I glanced up I saw a flock of birds flying northward so high that I knew they intended to cross the sea. I seemed to hear the rustle of their wings and their honking, and at that moment I knew that the moment of departure was near.

I did not drink or eat, but continued directly across the forest to the mountain slope and climbed atop some jagged rocks to listen to myself and to study the omens. Having left so abruptly, I had no other weapon with me than a worn knife. While climbing the slope I had caught the smell of a wild animal and heard whimpering. After a search I found the den of a wolf, some gnawed bones, and a small wolf cub tottering helplessly at the entrance to the cave. A wolf is a formidable opponent when it is defending its young, but I concealed myself in some bushes to see what would happen. When the she-wolf did not appear and the cub whimpered in hunger, I took it in my arms and went down the mountain.

Both Hiuls and Misme were captivated by the woolly cub, but the cat crept around it with arched back. I kicked the cat away and asked Hanna to milk the goat which the Siccanians had stolen from the Elymi. The cub was so hungry that it greedily sucked the goat's milk as Hanna thrust her fingers into the cup for it. The children laughed and clapped their hands and I laughed also.

At that moment I realized what a beautiful maiden Hanna had become. Her brown limbs were straight and smooth, her eyes large and bright and her mouth smiling. She was wearing a flower in her hair and that is probably why I looked at her with different eyes.

Arsinoe followed my glance, nodded and said, "We will get a good price for her when we sell her upon our departure."

Her words pierced me, for I had no desire to sell Hanna in some coastal city for travel funds, no matter how good a position she might attain as the plaything of some wealthy merchant. But I knew that it was wisest not to let Arsinoe notice my fondness for the girl who had so willingly shared the dangers of the Siccanian forest and had served us and cared for our children.

So certain was Arsinoe of her power over me and of her beauty that she ordered Hanna to uncover her body and show herself from front and rear so that I might observe for myself what fine merchandise we had obtained as a gift.

Hanna avoided my eyes in shame, although she tried to hold her chin up. Suddenly she covered her face with her hands, burst into sobs and ran out of the cave. Her weeping frightened the children so that they forgot their games. The cat took advantage of the situation, snatched the wolf cub in its teeth and slipped out.

When I finally found it, it had killed the helpless cub and was gnawing on it. In blind fury I seized a rock and crushed the cat's head. As I did so I realized that I had always secretly hated the animal. It was as though, in killing the cat, I had freed myself of evil that had been haunting me.

I looked around to make certain that I was unobserved, found a crevice in the ground, quickly thrust the carcass into it and stopped it with a rock. As I bent to tear some moss with which to cover the evidence, I noticed that Hanna had approached silently and was scratching the ground as zealously as I.

Guiltily I looked at her and confessed, "I killed the cat in anger, although I didn't mean to."

Hanna nodded. "That was good," she whispered.

We scattered moss and leaves over the spot and as we did so our hands touched. The touch of her trusting girl's hand felt pleasant.

"I don't intend to tell Arsinoe that I killed it," I said.

Hanna looked at me with flashing eyes. "You don't have to tell her," she assured me. "The cat has often disappeared into the forest for nights at a time and our mistress has feared that it has fallen prey to a wild beast."

"Hanna," I asked, "do you realize that by sharing a secret with me you bind yourself to me?"

She raised her eyes, looked at me bravely and said, "Turms, I bound myself to you when I was a little girl, that night when you took me in your lap on the steps of the dog Krimisos' temple."

"This secret is insignificant," I said, "and only for the purpose of avoiding an unnecessary quarrel, you understand. Never before have I deliberately lied to Arsinoe."

I warmed to the brightness of her eyes, although I certainly did not desire her. Indeed, the thought did not even enter my mind that I could ever desire any other woman than Arsinoe. Hanna probably realized it, for she bowed her head humbly and rose so suddenly that the flower in her hair fell to the ground at my feet.

"Is it a lie, Turms, if one keeps secret what one knows?" she asked, moving the flower with her brown toes.

"It probably depends on the person himself," I said. "I myself know that I would be lying to Arsinoe if I let her believe that the cat disappeared and did not tell her that I killed it in rage. But sometimes it is kindest to refrain from saying what will hurt another, even though the lie will burn one's heart."

Absently she touched her heart, listened to it for a moment and conceded, "Yes, Turms, the lie is burning my heart, and I feel its sting." Then she smiled oddly, tilted her head and exclaimed, "How gloriously the lie burns my heart because of you, Turms!"

Quickly she ran away. We returned to the cave by separate paths and did not speak of the matter again. Arsinoe mourned her cat but she had enough to do with the two children. Nor did she mourn the cat for its own sake but from sheer vanity, since she had lost what no one else among the Siccani possessed.

Primarily I was troubled by a gnawing restlessness and the omens which I was as yet unable to interpret. I knew that I had to depart soon but had no idea in which direction to go. I didn't even have the means with which to return to civilization where one could purchase hospitality if one had no friends. My only friend was Lars Alsir, if he still lived in Himera. But a return to Himera would have meant certain death since both Arsinoe and I were known there. Besides, I was already indebted to Lars Alsir and the thought of the debt troubled me.

I realized that I was just as poor as when Tanakil had banished us from Segesta, for like the Siccani I possessed only the clothes I wore and my weapons.

In my anxiety I reproached the succoring goddess, saying "Holy virgin, the Amazons hung their breasts on your garments as offerings. You have succored me and my family so that we have not wanted for food or clothing. But you yourself appeared to me in Ephesus as Hecate and promised that I would never lack earthly riches whenever I needed them. Remember your promise, for now I need gold and silver."

A few days later, near the full of the moon, Artemis appeared to me in a dream as Hecate. I saw her three terrifying faces, she was waving a trident and a black dog was barking furiously at her feet. My whole body was enveloped in cold sweat when I awakened, for even in a kindly mood Hecate is an awesome sight. But the trident confirmed my belief that I must sail across the sea.

I was filled with such elation that I could no longer sleep but went out into the forest. By the sacrificial rock I met several Siccanians who were looking and listening in every direction. They claimed that strangers were approaching.

"Let us go toward them so that we will surely meet," I suggested. "Perhaps they are bringing salt and cloth."

On a bank of the river we found an Etruscan merchant who had brought salt in a small sailboat to Panormos, where he paid his taxes, and from there transported the salt by donkey to the forests of the Siccani. He was accompanied by three slaves and servants. They had built a fire for the night to protect themselves from the wild beasts and to indicate their peaceful intentions. They had likewise ornamented the donkeys and sacks of salt with fir branches and themselves slept with a fir branch clutched tightly in one hand. The Siccanian forest had a frightening reputation although the Siccani had not within the memory of man killed any merchant who ventured into their territory under the protection of a fir branch.

When dawn broke I could hardly contain my impatience, for beside the Tyrrhenian merchant I saw a strange man sleeping under a beautifully loomed woolen mantle. His beard was curly and the fragrance of fine oils carried to my nostrils. I could not understand what such a man could be doing in the Siccanian forest with a lowly merchant.

I watched him while the day grew lighter and the fish began to leap in the calm waters of the river. Finally the stranger turned in his sleep, awakened, and sat upright with a cry of terror. Seeing the Siccanians with their striped faces sitting silently by the fire he screamed again and reached for the weapon beside him.

The merchant awakened instantly and reassured the man, while the Siccanians rose and disappeared silently into the forest as though the earth had swallowed them, leaving me to bargain with the merchant as was their custom. Nevertheless, I knew that they saw and heard all I did even though we could not see them. Their habit of painting stripes on their faces enabled them to remain invisible, for at first sight one would believe an immobile Siccanian to be but the shadows of reeds or bushes.

When the stranger arose, rubbing the sleep from his eyes, I noticed that he was wearing loose trousers. I knew then that he had come far and that he served the Persian king. He was still young, his skin was white, and he soon donned a broad-brimmed straw hat to shield his face from the heat of the sun.

He asked in amazement, "Was I dreaming, or did I really see trees walking away from the campfire? At least I saw a strange god in my dream and was so alarmed that I awakened to my own cry."

In his bewilderment he spoke Greek, which the Etruscan did not understand. Not wishing to reveal that I was not a Siccanian, I replied to him in Greek mixed with Elymian and Siccanian words.

"How far have you come, stranger?" I asked. "Your clothes are odd. What are you doing in our forest? You are certainly not a merchant. Are you a priest or a seer, or are you fulfilling a vow?"

"I am fulfilling a vow," he replied quickly, happy that I spoke comprehensible Greek. The Etruscan understood little of what the man said, although he had permitted the other to accompany him for payment, as I learned. I pretended to lose interest in the stranger and began to talk to the merchant, tasting his salt and looking at his cloth. With a wink he indicated that he had concealed iron objects in the sacks of salt. He had presumably bribed the customs man of Panormos, for the Carthaginian tax collectors were not much concerned with the Elymian ban against selling iron to the Siccani.

With the Tyrrhenian I spoke the jargon of the sea, which contained Greek, Phoenician and Etruscan words. Because of this he believed me to be a Siccanian who as a boy had been caught and sold as a galley slave and who had returned to the forest at the first opportunity. Finally I asked him about the stranger.

He shook his head scornfully. "He is just a mad Greek who is wandering from east to west to familiarize himself with the different countries and peoples. He is buying useless objects, and I think he is interested in Siccanian flint knives and wooden bowls. Sell him whatever trash you wish so long as you pay me my commission. He doesn't know how to bargain and it's no sin to deceive him. After all, he is a pampered man who doesn't know how to dispose of his money."

The stranger watched us suspiciously and when he caught my eye explained hastily, "I am not a lowborn man. You will benefit more by listening to me than by robbing me." Tempting me as one would a barbarian, he jingled his money pouch.

I kissed my hand, not from respect toward him but in gratitude to the goddess who as Hecate had not deserted me. But I shook my head and replied, "We Siccanians do not use money."

He spread his hands. "Then choose what you will from among the merchant's goods and I will pay him. He understands the value of money."

"I cannot accept gifts before I know what is going on," I said gloomily. "I suspect you because of the garments you wear. I have never seen any like them before."

"I am a servant of the Persian king," he explained. "That is why I wear these garments which are called trousers. I come from Susa, which is his city, and I sailed from Ionia as the companion of Messina's former tyrant, Skythes. But the people of Messina apparently do not want Skythes, preferring to obey Anaxilaos of Rhegion instead. So I am wandering around Sicily for my own pleasure and to increase my knowledge of the various peoples."

I said nothing. He looked at me intently, then shook his head and asked mournfully, "Do you understand at all what I am saying?"

"I understand more than you think," I replied. "After all, Skythes dug the pit for himself by inviting settlers from Samos to found a new colony. But what does the Great King hope to benefit from Skythes?"

He was elated to discover that I knew something of politics. "My name is Xenodotos," he explained. "I am an Ionian and a pupil of the famous historian Hecataeus, but I became a slave of the King during the war."

At my look of loathing he hastened to say, "Don't misunderstand me. I am a slave in name only. If Skythes had regained Messina, I would have become his adviser. Skythes fled to Susa because the King is the friend of all exiles. He is also a friend of knowledge, and his Crotonian physician has awakened his interest in the Greek cities of Italy and Sicily. But the King is interested in all other peoples as well, even in those of whom he has not yet heard, and is ready to send gifts to their leaders and to know more of them."

He looked at me closely, stroked his curly beard and continued, "In enlarging his knowledge of the world's peoples, the King is enlarging the whole sphere of knowledge and thus serves humanity. Among his treasures is a copy of Hecataeus' map of the world etched in bronze, but in his thirst for knowledge he wants to know even the shore lines, the course of the rivers, the forests and mountains of the various countries. Nothing is too insignificant for him to learn, since the gods have destined him to be the father of all peoples."

"He treated the Ionian cities in a paternal manner indeed," I observed sarcastically. "Especially Miletus, the most gifted of his children."

Xenodotos demanded suspiciously, "How have you learned to speak Greek, you Siccanian with the painted face? What do you know about Ionia?"

I thought it best to boast. "I even know how to read and write and have sailed to many lands. Why and how it happened is no concern of yours, stranger, but I know more than you think."

He became even more interested. "If that is so, and you really know and understand matters, you surely realize that even a lenient father is compelled to chastise his obstinate children. So much for Miletus. But to his friends the King is a most generous master, wise and just."

"You are forgetting the envy of the gods, Xenodotos," I said.

"We are living in new times," he replied. "Let us leave the tales about the gods to the babblers. The sages of Ionia know better. The only god served by the King is fire. Everything has its origin in fire and ultimately returns to it. But of course the King respects the deities of the peoples he rules and sends gifts to their temples."

"Doesn't one of the Ionian sages teach that everything consists only of movement and currents and the tremor of fire?" I asked. "Herakleitos of Ephesus, if I remember correctly. Or do you think he borrowed his doctrine from the Persian?"

Xenodotos looked at me with respect and admitted, "You are a learned man. I would gladly have met Herakleitos in Ephesus, but he is said to have become embittered toward the world and to have withdrawn to the mountains to eat herbs. The King had a letter written in which he asked for the details of the doctrine, but Herakleitos rejected the letter. In fact, he stoned the messenger and refused to accept the gifts that had been left for him. The King, however, did not take offense but said that the older he becomes and the better he learns to know people, the more he himself feels like bleating and eating grass."

I laughed. "Your story is the best I have yet heard about the Great King. Perhaps I would want to be his friend had I myself not withdrawn to the forest and donned pelts."

Xenodotos stroked his beard again and intimated, "We understand each other. Conclude your trade with the Etruscan and thereafter I want to enjoy your hospitality, see your home, become acquainted with the Siccanian chiefs, and talk more with you."

I shook my head. "If you succeed in laying a hand on the sooty stone of a Siccanian's hearth, you will enjoy his hospitality and that of his tribe to the end of your days. You see, the Siccani will not show themselves to strangers except in battle, and even then their chiefs wear wooden masks and the warriors paint their faces until they are unrecognizable."

"Are they skilled warriors? What weapons do they use? And how many tribes and families are there?" he asked quickly.

Knowing that the Siccanians were watching me, I kicked at the sacks of salt brought by the Etruscan and pretended to inspect the cloth as I replied, "They are useless on the plains, and the sight of a horse or dog fills them with panic. But in their own forests they are incomparable warriors. They make arrowheads of flint and temper the metal tips of their wooden spears in fire. Iron is their most precious metal and they know how to forge it if they can only obtain it."

To indicate what I meant, I opened a sack of salt and dug out an Etruscan knife and axe blade. When I held them up the entire forest seemed to stir. Xenodotos looked around in amazement, while the Etruscan boxed the ears of his servants and ordered them to hide their faces in the ground. Thereafter he willingly opened the sacks of salt and produced the iron objects that he had smuggled. We sat on the ground to bargain over them.

Soon Xenodotos grew impatient, jingled his pouch and asked, "How much do they cost? I will buy them and give them to the Siccanians so that we may proceed to our matter."

His stupidity displeased me. Accepting the pouch I said, "Take a walk along the river and watch the flight of the birds with the merchant. Take the servants with you. When you return at midday you will know more about the Siccani."

He became angry and called me a thief until the Etruscan seized him by the arm and pulled him away. When they had disappeared from sight the Siccanians appeared from the forest, accompanied by members of other tribes, also with their wares. When they saw the iron objects they flung their burdens to the ground and ran back for more. Those who had accompanied me began to dance the Siccanian sun dance in sheer joy.

By midday more than a hundred men had passed by the campfire to leave their wares, to which they had added game, wild ducks, a deer and fresh fish. But still no one touched the merchant's goods for fear that the Siccanian wares did not suffice as payment. It was the merchant's responsibility to separate the amount he deemed sufficient to pay for his goods.

To prove my honesty I also showed my tribal brothers the Persian gold coins in Xenodotos' pouch, but they were not interested. They stared greedily only at the iron objects. I myself chose a razor shaped like a half moon since I needed one for transforming my appearance. It was of the finest Etruscan iron and effortlessly cut even a heavy beard without wounding the skin.

Upon his return Xenodotos saw the trampled area and the heaps of goods around the campfire. Now he believed me when I said that I could call forth a hundred or even a thousand Siccanians from the forest if need be. I explained that no one knew the total number of Siccanians, not even they themselves, but if it became a question of defending the forest against a conqueror, every tree would change into a Siccanian.

"The Siccani retreat only from the path of cultivated land, villages and cities," I explained. "They will not begin a war of their own volition even against the Elymi. If they raid the Siculian and Elymian settlements in small groups, they are content to steal only a few goats and do not willingly kill anyone. But if the Segestan soldiers push their way into the forest with their dogs, the Siccani kill everyone they meet and in the most brutal manner."

When he had had time to ponder on my words I returned his pouch and said, "I have counted your money and you have eighty-three gold coins of Darius as well as silver coins of various Greek cities. Apparently you don't care to carry copper, so that even as a slave you are a noble. But keep your money. You cannot buy me for such a small sum. You may have my knowledge as a gift since it will probably rebound to the advantage of the Siccani. They would only make jewelry of the coins for their women and would value them no more than a shining feather or a colored stone."

Innate Ionian greed struggled for a moment with the generosity that he had learned at the court of the Persian king. Then he overcame himself, extended the pouch once more to me and said, "Keep the money as a memento of me and a gift from the Great King."

I told him that I accepted the money only in accordance with civilized custom, to spare him a refusal. However, I asked him to hold the pouch for me temporarily so that it would not be necessary for me to share its contents with the members of my tribe. Then I accepted some of the iron objects and a quantity of salt and colored cloth for the tribe but permitted the merchant to retain some of his supplies for the other tribes. My own tribe would have been suspicious had I received a better price than usual for their goods.

The Etruscan stored the wares that he had received under bark, and marked the place clearly, knowing that no Siccanian would touch it. Then he had his servants cook the game that the Siccanians had brought in an iron pot, salted it heavily, sacrificed some to his god Turnus, and spread the remainder on sprigs of fir. By then it was evening and he again took Xenodotos and the servants on a walk along the river. This time, however, they went armed, for at dusk the peaceful animals of the forest came to the river to drink and wild beasts lay in ambush. Like any civilized person Xenodotos greatly feared the darkening forest and jumped at every noise, but the merchant promised to shield him from the evil spirits of the Siccani. As evidence he showed the amulets that he wore around his neck and on his wrists, the most important of which was a bronze sea horse, green with mildew.

The sight of it made me tremble, but when the men had departed I signaled the Siccanians. They appeared silently, gulped down the salty food and peacefully shared the goods according to the needs of each. The priest of the tribe had come to view the strangers from curiosity but chose nothing for himself, since he knew that he could always obtain whatever he needed and did not wish to burden himself unnecessarily.

I said to him, "The stranger accompanying the merchant comes from the east beyond the sea and has good intentions toward the Siccani. He is my friend and inviolable. Protect him on his journey through the forests. He is a clever man among his own kind but in the forest a

214

snake may bite his buttock if he steps from the path to take care of his needs."

"Your blood is our blood," conceded the priest, and I knew that unseen eyes would watch over Xenodotos and that the youths of the tribe would protect him from all danger as he accompanied the merchant on his round.

The Siccanians picked up their goods and disappeared as silently as they had come while I remained by the glowing embers of the fire. The forest darkened, the night cooled and the fish made glimmering circles in the river. I heard the cooing of wood doves ceaselessly until finally a whole flock fluttered into flight just above me so that I felt the breath of air from their wings.

That was the final sign. Sated and content, I knew that all was well. Artemis as Hecate had fulfilled her promise and Aphrodite jealously wished to indicate that she had not abandoned me either.

I remembered my guardian spirit's winged body of fire, and at that moment it seemed as though she were within arm's reach. My heart glowed and I extended my arms to embrace her. Then, on the border between slumber and wakefulness, I felt the touch of slender fingertips on my bare shoulder and knew that she also had given me her sign although she could not appear because I was unprepared. Never have I experienced anything more glorious than the touch of my guardian spirit's fingertips on my shoulder. It was like the flick of a flame.

4.

When I heard the approaching steps of the Tyrrhenian and his companions I stirred the fire and added some of the wood that the Siccanians had brought, for the cooing of doves augured a cold night. Despite their woolen mantles Xenodotos and the merchant shivered with cold and hastened to the fire to chafe their limbs.

"Whence do you come and where do you obtain your salt?" I asked the Etruscan, to pass the time while waiting for Xenodotos to open our conversation. I did not wish to appear too anxious.

The Etruscan shrugged his shoulders and replied, "I come from the north beyond the sea and will return with the south wind directly home so that I will not have to follow the shores of Italy and pay taxes to the Greek cities. The Greeks make their own salt in Sicily but mine is cheaper."

From my purse I took the sea horse of black carved stone which Lars Alsir had sent to me upon our departure from Himera. I showed it to him and asked, "Do you recognize this?"

215

He whistled as though calling for the wind, raised his right hand, touched his forehead with the left and demanded, "How have you, a Siccanian, obtained such a sacred object?" He asked to hold it, stroked its worn surface and finally asked to buy it from me.

"No," I said. "You know well that such objects are not sold. In the name of the black sea horse I ask you to tell me exactly whence you come and where you obtain your salt."

"Do you intend to compete with me?" he asked. But the very thought made him laugh. No one had ever heard of Siccanians sailing the seas. Their boats were tree trunks hollowed by fire or reed rafts with which they crossed rivers.

"I get my salt from the mouth of one of the great rivers of my homeland," he told me. "We Etruscans have two large rivers of which this is the southerly one. The salt is dried on the shores of the sea, but higher up the river is the city of Rome which we founded. The salt road leading across the Etruscan country begins there."

"Up the river, you said." My curiosity was whetted and I remembered the willow leaf which had fallen before me onto the surface of the spring.

The Tyrrhenian's face darkened. "Yes, that city was ours and we built a bridge across the river. Several decades ago the mixed peoples populating the city banished the last Etruscan king who was of the cultured house of the Tarquins. Now the notorious and the criminal seek refuge in Rome. Its customs are crude, its laws severe, and all that they know about deities is what they learned under our kings."

"Why don't you retake it from the usurpers?" I asked.

He shook his head. "You don't understand our customs. Among us each city rules itself as it wishes. We have kings, tyrants and democracies like the Greeks. Only the inland cities are still ruled by Lucumones, and Tarquinius of Rome was not a holy Lucumo. Each autumn the leaders of our twelve cities gather on the shores of our sacred lake, and it was at such a meeting that the banished Tarquinius spoke on his own behalf and lots were drawn for Rome. When no one accepted the lot, the famous inland ruler Lars Porsenna finally took it. He conquered Rome but relinquished it because of the conspiracies against his life by the youths of the city."

"You have no love for Rome," I observed.

"I am a wandering salt merchant who obtains his salt from the merchants of Rome," he replied. "A trader does not love or hate anything so long as he makes a profit. However, the Romans are not people of the sea horse, but people of the wolf."

The hairs of my neck stood on end as I remembered the sign I had received. "What do you mean by 'people of the wolf'?"

"According to their tale the city was founded by twin brothers whose mother was the virgin of the sacred flame in a city farther up the river. The girl claimed that the god of war had made her pregnant. The city's Lucumo had the newborn placed in a willow basket which was tossed into the flooding river. The basket floated to the foot of a hill where a she-wolf found the babies, took them to a cave and there suckled them with its own cubs. If that is true, some god may well have made the girl pregnant and thus have protected his heirs. But it is more probable that their father was of alien blood, for when the boys were grown, one murdered the other and he in turn was murdered by the people of the city they had founded. The Etruscans then took over the government and brought order to Rome. But no Lucumo was willing to rule so violent a city, hence its rulers were merely kings under the Tarquinian Lucumo."

Although the Tyrrhenian's tale was alarming I did not hesitate, for the signs were too clear to be misunderstood. The willow leaf meant a river, the wolf cub Rome, and the birds had flown northward with loud honkings. There I must flee with my family, nor would I have anything to fear in a city which, after banishing its king, welcomed even criminals and outlaws.

Xenodotos had been listening to our conversation impatiently and asked finally, "What are you talking about so busily, or have you already tired of conversing with me, you civilized Siccanian?"

"The merchant is telling me about his home town, although the Etruscans usually are not garrulous," I replied. "But let us speak Greek again if you wish."

The merchant said irritably, "I would certainly not have become talkative if you had not shown me the sacred sea horse. It is the work of the ancients and more valuable than my own bronze emblem." Then regretting his candor, he went to rest and covered his head with his cloak. The servants also settled down to sleep.

When Xenodotos and I were alone I said to him, "I have a wife and two children, but because of the signs and omens that I have received I am compelled to leave the forest of the Siccani."

"Come with me when I sail with Skythes back to Ionia and from there to Susa," he suggested. "The Great King will give you a place among his escorts as the Siccanian chief. Perhaps when you have learned the Persian language and customs the King may even make you the king of the Siccani."

I shook my head. "My signs indicate the north and not the east. But if you will take me under your protection until I can sail from Sicily I will teach you all that I know about the Siccani and the land of Eryx, and that is not little."

He protested and called me mad for not seizing an opportunity the like of which came but once in a lifetime to my kind.

I remained firm, however, and said, "As an Ionian you were born a scoffer and knowledge has deepened your skepticism. But even a skeptic must believe omens, if only in the same manner as Darius' competitors when his horses were the first to whinny."

We laughed together, but soon Xenodotos glanced toward the black forest, covered his mouth with his hand and said, "Still, I don't reject heavenly or subterranean spirits. I know well that there are wanton shades which can chill a person's blood."

We talked of many other matters as well, while he cared for his beard, oiled his face and braided his hair for the night. He regretted not being able to serve wine because of the difficulties of transportation.

"But your friendship is more intoxicating to me than wine," he said courteously. "You are a powerful man. I admire your strong muscles and your beautifully browned skin." He began to caress my shoulders and cheeks with soft hands and insisted that I kiss him as a token of our friendship. Although he was a charming man and smelled sweet, I did not comply for I knew well what he wanted.

When he had returned to his senses we agreed that he would follow the Etruscan to the other trading places in order to see as much as possible of the Siccanian territory and to mark on a map the rivers, springs, trading posts and mountains to the extent that it was possible in the bewildering forest. I said I would meet him at that same spot with my family when the merchant's goods had been exhausted. Xenodotos wondered why I did not determine the day and moment of our meeting in advance. It was difficult for me to convince him that I would know of his coming anyway.

As I approached our home cave through the thickets, I heard the children's merry voices, for Hiuls and Misme did not know how to play silently like the Siccanian children. In the Siccanian manner I entered without a greeting, seated myself on the ground and touched the warm hearthstones. The children hastened to clamber onto my shoulders and from the corner of my eye I noticed the dumb joy in Hanna's dark face. But Arsinoe was angry, slapped the children and demanded to know where I had again been without leaving word of myself.

"I must talk to you, Turms," she said and sent the children into the forest with Hanna.

I tried to embrace her but she thrust me away. "Turms, my patience is at an end. I can bear no more. Doesn't the sight of your children growing into barbarians without proper companions make you suffer? Soon it will be time for Hiuls to receive instruction from an able teacher in some civilized city. I don't care where we go so long as I can breathe city air, walk on paved streets, visit the shops and bathe in warm water. You have made me so poor, Turms, that I don't demand much of you. But this much at least you owe me, and think also of the children's good."

She talked so fast that I had no chance to speak, and when I tried to put my arms around her she again pushed me away.

"Yes, that's all you want of me and it makes no difference whether I am lying on coarse moss or on a triple mattress. But I have listened to your excuses long enough, and you will not touch me until you have promised to take us away from here. Otherwise I will leave with the first merchant who comes along and take the children with me. I think I am still enough of a woman to be able to entice a man although you have done your best to destroy my beauty and health."

She paused for breath. I stared at her through new eyes and felt no desire to embrace her. Hatred had made her face hard as a rock, her voice was shrill and the strands of her black hair wriggled on her shoulders like snakes. An evil spell caught me in its grip as though I were staring at the face of Gorgon. I rubbed my eyes.

Thinking that I was searching for new excuses to remain with the Siccani, she stamped her foot and raged, "Cowardice makes you hide behind the trees and be content with a worthless life. If I had believed Dorieus I would be the queen of Segesta and the personification of the goddess for the entire land of Eryx. I don't understand how I could ever have loved you and I don't regret that I have had my own joys of which you are unaware."

Realizing that she had said too much she corrected herself smoothly. "I mean that I have met the goddess and that she enters my body as before. Now that the goddess has forgiven me I no longer have any reason to avoid people."

It was her turn to evade my glance. She softened, seized my arms and said, "Turms, remember that you can thank only me for your life when Dorieus planned to kill you."

Having learned to lie to Arsinoe, it was easy to conceal my thoughts from her, although there was a roaring in my ears and comprehension came to me in a sudden flash as though a layer of dark clouds had been rent.

Controlling myself, I said to her, "If the goddess actually has appeared to you that is a sufficient sign. We shall leave within a few days, for I have already arranged everything. But the pleasure of my surprise is spoiled by your cruel words."

At first she did not believe me, but when I told her about the Etruscan and Xenodotos she burst into tears of joy, came to me tenderly and would have embraced me in gratitude. For the first time she had to coax me before I consented to take her in my arms. When I had relented I jestingly told her about Xenodotos' attempt to seduce me.

Arsinoe stared past me with eyes like dark pools and said, "He is much mistaken in believing that he can find greater joy in a man than in a woman. If you were not so ridiculously jealous, Turms, I could prove that to him with the aid of the goddess."

She proved it to me in such an agonizingly rapturous manner that my joy was closer to torment than ever before, and I knew that I loved her no matter what she had done just because she was what she was and could be nothing else. Throwing her arms violently over her head, she breathed hotly into my mouth, stared at me through narrowed eyes and whispered, "Turms, Turms, in love-making you are like a god and there is no more wonderful man than you!"

She raised herself lazily onto her elbow and began to caress my neck. "If I understood you correctly, that Xenodotos would take you safely to the court of the Persian king. We would see the big cities of the world and you would receive royal gifts in the name of the Siccani. I'm sure that I could win many friends for you among the eyes and ears of the King. Why then have you chosen barbaric Rome of which you know nothing?"

"Only a moment ago you said that you would be content with any city if only I took you away from here. Your appetite seems to grow as you eat, Arsinoe."

She wound her arms around me, widened her eyes and breathed, "Yes, Turms, my appetite grows as you well know, or have you already tired of me?"

I did not resist although I realized with painful clarity that she tempted me only to bend me to her will. When she again began to talk of Susa and Persepolis I rose to stretch my limbs and went to the entrance of the cave.

"Hiuls!" I called. "Hiuls!"

The boy crawled to me like a Siccanian, rose upright against my knee

220

and looked at me admiringly. In the bright sunlight I studied the muscular limbs of the five-year-old, his morose lower lip, his brows and eyes. Nor did I have to see the birthmark of the Heraklidae on his thigh to know that it had not been etched there after birth. Dorieus' melancholy eyes looked at me out of his eyes, and in his chin, mouth and brows I saw Dorieus' merciless face.

I did not hate the boy because of it, for how could I have hated a child? Nor did I hate Arsinoe, because she was what she was and could not help it. I hated only my own stupidity for not realizing the truth earlier. Even Tanakil had been shrewder than I and the Siccanians in their secret wisdom had immediately named the boy Erkle when they met him by the sacred rock. But love blinds a person even to what may be as clear as day. I wondered whether my love for Arsinoe was beginning to fade despite my bittersweet enjoyment of her, or whether I had merely outgrown the period of blindness.

I was quite calm as I entered the cave with the boy. I sat down beside Arsinoe and when she again began to chatter about the glories of Susa and the King's favors, I drew the boy to me.

Holding him between my knees and patting his coarse hair I said with assumed indifference, "So Hiuls is Dorieus' son. That is why Dorieus wanted to kill me, to obtain you and him."

Arsinoe continued her own thoughts and had time to say that Susa would be best even for the boy before she comprehended my words. She sat up in alarm, covering her mouth.

I gave a short laugh. "That is why it was so easy for you to swear by our son. I should have believed your hair instead of your lying tongue."

Arsinoe was amazed by my lack of anger. What would I have gained by poisoning myself with hatred when it would have been to no avail?

She pulled the boy into her lap protectively. "Why are you always so cruel, Turms? You always begin to pry into old matters during our moments of happiness. Of course Hiuls is Dorieus' son although I myself wasn't quite sure of it until I saw Dorieus' birthmark on his thigh. I was terribly afraid that you would be angry. I would have told you earlier but I was sure that you would notice it yourself in time. As a woman I am sometimes compelled to lie to you because of your hot temper."

I wondered which of us really was quicker to anger but said nothing. Taking out my worn knife I gave it to the boy.

"You may have a knife because even as a boy you must be a man and worthy of your birth. I have taught you all that you can comprehend at this age and will leave you my own shield and sword since I once tossed

221

your father's shield into the sea as an offering in a moment of danger. Always remember that the blood of Herakles and the goddess of Eryx flows in your veins and that you are therefore of divine birth. I don't doubt that after our departure the Siccanians will ask the Pythagorean to educate you to your prospective rank, for I'm sure they expect much of you."

Arsinoe began to shriek. "Are you out of your mind? Do you intend to leave your only son among barbarians?"

She tore at my hair and hammered at my back with her fists as I went to a corner of the cave and from under a stone slab pulled forth the shield that I had hidden there. The boy was at first alarmed by her screams but soon began to play with the metallic shield and sword. One had only to see him clutch the sword hilt in his tiny fist to realize that he was Dorieus' son.

Realizing that nothing could shake me, Arsinoe sank onto the ground and began to weep bitterly. Her tears were not false, for she loved the boy more intensely than a she-wolf its cub. Touched by her sorrow, I sat beside her and began quietly to caress her black hair.

"Arsinoe, I am not leaving the boy here because of hatred or a desire for revenge. If I could, I would gladly take him with us for the sake of the friendship that bound Dorieus and me. I don't bear a grudge against Dorieus because you are as you are and he could do nothing. What man could resist you?"

Vanity prompted her to listen to me. "This is Hiul's place," I said, "because he is the son of Dorieus and thus the heir to the land of Eryx. The Siccanians have always called him Erkle and have smiled every time they have looked at him. Indeed I don't think they would permit us to take the boy away but would rather kill us. Nothing, however, hinders you from remaining with your son if you wish."

"No, no," she said hastily. "I wouldn't remain in the forest at any price."

To assuage her sorrow I talked to her encouragingly. "I will mention Hiuls to Xenodotos. Through him the Persians will learn that a future king, a descendant of Herakles, is growing up in the Siccanian forest. Perhaps your son will some day rule not only the forest and the land of Eryx but all Sicily under the protection of the Persian king. I shall see to that, for the Great King will soon rule the entire known world, perhaps during our lifetime."

Arsinoe's eyes began to gleam at the thought and she clapped her hands. "Your plan is wiser than Dorieus'. He came to Segesta as a stranger and no one there loved him except Tanakil."

"Now that we are in agreement thus far," I said with a heavy heart, "let us talk also about Misme. I remember how sarcastically you smiled when I gave her that name. Was it because of the fact that Misme and Mikon are a bit alike? Something already then must have told me the truth and made me give the girl a name that is suggestive of Mikon."

Arsinoe pretended amazement but I seized her wrists, shook her and declared, "The time for lies is past. Misme is Mikon's daughter. You slept with him on the journey from Eryx to Himera and it was because of you that he began to drink. You played with him as a cat plays with a mouse, to feel your power, and finally became pregnant by him. That was too much for him. He drank the Siccanians' poisonous potion and drowned himself in the swamp because he could no longer meet my eyes. That is the truth, isn't it? Or shall I call Misme and show you Mikon's round cheeks and full mouth?"

Arsinoe beat her knees with her fists and shouted angrily, "At least she has my eyes! The goddess was spiteful to let the poor girl inherit Mikon's short stature, but perhaps her limbs will yet straighten. Let it be as you wish, Turms, but it is all your fault for leaving me alone for days at a time. Poor Mikon loved me so bitterly that I could not help pitying him now and then, although I certainly didn't intend to become pregnant. Even that is your fault for taking me away from Segesta so quickly that my silver ring remained behind."

Noticing my calmness, she began to chatter in relief. "Mikon boasted so often of his experiences on the golden ship of Astarte that I was tempted to show him what else a man can experience in a woman's arms. He believed himself irresistible because Aura lost consciousness at his touch, but that was just her weakness. He could not compete with you in that respect, Turms, although he had his pleasing features."

"I don't doubt that!" I shouted, finally losing my temper. "I understand and forgive everything, but what is wrong with me? Am I sterile or does someone else always manage to dabble in the spring at full moon ahead of me?"

Arsinoe thought for a moment. "I think you really must be sterile but don't let it trouble you. A man who is given to meditation doesn't need children and in our times many a man might envy you for having everything without assuming responsibility for the consequences. Perhaps it resulted from the thunderbolt of which you have told me, or perhaps you were ill as a child. Or it might be a gift of the goddess, since she has always favored pleasure and only with reluctance has submitted to its consequences."

I would not have believed it possible that I could discuss such difficult matters with Arsinoe so understandingly and without the desire for revenge. It proved how much I had grown during my years with the Siccani without even realizing it. For once a dish is broken, anger is of no use. Instead, it is best to collect the pieces and make of them what one can.

But when I had confirmed the fact that Misme was not my child either, I felt myself naked and so cold that nothing could warm me. As a man I had to provide my own purpose in life, and probably nothing is more difficult. It is easier to beget children and to thrust the responsibility on them while washing one's own hands.

I felt myself so naked that I retired to the solitude of the mountain for a few days. I did so not to see signs and omens but merely to listen to myself. Doubt swept over me and I no longer believed in my power to summon the wind. Everything was but blind chance. It was for Dorieus that the earth had trembled and the mountain spat fire when we had approached the Sicilian shore. Again it had rumbled at the moment of his death. He had even begotten a son. I alone was vagrant without knowing whence I had come or where I was going or why. I was sterile as a stone and my love brought suffering rather than joy.

5.

Upon my return from the mountain I collected a few Siccanian objects such as a bow and some flint-tipped arrows, a painted drum, some cloth made of tree bark, a wooden spear, snares and bone hooks, a wooden whistle for luring animals and a necklace of wild animals' teeth, which I intended to send with Xenodotos to the Great King as a gift. No one forbade me to take anything since the Siccani do not take from one another unless in need.

The half moon shone in the sky during the day as though Artemis herself were benignly following my activities. When the sun was still up the Siccanians became restless and at dusk I took Hiuls by the hand and led him to the sacred rock. Like the Siccani I had become sensitive to events and no longer had to be invited.

Twelve old men, all wearing fearful wooden masks, were awaiting us by the sacred rock. I recognized them by their animal tails as priests, chiefs and holy men of the various tribes. They did not speak to me but upon our arrival they anointed the rock, lifted Hiuls atop it and gave him sweet berries to eat to pass the time.

They indicated that I was to take off my clothes. When I had done so they garbed me in a deerskin and covered my face with an antlered mask that was skillfully carved and painted. Thereafter everyone in turn, according to rank, drank a drop of the sacred potion from the wooden cup. I was last. Then they formed a line and began walking around the rock. I joined the end of the line. The beat of drums and the pipe of wooden whistles began to sound in the forest. Our walking changed to leaping and as the potion made itself felt the dance grew wild, with each of us emitting his animal cry. Hiuls was greatly amused by it, and whenever one of us imitated the cry of the animal whose tail he bore, Hiuls hooted like an owl. The Siccanians considered that a good omen.

The dance grew increasingly violent, the earth thinned into a veil around me and my blood throbbed in time to the drumbeat. Suddenly, to my amazement, I saw that animals were appearing from the forest, pushing through our circle to the rock and again fleeing. A wild boar crashed from the thicket with slavering tusks but no one attacked it and it thrust its way back into the woods. The last to appear was a gentle doe which paused by the rock to sniff at Hiuls with upstretched neck and then bounded back.

I cannot explain how the Siccanians accomplished this. There were many of them in the forest, as the sound of the drums and the whistles indicated. Perhaps they had smeared the rock with tempting smells or had captured the animals for the purpose of releasing them during the dance. But the animals might have been merely shades conjured up by the Siccanians and made visible by the sacred potion. If that was so, I cannot explain how Hiuls could see them and afterwards describe every animal.

With the disappearance of the animals the dance ended and the Siccanians lighted a fire. Then they lifted Hiuls down from the rock and placed around his neck a necklace made of wild animals' teeth and tied colored strips of hide around his ankles and wrists. Each slashed a wound into his own arm with a stone knife and let Hiuls suck it. They indicated that I also should slash my arm and let Hiuls taste my blood. When this had been done, the Siccanians burst into joyous laughter and sprinkled their blood over Hiuls until the boy was covered with it from head to toe.

Suddenly each seized a branch from the fire and disappeared into the forest. The priest of my tribe and I each took his burning branch and between us led Hiuls from the sacred rock. When the pine branches had burned out we tossed them away. The priest took off his mask and carried it in his hand. I also took off the deer mask that I had worn. We brought Hiuls home and put him to bed, but the priest forbade us to wash him until all the blood had worn off his skin.

I thought that that was the end of the matter but early the next day, before dawn, the priest came for me. He took me back to the sacred rock and laughingly showed me the marks of animals' hoofs and nails on the ground, touched the rock and said that during the night the animals had licked the rock clean so that a stranger could no longer distinguish it from other rocks.

When we had crouched on the ground I said to the priest, "I am leaving the Siccani, for the time prescribed for me to rest with you has ended. Hiuls will remain with you, but his mother, Misme, and our slave Hanna will accompany me."

The priest smiled, pointed northward and waved his hand as though in farewell. "I know that," he said. "We were afraid that you would take the boy with you. Our tradition has predicted his arrival for as long as we can remember."

Leaning on one elbow, he began drawing on the ground with a stick. "I am an old man," he said. "With these eyes I have seen much happen. Fields are now being plowed with teams of oxen where formerly my father hunted wild animals. There are Siccanians who have built huts on the edge of the forest and grow peas. During my lifetime the Greeks have spread further than the Elymi ever have. They breed like vermin and have constrained the Siculi to cultivate land and build cities. He who builds a hut is the slave of his hut. He who cultivates land is the slave of his land. Only Erkle can now save us Siccanians but how it will happen we do not know."

He covered his mouth with his hand, laughed, and continued, "I am only a foolish man and soon, when my knees fail me and my knowledge no longer serves my tribe, it will be time for me to go into the swamp. That is why I am talking so much, for I am very pleased. If you had tried to take the boy with you we would have had to kill you. But you brought Erkle to us and are leaving him here. That is why we consecrated you a deer and why you may have whatever you wish upon your departure."

I took advantage of the situation to ask for a hornful of the sacred potion and a few of the poisoned thorns that the Siccani scattered on the ground when the Segestan nobles and their dogs were in pursuit.

He smiled again and said, "You may have what you wish. The Siccani no longer have any secrets from you except for certain holy words which you will not need. Don't you really want anything else?"

I remembered the glitter of gold and silver that I had seen under the sacred rock while in a trance and realized that unwittingly they had consecrated me in the sign of Artemis' sacred deer. The goddess had appeared to me as Hecate and all this was part of her game in which the Siccani were merely instruments of her will.

I pointed to the sacred rock and said, "You have your secret treasure of gold and silver under the rock."

The priest stopped laughing. "How can you know that?" he demanded. "Knowledge of it passes among the priests as a heritage from father to son and the treasure has not been touched in generations."

Probably the Siccanian leaders would have given me some of the treasure even if I had not asked for it since I had brought them their Erkle. The treasure, however, was not under the sacred rock as I had erroneously believed. On the contrary, the priest took me half a day's journey away to a dangerous oak forest full of Siccanian snares and poisoned thorns. There he showed me a cave so well concealed that a stranger could not have found it. Together we cleared away the stones and earth until we found a hollow covered with bark and in it a wealth of silver and gold dishes and amulets. The priest was unable to explain how the Siccani originally had obtained the treasure but he believed it to be war booty from the time when the Siccani had ruled all Sicily.

The objects had apparently been collected at various times for some were of finer, some of clumsier workmanship. The most valuable was a golden bull's-head which weighed a talent. The priest urged me to choose what I wished and as I did so he watched keenly to see whether greed overcame me. In that case he might have killed me, for he held a spear in his hand throughout. The disclosure of the treasure was presumably the final test to determine whether I was worthy of their confidence and whether they could permit me to leave in peace.

I selected only a simple golden goblet which weighed perhaps fifteen minas, a small golden hand which weighed less than one mina, but which pleased me as an amulet, and in addition a spiral bracelet which weighed perhaps four minas and which I intended for Arsinoe. I took only gold objects since they were easiest to carry and conceal, and because gold had become more valuable than silver now that most of the Greek cities had begun to mint silver money. More than that I did not take. Because the goddess had proved that she kept her promise as Hecate I knew that I would obtain material wealth whenever I needed it.

The Siccanian priest released his hold on the spear and together we returned the treasure to its place of concealment. As we departed along the path indicated by the priest I made no attempt to mark the trees or to memorize the mountain peaks or the direction. This pleased him, and when we were once again in the safe forest he began to jump for joy.

Knowing that he trusted me, I asked him to send for the wandering Pythagorean or some other Greek teacher to undertake the education of Hiuls after our departure. I impressed upon him the fact that Hiuls must learn to read and write, to count, and to draw figures and measure them. In addition to the Siccanian and Greek languages, he must learn to speak Phoenician and Elymian, the better to fulfill his task as the best of the Siccani. The Etruscan language might also prove useful, if he should show a readiness for learning, nor would practice on a stringed instrument hurt him. I was not concerned about his physical development, for life in the forest would see to that. As for the use of weapons, Hiuls' own heritage would be the best teacher. Still my heart was filled with sadness at the thought of leaving Hiuls among the Siccani, although I knew that they would cherish and protect him better than I could.

And so I hardened my heart and advised the priest, "Teach him to obey his tribe. Only one who himself has learned to obey can some day command. If you see him killing merely for the sake of killing, kill him with your own hands and renounce Erkle."

Arsinoe was pleased with the bracelet and claimed that it was old Cretan workmanship and that the collectors of antiques in Tyre would pay many times more than its weight in gold. I did not tell her where I had obtained it but said merely that the Siccanians had given it to her in gratitude for her having entrusted the boy to them.

The gift eased Arsinoe's pangs at the moment of parting and Hiuls indicated no desire to follow us. In the Siccanian manner we left without farewell, arranging our departure so that we met Xenodotos and the Etruscan just as they arrived at the merchant's storage place on the bank of the river.

The merchant declared that we were the first Siccanians he had seen appearing as a family before strangers, while Xenodotos rejoiced at the Siccanian objects I had brought with me. After resting that night by the fire, we began our journey toward Panormos.

In my Siccanian guise and after the lapse of so many years I did not fear recognition in Panormos. Nor did I think that Arsinoe, with her dark hair and changed face, would be recognized if she were careful. The Elymi did not attack unarmed Siccanians who arrived in the cultivated areas with a fir branch in their hands, as happened occasionally. I also had faith in the protection of Xenodotos, for it was doubtful whether anyone would wish to offend the Great King's servant who had arrived in Sicily with Skythes.

Our journey progressed slowly because of the successful trading engaged in by the merchant along the way. Thus the journey did not tire Arsinoe, although she had to walk, nor did Hanna feel the burden of carrying Misme.

At night as we lay under the open sky or within some Elymian log hut, I told Xenodotos as much about the Siccani as I thought might benefit them. I also entrusted him with the secret of Hiuls and the fable about Erkle, but swore him to secrecy, asking him to reveal it only to the King himself or to his most trusted advisers in matters pertaining to the West.

"I am not concerned with when and how the Great King utilizes this knowledge," I said, "but it may be beneficial for him to know that the Siccani are rearing Erkle. Nor do I think that the Siccani will survive as a nation save under the protection of the King, for they are oppressed both by the Elymi and the Greeks. The King himself will know best against whom to send the Siccani so that they may redeem the right to live in the forest and to survive as a nation."

Xenodotos declared that I was the most beautiful man he had ever seen and that he liked me even more now that I had bared my chin by shaving.

He brought his nose far too close to me in sniffing the smell of resin and smoke that clung to my skin after my years in the forest. He also assured me that my eyes were like those of a deer. Nor did he say all that merely to be courteous. Day by day he seemed to be increasingly attracted to me and it was with difficulty that I parried his approaches without hurting him too much.

But although I was sure of his friendship I did not reveal my name or identity and warned Arsinoe against placing too much confidence in him. When he had realized the futility of his approaches and saw that I had no intention of accompanying him to Susa, he as an intelligent man began to pay attention to Arsinoe. And because he was not susceptible to Arsinoe's charms as a woman he was able with greater shrewdness to bend her to his will.

I did not suspect his intentions, but I felt only relief that he left me in peace and talked with Arsinoe about the goddess of Eryx, the ancient fountain and the rites. Xenodotos' curiosity was inexhaustible. While they conversed I had the opportunity to talk to the merchant and tried to obtain some information about Rome. But he was an uneducated man interested only in his trade. I did, however, learn that Rome quarreled perpetually with its neighbors and that the rivalry between its rich and poor was so intense that the poor now and then rebelled against military service in order to gain concessions for themselves.

That did not alarm me, for a similar situation prevailed in all other cities. The dance of freedom had been glorious in the days of my defiant youth when I was a stranger and wanted to become the equal of other youths in Ephesus for the sake of Dione. But I had already forgotten Dione's face, and even as the burning reeds had flown through the air in Sardis and left ineffaceable burns on my arms, I had begun to tremble in realization of what I had done. True, I had gained the favor of Artemis, but Ionia's fate had been billowing smoke and the stench of death.

I thought of all that as I crouched by the fire under the autumn stars of Eryx talking to the sullen Etruscan while Xenodotos chatted animatedly with Arsinoe on the other side of the campfire. Misme slept the sound sleep of a three-year-old in her sheepskin and in the glow of the fire I occasionally met Hanna's sparkling glance. Absently I drew designs on the ground with a stick and knew that I lived in a period of tumult until such a time as the Persian king would restore harmony to all lands.

6.

We arrived in Panormos as in a festival procession with the curious thronging about us. We went directly to the harbor, to the Etruscan's ship, and my heart sank when I saw it. It was round and slow and only partly covered with a deck, and I wondered how it had managed to make the long voyage from Rome to Sicily with its heavy cargo.

The customs men installed by Carthage greeted the Etruscan laughingly and politely raised their hands in amazement at the success of his trade. They treated Xenodotos with respect and were content to look from afar at Arsinoe and at my wooden mask without daring to finger our clothes. They said to one another that it was a good sign when highborn Siccanians ventured out of their forest into the civilized world to learn languages and sensible customs. It furthered trade and thus the interests of Carthage.

Panormos and the entire land of Eryx had good reason to be on conciliatory terms with the Etruscan from Rome, for during the previous years the administrators of Rome had bought vast quantities of grain from Eryx to avert a famine caused by the disorders.

The people of Eryx hoped that the trade in grain would be continued in the future. Panormos especially benefited by it since Rome shipped its grain not only on Etruscan vessels but on those of Panormos as well.

But the Etruscan, who as a merchant was never content, said bitterly, "If times were as they used to be and reasonable trade were possible, I could sell the Siccanian goods here in Panormos, buy grain at a low price and then sell it at a high price in Rome. But the Roman praetors have set a limit on the price of grain just as they have taken over the salt trade and determined its price in Rome. Formerly I could have sailed to Cumae and bartered the Siccanian goods for Attic vases whose beauty and graceful decorations we Etruscans admire so deeply that we even put them in the tombs of our rulers and Lucumones. But the Greeks have become arrogant after their victory at Marathon and the tyrant of Cumae confiscates the Roman grain ships arriving there."

He cursed the Greeks and continued, "No, I dare not sail to Cumae. All I can do is to await a strong south wind and surrender myself to the dangers of the open sea in sailing back to the mouth of the Roman river."

Sack by sack, bundle by bundle and basket by basket he loaded his vessel. The customs men entered the cargo on their wax tablets and with a deep sigh the Etruscan paid for the donkeys he had hired and chased the drovers away with curses, saying that in no country had he met such thieves as in the land of Eryx. Of course this was a lie since the people of Eryx allowed him to trade freely with the Siccani while he himself had violated the laws of Eryx by smuggling iron goods to the Siccani.

I myself said hardly a word to the Carthaginians since I considered it wiser to let them believe that as a Siccanian I did not know their language. Even Arsinoe managed to control her tongue. But when we were within the walls of the house that the council of Panormos rented to strangers and in which the slaves and companions of Xenodotos greeted him with the utmost humility, Arsinoe could no longer restrain herself.

Tearing the cloth from her head, she stamped her foot and cried, "I have already risked enough for your sake at sea, Turms! Never will I consent to set foot on that Etruscan's smelly tub. Even if I am not afraid for myself, I must think of Misme. In the name of the goddess, Turms, what are we doing going to Rome when your friend Xenodotos is ready to smooth the road to Susa for you and arrange a secure future for you in the King's court as the Siccanian ambassador?"

Xenodotos was a changed man now that he was once more among his companions. He carried his curly-bearded chin proudly upright and watched me stealthily.

"Let us not quarrel as soon as we have stepped over the threshold," he said placatingly. "Let us first bathe and have the rigors of the journey rubbed and anointed from our bodies. Let us eat seasoned food like civilized people and freshen our minds with wine. Only then let us confer with one another—you, Turms, who have not even revealed your name to me. Now I shall carefully remember it and I assure you that your wife is wiser than you. Do not scorn her intellect."

I guessed that they had allied themselves for the purpose of making me accompany Xenodotos and Skythes back to Ionia and from there to the Great King's presence in Susa. I also suspected that Arsinoe had rashly told Xenodotos things that should have been left unsaid.

But I had learned, while among the Siccani, to control my face. I said nothing, merely followed Xenodotos calmly to the bath which his servants had prepared. Arsinoe followed us since she was unwilling to leave us by ourselves.

Thus the three of us bathed together and the warmth of the water and the fragrance of fine oils made us languid after the hardships of our journey. Xenodotos watched me rather than Arsinoe, although he courteously lauded her beauty, saying that he could not believe that she had ever had children and assuring her that not many women in the Persian king's court could compete with her.

"Watching you," he said ingratiatingly, "I regret that the gods have made me as I am. The more fortunate is Turms who is able to enjoy your unparalleled beauty. Indeed, looking at you both I find it difficult to believe that you are native Siccanians and true members of that dark-skinned and bowlegged people."

Afraid of his curiosity I demanded bluntly, "How many Siccanians did you see during your journey, Xenodotos? Real Siccanians are straight and beautifully developed. Look at our slave Hanna. You saw only tribal outcasts who grow peas around their miserable huts."

But Arsinoe said frankly, "But Hanna is not a Siccanian. She is an Elymian, born in Segesta. I admit, though, that there were some surprisingly strong men among the Siccani."

She extended her white limbs in the warm water, called a servant and rose to have her hair washed.

At that moment her allure aroused only revulsion in me and I could not forgive her for having babbled about us to Xenodotos. My anger increased as we ate and drank. Both of us had been without wine for so long that we quickly became intoxicated. Then Xenodotos cleverly provoked a quarrel between us.

Finally I sprang up from the convivial couch and swore by the moon and the sea horse. "My omens and signs are more potent than your greed, Arsinoe. If you don't want to accompany me I shall go alone."

"Sleep your head clear before you swear such a pernicious oath," warned Xenodotos.

But I was intoxicated by wine and bitterness and shouted recklessly,

"You, Arsinoe, follow Xenodotos if you want to obtain more security than I can give you. He'll be able to sell you to some noble Persian. But I suspect that, once behind the grating of a woman's house, you will begin to yearn more for your freedom than for a life of luxury."

Arsinoe flung her wine across the room. "You know what I have sacrificed for your sake, Turms. I have even risked my life for you. But I must think of my child. Year by year you have become increasingly stubborn and foul-mouthed and I wonder now what I ever saw in you. Xenodotos is waiting for a west wind to take him to Rhegion, where he will meet Skythes. The wind may turn tomorrow, and that is why you must decide which to choose. I myself have already decided in the name of the goddess."

When she saw that I was not alarmed by her threat, she became even angrier and screamed, "Let us be separated from each other as of this moment, and don't dare try to force your way into my bed! I have had enough of your sour face and so abhor your barbarically hard limbs that I could vomit."

Xenodotos tried to stifle her words but she bit his finger, began to howl from the bottom of her heart and vomited the wine she had drunk. Whereupon she fell asleep, wet from the wine. I carried her to bed and bade Hanna take care of her for I myself was so embittered that I had no desire to sleep in the same room.

Upon my return to the banquet room Xenodotos sat beside me, placed his hand on my knee and said, "I know you for a Greek, Turms, from all Arsinoe has told me. But trust in me. If you are an Ionian refugee and fear the King's wrath, I can assure you that the Persian does not desire revenge for the sake of revenge. The service that you are offering him will weigh more heavily in the scales than the possible mistakes in your past."

I did not doubt his words, but how could I disregard the signs that I had received? I tried to explain the matter to him but he became stubborn in his zeal.

After coaxing me a while he warned, "Don't aggravate me too much, Turms. If you are thinking of the temple at Sardis, don't be afraid. Your wife was wise in entrusting your fears to me. I even know that you have been guilty of piracy. You are in my hands, Turms. I have only to call for the city guards and you are lost."

At that moment I hated Arsinoe for wantonly having placed me at the mercy of a stranger so that I would be compelled to abandon my purpose and follow Xenodotos to the East. My long-dormant hatred

233

burst forth like molten rock from a quaking mountain and scorched me until nothing mattered any more.

I thrust Xenodotos' hand from my knee and said, "I thought you were my friend, but now I know better. Very well, I will call the police and surrender myself to be skinned alive as a pirate by the priests of Carthage. But at the same time let Arsinoe be sold in the market as an escaped temple slave and Misme as the daughter of a slave. I am sure that your reputation will be greatly enhanced in the eyes of the King by such a public disturbance in Panormos."

I said further, "My omens are clear and indisputable, and the Ephesian Artemis and Aphrodite of Eryx vie with each other in bestowing their favors on me. By hurting me you hurt them, and I warn you of their power. I myself am fulfilling the fate within me which no human power can deflect. I will not follow you to Susa."

When he realized that my decision was unalterable, Xenodotos tried to placate me and apologized for his threat. He urged me to reconsider the matter after I had slept my head clear. On the following day Arsinoe also suddenly changed and tried by every means at her disposal to weaken me. But I remained resolute and did not touch her. Whereupon she sent Hanna to the temple of the goddess to purchase beauty preparations, secluded herself in her room and then climbed to the roof to dry her hair in the sunshine. She had succeeded in dyeing her hair golden once more, and as she rested on the roof with her hair outspread she was a lovely sight to behold. However, her hair had a new reddish gleam for which she blamed Hanna, claiming that the stupid girl had accepted inferior dyes.

I thought she was senseless to restore her former appearance in Panormos where the curious stared at her from other housetops. But she risked the danger in order to make herself as attractive as possible and thus irresistible to me.

Xenodotos took me to the harbor to show me the trim ship that he had chartered at Rhegion after leaving Skythes there to confer with Anaxilaos. I asked him of Kydippe and learned that, since her marriage to Anaxilaos, she had had several children, drove a pair of mules and kept rabbits in her house. She was famous for her beauty throughout Sicily as well as the Greek cities of Italy, and her father ruled Himera.

Xenodotos' comfortable ship did not tempt me. Instead, I went to the wooden-pillared Etruscan temple where the salt merchant was praying for a good south wind, and asked whether he would take me with him to the mouth of the Roman river. He was elated to get a man who might prove helpful at the oars and sails but as a merchant concealed his feelings and declared that I must bring my own provisions and pay for the voyage.

The Etruscan's prayers were effective to such a degree that a few days later the wind turned west and began to blow briskly. This suited Xenodotos' plans perfectly and he said to me, "I shall wait until evening for you to recapture your senses, Turms. But at dusk I shall put to sea, for I have been told that that is the most favorable time to sail eastward from Panormos. I implore you to accompany me, for I have given my oath to take with me your wife Arsinoe, her daughter Misme and her servant Hanna."

I hardened my heart, went to Arsinoe and said, "The moment of parting has arrived, but only because you wish it, not I. I thank you for the years that you have given me and will not remind you of the grief you have caused. I shall remember only the good that we have shared. In addition to the Siccanians' gift I shall give you the gold coins given to me by Xenodotos and shall retain only enough money to pay for my voyage to Rome. But Hanna you cannot take with you. I know well that in your greediness you would sell her at the first opportune moment, and I want no harm to befall her."

Arsinoe burst into tears and shouted, "Your heart is like stone! I am too proud to remind you of the sorrow that you have caused me, but it is only natural that you should give me your money. A few gold coins are small compensation indeed for all that I have lost because of you. Nor have you any right to Hanna. I am the one who has raised and taught her, and she even spoiled my hair."

We argued about Hanna until I produced the golden goblet I had chosen from the Siccanian treasure and gave that also to Arsinoe. I concealed from her only the small golden hand which had more value as an amulet than as money.

Arsinoe weighed the goblet in her hand, glanced at me suspiciously and demanded, "What do you want with that girl and how does her fate concern you?"

Indignantly I exclaimed, "I shall marry her to some good man with her own permission. That much I feel that I owe her because she took care of both your children."

"Of course I can buy a more skilled slave in Rhegion," she retorted. "It will be a relief if you take that clumsy girl off my neck, for she has been looking at me malevolently for a long time. Even without her, though, you will have more than enough trouble. Remember my warning when calamity befalls you, Turms."

Even in my anger I glowed and trembled at her nearness and I did not know how I could live without her. We had spent many days in Panormos during which she had not humbled herself and I had not touched her. She had hoped to bend me to her will by arousing my desire and was greatly disappointed when I did not attempt to put my arms around her even at our moment of parting. Yet had I done so, I would once again have been in her power, so I controlled myself.

As the day began to close I took her from the city to the harbor, kissed Misme farewell and assured Xenodotos of my good wishes.

"For the sake of our friendship," I requested, "if the weather compels you to stop at Himera, look up the highborn Etruscan merchant, Lars Alsir. Give him my regards and pay him whatever I owe, for it is difficult for me to leave a country in which I am indebted. He is a cultured man and can give you much valuable information about the Etruscans."

Xenodotos promised to do so but Arsinoe reproached me bitterly. "Is this your only farewell to me? Are you really more concerned about your debt to a stranger than about your debt to me?"

Covering her head, she climbed up the ladder onto the ship and Xenodotos followed with Misme. Until the last moment I expected Arsinoe to be overcome by remorse and to jump off the ship, but the sailors pulled in the ladder, tied it to the railing and with the oars thrust the ship onto the water. As they left the shore they raised the sail, the sunset colored the ship red and I believed Arsinoe to have disappeared from my life forever. There on the shore of Panormos I dropped to my knees in grief and buried my face in my hands. Disappointment overwhelmed me and in my heart I cursed the gods who trifled with me. Nor did I feel relief in remembering Arsinoe's greed and frivolity, for she had in truth forsaken all in Segesta to follow me. And I had until the last moment expected her to do so again.

Then I felt the shy touch of fingertips on my shoulder and heard Hanna's warning voice, "The Phoenicians are looking at you."

Remembering my hazardous position and my Siccanian appearance, I donned the antlered mask once more and tossed over my shoulder the colored woolen mantle which Xenodotos had given me on parting. Head proudly erect, I strode to the Etruscan's ship and Hanna followed behind with a hide bundle of our few effects on her head.

Only the Etruscan's limping helmsman was on guard. When I stepped aboard the ship he thanked the gods and said, "It's good that you came, Siccanian. Keep an eye on the cargo and the ship so that I also can sacrifice and pray for wind."

As the night darkened the sound of Phoenician musical instruments and the bawling of drunkards began to carry from the market place, so that I well understood why the helmsman had jumped for joy at being able to join in the sacrifice. When he had left, Hanna and I found a place for ourselves on the ship. In the protective darkness the hot tears finally burst from my eyes. I wept for my loss and the compulsion of my omens and could think of nothing but Arsinoe.

In the dark of the ship I felt Hanna creep beside me as I lay on the stinking bundles. She touched my face with her fingertips, wiped the tears from my eyes, kissed my cheeks, caressed my hair and in her distress began to weep also. She was only a young girl, but in my sorrow the mere presence of another person exuded compassion. Hanna's sadness assuaged my own pangs, nor did I want her to weep because of me.

"Don't weep, Hanna. My tears are but the tears of weakness and will cease of themselves. But I am a poor man and my future is uncertain. I don't know whether I did the right thing in taking you with me. Perhaps it would have been better for you to have followed your mistress."

Hanna rose to her knees in the darkness and declared, "I would rather have jumped into the sea! I am thankful that you are taking me with you wherever you go." She reached for my face. "I shall be whatever you wish, and will gladly work for you. If you wish you may brand my forehead or loins with the sign of the slave."

Her fervor touched me. Stroking her hair, I said, "You are not a slave, Hanna. I shall protect you as best I can until you find a man you can accept."

She rejected the thought. "No, Turms. I don't think I will find such a man. You keep me, please. I'll try to be as useful as possible." She added hesitantly, "Arsinoe, our mistress, explained that I could earn the most money by offering myself to some brothel in a big city. If you wish, I am ready to earn money for you even in that way, although I would not do so gladly."

Her suggestion so horrified me that I put my arms around her. "Don't even think of such a thing. I would never permit it, for you are an untouched and good girl. I want to protect you and certainly not lead you to destruction."

She was highly pleased at having made me forget my sorrow momentarily and forced me to eat and to drink the wine that she had brought along. We sat dangling our feet over the side of the ship, looked at the reddish lights of the harbor and listened to the blare of the Phoenician instruments. Hanna's nearness warmed me because I at least had someone with whom to talk.

I don't know how it all happened, but the wine and the music and the trusting presence of a young girl must have been responsible. Nor have I any defense other than that in his deepest sorrow man is so shaken that in his receptivity to another's presence he seeks oblivion in the roar of his own blood. Arsinoe had denied me herself, and the good food and idleness in the city had made my body sensitive to temptation. I cannot blame only Hanna but myself as well. For when we had gone to rest I was overwhelmed with desire at the touch of her smooth limbs. Without protest she surrendered to me and wound her arms around my neck. But even as I delighted in her I knew that her slender limbs were not Arsinoe's limbs and that her body could never compete with Arsinoe.

When I drew away from her we lay silent in the darkness for a long time until I heard her stifled sobs.

I touched her bare shoulder and said with bitterness, "Little did I think that on the very first night you would have to weep because of me. You see now what kind of a man I am. I have hurt you and spoiled your chances for marriage. I can well understand why you are weeping."

But Hanna pressed against me passionately, whispering, "I'm not weeping because of that. These are tears of joy that you should have cared to touch me. I'm not regretting the loss of my virtue, for I have been saving it for you. I have nothing else to give you."

She kissed my hands and shoulders fervently. "You have made me so happy! I have been waiting for this moment ever since that moonlit night when you held me in your lap when I was but a child. Don't heed my tears, for I am weeping only at my worthlessness. How could cheap copper satisfy one who is accustomed to embracing gold?"

"Don't say that," I protested. "You were most winsome in my arms, and I have never before embraced an untouched girl. But I did you a great wrong. My only consolation is the knowledge that I am sterile and that you need have no fear of the consequences. You probably knew that Hiuls was not my son nor Misme my daughter."

Hanna said nothing. I guessed from that she had known, and I admired her understanding. She must have wanted to warn me many times, but in my blindness I would not have believed her. I could almost hear Arsinoe saying sarcastically, "Would you rather believe a jealous slave girl than me?"

I seemed actually to hear Arsinoe's voice and to feel her nearness. To forget, I took Hanna in my arms once more and embraced her as violently as I would have Arsinoe. Once the damage was done there was no harm in repeating it.

Finally she cried out hoarsely, began to kiss my face with fervor and breathed, "Oh, Turms, I love you and have loved you from the first moment and I don't think that anyone could love you so much, even though you don't care much for me. But if you like me even a little, I'll follow you wherever you go. Your city will be my city and I have no other gods but you."

My conscience told me that I did wrong in warming my disappointment with a young girl's life, but reason cold-bloodedly assured me that it would be better if I had a willing companion and it mattered little whether I loved her or not if she were content. It was useless for me to ponder or regret since everything happened as it happened and I was unable to prevent it.

At last she rose to wash herself and I did likewise. When I touched her I felt that her cheeks were still flushed and the veins in her neck throbbed. She aided me to sleep and wound herself around me. Faintly I heard the Etruscan and his men clamber onto the ship and argue about sleeping space. I seemed to feel the presence of my guardian spirit as Hanna's slender girl's body warmed me and I in turn warmed her with my own. In that shadowy state between sleeping and waking I felt as though the goddess whom I had known only as a capricious being wanted to indicate to me through Hanna an entirely new side of herself. With a sigh I sank into a deep sleep until bright daylight.

7.

Surely my guardian spirit must have watched over me and caused Hanna to awaken at dawn and creep away. I myself awakened only when Arsinoe, with Misme in her arms, kicked me in the ribs and then in the head with her silver-ornamented sandal.

At first I could not believe my eyes and thought I was dreaming. But there she stood, nor did it take me long to realize her treachery. I myself had wondered how anyone could sail westward in the evening. Xenodotos and Arsinoe had, of course, laid the scheme together, hoping that I would join them at the last moment. When I had not yielded, they had cruised before the harbor all night and brought Arsinoe to shore in a fishing boat. Xenodotos, however, was wise enough not to remain behind but had continued his voyage eastward with a brisk west wind.

When Arsinoe had given vent to her anger she suddenly turned humble, cast her eyes down and said, "Turms, did you really think that I could give you up so lightly? After all, I have no other life but you since the goddess has bound us to each other. You don't know very much about love since you were ready to let me go because of your foolish omens."

My trembling body and groping hands placated her and she smiled. The beauty of her face brightened the dirty ship like sunshine and she said in a low voice, "Now, Turms, summon a south wind, you who think you rule the winds. Summon the wind, for it, like the storm, is already in me."

Hanna had approached us on bare feet and stood petrified at sight of Arsinoe. Guilt shone on her face, but fortunately Arsinoe could not even have imagined that she had a competitor, least of all a bare-footed girl in a tree-bark dress.

She mistook Hanna's shock for mere surprise, thrust Misme into her lap and snapped, "Feed the child, change her clothes to something appropriate to this filthy ship and disappear from sight. We want to be alone to summon the wind."

A violent glow spread through me, I felt my strength and in looking at Hanna I could no longer understand how I could have been attracted to the dark-skinned girl even for a moment while Arsinoe was in the same world with me. The magic of the goddess seized me and I ran to shake awake the Etruscan and his limping helmsman and drove the head-scratching slaves off the ship.

"Make haste to pray for wind with your men," I ordered. "I intend to fly your boat to Rome on the wings of a storm faster than you have ever sailed before. Make your sacrifice quickly, for by midday we will raise the sail."

In a drunken stupor the Etruscan obeyed me. It was good that he did, for otherwise I would have thrown him off his own ship so that I might be alone with Arsinoe. Eagerly we ran into each other's arms. She had a scorching wind in her body and I had a storm in my blood.

An ecstasy came over me, the holy dance began twitching my limbs and I vied with Arsinoe in calling for the wind. Three times, seven times and twelve times I summoned the south wind, until we stood at the stern, hand in hand, shouting for the wind in a holy frenzy. I don't know how long it lasted and whence the words spilled into my mouth, but we did not cease until the air had blackened, the wind turned and the clouds, black-haired and with the glint of lightning in their eyes, had begun to roll over the hump-necked mountain of Panormos to the sea. Beyond Panormos the mountain peaks of the land of Eryx darkened and whirlwinds swept up the merchants' shelters and baskets in the market place, we heard the slam of gates even from the city, and clumps of reeds, torn from the roofs by the wind, began swirling in the air.

Only then we ceased. Our holy frenzy died down and we looked around in amazement. We saw the merchant and his men run toward the ship with fluttering clothes as the Carthaginian soldiers and customs men stood on the shore, staring at our ship with hands over their mouths.

Just as the Etruscan reached the ship a strong eddy flung the stern from the shore into the water. Quickly he shouted to his men to raise the sail and seize the steering oars to keep us with the wind. The Phoenicians on shore flew black strips of cloth as storm warnings and raised a shield to prevent our departure. But the wind snatched the shield from the arms of the man holding it and carried it out to the foaming sea. Swaying and slapping the water under its round prow, the ship sped to the open sea, drawn by its patched sail.

As the waves rumbled against the sides of the ship and the wind whistled in the ropes, Misme began to weep in terror and Hanna crouched among the cargo. But Arsinoe was not afraid now that she had found me. I myself saw how sturdily the ship responded to the waves and noticed that the Etruscan's helmsman knew his trade. Laughingly I showed him the black stone sea horse in my palm and indicated that he could easily give us more sail.

But despite my ecstasy I bore such a grudge against Xenodotos that I suddenly wished that the southerly gale would blow out to sea and endanger his sleek ship. The wind did in fact blow him off his course, driving him along the Italian coast as far as Poseidonia. Only there was he able to land and he suffered great humiliation because of his Persian trousers. Hence he left his ship there for repairs and traveled by land along the old trade route of Sybaris to Croton and from there to Rhegion where he met Skythes.

But all that I learned only much later. I myself sailed northward in a creaking ship on the wings of a storm, as the omens had ordained. After helping the Etruscan and the helmsman in holding the steering oars, I went to see how Arsinoe felt. As I swayed with the movement of the ship among the cargo, my eye was caught by a smooth pebble which had clung to one of the bundles on shore and had dropped loose only on the ship. Without realizing what I did I stooped to pick it up and remained holding it in my hand. Its gray-and-white color reminded me of a dove. I knew then that it was intended for me, and I put it into my pouch with the other pebbles as well as the golden hand and the stone sea horse.

They were my only possessions as I left Sicily, for Arsinoe's scheme had benefited her at least to the degree that she had all my money. But it did not trouble me, for I had strong faith in Hecate.

I no longer looked behind at the mountains of Eryx as I sailed from Sicily. I looked only ahead and to the north.

BOOK EIGHT

The Omens

.

WITH our hair stiff from the splashing brine, our faces gray from lack of sleep and our hands chafed by the rope, we sighted the shore of Italy. The helmsman immediately recognized the landmarks and declared that we were but a day's voyage from the mouth of the Roman river. The Etruscan clasped his hands and swore that never before had he experienced so swift a voyage and so even a south wind once we had left behind the first day's storm.

At the mouth of the Roman river we met ships of all nations, large and small, on their way up or down the majestic river. From afar I saw the dazzling white glimmer of the salt basins which nature had bountifully bestowed upon Rome. The slaves were wading knee deep in the salt as they shoveled it together and carried it away.

Without pausing at the mouth of the river the merchant hired oxen and slaves and had a rope fastened to the upturned prow to tow the ship up the swiftly flowing river. So broad and deep was the water that even large seagoing ships could sail as far as Rome where, at the shore by the cattle market, they met the vessels from the upper reaches of the river.

Boats on their way downstream passed us continually, and majestic tree trunks, tied into rafts, floated slowly by on their way to the shipyards. The men on the ships called out to us in the language of the sea, but the timber floaters spoke Etruscan while the ships' towers employed Latin and its numerous dialects. Hearing them, the merchant said derisively that the Roman language was not a real language and that all the words pertaining to cultural matters had been borrowed from the Etruscans and distorted in a barbaric manner.

The drover mercilessly lashed his slaves and goaded the oxen to speed the journey and earn his money the sooner. But I had time to see the willow bushes on the banks, the restless flocks of birds fluttering over our ship and the hawks circling the endless harvested fields and meadows with motionless wings. It seemed to me that the outskirts of Rome were nothing but fields and gardens, and I had difficulty in believing that so prosperous a city found it necessary to ship grain all the way from Sicily to stave off famine.

But the merchant pointed out the ruins of many huts burned by the Romans themselves. In their intramural quarrels the people of Rome did not even spare their own, and in the yearly wars the cultivated areas had suffered as Rome expanded its power. Once the Etruscans had made an immense plain near Rome fruitful with canals and drains. Under the rule of the Etruscan kings the brutal people of Rome had been held within bounds, but when the Romans had expelled their king, agriculture and trade had suffered from the ceaseless warring and no neighboring city felt itself safe from Roman rapaciousness.

Then I saw the hills of Rome, their villages, the wall, the bridge and a few temples. The bridge which the Etruscans had built to link the innumerable cities that were separated by the river was expertly constructed of wood and was the longest I had ever seen, although an island helped to support it. Indeed, the Romans considered this bridge so important that their high priest had inherited from the Etruscan period the title of "High Bridge Builder." The crudity of Roman customs is well conveyed by the fact that the maintenance of the bridge had fallen to the high priest, although the Etruscans had intended the title to mean a builder of bridges between man and the gods. To them the wooden bridge was merely the symbol of the invisible bridge, but the Romans took literally all that the Etruscans taught them.

When the harbor custodians had indicated a place for us on the muddy bank that was supported by piles, the inspectors boarded the ship. Nor did the Etruscan even attempt to offer them gifts or to invite them to join him in a sacrifice. He declared that Roman officials were incorruptible because of the stringency of their laws.

On the edge of the cattle market, beside a pillar, stood an executioner ready to fulfill his duty. His symbol, which the merchant said had been inherited from the Etruscans, was a long axe surrounded by whips. The Romans called these executioners "lictors." Instead of a king, they elected two officials annually, and each of these praetors was accompanied by twelve lictors. In obvious cases a lictor could halt a criminal on the street, flog him or chop off the thief's hand with his axe. Because of this, exemplary order prevailed in the harbor and one did not have to fear thieves as in all other harbors.

The Etruscan let the quaestor inspect Arsinoe's and my goods first, and they wrote down our names and believed us when we called ourselves Siccanians from Sicily. The merchant forbade us to conceal anything from them, and they carefully counted Arsinoe's gold coins and weighed our gold objects. We had to pay a high tax for bringing them into the city since only stamped copper was accepted as currency in Rome. When they asked whether Hanna was slave or free, Arsinoe declared quickly that she was a slave and I maintained that she was free. The officials, who understood little Greek, called an interpreter but since Hanna was unable to defend herself, she was declared to be a slave, the quaestors thinking that I had called her free merely to evade payment of the tax on slaves.

Benevolently they let the interpreter explain that if they had entered Hanna on their tablets as a free person, she could have gone where she wished and enjoyed the protection of Roman laws. Thus, by lying to them, I had been on the verge of losing a small fortune. They considered it a fine jest and laughingly pinched Hanna as they tried to guess how much she would bring on the market. But they respected Arsinoe and me because of our gold. The Romans were greedy, dividing their people into various classes according to their possessions, so that the poorest citizens were only rarely permitted to vote on municipal affairs. In military service, however, the wealthy were given the most difficult tasks, while the poor escaped with less and the poorest did not have to serve at all because the Romans considered rabble to be but a burden to the army.

When we left the ship the merchant led us quickly to a new temple of Turnus to sacrifice. Actually the Romans worshiped the god as Mercury, but in the same temple the Greeks of Rome worshiped him as Hermes, so presumably he was the same god.

The temple was full of chattering merchants from various cities, all asking the latest prices on copper, ox hides, wool and timber, for the prices were determined each day anew in the temple of Mercury, rising or dropping in accordance with demand and supply. Only the price of grain had been fixed by the Roman officials, for they had so offended the neighboring peoples and the Etruscans that these sources refused to sell them grain.

When we had sacrificed and left our gifts in the temple, the Etruscan bade us farewell.

He did not accept payment for the voyage although I thought he had brought me to the temple for the purpose of settling the matter before the eyes of the god. On the contrary, he even thrust back the deposit I had made in Panormos.

"I don't think I would have good luck if I were to accept payment for the voyage. I remember all too well how black magic launched the ship and how the ship grew wings so that my cargo did not get wet in the storm. Just give me, a poor man, your blessing. That will suffice as payment, although I ask you not to remember me otherwise."

I put my hand on his shoulder and with my left hand covered my eyes to bless him, but why I made that holy gesture I do not know. Immediately the merchant became so alarmed that he forthwith fled to the shore, glancing back at me through his fingers.

In that manner Arsinoe, Hanna, Misme and I were left outside the temple of Mercury with our possessions. And since I did not know the city and its customs or even understand its language I decided to remain there until an omen should indicate our next move.

Arsinoe did not tire of watching the crowds pass, for many men looked at her and even looked back. She pointed out that all the people wore shoes and only slaves were barefoot, but she considered the women morose and bloated and declared that their clothes were ugly. More than that she had not time to say, for just then we were approached by an old man carrying a crooked staff. His robe was soiled and stained with food, his eyes were red and his gray beard was dirty.

"Do you wait for something, stranger?" he asked.

I guessed his trade from the staff although his appearance was not such as to arouse confidence. But since he was the first person to speak to me I replied kindly, "I have just arrived in the city and am awaiting a favorable omen."

He became greatly interested, and the crook began to tremble in his hand as he explained, "I guessed that you were Greek, although more from your wife's appearance than your own. If you wish, I will study the birds for you, but I could take you to an associate who will sacrifice a sheep for you and read the omens from its liver. That is more expensive, however, than studying birds."

His knowledge of Greek was weak, and so I suggested, "Let us speak your own language, that I may understand you better."

He began to speak the language of the city which sounded as harsh and merciless as its residents were said to be. I shook my head. "I understand not a word. Let us speak the old and true language. I have learned it somewhat by associating with an Etruscan."

In talking with the merchant it had been as though the Etruscan that I had learned from Lars Alsir in Himera had burst forth again after years of dormancy. Or as though I had once known the language and then forgotten it. The words had come to my lips so easily that the merchant had gradually stopped speaking the polyglot language of the sea and begun speaking his own language with me.

The old man waxed even more interested. "You are truly an exceptional Greek if you know the holy language. I myself am an Etruscan and a real augur, not one who merely recites by rote. Don't despise me even though my weak eyes make it necessary for me to seek a livelihood since people no longer come to me."

He shaded his eyes with a hand, looked closely at me and asked, "Where have I seen your face before and why is it so familiar to me?"

Although such talk is usual on the part of wandering seers in every country, he spoke so sincerely and was such a venerable old man despite his poverty that I believed him. I did not, however, reveal my certainty that the gods had sent him to me at that precise moment and place.

Arsinoe immediately became envious, thrust her beautiful face before the old man's nose and demanded, "What of me? Don't you recognize my face, if you are a true augur?"

The old man put his hand to his forehead, stared into her eyes and began to tremble. "Of course I recognize you, and the days of my youth return to me when I look at your face. Are you not Calpurnia whom I met by the spring in the woods?"

He recovered himself and shook his head. "No, you cannot be Calpurnia, for she would be an old woman if she were alive. But in your face, woman, I see all the women who have made me tremble during my lifetime. Are you perhaps the goddess herself in a woman's guise?"

Arsinoe laughed delightedly, touched his arm and said to me, "This old man pleases me. He is surely a true augur. Let him study the omens for you, Turms."

But the augur was staring at me again in bewilderment. "Where is it that I have seen your face?" he asked in Etruscan. "I seem to remember having seen a smiling likeness of you during my travels to the holy cities to learn my profession."

I laughed again. "You are mistaken, old man. I have never even visited any Etruscan cities. If you really recognize my face, you have perhaps seen me in a dream to enable you to give me my omens."

He drooped again and the glow in him was extinguished. Humbly he said, "If that is so and you desire it, I shall study the omens gratuitously, although I have not eaten much these past days. Some soup would strengthen my body and a drop of wine would cheer an old

246

man's mind. But don't consider me a troublesome beggar even though I do reveal my need."

"Don't worry, old man," I assured him. "I shall reward you for your trouble. It would not even become my dignity to accept something free. I myself am a giver of gifts."

"Giver of gifts," he repeated and raised his hand to his mouth. "Where have you learned those words and how dare you say that of yourself. Aren't you a Greek after all?"

I realized from his alarm that I had unwittingly used the secret name of some Etruscan god, but how the words had come to me I did not know. Nevertheless I laughed, placed my hand on his shoulder and said reassuringly, "I speak your language poorly and use the wrong words. In no way do I want to insult you or your religion."

"No," he protested, "your words were correct but in the wrong place. They are the words of the holy Lucumones. Times are bad and we are living in the day of the wolf, if even a stranger can repeat holy words like a raven which has learned to talk."

I did not take offense at his abuse. Instead I asked with curiosity, "Who are the Lucumones? Explain the matter to me so that I will never again err in using the right words in the wrong place."

He looked at me with hostility and explained, "The Lucumones are the holy rulers of the Etruscans. But they are born rarely these days."

We soon found ourselves in that part of the city where the visiting peasants and cattle merchants had their lodgings. But the hairy-armed innkeepers tempting us with their ladles did not please us nor did I understand their language. The narrow alleys were dirty and muddy, and Arsinoe declared that she could see from the women's faces what profession they practiced. The place, which the old man called Suburra, had been cursed and the only people who lived there were the disreputable elements and the people of the circus.

The old man showed us the altar which the Greeks had erected to Herakles and asked us whether we desired to find lodgings among the Greeks who had come there as exiles to practice their various trades. The altar looked quite ancient and the augur explained that, according to the Greeks, the founders of Rome were the descendants of Aeneas who had fled there following the fall of Troy.

"Let him who will, believe it," he said. "The Greeks are talkative tellers of tales and quickly infect the primitive peoples with their customs wherever they may settle. If it did not offend you I would say that the Greeks with their customs are everywhere like a contagious disease."

247

"You don't offend me and I don't want to live among the Greeks," I said.

He explained that Rome also had Phoenician merchants and artisans who had come there both from the eastern lands and from Carthage. But I did not wish to live among them, either. Finally the old man showed us an ancient fig tree to whose foot the newly born twin brothers Romulus and Remus had drifted in their willow basket in the flood. There the she-wolf had suckled them until their rescue by shepherds.

"Their names have been distorted," declared the old man. "Their real names were Ramon and Remon for the two rivers, until the river Ramon straightened its course and overcame Remon. Now the Romans call it the Tiber, for a certain Tiburinus who was drowned in it."

I noticed that as we had talked we had reached a street paved with flagstones. The old man explained that this was the Etruscan quarter and that the street was called the Vicus Tuscus because the Romans called the Etruscans "Tuscans." Here lived the wealthiest merchants, the most skilled artisans and the old Etruscan families of Rome. They comprised one third of Rome's noble families, just as one third of the Roman cavalry consisted of descendants of old Etruscan families.

Looking around him the augur said, "My feet are tired and my mouth is dry from much talking."

"Do you think that some Etruscan would consent to give lodgings to me and my family although I am an alien?" I asked.

He did not wait for more but immediately rapped with his crook on a painted gate, entered and led us to a pillared, half-covered court with a rain-water pool in the center and the household gods on their altars along the edge. Around the court were buildings which were rented to travelers, while the main house contained a number of rooms with wall paintings, tables and seats. The innkeeper was a reserved man and did not greet the old augur with great warmth. But when he had studied us he accepted us as his guests and bade his slaves prepare food. Leaving Hanna and Misme in one of the buildings in the yard to guard our possessions, we went inside to eat.

The room contained two couches, and the augur explained, "The Etruscans permit a woman to eat in the same room with men, reclining on a couch. She may even lie on the same couch with her husband if she wishes. The Greeks permit a woman merely to sit in the same room, but the Romans consider it indecent for a woman to eat in the company of a man."

He himself leaned humbly against the wall to await our crumbs of charity. But I asked him to share the meal with us and the slaves to

248

bring in another couch. Immediately he went to wash himself and the innkeeper brought a clean robe to protect the double cushions on the couch. As we ate the well-prepared food and drank the country wine, the old man's face began to glow, the wrinkles on his face eased and his hands ceased trembling.

Finally he leaned back, the wine goblet in his left hand and a pomegranate in his right, while the staff lay on the couch at his left. I was overcome by a strange feeling that I had once before lived that same moment in a strange city and a strange room under a roof ornamented with painted beams.

The wine rose to my head and I said, "Old man, whoever you may be, I have seen the glances that you have exchanged with the innkeeper. I am not familiar with your customs, but why am I served from black cups when my wife has been given a silver plate and a Corinthian goblet?"

"If you don't know and understand it makes no difference," he said. "But it is not a sign of disrespect. They are old dishes."

The innkeeper himself hastened to offer me a beautifully hammered silver goblet to replace the black clay cup. I did not accept it, however, but continued to hold the clay cup. Its shape was familiar to my palm.

"I am not a holy man," I said. "You are surely mistaken. Why otherwise would you let me drink from a sacrificial cup?"

Without replying the augur tossed the pomegranate to me and I caught it in the shallow clay cup without touching it. My robe had slipped so that the upper part of my body was bare. Thus I reclined on the couch, resting on one elbow with the black clay cup in my left hand. The pomegranate which I had not touched with my hand lay in its round hollow. When he saw it the innkeeper came to me and placed a garland of autumn flowers around my neck.

The augur touched his forehead with his hand and said, "You have fire around your head, stranger."

"It is your profession to see what does not exist," I protested, "but I forgive you since I myself am serving you wine. Don't you see fire also around my wife's head?"

The old man looked at Arsinoe carefully, then shook his head. "No, there is no fire, merely fading sunshine. She is not like you."

Suddenly I realized that I was beginning to see through the walls. Arsinoe's face changed into that of the goddess and the old man lost his beard and seemed like a man in the prime of life. The host was no longer merely an innkeeper but rather a scholar.

I burst out laughing, "What do you mean by putting me, a stranger, to the test?"

The old man raised a finger to his lips and indicated Arsinoe who was yawning deeply. Within a moment she was asleep, and the augur rose, raised her eyelid and said, "She is sleeping soundly and nothing will happen to her. But you, stranger, must have your omens. Don't be afraid. You have not eaten or drunk poison, you have only tasted the sacred herb. I myself have also tasted it to clear my eyes. You are not an ordinary man and an ordinary omen will not suffice. Let us leave and ascend the holy hill."

Filled with radiance, I left Arsinoe sleeping and followed the augur. But I made the mistake of going through the wall directly to the court-yard, whereas the augur had to leave by way of the door so that I was in the courtyard to meet him. Then I saw my body obediently walking behind him and instantly returned to it since I could speak only with its aid. Never had I experienced anything so absurd and I greatly feared that I had drunk more wine than was good for me. My legs were not unsteady, however, and the augur led me to the market place, indicating with his staff the senate building, the prison opposite it and many more sights. He wanted to take me along the sacred way but after walking some distance I stepped to the side and went toward a steep cliff.

Looking around I saw a round temple with wooden pillars and reed roof, and cried, "I feel the nearness of a holy place!"

"That is the temple of Vesta," explained the old man. "Six unmarried women guard the holy fire in it. No man can enter there."

I listened. "I hear the murmur of water. Somewhere there is a sacred spring."

The old man protested no longer but allowed me to lead the way, ascend the steps that had been hewn out of the rock and enter the cave. Inside was an ancient stone trough into which water trickled from a crack in the wall, and on the edge of the trough lay three wreaths, as fresh as though someone had just placed them there. The first was formed from a willow branch, the second from an olive branch while the third was of ivy.

The augur looked about in alarm. "Entering here is forbidden, for this is the home of the nymph Egeria whom we Etruscans call Begoe. The only Lucumo to have ruled Rome comes here at night to meet her."

I dipped both hands in the cold water, sprinkled some over myself, took the ivy wreath in my hand and said, "Let us continue to the mount. I am ready."

Just then the cave darkened and I saw at its entrance a woman enveloped in coarse cloth. It was impossible to say whether she was old or young for she had covered her head, her face and even her hands so that only the fingertips holding the brown cloth were visible. She looked at me searchingly through a slit but stepped aside and said nothing.

Nor do I know how it happened, but at that moment, as I stepped from the dimness of the ancient cave back into the daylight, I, Turms, realized my immortality for the first time with heartrending certainty. I heard the roar of immortality in my ears, I smelled the icy odor of immortality in my nostrils, I felt the metallic taste of immortality in my mouth, I saw the flame of immortality before my eyes. Experiencing that, I knew that I would one day return, climb the same stone steps, touch the same water and, in doing so, know myself again. Nor did this perception last longer than the moment it took me to place the ivy wreath on my head. Then it disappeared.

I kissed the earth, the mother of my body, foreseeing that some day the eyes of my body would see more than merely the earth. The shrouded woman moved aside without a word. Once a similarly shrouded woman had sat on the divine seat under a parasol and I had kissed the earth before her. But whether that had happened in a dream or in reality or in some previous life I did not know.

A fine mist began to descend into the valley between the hills, dimming the outline of the houses and hiding the market place from view. The augur said, "The gods are coming. Let us hasten."

He climbed a steep path ahead of me, growing breathless as he climbed until his legs began to tremble and I had to support him. The youthful brightness induced by the wine died from his face, his cheeks became furrowed and his beard grew longer with every step. The higher we rose the older he became, until he was as ancient in my eyes as an oak.

The summit was clear, but below, on the other side of the crest, the track at the circus was veiled with mist. Unerringly my steps led me to a smooth rock.

The augur asked, "Within the walls?"

"Within the walls," I assented. "I still am not free. I still do not know myself."

"Do you choose the north or the south?" he asked.

"I do not choose," I replied. "The north has chosen me."

I sat on the rock with my face to the north, nor could I have faced the south if I had tried, so firmly was I in the grip of my power. The old man settled himself to my left with the staff in his right hand and measured and determined the four cardinal points, repeating them aloud. He said nothing about birds or how he expected them to fly.

"Will you be content with merely an affirmative or a negative reply?" he asked, as an augur must.

"I will not," I replied. "The gods have arrived. I am not committed, but the gods are obliged to give me their signs."

The augur covered his head, changed the staff to his left hand, raised his right to the crown of his head and waited. At that moment a gentle breeze rustled the treetops and a fresh oak leaf fell to the ground between my feet while somewhere in the distance, from another hill, I heard the muted cackle of geese. A dog came from nowhere, circled us, muzzle to the ground, and disappeared again as though eagerly following a scent. The gods seemed to be vying with one another in proving their presence, for farther away the thud of a fallen apple sounded in the stillness, and a lizard scampered over my foot, disappearing into the grass. Presumably the other seven gods were also present although they had not given clear indications of themselves. When I had waited yet a while I called to the gods who had revealed themselves.

"Master of the clouds, I know you. Gentle-eyed one, I know you. Fleet-footed one, I know you. Foam-born, I know you. You of the underworld, I know you."

The augur repeated the true and holy names of these five gods and then came the omens.

From the reeds in the river a flock of water birds rose, flying northward with extended necks, and disappeared from sight.

"Your lake," said the augur.

A high-circling hawk struck at the ground and again rose. A fluttering flock of doves rose from the mists and flew swiftly to the northeast.

"Your mountain," said the augur.

Then came the black ravens, circling lazily over our heads. The augur counted their number.

"Nine years," he said.

That marked the end of the omens, but onto my foot climbed a black and yellow beetle. The augur again covered his head, changed his staff into the right hand and said, "Your tomb."

In that manner did the gods remind me jealously of my body's mortality and try to frighten me. But I kicked away the beetle, rose and spoke. "The act is ended, old man, and I will not thank you for the omens since one does not express thanks for them. There were five gods, and of them only the ruler of thunderbolts was male. There were three omens, two of which concerned places and the third the period of my imprisonment. But the gods were only earthly gods and their omens concerned only this life. They reminded me of death because they know that a human's fate is death, but they themselves are bound to the earth as men are and thus, even as immortals, they are like men. I myself worship the veiled deities."

"Speak not of them," the augur said warningly. "The knowledge of them suffices. No one can know them, not even the gods."

I replied, "The earth does not restrain them. Time and place do not restrain them. They rule the gods, as the gods rule men."

"Don't talk," said the augur once more. "They exist. That is enough."

2.

We returned to the streets of the Etruscans and stepped into the inn so that I might give the augur his gift. There the host met us, wringing his hands.

"It's good that you returned, stranger, for things are happening here that I don't understand. I don't know whether I can let you and your family remain in my house. My trade will suffer if people begin to fear this place."

The slaves bustled about, shouting that objects had fallen from the walls and the household god had turned its back on the hearth. Quickly I went into the room in which we had eaten. Arsinoe was sitting on the edge of the couch with a guilty look, munching on an apple, and on a bronze-legged chair beside her sat a withered old man propping the drooping lid of his right eye with a finger. He wore a bleached robe bordered in purple and on his thumb was a gold ring. When he noticed me he began painfully to explain something in Latin, but the host urged him not to exert himself.

"He is one of the city fathers," explained the innkeeper. "Tertius Valerius, the brother of the plebeian's friend, Publius Valerius. The events of the past years have touched him deeply ever since he had to permit both his sons to be killed in accordance with a law which his brother introduced and the Senate ratified. A short while ago he was in the Senate when the tribune was impeaching Caius Marcius, conqueror of the Volsci, and the people rioted. He lost consciousness and was carried into my house since the slaves were afraid to take him to his own house lest he die on the way. When he regained consciousness he claims he saw his wife although she died of sorrow after the loss of her sons."

The old man began to speak in Etruscan and declared, "I saw my wife, touched her and discussed matters that only we two know. I don't know what it means, for finally everything darkened and my wife changed into the woman before me."

"The most amazing thing is that shortly before that I also saw my wife," said the host, "although I know that she is visiting relatives in Veii and Veii is a full day's journey from here. But with my own eyes I saw her walking in the court. In the name of my guardian spirit I swear that I saw her and touched her, for I ran to embrace her, asking, 'When did you return from Veii and why so soon?' Only then did I realize that I had touched this woman who had awakened from a sleep and was walking about the house."

"He is lying," declared Arsinoe. "They are both lying. I awakened only now and can remember nothing unusual. The old man was just staring at me. He hasn't tried to lie with me nor would he be capable of it."

I said angrily, "You could turn any house upside down with your pranks, but perhaps the goddess entered you as you slept and you really don't know what happened."

Tertius Valerius was sufficiently educated to stammer a few words in Greek. Turning to him I said, "You saw the vision in a twilight condition. Undoubtedly a blood-vessel in your brain burst from the shock you experienced at the market place, as I can see that from your drooping eyelid. Your wife appeared to you in the guise of my wife to warn you to take care of yourself and not to become involved in disputes that only injure your health. The vision signified no more than that."

"Are you a physician?" asked Tertius Valerius.

"No, but I was friend to one of the renowned physicians of the island of Cos. He knew that a certain Alcmaeon has proved that disturbances in the head affect various parts of the body. Your injury is within your skull and the paralysis of your body is an indication of that and not an illness in itself. So we are told."

The old man thought for a moment, made his decision and said, "Clearly the gods sent me to this house to meet your wife and you and to find peace of heart. I believe my wife. Had I believed her in time, both my sons would still be alive. Ambition blinded me and I thought I was the equal of my brothers and was not content to remain silent on public matters. Now my hearth is cold, my old age cheerless and the Furies whisper in my ears as I sit alone in the dark."

He clutched Arsinoe's hand and continued, "Both of you must accompany me to my house as my guests."

The innkeeper took me aside. "He is a respected man and owns thousands of jugera of land. But he has been muddled for a long time and the illness has hardly improved his reason. I would doubt his vision had I myself not seen a similar one. You will be hated by his relatives if you remain in his house as his guest."

I pondered the matter and said finally, "It is not up to me to doubt events. I thank you for your hospitality, for which I will pay you when you have counted on your tablet how much I owe you. I shall accompany this old man, my wife will put him to bed and our own servant will care for him. That is my decision."

Face flushed, the host pulled the tablet from his belt and began to write eagerly with the stylus. He glanced at me apologetically and said, "You must realize, stranger, that I would much rather offer you my hospitality without a price on it. I would even, for certain reasons, worship you on my knees, but this is my trade and we are in Rome."

He looked about him but saw only Tertius Valerius clutching Arsinoe's hand tightly as though seeking protection. "Perhaps the gods wish you to go to Tertius Valerius' house. But remember that his oldest brother was a many-time praetor who incurred the wrath of the patricians because of his law of appeal. His other brother has also been a praetor, and this brother's son Manius even a dictator and so successful in war that an ivory seat of honor at the circus was bestowed on his family. Throughout his life Tertius has striven to equal his brothers. Sheer ambition prompted him to send his sons to the executioner's pillar when Publius sent his own sons, and to try to watch his sons' flogging and execution as impassively as his brother. The youths had gathered in secret to pledge their support for the last Tarquinius."

As the host prattled on, he rapidly entered number after number in Etruscan numerals. Finally he extended the wax tablet to me with a sigh. Both sides were filled from right to left and from bottom to top.

"All this you have eaten and received," he assured me. "Included also is what your wife and daughter and slave have eaten and what you in your generosity gave to my slaves and to the poor."

I began to add the figures and was horrified. "You have fed the entire city of Rome at my expense! That was not my intention."

Arsinoe stroked Tertius Valerius' veined hand. "Don't always be so petty, Turms," she murmured, and tilted her head to catch the old man's glazed glance.

Tertius Valerius rose immediately and wrapped his purple-bordered toga tightly around himself. "Leave the account to me," he declared. "The innkeeper can send his slave to my house to fetch the copper. Let us depart."

I tried to protest but he was stubborn and called us his friends as the host scratched his neck with the stylus in bewilderment and exclaimed, "If I once doubted, I doubt no more! A Roman paying a guest's account? No, when his head has cleared he will begin to haggle and run my slave back and forth between our houses until my hair turns gray before I get my money."

The old man angrily snatched the tablet from the host's hand and with trembling fingers drew his initials in the wax. Then, without another glance at the innkeeper, he seized Arsinoe's arm.

"You lead me, my dear deceased wife, for I am old and my knees shake. And do not reproach me for my extravagance. It will happen only this once from the sheer joy of meeting you again as youthful and beautiful as you were during our happiest days."

When I heard that I began to regret my hasty decision but it was too late, for Arsinoe was already leading the old man quickly through the room to the courtyard where his slaves were waiting to carry him home.

The journey was not long, and we soon arrived in the courtyard of Tertius Valerius' old-fashioned house which, in imitation of his brothers, he had built at the foot of Velia. The gatekeeper slave was as old and trembling as his master and the link fastening his fetter to the gatepost had long ago rotted, so that he wore it only for the sake of appearances when guests arrived. Otherwise he limped about the courtyard or in the street in search of a sunny place in which to warm his aged body.

The slaves carried the litter inside to the court, where Arsinoe gently awakened the old man. We had the slaves lift him into bed and bring a brazier to heat the half-dark room, noticing as they did so that his household, run by decrepit slaves, was badly neglected. With a deep sigh he turned his cheek to the pillow but remembered to tell the slaves to obey us, his guests. Then he motioned us closer, and as we leaned over him he stroked Arsinoe's hair and from courtesy also mine. Arsinoe laid her hand on his forehead and bade him sleep. He did so immediately.

When we returned to the court I asked the slaves to return to the inn for Hanna, Misme and our goods. Instead, however, they looked at us disdainfully and shook their heads as though they did not comprehend. But the white-haired housekeeper finally bowed his head before my stern look, admitted his Etruscan birth and ordered them to go. He said that he still understood the language well, although Romans avoided speaking it in public following the king's exile. The more fanatical among them did not even wish their children to learn the old language, he explained, but the truly noble sons of Fathers still sent their own sons either to Veii or Tarquinia for a time in their youth to learn culture and good manners.

"Tell me your name and family and your wife's name and whence you come, so that I may address you properly," he said humbly.

I had no desire to conceal my real name from the housekeeper who enjoyed Valerius' confidence. "I am Turms of Ephesus and an Ionian refugee as you can guess. My wife's name is Arsinoe. She speaks only Greek and the language of the sea."

"Turms," he repeated. "That is no Greek name. How is it possible that an Ionian speaks the holy language?"

"Call me whatever you wish!" I exclaimed, and had to laugh.

In a friendly gesture I placed my hand on his shoulder, but the touch of it made him tremble. "The Romans distort the name Turms into Turnus," he explained, "and it may be best for you to call yourself Turnus here. I will not ask anything more but will serve you as best I can so forgive my curiosity, which is a weakness of old age. I thank you for having deigned to touch me, a lowly person."

His back erect, he walked effortlessly before us to show us the rooms. I asked him to speak to me in Latin, which was the language of the city, so that I might learn it, and he began by naming every object, first in Latin and then in Etruscan. Arsinoe, too, listened so attentively that I realized that she wished to learn to speak to Tertius Valerius in the city's own language, and I feared the consequences.

3.

Tertius Valerius did not have another paralytic stroke despite the fervent wishes of his relatives who had long suffered the taunts of the man they considered simple-minded. Even as a youth he had been so untalented in comparison to both his intelligent brothers that he had been called simply Tertius, the third son, while in the Senate he was known as Brutus, the imbecile.

But he was not untalented. His gifts were merely of another kind than those of his politically astute brothers who performed glorious deeds for Rome and rose to be first among the first. Every man, even an apparently simple one, has his own talent which is peculiar to him and which is perhaps never recognized by those around him if he has no opportunity to reveal it. Others are given the opportunity only once. Such, among the Romans, was the one-eyed Horatius who, although only a stupid, brawny man, remained alone on the Etruscan shore to defend the Roman bridgehead until the others behind him had time to destroy the bridge. Bullheaded stupidity was his talent, even though Lars Porsenna did conquer the city despite his stand.

Such lands and wealth as Tertius Valerius possessed could not have been accumulated by a stupid man. Nor was it ambition, in my opinion, that drove him to yield his sons to the lictors but rather an excessive sense of responsibility as a Roman and a desire to emulate his admired brothers. The Etruscans who were descended from patrician families strove to be even more Roman than the Romans themselves, attempting by their actions to dispel the understandable skepticism of the plebeians. One would have thought that those of Etruscan origin would have desired the return of Etruscan kings to Rome, but they did not. They preferred to rule the city and the people as patricians, senators and state officials.

Because of Arsinoe's nearness and my simple care, Tertius Valerius quickly recovered from his paralytic stroke and was deeply grateful to us both. When he had emerged from his twilight condition he no longer imagined Arsinoe to be his deceased wife, although he remembered well that he had done so. He believed merely that his wife's spirit had fleetingly transferred herself to Arsinoe's body so that she might care for him tenderly. He declared himself fortunate to have been able to beg her forgiveness for having disregarded her pleas and sacrificed their sons.

When he was again able to move about, I had a skilled massager manipulate his face carefully so that his eyelid no longer drooped as badly as before. Saliva still trickled from his twisted lip, but Arsinoe wiped his beard like a devoted daughter with a warm linen towel that she kept nearby. She also began to supervise the household, patiently advising the old slaves and servants, so that the old man received better food than formerly. Likewise the rooms were swept every day, the dust was wiped from the Penates and the dishes were kept clean. I hardly recognized her, for she had never before seemed domestic.

As I expressed amazement she said, "How little you know me, Turms. Haven't I always declared that as a woman I ask for no more than security and four walls and a few servants to command? Now that I have them, thanks to this grateful old man, I can ask for nothing more."

But I was not pleased when, upon my approaching her in bed, she submitted meekly to my caresses with her thoughts obviously elsewhere. In a way I should have been content, for when she was restless she created mere disorder, but when it had happened several times I complained bitterly.

"Oh, Turms, doesn't anything that I do please you?" she exclaimed. "After all, I do show you that I still love you. Forgive me if I can no longer participate wholeheartedly, but your blindness and my own body have already caused me sufficient grief. My terrible life in the Siccanian forest made me realize that any other condition would be more desirable. After all, it was my mad passion for you that plunged me to the level of the lowest barbarian. Now at last I feel myself secure. Security is a woman's greatest happiness so permit me to retain it."

Concerning the events in the city, I can relate that the same assembly at which Tertius Valerius had suffered his paralytic stroke impeached the former hero Caius Marcius. Pursuing the fleeing Volscians alone, he had once forced his way into the city of Corioli, set fire to the nearest houses and held open the gate long enough for the cavalry to follow him. For that deed he had been given the privilege of participating in the triumph, standing beside the consul who had led the army and receiving the honorary appellation of Coriolanus from the people. Now the people were impeaching him for despising them and accusing him of secretly harboring designs of autocracy. It is true that he felt bitterness toward the people, for when the plebeians had ascended the holy mountain they had sacked and burned his country house together with the others', and had marched him under a yoke. His pride had never been able to forgive that humiliation. The plebeians had been pacified with the acquisition of two tribunes, who had the privilege of discontinuing the enforcement of any official edicts which they considered detrimental to the people's interests. But Coriolanus compelled the tribunes to step aside when they passed, spat before them and jostled them.

Coriolanus knew well that his own kind could not protect him from the wrath of the people during the trial. Fearing for his life, he evaded the lictors guarding his house, escaped over the wall, stole a horse from the barn at his own country house and rode through the night across the border south to the land of the Volsci. It was said that they greeted him with honors, gave him new clothes and permitted him to make sacrifices to the Volscians' city gods. The Romans were so famous for their military strategy that it is no wonder the Volscians welcomed a Roman commander to train their troops.

That same autumn the seven-day games at the circus had to be repeated because of an error that had occurred during the original celebration. The gods had revealed their displeasure through an unfavorable omen, and so the Senate undertook to repeat the expensive games rather than insult the gods. True, Tertius Valerius observed venomously that the Senate accepted the omen only because it wished to take the people's mind off other things, but this was merely his opinion.

Through him we obtained seats in the Senate's stand, and the Circus Maximus was truly something the like of which we had never seen before. Its fame had spread even to the neighboring peoples, so that crowds streamed to it from every direction, even from Veii, which was an incomparably finer city than Rome and only a day's journey away. A large group of Volscians arrived from Corioli with their families, but hardly had they seated themselves than a disturbance broke out and the people began to scream with one voice that the Volscians were the enemies of Rome and planned to seize the city during the games.

Even the patricians rose from their benches and finally the members of the Senate joined in the demand that the Volscians be ousted not only from the stand but from the entire city to restore order. The consuls ordered the lictors to remove the Volscians from the circus and to see that they immediately went to their lodgings, gathered their things and left the city. A better reason for war could not have been devised.

The Roman circus was completely unlike the Greek athletic games in which free men competed among themselves, but differed little from the Segestan games in which paid athletes and slaves boxed and wrestled. But horse races were the main attraction. The Romans had adopted the spectacle from the Etruscans, but the combats had lost their original significance and retained only their superficial aspects. Although the high priest determined the combatants' clothes and weapons, such as a trident and net against a sword, according to instructions that had been preserved, he hardly remembered their allegorical purpose.

Why should I describe the circus, which has changed from a worship of the gods to bloodshed for the sake of bloodshed? The Romans were truly wolf people, for each time they bestowed the greatest acclaim on the Kharuns who stepped into the arena with their sledge-hammers to crush the skulls of the vanquished. The combatants were slaves, prisoners of war and criminals, and not voluntary sacrifices to the gods as they had been under the Etruscans. Why shouldn't the Roman Senate have permitted them to slay one another for public amusement to divert the commoners' minds from their own problems? The same thing will presumably happen throughout the ages. Thus it is useless for me to describe further the various performances, or even the horse races despite the magnificent teams that had arrived even from the Etruscan cities.

I shall describe only Arsinoe's enchantment with the scene and her glowing eyes during those late autumn days as she clapped her white hands whenever blood bubbled forth onto the sands of the arena, or the horses plunged by with streaming manes and snorting nostrils. But even in the excitement she did not forget to adjust the blanket on Valerius' knees or to wipe the saliva from his beard as he cackled with glee at the familiar scenes.

I shall say no more about the laughter and excitement, the horror and cruelty of the circus. They will always remain although the form may change, and I shall not need to be reminded of them. I want only to remember Arsinoe's face in those days, still youthful and glowing. I want to remember her as she sat on a red cushion in the midst of a screaming crowd of ten thousand. Just so do I want to remember her, because I loved her.

The Romans dedicated the darkest days of the year to the earth god Saturn who was so old and sacred that they hardly dared strengthen the rotted wooden pillars of his temple. He was older even than Jupiter on the Capitoline hill, whose temple their first king, Romulus, had erected. They themselves declared that he was as old as the earth.

They celebrated him with the Saturnalia that lasted for days in which all work ceased and normal life turned upside down. People gave one another gifts even though Romans under ordinary circumstances did not willingly do so. Masters served their slaves and slaves ordered their masters and mistresses about to compensate for the heavy days of the remaining year. The position of slaves was not an easy one in Rome where fear ruled because of the city's own violence. Thus many had their male slaves castrated, not to protect the chastity of their wives and daughters as was the case in the eastern lands and in Carthage, but to destroy the slaves' virility and rebelliousness. During the Saturnalia, however, the wine flowed, master and slave exchanged places, patrician and plebeian met as equals, strolling players performed on street corners and no jest was too daring.

Those distorted days changed Roman life completely, abolishing dignity, severity and even frugality. Arsinoe received many presents, and not only the customary clay bread, fruit and domestic animals, but valuable jewelry, perfume, mirrors and wearing apparel. She had attracted much attention despite her modest demeanor as she walked in the streets and market places accompanied by Hanna or one of Valerius' old slaves. She accepted the gifts with a wistful smile, as though a secret sorrow were preying on her. As return gifts Tertius Valerius bestowed upon the givers, on her behalf, a clay oxen or lamb to remind the recipient of the simplicity of traditional Roman customs.

But Arsinoe declared, "These festivities are nothing new to me. The celebrations in Carthage which honored Baal were much wilder. I can still hear the furious music of the drums and the rattles in the days when I was young and attended the temple school. The youths became so frenzied that they slashed their bodies like the priests, and wealthy merchants presented fortunes, houses and ships to the women who could please them. This primitive festival is really quite tame compared to the festivals of my youth."

She met my glance and explained hastily, "Not that I long for those

261

days of futile passion. It was passion that plunged me to destruction, causing me to lose for your sake all that I had achieved. But surely I can think of my youth with a sigh now that I am a mature woman who is content with her lot in a secure house and a place in a bed beside a useless man."

In that manner she reminded me that I was but a guest in Tertius Valerius' house and even that only through her efforts. But she was so under the spell of the gifts, the festivities and the excitement that she drew me to her in the dark of night. I felt the glow of the goddess in her body and once again she flung back her white arms and breathed her hot breath into my mouth.

But as we lay in the darkness and I felt myself happy once more she began to talk. "Turms, beloved, months have passed and you have done no more than gape about you. Soon Misme will be four years old and it is time for you to become sensible. If you won't think of me and my future, at least think of your daughter and her future. How does she feel, seeing that her father is a mere idler who is content with crumbs of charity? If you were even a driver of race horses or a skilled horn blower, you would be something. But now you are nothing."

Her caresses made me so happy that her words did not anger me, nor did I care to remind her that Misme really was not my daughter. I was very fond of the little girl and enjoyed playing with her, while she liked me more than Arsinoe who rarely had time for more than scolding.

I stretched my limbs in the bed, yawned deeply and said in jest, "I trust that you are still satisfied with me as a lover. If you are, that suffices for me."

She let her palm slide down my bare chest.

"You don't have to ask that," she whispered. "No man has ever loved me so divinely as you. You know that."

Then she raised herself on one elbow, blew into the brazier so that her face was lighted by its reddish glow, and said thoughtfully, "If that is your only skill, Turms, at least take advantage of it. Although Rome is superficially strict in its habits, I doubt whether it actually differs much from other lands. Many a man has risen to high position merely by choosing the right bedchamber."

Her cold-blooded suggestion made me sit upright. "Arsinoe," I exclaimed, "do you really mean that you would want me to sleep with a strange woman for the purpose of obtaining political or material benefits from her husband or friends? Don't you love me any more?"

"Of course I would be slightly jealous," she hastened to assure me. "But I would forgive you knowing that it happened for the good of our future. Only your body would be involved, not your heart, and thus it would mean nothing."

She caressed my limbs and laughed lightly. "Truly, your body is so beautifully formed and is so appropriate to its task that I fear it would be wasted if it made only one woman happy."

"The same is true of your own body, Arsinoe," I said coldly. "Is your suggestion a threat?"

She raised her hand to her mouth and yawned. "It was so unnecessary for your tone to harden," she said reproachfully. "You yourself have noticed the change in me. No, Tertius Valerius would not understand and forgive me if he saw that I were wanton. But forget what I have said. I merely spoke what came to my head. Some other man would have considered my words a compliment. Only you are as hard-headed as ever."

Only a few days later, when the palling after-effects of the festival were still felt throughout the city, and I myself was depressed to think that I was nothing, Arsinoe came to me in great haste. Her face was set in a hard white mask, not beautiful but horrifying as a Gorgon in my eyes.

"Turms," she said sharply, "have you looked at Hanna recently? Have you noticed something different about her?"

I had not looked at Hanna especially although I had felt her presence and bright glance whenever I played with Misme. "What is wrong?" I asked in surprise. "Perhaps her face is thinner. Surely she is not ill?"

Arsinoe struck her hands together in impatience. "How blind you men are! Still, I myself have been just as blind in trusting that girl. I thought I had reared her well, but now she is pregnant."

"Pregnant—Hanna?" I stammered.

"I happened to look at her and demanded an explanation," said Arsinoe. "She had to confess, for she can't hide her condition much longer. That stupid slut obviously thought that she could deceive me, her mistress, and began to sell herself. Or perhaps, in even greater stupidity, she became fond of some handsome lictor or wrestler and slept with him. But I'll teach her!"

Only then did I remember my own guilt with a pang. It was I who had warmed my loneliness with her virginity in the harbor of Panormos. But Arsinoe had assured me that I was sterile, so Hanna could not have become pregnant by me. I had merely opened the way, and it was my fault if she had succumbed to temptation in a city like Rome. But that I could not confess to Arsinoe.

Arsinoe became calmer and pondered on the matter coldly. "She has

263

betrayed my trust. What a price I would have received for her if she were undefiled, and how well I would have arranged everything for her! She could have even earned enough to buy her freedom in accordance with Roman laws. But a pregnant female slave will be bought at best by some overseer who wants to increase his workers. But why weep over a broken crock? We'll sell her quickly, that's all."

Horrified, I declared that Hanna had, after all, taken good care of Misme and that Arsinoe should not have been concerned with her support since Tertius Valerius bore the cost of it.

Arsinoe screamed shrilly at my stupidity, shook my shoulders and exclaimed, "Do you want a harlot to care for your daughter? What manners do you think she will teach Misme? And what will Tertius think of us for not keeping an eye on our servant? First the girl must be flogged, and I myself shall see to it that it is not done clumsily."

And again I can plead no defense save that everything happened too rapidly and that my own feeling of guilt stunned me. As Arsinoe rushed out I sat with my head between my hands staring at the colored tiles of the floor and was roused only by screams of agony coming from the courtyard.

Running outside, I saw Hanna tied by her wrists to a stake and the stable slave lashing her bare back so that welts had formed on her smooth skin. I snatched the whip from the slave's hand and, blind with rage, struck him across the face with it. Arsinoe stood nearby, red-faced and quivering.

"That's enough," I said. "Sell the girl if you wish, but she must be sold to a good man who will take care of her."

Hanna had slumped to the ground, hanging by her wrists, and sobs shook her body although she tried to control them. Arsinoe stamped her foot and her eyes were round.

"Don't interfere, Turms! The girl must confess who has raped her and with how many she has slept and where she has hidden the money that she has earned. It is our money and we can collect something from the rapist if we threaten him with legal action."

At that I slapped Arsinoe across the face. It was the first time that I had hit her and I was frightened by it myself. Arsinoe turned pale and her face twisted, but to my surprise she remained calm.

When I took out my knife to free Hanna, Arsinoe signaled to the slave and said to me, "Don't cut the costly thongs. Let the slave open the knots. If the girl is so dear to you that you don't want to know what happened, so be it. Let her be led immediately to the cattle market to be sold. I myself will accompany her there to make certain that she finds a respectable master, even though she doesn't deserve one. But you have always been tender-hearted and I must obey your wishes."

Hanna raised her face from the ground, her eyelids swollen from weeping. She had bitten her lips raw, for despite the flogging she had refused to divulge a word although it would have been easy for her to name me as the one who had led her down the wrong path. But her glance was not accusing. She merely opened her eyes as though in joy that she could see me defending her.

A cowardly relief came over me when I caught her glance and it did not occur to me that Arsinoe might be untrustworthy. Nevertheless I felt sufficiently skeptical to ask, "Do you swear to look out for the girl's good even though it means getting a lower price for her?"

Arsinoe looked me in the eye, took a deep breath and assured me, "Of course I swear it. The price makes no difference so long as we get rid of the girl."

One of the household slaves brought her the large stole worn by Roman women and draped it over her head and shoulders. The stable slave pulled Hanna to her feet, tossed a rope around her neck and so they departed through the gate, the slave first, leading Hanna by the rope, and Arsinoe last, tightly wrapped in her stole.

I ran after them, touched Arsinoe's shoulder and begged in a tearchoked voice, "At least take down the name and city of the purchaser so that we will know where Hanna is."

Arsinoe paused, shook her head and said gently, "Turms dear, I have already forgiven you, for I understand your ugly behavior. Apparently it is as though you had to let some beloved animal be killed because of sickness. In such a case, doesn't the kind master entrust the deed to a dependable friend without seeking to know how and where it happens or where the carcass is buried? For your own sake it is better that you don't know where the girl goes. Trust me, Turms. I will take care of everything for you since you are so sensitive."

She brushed my cheek with her hand and hastened after the slave. I had to admit that Arsinoe's words sounded reasonable, but doubt gnawed at my heart and I felt guilty no matter how I tried to persuade myself that as an Elymian Hanna was innately wanton. Otherwise she would not so readily have flung herself into my arms. It would be better for me if I thought no more of the matter.

In that Arsinoe helped me, for when she returned that afternoon she was so considerate that she did not even mention the price that she had obtained for Hanna. Nor did she say one word about the matter even later. That in itself should have made me suspicious, but instead it helped me to forget. So settled was I in everyday life in Tertius Valerius' house.

4.

It was probably meant that I should struggle within walls for the nine long and certainly hard years indicated by the ravens, so that I would better learn to know life and achieve the proper age. That is undoubtedly why Arsinoe was ordained to be my companion, for it is doubtful whether any other woman would have succeeded in keeping me fettered to the earth and everyday life for such a long period. Indeed, it was because of her that Tertius Valerius took me aside one day to talk to me in his kindly old man's way.

"My dear son Turnus," he said amiably, "you know that I am fond of you and that your wife's presence brightens my old days. But my illness in the forum was a healthy reminder of mortality. You yourself know that any day I may fall lifeless to the ground. And that is why I am so concerned about your future.

"You see, dear Turnus," he continued in his quavering voice, "as much as I like you, permit me as an old man to say that the life you are leading is not worthy of a man. You must brace yourself. You have looked around long enough to understand Roman customs and you even speak the language better than some Sabine or other person who has been transplanted here to increase the population. You can pass for a Roman as well as anyone else if you but choose."

He shook his head, smiled with wrinkled eyes and observed, "You probably think, as I do, that this is a brutal and merciless city. I myself would wish it to return to Saturn's power, but the war god's wolf is the suckler of Rome. The gods have decreed it and we can only submit. I don't consider all Rome's principles correct or its wars just. Greed is our weakness and we do not wish to yield even a portion of our land until we are compelled to do so."

Again he shook his head, laughed and said, "Forgive an old man if I stray from the subject and return to the same old matter that has given me the reputation of a simpleton among my friends and relatives. But right or wrong, Rome is my city and that of my family ever since our progenitor left Volsina one hundred and fifty years ago to build a future for himself in a new land. Only a stupid man tries to turn his mistakes into virtues and rejoices in them. I am not proud of the death of my only sons. It was the bitterest error of my life even though the people point to me in the forum and fathers whisper to their sons, 'There goes Tertius Valerius, who surrendered his own sons to the lictors to protect Rome from autocracy.' I don't turn around to shout that it was a horrible mistake, for it is better that people believe in a lie if it benefits Rome and helps the young to withstand future ordeals. And such there will be."

His body began to tremble and saliva trickled from the twisted corner of his mouth. Arsinoe entered the room as though she had passed the doorway by chance, wiped the old man's beard with a linen towel, gently stroked his sparse hair and spoke to me angrily. "Surely you are not tiring our host or distressing him?" Tertius Valerius ceased trembling as soon as he clutched Arsinoe's hand, looked at her lovingly and said, "No, daughter, he has not been tiring me. Rather, I have tired him. I should remember that I am not speaking in the Senate. I have a proposition to make to you, Turnus. If you wish, I can obtain Roman citizenship rights for you in a fairly good tribus. As a plebeian, of course, but you had sufficient means upon entering the city to meet the property demands for a heavily armored soldier. You cannot enter the cavalry because that is separate, but you can enter the army and you have experience in warfare as your wife has related and your scars prove. There is your opportunity, Turnus. After that, everything depends on yourself. The gate to the temple of Janus is always open."

I knew that a serious war was expected because the traitor Coriolanus was training the Volscians' best warriors in Roman battle tactics. I surmised that I could become a Roman citizen by merely petitioning it since I had sufficient means to pay for my arms, and under those conditions I did not need Tertius Valerius' recommendations. While it is true that he thought of my interests, as a Roman he also thought of the city's. Even one experienced heavily armored soldier strengthened the army, and as a new citizen I could be expected to fight as well as possible to gain a reputation.

His suggestion was sensible, but I had had enough of war with Dorieus. The very thought of war made me feel ill.

I could not explain my feeling but it was so strong that I replied, "Tertius Valerius, don't be angry with me but I don't feel that I am yet ready for Roman citizenship. Perhaps later, but I cannot promise anything."

Tertius Valerius and Arsinoe exchanged glances. To my surprise they did not attempt to persuade me.

Instead, Tertius Valerius asked carefully, "Then what do you intend to do, my son? If I can advise you in any way, speak."

The thought had surely matured in me although it burst forth only in response to his question. "There are other lands besides Rome," I said. "To increase my knowledge I intend to travel to the Etruscan cities. A great war is brewing in the East. Of that I have certain knowledge, and it may be that its repercussions will even extend to Italy. Before such an avalanche even Rome would be but a city among cities. Knowledge of other countries is always needed, and my knowledge and political astuteness may some day benefit Rome."

Tertius Valerius nodded enthusiastically. "Perhaps you are right. Political advisers on distant lands are always needed, and Roman citizenship would be only a hindrance to you in obtaining this experience since it would obligate you to military service. I can give you letters of introduction to influential persons in both Veii and Caere, the nearest of the large Etruscan cities. It would also be wise for you to become acquainted with the Etruscan coastal cities of Populonia and Vetulonia, on which we are completely dependent for iron. In fact, the armed strength of Rome is founded on the free import of iron from the Etruscan cities."

When Arsinoe stooped to wipe his dripping mouth I took advantage of the moment and said with a smile, "I have enjoyed your hospitality far too long, Tertius Valerius. I cannot impose upon you still more by requesting letters of recommendation. I shall probably wander alone and freely and I don't know whether the recommendation of a Roman senator would benefit me in trying to befriend respected Etruscans. It is better for me not to tie myself to Rome even with your recommendations, as much as I value your friendship."

He placed his hands cordially on my shoulders and said that I should not hasten my departure. As his friend I would always have a place by his hearth, whenever and for as long a time as I wished it. But despite the warmth of his voice I was certain that this was farewell. For one reason or another he and Arsinoe wanted me to leave Rome. My suggestion pleased them both.

Their behavior wounded my vanity to the extent that I was determined to get along on my own assets and if possible to augment my resources along the way. Thus Arsinoe bound me to the earth and to everyday life even more tightly than if I had remained with her. She sent me forth among the ordinary people to gauge the possibility of profit and if necessary to work with my hands, which I had never before done. For that reason my journey was to constitute a period of learning in which I would discover the needs of a simple person in a civilized world.

I exchanged my delicate footwear for heavy-soled Roman travel shoes and donned a simple shirt and gray woolen mantle. My hair had grown again and without anointing it I braided it into a knot at my neck.

Arsinoe laughed at my appearance until the tears came, thus easing the pangs of parting.

Tertius Valerius said, "You are right, Turnus, from the ground one sometimes sees more than from the ridge of a temple. At your age my palms were calloused and these hands of mine were as broad as shovels. When I see you like that I respect you more than before."

I should have realized from that that I was setting forth on a new blind path. Naturally I still was accompanied by Hecate's luck since she provides aid in small as well as large matters. So when I paused on the bridge to look at the flooding yellow waters of the Tiber, a skittish herd of cattle pushed past me and would have crushed me against the railing if I had not leaped over it in time. The angry cries of the guards added to the confusion, and finally the drover called for help and his half-grown daughter burst into tears. I jumped back onto the bridge and seized the lead bull by the nostrils, squeezing them as hard as I could. The bull tossed his head in vain and finally quieted down as though realizing that he had met his master. Then the entire herd grew calm and obediently followed the bull until we left the bridge and I guided the herd to the side of the road near the slope of Janiculum.

There I released the bull and wiped the mucus from my hand. The drover approached me limpingly and holding his back, for at the end of the bridge the guard had struck him with the shaft of a spear. He blessed me in the name of Saturn, from which I deduced that he belonged to the simple country people of Rome, while his daughter wiped her tears and hugged her cows.

The drover seated himself on a hummock and rubbed his back. "Now what, master? I can see from your face that you are not our kind. We are living in bad times and at our master's command we are taking our cattle to the market at Veii before the Volscians arrive and steal them. They have never been so wild and I do not know how my daughter and I will be able to control them now that my back is hurt."

His helplessness touched me and his daughter was a pretty girl although barefooted. "I don't know much about cattle," I said readily, "but I am on my way to Veii and in no hurry. I will gladly help you herd your cattle although I don't know how to milk them."

He was greatly cheered by my words. "That new god Mercury must be of some use, after all. As I was about to leave I made a hasty bow at the door of his temple, and look how soon that young and kind god has sent you to my aid."

We joined forces and, paced by the slow herd, set off for Veii along the worn road. I picked up a switch but we soon noticed that we made the best progress if I walked ahead with my hand on the lead bull's neck while the drover and his daughter followed behind, chasing the cows that paused at the roadside. Soon the journey progressed so well that the girl began to sing an old shepherd's song. The sun shone between the clouds and my mind brightened after the sadness of parting. At dusk I was grateful for the slowness of our journey, for the new shoes were rubbing blisters in my heels. I took off the shoes and flung them over my shoulder. For the first time I felt how gloriously the earth's dust responds to the steps of a bare foot.

When darkness fell we found a deserted cattle enclosure whose fence assured us a restful sleep, for otherwise we would have had to guard the cattle alternately. We made a fire to warm us in the biting dampness of the early spring. Father and daughter began to milk the cows, and when I noticed how painfully the man stooped because of his injured back I offered to help them. Laughingly the girl showed me how to use my hands, and the touch of her tanned fingers thrilled me, not with desire, but merely with the nearness of a young person. I was surprised at the smoothness of her palms and she explained, laughing at my stupidity, that it was caused by milking and milk fat. She said that noble Etruscan women even bathed in milk, but that in her opinion it was a crime against the gods because milk, butter and cheese were intended for human nourishment.

I said that to me it was as great a crime to let warm milk flow onto the ground.

The girl became serious and explained, "Necessity knows no law. We could not take any vessels with us and the cows must be milked. Otherwise they will suffer and their udders will become inflamed and we will not get the price that our master demands for them."

She glanced at her father and confessed ruefully, "We will hardly get it anyway, for I see by the innumerable hoofprints on the road that all the patricians have had the same idea at the same time. I am afraid that the cattle merchants of Veii will pay whatever they wish for Roman cattle. No matter what price my father obtains for them our master will be dissatisfied and will beat him."

"What a severe master you must have," I observed.

But the girl immediately began to defend him and said proudly, "He is no more severe than the others. He is a Roman and a patrician."

There were not many milch cows and they had a dipper with them so that each of us could drink his fill of warm milk. When he had closed the gate of the pen the drover gathered the cleanest of the straw and said contentedly, "I didn't expect us to have such a fine bed. Sleep well, master."

He removed his mantle and flung himself on the straw, covering himself with the coarse cloth. The girl stretched out beside her father and he covered her likewise.

When I remained standing in doubt, the girl sat up and urged, "Do lie down, friend. Let us warm one another, for otherwise it will be a cold night."

Already in the Ionian war I had learned to sleep side by side with my comrades but this was something new and the smell of manure in the straw was repulsive. To avoid hurting the girl I removed my woolen mantle, lay down beside her and covered myself and her with it. One corner of it even reached her father.

The girl sniffed the odor of wool in the new mantle, fingered the fabric and said, "You have a fine cloak." Suddenly she turned around, wound her arm around my neck, pressed her cheek against mine and whispered, "You are a good man."

As though ashamed of her outburst she buried her face in my chest and a moment later I realized from her breathing that she had fallen asleep in my arms. Her body warmed mine delightfully as a little bird throbbingly warms the hand. I still felt the quick touch of her cheek on mine and happiness filled me. The night sky grew clear, the stars shone brightly and in the air was the cold breath of the mountains of Veii. I slept more soundly than I had in years, without a dream. So close to the earth and to humans did I become on the first day of my journey.

The next day as the mountains gleamed and the sky shimmered with sunshine we drove the herd up an increasingly steep road until before us, on an unconquerable mountain, rose splendid Veii, surrounded by its wall. The painted temple roofs with their statues of deities shone from afar. All the while we were met by Roman shepherds, who warned us against continuing our journey since the cattle merchants of Veii were taking advantage of Rome's plight by paying wretched prices even for the best cattle. They themselves regretted their sales and urged us rather to drive our cattle back, for the rumors of a Volscian attack were probably exaggerated. Very likely it would take a long time for the Volscians to equip a real army that would dare advance within sight of Rome.

But despite his doubts the drover had to obey his master's order. Sadly we drove the herd through the massive archway and the guards indicated where we should take the animals. In contrast to Rome, whose walled area included large meadows and swamps, Veii was a closely built great city with little pasturage even in the event of war. Its population was twice that of Rome, its wall longer than Rome's flimsy wall, and its two main streets, which crossed each other, were broad and straight in comparison to the streets of Rome. They were paved with stone slabs worn deep by the traffic, and the fronts of the houses facing them were ornamented with molded and brightly colored clay statues and decorations. Even the people differed from those in Rome. Their faces were long and fine-featured, they smiled attractively and their clothes were gracefully cut and adorned.

Hardly had we reached the cattle market when a group of brawny men hastened toward us to inspect the bulls, try the udders of the milch cows and measure the distance between the heifers' horns. When they had done so they spread their hands in customary dismay, began to criticize the cattle and called them worthless. In wretched Latin they declared that they were at best suited for slaughter and that even their hides had little value. Nevertheless, they hastened to make their offers while glancing at one another surreptitiously. Thus we learned that a large number of cattle merchants had just arrived in Veii from the inland Etruscan cities, tempted by the news that the Romans were selling their cattle at ridiculous prices because of the threat of war. Roman cattle were famous because the Romans had stolen the finest breeding stock during their wars against their neighbors and the Roman patricians were known to be skilled breeders.

The cattle merchants of Veii had joined forces and until that moment had been paying a low price upon which they had agreed and sharing the cattle that they bought. But the competition offered by the strange merchants broke down the ring of resistance and induced the city's merchants to compete with the strangers and one another. The last sellers to depart from the city had clenched their fists and sworn to spread the word around Rome that it no longer paid to drive cattle to Veii, hence the cattle merchants feared that they would obtain no more good Roman cattle.

The injudicious drover would happily have accepted the first offer that met the price set by his master. But when I saw how matters stood I urged him to be calm and pointed out that it was still a long time until sunset. Leisurely we seated ourselves on the ground, ate our bread and cheese, and I called to a peddler for wine which he served from beautifully painted clay cups. The wine cheered our spirits and the weary cattle calmly chewed their cud around us.

The girl looked at me with smiling eyes. "You brought us good fortune, friend."

I remembered then that it was necessary for me to earn my bread among people like the others. And so I suggested to the father, "The bread and cheese you have given me suffice to pay me for my help in driving the cattle safely here. Permit me now to participate in the bargaining. I ask half of whatever amount exceeds the price set by your master. That would seem only just."

The drover was not at market for the first time. He had enough peasant shrewdness to reply instantly, "I can drive my own bargains, but I don't understand the language of these strange Etruscans. You are probably wiser than I anyway and they would not dare to cheat you as much as me. But half the profit is too much for I must think of my master. If you will be content with one fourth I will shake hands on it gratefully."

I pretended to hesitate but then extended my hand and we sealed the agreement. That was all I had wanted, for I would have been ashamed to accept more than one fourth of the good man's profit that would spare him a beating. I rose from the ground and let my tongue sing from the joy of wine. I praised our cattle in Latin and Etruscan and even Greek which was well understood by the Tarquinian merchants. As I sang their praises the bulls, cows and heifers seemed to brighten in my eyes until they were almost like divine cattle, and the merchants began to feel them again with new respect. Finally the merchant who had come the farthest offered the highest price. The others covered their heads as though crushed, but behind the edge of their robes they laughed.

When we had weighed the silver and computed its equivalent in Roman copper, it became apparent that my eulogies had brought more than twice the price set by the patrician and almost equaled the actual value of the cattle in peacetime. The drover kissed his hands in joy and his daughter began to dance. Unhesitatingly the father paid me one fourth of the profit in good silver and whispered that he had hidden the best bull in the forest where the Volscians would hardly find it. There would be the beginning of a new herd when peace returned.

I thought it best to leave the drover for I was impatient to become acquainted with the gay and civilized city that differed so greatly from the previous cities I had known. The mountain height made its air fresh and its stone streets had none of the usual vile-smelling rubbish, for all dirt was carried away by sealed sewers under the streets.

I remained and thrived in Veii until summer, living in a neat inn where no one was unduly curious about me or asked about my comings and goings as was the custom in Greek cities. The silence and courtesy of the service pleased me. When I remembered the noisy and chattering Greek cities I felt as though I were in another, more noble world. In itself the inn was modest and appropriate to my appearance but not even there was it customary to eat with two fingers. Instead, a two-pronged fork was used at meals. From the very beginning the servant brought me a silver fork as though the world contained no thieves.

I did not attempt to make friends, but as I walked in the streets and the market places I enjoyed the composure of the people and the beauty of the city and began to feel that, compared to its neighbor, Rome was a barbaric place. Presumably the residents of Veii thought likewise although I did not hear them speak unkindly of Rome. They lived as though Rome did not exist, having signed a twenty-year pact of non-aggression with it. But there was something sad in the faces and smiles of the people of Veii.

On the first morning when I was content only to breathe the air of Veii, which was like medicine after the Roman swamps, I found myself in a small market place and sat down on a worn stone bench. I saw the shadows of people hastening by. I saw a donkey with its neat forelock and its basket of vegetables. I saw that a country woman had placed cheeses on display on a clean cloth.

With a catch of my breath I realized in a sudden flash of perception that once again I had previously lived that same moment of happiness. As in a dream I rose and turned a familiar corner. Before me rose a temple whose pillared front I recognized.

The mysteriously splendid and deep-hued statues on the temple roof represented Artemis defending her deer against Herakles while the other gods watched the scene with smiles on their divine faces. I ascended the steps and entered the gate behind which a sleepy temple servant sprinkled holy water over me with his whisk. I became increasingly certain that I had once before lived that moment.

Against the dimness of the walls, in light that streamed down from an opening in the roof, stood the divinely beautiful goddess of Veii on her pedestal, a dreamy smile on her lips. A child was in her arms and at her feet was a goose with arched neck. Nor did I have to inquire to know that her name was Uni. I knew it and recognized her by her face, the child and the goose, but how I knew it I cannot explain. My hand rose to my forehead and I raised my right arm in sacred greeting, bowing my head. Something in me knew that the image was sacred and that the spot on which I stood had been holy even before the temple and the city had been built.

No priest was visible but the servant guessed from my attire that I was a stranger and rose from his seat to describe the votive offerings and sacred objects along the walls. My devotion was so deep that I motioned him away, for I did not wish to look at anything in the temple save Uni, the divine personification of womanly tenderness and goodness.

Only afterward did I remember that I had seen that vision in the goddess's dream at the temple of Eryx. In itself it was not unusual, for a person frequently dreams that which happens only later, but I wondered why my dream in the temple of Aphrodite had led me to the sacred house of compassionate love and maternal happiness unless it was merely the goddess's mockery at my expense.

On the threshold of summer, news came to Veii that the Volscian army under Coriolanus was marching on Rome to avenge, as they said, the insult suffered by the Volscians at the circus. But the Roman forces did not advance to meet the enemy in open battle as they usually did. From that it was surmised that Rome would be in a state of siege, as unbelievable as it seemed.

By walking briskly I could have reached Rome in a day, but instead I turned away from it, first northward to see the lake of Veii and from there over the mountains westward along shepherds' trails to the city of Caere, which was near the sea. For the first time in my life I saw the limpidity and red glow of a large lake at sunset. I do not know what so inexpressibly stirred me at the sight of that lake surrounded by mountains, but the mere rustle of the reeds and the smell of the water, so different from the stench of brine, made my breath quicken. I myself thought that I was only a traveler who wished to see something new, but my heart knew better.

In the city of Caere I suspected for the first time the true mightiness of the twelve Etruscan states when I saw the immense necropolis that rose, beyond a deep valley. On either side of its sacred way was a series of circular burial mounds heaped on stone bases within which were entombed the city's ancient rulers surrounded by their sacrificial gifts.

Life in Caere was noisier than in noble Veii. From morning to night one heard the clink and clank of artisans in innumerable workshops, and sailors from all countries wandered through the streets glancing about in search of their customary diversion on land. Although the port of Caere was far away at the mouth of the river, the fame of the Etruscan cities' splendor and gaiety had traveled so far that alien sailors willingly climbed the steep road to the city.

Instead of walking in the restless streets, I preferred to breathe the air of the holy mountain and the fragrance of mint and laurel shrubs in the city of tombs. The guard explained that the sacred roundness of the tombs had its origin in ancient times when the Etruscans had still lived in hive-shaped huts, and because of that the oldest temples, such as the temple of Vesta in Rome, were also round. He spoke of Lucumones instead of kings and I asked him to explain what he meant.

He spread his hands in a manner that he had learned from Greek visitors and said, "It is difficult to explain to a stranger. A Lucumo is that which is."

When I did not understand he shook his head and tried again. "A Lucumo is a holy king."

Still I did not understand. Then he pointed to several gigantic mounds and said that they were the tombs of Lucumones. But when I indicated the most recently built tomb on which the grass had not yet had time to grow, he made a negative gesture and explained as though to a barbarian, "Not a Lucumo's tomb. Only a ruler's tomb."

My insistence made him impatient because he found it difficult to explain what seemed apparent. "A Lucumo is a ruler chosen by the gods," he explained crossly. "He is found. He is recognized. He is the high priest, the supreme judge, the supreme lawgiver. An ordinary ruler can be dethroned or his power can be inherited, but no one can deprive a Lucumo of his power because the power is his."

"How is he found, how is he recognized?" I asked in bewilderment. "Is not a Lucumo's son a Lucumo?" I gave the guard a piece of silver to pacify him.

But he could not explain how a Lucumo is recognized and what distinguishes him from an ordinary person. Instead he said, "A Lucumo's son is not usually a Lucumo although he may be. Very old, very divine families have given birth to Lucumones successively. But we are living in corrupt times. Lucumones are born but rarely these days."

He pointed to a majestic tomb that we were passing. Before it was a white stone pillar topped by a round, instead of a peaked, headdress.

"A queen's tomb," he explained with a smile, and said that Caere was one of the few Etruscan cities which had been ruled by a queen. The reign of the famous queen was remembered by the people of Caere as a golden age, for the city had prospered more than at any other time. The guard declared that she had reigned in Caere for sixty years, but I suspected that he had learned the art of exaggeration from Greek visitors.

"But how can a woman rule a city?" I asked in amazement.

"She was a Lucumo," explained the guard.

"Can even a woman be a Lucumo?" I asked.

"Of course," he said impatiently. "It happens rarely, but through a whim of the gods a Lucumo can be born a woman. That is what happened at Caere."

276

I listened and did not understand because I listened with prosaic ears and had bound myself to lead an ordinary life among people. But many times I traversed the difficult road and returned to the giant tombs that exuded an air of mysterious power.

In the city itself I saw another sight that moved me strangely. Beside the wall was a row of potters' stalls, most of them selling cheap red funerary urns to the poor. In Caere the deceased were not buried as they were in Rome but were cremated and their ashes buried in a round urn which could be of expensive bronze decorated with beautiful designs or of plain red clay such as the poor used. Only the lid had some clumsy image as a handle.

I happened to be looking at the red urns when a poor country couple, hand in hand, came to select a resting place for their deceased daughter. They chose an urn with a lid bearing a crowing cock. When they saw it they smiled with joy and the man immediately pulled out a stamped copper ingot from his pouch. He did not haggle over the price.

"Why isn't he bargaining?" I asked the potter in surprise.

The man shook his head. "One does not bargain over sacred things, you stranger."

"But that vessel is not sacred," I insisted. "It is merely clay."

Patiently the man explained, "It is not sacred when it leaves the potter's kiln. Nor is it sacred here on this table. But when the ashes of that poor couple's daughter have been placed in it and the lid has been closed, it is sacred. That is why the price is modest and unconditional."

Such a manner of selling was un-Greek and new to me. Indicating the crowing cock on the lid of the urn, I asked the couple, "Why did you choose just a cock? Would not it be more appropriate for a wedding?"

They stared at me in astonishment, pointed to the cock and said in unison, "But it is crowing."

"Why is it crowing?" I asked.

They looked at each other and smiled mysteriously despite their grief. The man put his arm around his wife's waist and said to me as to the most stupid of persons, "The cock is announcing the resurrection."

They left the urn, and I remained staring after them with tears in my eyes. How touchingly and with what strange certainty and insight did the words pierce my heart! That is what I remember about Caere. Nor could I explain the great difference between the Greek and Etruscan worlds more effectively than by remembering that to the Greeks the cock is the symbol of lust, to the Etruscans of resurrection.

I had intended to return to Rome from Caere but word spread of Coriolanus' liberation of one city after another that had been occupied by the Romans. He had conquered Corioli and even Lavinium which the Romans considered an important city. It seemed only a matter of time before the salt basins at the mouth of the Tiber would fall into the hands of the Volscians. For that reason I preferred to continue northward to see Tarquinia, which was considered the most significant and politically important city in the Etruscan league.

As I journeyed through the freshness of summer I did not know what to admire the most, the security of the roads, the hospitality of the country people, the long-horned cattle in the pastures or the fertile fields that had been created from the swamps by drains. The earth around me was richer and more fruitful than any I had seen before. The draining of the swamps and the clearing of the forests had demanded generations of skill and hard labor. And yet the Ionians scornfully called the Tyrrhenians pirates and the Etruscans a tyrant nation which had degenerated through debauchery.

Tarquinia is presumably an eternal city on earth, and so it is not necessary for me to describe it. Many Greeks lived there, because the Etruscans in that advanced and lively city admired a stranger's skill and were interested in everything new just as women are attracted to alien soldiers because of their odd-plumed helmets. Only in religious matters did the Etruscans know that they were superior to all other nations.

The residents of Tarquinia were eager to learn. Among them I found friends and despite my appearance was invited to banquets at the homes of the nobles when it became known that I had fought in Ionia and knew the cities of Sicily. I had to buy new clothes so that I might appear worthy of my companions. Gladly I donned Etruscan clothes of fine linen and thin wool and wore a low, dome-shaped cap. I began anointing my hair once more, carefully shaved my beard and allowed my braid to hang freely to the shoulder. Looking at myself in a mirror I could no longer distinguish myself from a native Etruscan.

At banquets I willingly replied to such questions as were asked, even about Rome and its internal political problems. When the young men noticed that I was not sensitive about my Ionian blood they began to upbraid the Greeks.

"In ancient times the power of the twelve Etruscan cities extended from north to south on the Italian mainland. We had colonies along the shores and islands as far as Iberia, and our ships sailed all the seas to Greece, Ionia and Phoenicia. But with the passing of time more and more new hungry nations came from the north. We permitted them to settle on our land and civilized them, although some we destroyed, but still they came from the mountain passes. The worst, however, are the

Greeks who have spread their colonies even to Cumae and are sitting on all the shores as thickly as frogs. In the north we are being crushed by the recently arrived Celtic tribes and in the south the Greeks are destroying all reasonable trade."

Thus we exchanged thoughts while drinking wine, but I myself spoke only when questioned and otherwise kept my mouth closed. By being an understanding listener I won many friends, for the Etruscans in that respect did not differ from other peoples.

Tarquinia was a city of painters just as Veii was the home of sculptors. Not only were there decorators of house walls and painters of wooden chests, but also a guild of tomb painters who were the most respected of all and whose few members had inherited their talent from their fathers and practiced it as a sacred craft.

The burial ground of Tarquinia was on the other side of a valley atop a bluff from which one could look westward over gardens and fields, olive groves and orchards to the sea itself and even beyond. The tumuli, while not so imposing as the tombs of Caere's rulers, were more numerous, extending as far as eye could see. Before each was an altar for sacrifices and from a door steep stairs descended into the tombs hewn out of the soft rock. For centuries it had been the custom to decorate the walls of the tombs with sacred paintings.

As I wandered along the holy field I noticed that the temporary wooden door of a recently completed tomb was open. Hearing voices from the depths I called down and inquired whether a stranger might enter to look at the artist's sacred work. The painter bawled back such a coarse oath as I had not heard from even the lips of a shepherd during my journey, but a moment later his apprentice ran up the stairs with a smokeless torch to light my way.

Cautiously I descended the uneven steps, leaning against the wall, when to my amazement I noticed the outline of a shell etched in the wall as though the goddess were indicating by a secret sign that I was on the right path. In that manner the gods now and then revealed themselves playfully to me in the course of my journey, although I paid little heed to the signs. Probably my heart was on a pilgrimage all the while although I did not realize it and although my body, bound to the earth, wandered with earthly, curious eyes.

The apprentice preceded me with the torch and soon I was in a chamber from whose walls had been carved benches for both the deceased. The artist had commenced his work from the ceiling and the broad central beam was ornamented with circles and capriciously scattered heart-shaped leaves of various colors. Both the slanting sides of the ceiling had been divided into red, blue and black squares as was the custom in Tarquinian houses. The painting on the right wall was already completed. There, reclining side by side on their left elbows on a cushioned couch, were both the future deceased in their festive garments and with wreathed heads. Eternally young, the man and his wife looked into each other's eyes with hands upraised while dolphins played below them in the eternal waves.

The joy of life that exuded from that fresh painting so gripped me that I remained staring at it before moving on to the discus thrower, the wrestler and the dancers who played their eternal games along the walls. Several torches were burning in the chamber and a sweet fragrance emanated from the high-legged censer to dispel the smell of damp stone and the metallic odor of the paints. After he had granted me sufficient time for looking about, the artist swore again in Greek, thinking perhaps that I understood nothing else.

"Tolerable, perhaps, stranger," he remarked. "Worse pictures have been painted in tombs, eh? But at the moment I am struggling with a horse which will not assume the shape that I wish. My inspiration is fading, my jug is empty and the dust of the paints is smarting unpleasantly in my throat."

I looked at him and saw he was not an old man but approximately my own age. I seemed to recognize his glowing face, oval eyes and swollen mouth.

He looked eagerly at the clay bottle which I carried in its straw sheath, joyously raised his square hand with its blunt fingers and exclaimed, "The gods sent you to me at precisely the right moment, stranger. Fufluns has spoken. Now it is your turn to speak. My name is Aruns in honor of the house of Velthuru which is my patron."

I kissed my hand respectfully and said with a laugh, "Let my capacious clay bottle speak first. Undoubtedly Fufluns sent me to you, although we Greeks call him Dionysus."

He took the bottle before I even had time to remove the cord around my neck, and tossed the stopper in the corner as though to indicate that I would no longer need it. With incomparable skill he sprayed the red wine into the right place without wasting a drop, wiped his mouth with the back of his hand and sighed in relief.

"Sit, stranger," he urged me. "You see, the Velthurus were angry at me this morning and accused me of delaying my work. How could nobles understand an artist's problems? And so they had water thrown over me and had me lifted into a cart with only a jar of Vekunian spring water as provisions. They even said sarcastically that it should provide sufficient inspiration for painting a horse since it had inspired the nymph to recite an eternal incantation for Tarquinia."

I seated myself on one of the stone benches and he sat beside me with a sigh and wiped a bead of sweat from his brow. From my knapsack I took a thin silver goblet which I carried with me to prove if necessary that I was not a humble man, filled it, splashed a drop onto the floor, drank from it and offered it to him.

He burst into laughter, spat on the floor and said, "Don't trouble to pretend. A man is known by his face and eyes, not by his clothes or his sacrificial habits. The rich flavor of your wine speaks more for you than the silver goblet. I myself am such a close friend of Fufluns that I would consider the sacrifice of a single drop to him sheer waste.

"So you are a Greek," he went on without inquiring my name. "We have Greeks in Tarquinia and in Caere they make fairly attractive vases. But it's best for them not to attempt sacred paintings. Sometimes we compare our designs with such enthusiasm that we break empty dishes over each other's heads."

He gestured to the youth who brought a wide roll. Aruns opened it and stared at the well-drawn and colored dancers and wrestlers, musicians and horses. He pretended to show me the traditional designs for the paintings but his eyes and wrinkled forehead betrayed his preoccupation with his unfinished work.

"These are of course helpful," he said absently, groping for the silver goblet and emptying it without even realizing it. "One knows the right colors without guessing and the apprentice can scratch the outlines of the traditional pictures in advance. But a pattern is helpful only so long as it does not fetter but frees and eases the play of one's own imagination."

He thrust the roll of pictures into my lap without even troubling to wind it, rose and stepped to the opposite wall with a metallic graver in his hand. He had under way a picture of a youth holding a race horse by the neck. Most of it was completed, with only the horse's head and neck and the youth's hands still missing. When I carefully stepped closer I noticed that their outlines had already been scratched in the soft rock. The master, however, was not pleased with them. Suddenly he began scratching a new outline. The horse's head rose more expressively, its neck arched more muscularly, it lived. The work took only a moment, then in a frenzy Aruns applied the color to the horse's head without even following precisely the outline he had just made but improving on the position even as he painted.

Tiring a little, he mixed a light brown paint and effortlessly painted the youth's hands around the horse's neck without even troubling to etch the outline. Finally he outlined the arms with black so that the muscles fairly bulged to the blue border of the short-sleeved shirt.

"Well," he said wearily, "This will have to do for the Velthurus for today. How could an ordinary person understand that I was born, I grew, learned, drew, mixed paints, raged and spent an entire life merely for these few moments? You, stranger, saw that it lasted but a few moments and probably thought, 'He is very skilled, that Aruns.' But it is not skill. There are enough and even too many with skill. My horse is eternal and no one has ever painted one precisely like it. Therein lies the difference which the Velthurus don't understand. It is not merely color and skill but suffering and ecstasy almost to the verge of death that enables me to reveal life's game and caprice in all its beauty."

The youth said consolingly, "The Velthurus understand that. There is only one Aruns the painter. Nor are they angry at you. They are only thinking of what is best for you."

But Aruns was not so easily appeased. "In the name of the veiled gods, take away this dreadful burden! I must swallow an ocean of gall before I can squeeze a drop of joy from it and for a few fleeting moments be content with my work."

Hastily I filled the silver goblet and extended it to him. He began to laugh. "You are right. A few vatfuls of wine have of course gone down with the gall. But how else could I free myself? My work is not so easy as people believe. This sober youth will understand it when he has reached my age if he develops as I expect."

He placed his hand on the youth's shoulder. I suggested that we return to the city and eat together, but Aruns shook his head.

"No, I must remain here until sunset. Sometimes I remain even longer, for here in the bowels of the mountain there is neither night nor day. I have much to think about, stranger."

He indicated the blank rear wall and I saw how the pictures alternately leaped alive and faded to a mist before his eyes. Forgetting my presence he mumbled to himself, "After all, I was at Volsinii when the new nail was struck into the pillar of the temple. The Lucumones permitted me to see that which an ordinary man does not see until the curtains fall. They believed in me and I must not betray their confidence."

Once more he remembered me and my silver goblet. "Forgive me, stranger. Your face is still smooth although you are probably my age. I myself can see this swollen mouth, these tired eyes, the wrinkles on my forehead and the lines of discontent at the corners of my mouth. But I am discontented only with myself. Everything else goes well. I am gnawing at myself only to create that which has never before been created. May the gods be with me and with you also, stranger, for you brought me good luck and I was able to solve the problem of the horse to my own satisfaction."

I understood his words as a farewell and did not wish to disturb his thoughts further, for he was staring at the blank wall and making impatient gestures in the air.

He was probably ashamed of having banished me so abruptly, for he suddenly said, "Well, stranger, those who do not understand are content with everything if it has the traditional lines and colors. That is why the world is full of skilled people and they are successful and life is easy for them. A real artist can compete only with himself. No, I have no competitor in this world. I, Aruns of Tarquinia, compete only with myself. If you wish me well, my friend, leave your clay bottle here as a memento of your visit. I feel that it is still half full and you will tire your fair shoulder if you carry it back to the city in the heat of the day."

Gladly I left the bottle for that remarkable man since he needed it more than I.

"We shall meet again," he said.

Not in vain had I noticed the goddess's sign on the stone wall when I descended into the tomb. It was intended that I should meet that man and see the completion of the painting that he then planned. But I met him also for his own sake, to enable good luck to help him in his work and to rescue him from a human's greatest despair. That he deserved. Already then I recognized him from his face and eyes. He, Aruns, was one of those who return.

5.

For several weeks I did not meet Aruns nor did I wish to descend again into the tomb for fear of disturbing him at his work. But at vintage time one moonlit night he came toward me with his drinking companions, so fearfully intoxicated that I had never before seen anyone in such a condition because of wine. Nevertheless he recognized me, stopped to embrace me and kissed my cheek with his wet mouth.

"There you are, stranger! I have missed you. Come, my head needs a cleansing from within before I begin working, so let us drink deep so that I may empty my head of all useless thoughts and thereafter vomit my body clean of all earthly filth before undertaking divine matters.

283

But why are you wandering through the streets at night with a clear head, stranger?"

"I am Turnus from Rome and an Ionian refugee," I thought it best to explain to his noisy companions. To Aruns I said, "The goddess troubles me at the time of the full moon and drives me from my bed."

"Join us," he suggested. "I'll show you living goddesses, as many as you please."

He linked his arm with mine and pressed onto my head the vineleaf wreath that drooped from his ear. I accompanied him and his friends to the house that the Velthurus had provided for him. His wife, awakened from her sleep, met us with a yawn, but she did not drive us away as I expected. Instead, she opened the doors, lighted the lamps, brought out fruit, barley bread and a jar of salted fish, and even tried to comb Aruns' tangled and wine-dampened hair.

As a sober man and a stranger in the city I was ashamed of forcing my way into the house of a casual acquaintance in the middle of the night. And so I mentioned my name and apologized to Aruns' wife.

"Never before have I seen such a wife as you," I said courteously. "Any other woman would have boxed her husband's ears, poured a tubful of water over him and driven away his friends with oaths even though it is vintage time."

She sighed and explained, "You don't know my husband, Turnus. I do, having lived with him more than twenty years. It has not been an easy time, I assure you. But year by year I have come to know him better, although some weaker woman would long ago have packed her things and left. He needs me. I have worried about him, for he has not tasted a drop in weeks, merely pondered and sighed, walked to and fro, broken wax tablets and torn expensive paper onto which he had drawn pictures. Now I feel better. This always happens when the pictures begin to take shape in his mind. It may last a few days or a week, but when his head has cleared he will don his work robe and hasten to the tomb even before dawn lest he lose precious moments."

While we talked Aruns had tottered to the yard and fetched a large wine crock which he had concealed under a heap of straw. He tore open the seal but was unable to remove the stopper. Finally his wife dexterously opened the crock, removed the wax and poured the contents into a large mixing vessel. She did not, however, insult Aruns and his friends by adding water to the wine. Instead, she brought out her best dishes and even filled a cup for herself.

"It is best so," she said to me with the experienced smile of a knowing woman. "The years have taught me that everything is easier if I also become intoxicated. Then I no longer worry about broken objects, ruined floors and gate posts which guests carry away with them."

She extended a cup to me. When I had emptied it I noticed that it was of the newest Attic ceramic ware with a picture of a cloven-hoofed satyr and a struggling nymph at the bottom. The picture remained in my memory as a symbol of that night, for soon two dancers appeared and we went into the garden where there was more room.

In Rome I had been told that even at their wildest the Etruscan dances are sacred dances, danced traditionally for the pleasure of the gods. That was not true, however, for when the women had danced awhile with fluttering garments they began to disrobe and with upper bodies bare danced joyously to permit us to enjoy their beauty. One of the guests proved to be a master at the flute and never in east or west have I heard such exciting melodies. They quickened my blood more than did the wine.

Finally those beautiful and ardent women danced on the grass in the moonlight with no clothing whatsoever save beads of pearls which one of the guests had indifferently tossed around their necks as gifts. I was told that he was the young Velthuru although he was dressed as modestly as his companions.

He spoke to me also, drank with me and said, "Don't despise these drunkards, Turnus. Each of them is a master in his own field and among them I am the youngest and the most insignificant. True, I ride fairly well and can use a sword, but am a master at nothing."

Carelessly he indicated the dancers, who were mature women. "I presume you have noticed that they also are masters in their own field. Ten and even twenty years of practice every day are required to enable a person to portray gods with his body."

"I fully appreciate both the sights and the company, you noble," I said.

Nor was he offended by the fact that I recognized him, for he was still young and vain even though he was of the house of Velthuru and no Velthuru need be vain because he already is what he is. He was of such an old family that he presumably instinctively knew me and hence did not inquire how I had joined the company. But that I realized only much later.

Since Aruns was so overflowingly at peace with the world and himself, I took advantage of the situation to inquire, "Why did you paint the horse blue, master?"

He stared at me with dull eyes. "Because I saw it blue."

"But," I insisted, "I have never seen a blue horse."

Aruns was not hurt. Shaking his head in sorrow he replied, "In that case I pity you, my friend."

We spoke no more of that matter but his words were a lesson to me. After that I often saw a horse as blue, regardless of its other color.

Hardly a week had elapsed when Aruns' apprentice breathlessly came to me at my lodgings and shouted with flushed face, "Turnus, Turnus, the work is completed! The master sent me for you so that you might be the first to see it as a reward for having brought him good luck."

I was so curious that I borrowed a horse and galloped down the valley and up the slope to the necropolis while the apprentice sat behind me clinging to my waist.

"The gods are looking at us," whispered the bright-eyed youth behind me and his hands tightened around my waist. I was overcome by a strange certainty that he was a herald of the gods.

When I descended into the tomb I saw that the entire rear wall had been covered with bright colors that breathed harmony, beauty and wistful joy. Aruns did not turn to greet me but remained staring at his own work.

The draped curtains of an open summerhouse circled the ceiling. In the center, incomparably above everything earthly, stood the convivial couch of the gods with its numerous cushions. Both white cones in their festive wreaths rose from their double cushions, while both robes hung at the foot of the bed, side by side. To the right of the gods' couch and far below on the humans' couch lay the festive couple behind whom stood youths extending their hands in greeting to the gods. To the left was a mixing vessel and a woman with upraised arms. Looking at the picture closely, I noticed that the artist had extended the folds of the tent to both side walls so that the scenes which Aruns had painted earlier formed a part of the whole lofty picture which was dominated by the couch of the gods.

"The feast of the gods," I whispered in the grip of a holy tremor, for my heart understood the painting even though my earthly mind could not explain it.

"Or the death of a Lucumo," replied Aruns, and for a fleeting moment I realized with dazzling clarity what he meant and why it had been ordained that I witness the birth of the painting. But my moment of perception passed and I returned to earth.

"You are right, Aruns," I said. "Probably no one has dared paint anything like this. The gods themselves must have guided your brush and chosen the colors for you, for you have attained the unattainable."

I embraced him, and he buried his bearded, paint-smeared face in my shoulder and began to weep. Sobs of relief shook his strong body until he finally collected himself and rubbed his eyes with the back of his hand, thus smearing his face still more.

"Forgive my tears, Turnus," he pleaded, "but I have been working night and day and have slept only the necessary moments on the stone bench until I have again awakened to the cold of the tomb. I have not eaten much. Colors have been my bread. I have not drunk much. Lines have been my drink. Nor do I know how I have been able to succeed or if I have succeeded at all. But something within me assures me that an entire era is concluded with this painting even though it may go on for another ten or twenty years. That is why I am weeping."

At that moment I saw with his eyes and felt with his heart the death of the Lucumo and knew that a new age was indeed coming, uglier, more bloated and more mundane than this age which was still illumined by the radiance of the veiled gods. Instead of guardian spirits and beautiful earthly gods, monsters and cruel spirits would well up from the underworld pits, just as a bloated person sees nightmares after he has eaten his belly too full.

I need say no more about Aruns and his painting. Before departing I sent his good wife an expensive gift but to him I sent nothing, since no gift could have repaid him for what he had shown me.

How was I, who had left Rome as a shepherd, able to give expensive gifts? One day I happened to be walking outside the city and passed a colorful canopy under which a group of noble youths were playing dice. Among them was Lars Arnth Velthuru who extended a white hand and called to me.

"Will you join us, Turnus? Choose your place, have a drink and pick up the dice."

His companions looked at me in surprise, for I was wearing my cheap traveler's clothes and on my feet were the heavy-soled shoes. I saw the ridicule in their eyes but no one dared oppose a Velthuru. I saw their beautiful horses tied to the trees and guessed that they, like Lars Arnth, were high-born cavalry officers.

I seated myself opposite Lars Arnth, wrapped my robe around my knees and said, "I have not played much but I am always ready to try with you."

The others exclaimed in surprise but Lars Arnth silenced them, dropped the dice in a beaker and extended it to me. "Shall we play for a whole?" he asked casually.

"As you will," I said, thinking that he was referring to a gold coin or perhaps, since such noble youths were playing, a whole mina of silver.

"Well!" cried the youths. A few of them struck their palms together and demanded, "Will you answer for that?"

"Silence!" snapped Lars Arnth. "He will. I guarantee it if no one else does."

I tossed the dice, then he took them in turn, tossed and won. In that manner I lost three times successively faster than I could swallow my wine.

"Three whole," observed Arnth Velthuru and indifferently tossed to the side three beautifully lettered ivory chips. "Would you like to draw breath for a while, friend Turnus, or shall we continue?"

I glanced at the sky and thought that three minas was a lot of money. Silently I called to Hecate, reminding her of her promise. As I turned my head I saw that a lizard had slipped onto a nearby stone to sun itself. The goddess was with me as Hecate.

"Let us continue," I suggested, finished my wine and tossed the dice once more, gloriously confident of victory. I leaned over to read my throw, for the Etruscans did not mark the sides of the dice with dots but with letters, and saw that I had made the best possible throw. Lars Arnth should not even have tried, but he did and lost. In that manner I won three times in succession.

The noble youths had forgotten their mockery and with bated breath were following the roll of the dice. One of them said, "I have never seen such playing! His hands do not even tremble and his breath is not quick."

That was true, for I watched the fluttering sparrows and rejoiced in the blue of the autumn sky fully as much as I participated in the game. A thin red had touched the slender cheeks of Arnth Velthuru and his eyes shone brightly although he cared little whether he won or lost, but merely enjoyed the excitement of the game.

"Shall we breathe?" he asked when we were even and he took back the third chip.

I let my wine cup be filled, drank with him and suggested, "Let us have one more throw to see which of us wins, which loses. Then I must leave."

"As you wish," he said and in his excitement made the first throw. He apologized immediately and remarked, "A bad throw but I deserved it."

I won by only one point, which was best since it softened his defeat, then I rose to leave.

"Don't forget your winnings," exclaimed Lars Arnth and tossed the

288

ivory chip to me. Laughingly I caught it in the air and remarked that winning was not really important. A greater joy had been in meeting him and playing the exciting game.

The youths stared at me open-mouthed but Arnth Velthuru smiled his thin attractive smile and said, "I shall send my slave to bring you your winnings either tonight or tomorrow morning. Remind me of it if I should forget."

But he did not forget the matter. Only when his handsomely clothed keeper of the money that same night brought to the inn a talent of silver in the form of twelve stamped bars did I realize that he had meant a whole talent.

A talent of silver was so much money that I could easily have built a house, decorated and furnished it beautifully, planted a garden and bought slaves to care for the house. I decided that after that I would no longer dice in Tarquinia and to that resolve I clung despite temptation.

So it was that I returned to Rome a wealthy man after the Volscians had quieted for the winter. Nevertheless I followed my original plan of supporting myself by my own hands and signed up as an ordinary sailor on one of the grain ships sailing from Tarquinia to Rome.

On a foggy day in late autumn I again arrived at the shore by the cattle market, but this time along the bank of the Tiber and with my shoulder bloody from pulling the heavy hawser of the grain ship. In an ordinary goatskin sack I had as the fruit of my journey as much good silver as a man could carry and as a lowly sailor I could perhaps have brought it ashore without the knowledge of the tax collectors. But I thought it best to reveal it to them so that they might enter it in the state records. It might prove useful to me to have it known that I had become wealthy through my own efforts, and I no longer wanted to be known as Tertius Valerius' parasite.

My silver aroused amazement in the captain and the sailors and they swore laughingly that they would not have hesitated to kill me and toss me overboard had they known of my treasure. But the bookkeeper paid my wages in copper without a murmur and I put the coins carefully in my pouch. A frugal man was respected in Rome.

With the sack of silver on my back, my clothes ragged, my face bearded and my shoulder rubbed raw by the hawser, I once again walked the narrow streets of Rome and breathed the marsh-polluted air. Near the temple of Mercury I saw the same half-blind augur with his worn staff and soiled beard waiting for some credulous stranger to whom he might show the sights of Rome and for whom he might predict a bright future. Rome was already familiar to me; the worn stones in the streets responded familiarly to my feet; the cattle bellowed familiarly in the market place. Longing burned my body as I hastened to Tertius Valerius' house.

The gate was open, but when I tried to enter, the gatekeeper slave began to shout and to wave his stick at me. Only when I called him by name did he recognize me. Tertius Valerius was at a Senate meeting, he said, but the mistress was home.

Misme, round-cheeked and curly-haired, ran across the yard to me and hugged my knees. I lifted her into my lap and kissed her, but Mikon's eyes looked back at me from her face. She wrinkled her nose, sniffed my clothes and said accusingly, "You smell bad." She struggled out of my lap.

That brought me to my senses. Carefully I went inside with the hope of seeing the housekeeper so that I might bathe and change my clothes before meeting Arsinoe. But at that very moment Arsinoe rushed in, paused to stare at me with her white forehead wrinkling in anger, and cried out, "You, Turms! And how you look. I might have guessed."

My joy died and flinging the sack from my shoulder I emptied it so that the bars of silver rang on the floor. Arsinoe stooped to pick one up, weighed it in her hand and stared at me in disbelief. I held out the new-fashioned earrings that I had bought in Veii and a brooch which the most skilled goldsmith in Tarquinia had made.

Arsinoe squeezed my hand with the jewelry and despite my dirty clothes she hugged me to her and kissed my bearded face time and again. "Oh, Turms, if you knew how I have longed for you and through what agonizing times we have lived under the threat of the Volscians! And you have wandered without a care through spring and summer until the dark of autumn. How could you?"

I reminded her coolly that I had sent word of myself to her whenever it was possible, just as I had heard that she was well. But I felt the warmth of her arm and the smoothness of her shoulder and had to relent. After all, she was Arsinoe, and no matter what she did or desired my glow was not diminished. I wondered that I had been able to live so long without her.

She read her triumph in my eyes, drew a deep breath and whispered weakly, "No, no, Turms. First you must bathe and eat and don clean clothes."

But I was no longer a Greek and clothes meant nothing. My mantle fell to the floor of the court, my shirt was dropped at the entrance to

Arsinoe's room and my worn shoes were kicked off beside her bed. She was Arsinoe, her nakedness responded to mine, her embrace to mine, her breath to my own hot breath. The goddess smiled from her capricious face and her darkening eyes, enticing, persuasive, unforgettable.

That is how I want to remember Arsinoe.

6.

During the winter I moved among the people of Rome, even among the disreputable elements of Suburra, that I might learn human nature. My journey had taught me not to be too careful of my company or to choose my friends because of the possible benefit that might result. I sought only people to whom I could feel close, and they could be found just as easily among the poor as among the nobles.

In a Suburran brothel I found myself playing dice with the bookkeeper of an iron ore ship from Populonia. The Roman smiths needed much iron that winter and when the bookkeeper had lost his money he tore his braid and thoughtlessly offered me a free voyage to Populonia for just one more throw. I won that also, and he swore to fulfill his promise since he well knew that he would not be welcome in Suburra if he failed to pay his gaming debts.

"I have brought difficulties upon myself," he said, "but I have probably deserved them because of my frivolity. At least you must wear Etruscan clothes and try to act like an Etruscan if you possibly can. I shall take you to Populonia as I promised but the rest is in your own hands. At the present time the custodians of iron ore do not welcome strangers."

I consoled him and indicated that I could speak Etruscan effortlessly although I had previously pretended to know little, and returned the money that I had won from him so that he might seek solace in wine and in the company of the girls of the house. When I greeted him at his ship the following morning I was clothed in my beautiful Etruscan attire with the peaked cap. He was happy to see that I was not an unsignificant person, declared that I could pass for an Etruscan as well as anyone else and assured me that he would keep his promise. But storms were raging at sea, and his commander wanted a return cargo from Rome. The Senate had promised to exchange the iron for ox hides but was laggard about it, as was its custom, and haggled about the price.

It was therefore spring before we could leave, and we sailed from the mouth of the Roman river just two days before the arrival of the Volscians. Pillars of smoke along the shore told of their coming, but having sailed down the river in time we caught a favorable wind and managed to elude them.

When we had sailed by Vetulonia and seen the Etruscans' famous ore island to the left of us, we reached the seamarks of Populonia and were escorted to the harbor by a guardship to make certain that the cargo or passengers were not discharged earlier. We passed many barges loaded to the gunwales which sought with sail and oars to reach the port of discharge. Along the shore behind sturdy unloading bridges were dark red hills of ore and beyond them puffs of smoke rose from the smelting pits.

When the stern of our ship had been fastened and the steps lowered, iron-clad guards surrounded us. Never before had I seen such a dismal sight, for their smooth armor bore not a single decoration or emblem. Even their shields were smooth, and their round helmets extended to the shoulders of their breastplates. Square openings had been cut into the helmet for the eyes and mouth so that the guards no longer resembled people or soldiers but were inhuman as beasts or hard-shelled animals. Their spears and swords likewise were without a single ornament.

Just as simply clothed were the gray-robed inspectors who climbed unarmed onto the vessel and to whom the commander showed his sailing tablet with the seals from the various ports to indicate his route. The bookkeeper presented the cargo list and thereafter every man was called before the inspectors to give an account of himself.

Each had to extend his hands and the inspectors looked at them to see whether they actually were the calloused hands of one who had spent a lifetime at the oars or hawsers. Only then they looked into the man's eyes and cared little for his nationality so long as he was an ordinary sailor who asked for no more in a port than a measure of wine and a cheap woman as his bed companion.

As a passenger I was last. The sight of the strict inspection made me glad that I had not attempted to reach Populonia as a sailor but was dressed in my Tarquinian attire with my braided hair on my shoulders.

To my amazement the inspector looked at my face and then glanced at his companions. The three gruff men stared at me, then the youngest of them raised his hand to his mouth. But his superior looked at him sharply and frowned, then took a simple wax tablet, impressed on it the head of Gorgon with his seal and extended it to me.

"Write your name on it, stranger. You may come and go in our city as you wish."

I saw an understanding flicker in his eyes and suspected that he had known in advance of my coming. Fearing that they wanted to lead me into a trap so that they might later imprison and condemn me for excessive curiosity, I therefore thought it wisest for me to reveal my plans immediately.

"I would also like to travel to the ore island to see the famous mines and visit the forests here on the mainland from which you obtain the coal for refining the ore."

The inspector lifted his slanting eyebrows and remarked impatiently, "Your tablet bears the picture of our Gorgon as its emblem. Just write on it the name that you wish to use."

Surprised, I tried to explain, "I am Turnus from Rome," but the inspector interrupted me and said, "I have asked nothing. Never claim that I have inquired your name or your family or your city."

Such treatment was amazing. The bookkeeper's mouth dropped open and he began looking on me with new eyes. I myself could not understand why I was treated so favorably in a city which was guarded from strangers as carefully as were the sea charts and war port of Carthage.

As a city Populonia was like its guards, bleak, severe and adapted to its purpose. Its people considered drudgery an honor and the smoke from the smelting pits had blackened the painted cornices of the houses. Gorgon was the emblem of the city and Sethlans with his sledge-hammer the god, so that in his temple Sethlans was in the center and Tinia and Uni in each side chamber. That is how greatly the residents of Populonia respected the god of iron.

I sailed in an empty ore vessel to the ore island of Elba, where I saw the mines and the as yet unbroken ore fields, and with my own eyes confirmed that such endless ore reserves and pure iron could be found nowhere else in the world. But I was even more curious about the temple of lightning of which I heard. It was situated near the ore fields atop the highest hill and was surrounded by hollow bronze statues worn green with age which represented the twelve cities of the Etruscan league.

Here, where the thunderstorms raged the fiercest and lightning flashed the brightest, the most experienced lightning diviner studied its omens for the Etruscan cities and nations. For that purpose a flat stone bore a bronze shield that was quartered and orientated like the vault of heaven and divided into sixteen minor parts inhabited by sixteen deities whose signs only the priests could interpret. In that temple those who sought to become lightning priests received their final secret knowledge and consecration after ten years of study in their own cities under the guidance of elders. But innate ability and perception were of even greater importance than study and tradition and endless precedents. A youth who possessed an apparent gift for studying lightning could be spared ten years of study on the basis of proven perception and could be consecrated at the age of eighteen.

During generations many a candidate for priesthood had been killed by lightning. But if he survived he needed no other consecration and was considered more holy than the other priests.

Divination by lightning was not done for individuals at that modest wooden temple. The omens concerned entire nations and cities and warned them about coming disasters or foretold good and fruitful years. After the short-haired candidates had shown me the temple and related the stories of the bronze statues, the temple elder himself received me and looked at me keenly. He did not say much but offered me bread baked in ashes and water to drink, and urged me to come to the temple during the next storm if I dared.

I did not have to wait many days before dark clouds began to roll from the mountains in the east toward the sea. So hastily did I climb the winding path to the hilltop that I bruised my knee on a rock and brambles scratched my legs and arms. I saw the sea foam and the distant lightning flash over Populonia and Vetulonia.

Noticing how eagerly I hurried to the temple the elder smiled the mysteriously beautiful smile of the wise and said that there was no hurry as yet. He led me into the temple and soon we heard the rattle of rain on the roof and the rush of water down the clay gutterspout and through the lions' maws at all twelve corners. Blue flashes now and then illuminated the interior of the temple and the black-painted face and white eyeballs of the god of lightning.

When the moment had arrived the elder bade me undress, donned a rain collar and head covering, and took me into the rain. The sky was black above us but he asked me, naked as I was, to seat myself at the center of the bronze shield facing northward while he himself stood behind me. I was wet through and before me forks of lightning crossed one another as they struck the ore fields of the island. Suddenly everything flashed white and a bolt that covered the entire northern sky leaped from the clouds and back again in a triumphant arc that in my dazzled eyes formed a complete circle against the heavens without touching the ground. At the same moment a crash of thunder deafened my ears.

The old man placed his hands on my shoulders from the rear and said, "The god has spoken."

Trembling with cold and shock, I followed him back to the temple where with his own hands he dried me and gave me a heavy woolen cloak to wear. But still he said nothing and made no prediction, merely looked at me affectionately as a father at his son.

Nor did I ask anything although something compelled me to tell him of my youth and how I had found myself at the foot of a lightning-cleft oak near Ephesus. I also confessed my most secret crime, the burning of the temple of Cybele, and when I had told him everything I bowed my head, awaiting his judgment.

But he laid a protecting hand on my head and declared, "What you have done you had to do. You need not fear the dark goddess, you fair visitor on earth. We Etruscans do not, like the Greeks, consider criminal a man who has been struck by a thunderbolt and survives. On the contrary, you yourself saw the sign a moment ago. What you have told me confirms the presentiment I had as soon as I saw your face."

Human curiosity prompted me to ask, "What was your presentiment?"

He smiled sadly, shook his old head and replied, "I have not the authority to tell you until you have found yourself. Until then you are a stranger on earth. If you are sometimes melancholy, if you are sometimes disconsolate, remember that kindly spirits are guarding you as are also the earthly rulers of our people from now on."

The radiance disappeared from the old man's face and I saw only his tired eyes, white beard and sparse hair. When the rain had ceased and the clouds had drifted out to sea he led me to the temple entrance and blessed me in the name of his god. The sun shone brightly, the air was clear and the earth glittered.

I continued my wanderings toward the source of the Tiber with the intention of following the river to Rome. Despite the autumn rains I found the narrow stream between the bleak mountain peaks. Stones cut my shoes, my mantle was torn and my only protection against the biting cold was an occasional shepherd's shelter.

The first snow flurries greeted me as I came out of the forest to the wealthy city of Perusia. There I had to spend the coldest part of the winter and when the warm winds began to melt the snows in the mountain peaks I continued my journey down the Tiber. I wandered through the entire Etruscan heartland in a wide, wavering arc before reaching my starting point. The end of the journey I made as a timber floater on an immense raft that was being transported down the Tiber by a timber merchant.

As we approached the bridge we saw, toppled on the ground, the siege tower built by the Volscians. We also saw signs of destruction, but the bright green grass had mercifully covered the sooty ruins. On both sides of the river new barns and cattle enclosures were being built, oxen were calmly pulling their plows in the fields and birds were warbling everywhere with ruffled throats.

I had left Rome on an early spring day. On an early spring day I returned. But I will not praise the spring in Rome, for when I finally saw Arsinoe a year after our parting I noticed that she was in an advanced stage of pregnancy, nor did she rejoice at my return.

BOOK NINE

The Lucumo

I.

AS I again stepped into the patrician courtyard of Tertius Valerius I could see that the rotted gateposts had been repaired and the gate painted. Once inside, I found I hardly recognized the house, so thoroughly had it been cleaned and so numerous were the expensive new seats and other pieces of furniture that had been obtained. A recently cast bronze statue of one of the Graces danced in the pool, clad in only a thin veil, and Tertius Valerius' beloved clay oxen with their plow had been placed in the darkest corner. All this I noticed as I paused to gain time after the first crushing realization of Arsinoe's condition.

As I continued silent Arsinoe fingered the edge of her matron's robe nervously, looked at the floor and said, "You frightened me with your sudden appearance, Turms, for I did not expect you yet. Of course I have many things to explain to you but in this condition I cannot bear to be agitated. Therefore it may be best that you first meet dear Tertius Valerius."

She quickly withdrew to her room, burst into tears and called for her servants. Alarmed by her weeping and shouting, Tertius Valerius rushed forth from his own room with upraised stick. But when he recognized me he lowered it and looked embarrassed.

"You, Turnus," he said slowly. "I did not expect you to return, for we received word that you had drowned in a storm at sea. It was Arsinoe herself who met the sailor when she was every day seeking news of you. She brought the man here and he swore, hand on the hearth, that he had seen you go down. We have lived through difficult times ourselves with the Volscians' siege, and I did not doubt his story."

I said quietly that I had been unable to send news of myself because of the siege. Then with some bitterness I added that the news apparently had not been missed and that it would have been better had I not returned.

Tertius Valerius replied hastily, "No, no, do not misunderstand, Turnus. You are always welcome in my house and I rejoice that you are alive and apparently well. Judicially it in no way affects the situation. After all, Arsinoe herself admitted that you have never understood each other and that circumstances compelled her to accompany you for lack of another protector because of her burning desire to return to the city of her birth. Where was I? Ah, yes. No, I bear you no grudge, nor does Arsinoe. After all, you were never legally married, at least not bindingly according to Roman laws. When her goddess made me virile again even at my age I considered it my privilege and even, because of her condition, my duty to marry her legally. Since then I have grown younger by ten, perhaps even by twenty years. Don't you agree that I am rejuvenated, Turnus?"

The heretofore sensible old man began to prance and arch his neck before me like a cock while the wrinkles hung like a wattle under his thin jaw. He had even shaved his beard and was clutching his purple-bordered toga as foppishly as a vain youth. So pathetic a sight was he that I did not know whether to weep or to laugh.

When I said nothing Tertius Valerius continued, "Of course there were many difficulties, since we first had to prove that she is a Roman citizen and a patrician. She has probably told you through what quirks of fate she found herself a helpless orphan in a strange land. But her bravery during the siege and the reputation she won for herself among the Roman women proved helpful, for the senators were made to understand by their wives that only a true Roman woman could have behaved so unselfishly. This was accepted by the Senate as evidence of her birth and she was accordingly recognized as a citizen and finally as a patrician. Without that recognition we could not have been married, for the law forbids marriage between a patrician and a plebeian."

He rapped on the floor with his stick and added, "Because of our legal marriage all other previous bonds are dissolved as a matter of course. From now on Roman law will protect the reputation, honor and property of the person concerned."

Summoned by the rapping, a new housekeeper dressed in splendid clothes appeared with a bow and Tertius Valerius bade him bring bread and wine with which to bid me welcome. Absently I had laid my hand on the hearth and his experienced eye noticed my gesture and he respected the tradition.

When we had drunk wine and broken bread we sat on the comfortable seats facing each other. The unaccustomed wine rose to the old man's head, and soon his cheeks and temples were deeply flushed.

"I rejoice that you are reacting sensibly to this matter," he said. "It shows you are an understanding man. Arsinoe had to admit that she sent you away because of her fondness for me and besides, you are sterile and could never give her the joy of motherhood. It was not her fault that that cruel Greek took advantage of her defenseless position and forced her to submit. But she herself is innocent and without a single evil thought. Indeed, I respect her greatly for having kept Misme although the sight of the girl must arouse dismal memories. I can well realize how much your return reminded her of those sad times. Women in her condition are very sensitive."

He began to titter. "I am a farmer at heart and accustomed to breeding cattle, so that I am not unduly shy in matters pertaining to the sexes. But I have never met more sensitive innocence than Arsinoe's among the women of Rome. Still, she is a heroine. As the most courageous of the Roman women she was instrumental, with the help of her goddess, in persuading Coriolanus to lift the siege and depart with the Volscians."

His brow darkened, he gripped the stick tightly and recollected, "As the Volscians left they burned and plundered even the patricians' houses, so that I suffered great material loss." Then he brightened again. "But the land remains and we are rid of Coriolanus. The Volscians no longer trust him because he lifted the siege without a battle, although by dint of great effort they had built siege towers and battering rams with which to break down the gates. Now the women of Rome believe in Arsinoe's goddess and worship her as Venus. I myself have vowed to erect a temple to her in Rome and intend to propose it in the Senate time and again. If it is not accepted I shall erect the temple, at least a small one, with my own money."

"I know Arsinoe's goddess," I said impatiently. "I don't doubt that the women of Rome will donate their jeweled hairpins and brooches to a collection for the temple."

"A splendid idea!" cried Tertius Valerius. "You understand me best of all, dear Turnus. Arsinoe has even predicted that the descendants of the goddess Venus will one day rule the world from Rome."

"Continue your story," I urged.

Tertius Valerius' mouth dropped open as he searched his memory. "Ah, yes. I began with the bulls and Arsinoe's modesty. Although I convinced the Senate I had a harder time persuading my relatives. Not until they saw with their own eyes did they believe that I had regained my manhood. We Romans are not unduly bashful in such matters, but before I could prove it I had to overcome Arsinoe's shyness, for although she is a mature woman she is as bashful as a young girl who for the first time submits to a man's embrace."

"Undoubtedly," I said with gall in my throat. "Undoubtedly."

Tertius Valerius recollected the event with enthusiasm. "My brothers, my brother's son and a representative chosen by the Senate saw with their own eyes that I could fulfill my conjugal responsibilities as well as anyone else. After that no one doubted that Arsinoe had become pregnant by me."

At this moment Arsinoe entered the room with tear-swollen eyes, lagging steps and downcast eyes. She stooped to kiss Tertius Valerius' forehead and in passing deftly wiped his chin and wattle with a linen towel.

"Surely you are not exerting yourself with tiresome matters, my dear Tertius," she said affectionately, and gave me a reproachful glance.

Tertius' head ceased wobbling and he straightened himself like the senator he was. "Unpleasant matters are best settled immediately," he declared. "Everything has turned out for the best and only certain financial matters remain. When you arrived in our city, Turnus, your property was mistakenly entered in your name, but I will not believe that you did so with calculated slyness. You probably wished only to protect Arsinoe's money since you did not know our city's laws and thought that it was not possible for a woman to own property. Similarly you had entered in your name that talent of silver which Arsinoe had you bring for her on your previous journey. After all, her pride demanded that she have a dowry as though I were not sufficiently wealthy."

He stroked Arsinoe's hand. In her defense I must say that she dared not meet my glance. "As a man of honor, Turnus," continued Tertius Valerius emphatically, "will you be so kind as to transfer Arsinoe's property to her name officially, just as I transferred certain estates with their slaves to her name at our marriage? No one can compel you to do so, of course, but I fear that your past would not stand a trial."

I looked at Arsinoe's beautiful face, at the glow of her eyes and the smooth whiteness of her bare arms. "I shall arrange the matter tomorrow," I said. "I am only too happy to serve Arsinoe as I have in the past. A silver talent and a moderate amount of gold in coins and objects is a dowry not to be scorned by even a Roman senator. Let it add to her fame among the noblewomen, although her most precious dowry, of course, lies in her modesty and irreproachable manners."

Arsinoe did not blush but merely nodded as she stroked the old dotard's thin hair.

Why didn't I fly into a rage at those contemptible lies? Why didn't I open Tertius Valerius' eyes to the kind of woman Arsinoe really was? Above all, why didn't I snatch her into my arms and carry her away as I had before?

Because at last I realized the futility of such actions. Arsinoe knew what she wanted and if she preferred wealth, security and a high position at the side of a friendly old man to me, why should I try to change her mind? The crock was broken and the wine had seeped out. Perhaps the crock could have been repaired somehow but why should I have tormented her and myself any longer? If Tertius Valerius was happy, why should I have disturbed his joy by arousing unnecessary doubts?

When I relinquished all my rights willingly and without haggling, Tertius Valerius glanced questioningly at Arsinoe as though seeking advice. She nodded.

Overcoming his innate miserliness Tertius Valerius said magnanimously, "You are a fine fellow, Turnus, and deserve compensation for rescuing Arsinoe from the heartless Greek and returning her safely to the city of her birth. Therefore, with my wife's permission, I have thought of giving you a small farm with fifteen jugera of land and the necessary farming implements as well as two slaves. The farm is on the opposite bank of the river some distance from the city and near the Etruscan border. I myself obtained it as security for a loan after a plebeian was killed in the war, and though the slaves are old, they are a dependable couple. The Volscians burned the house but the necessary sties and pens are being built and the slaves are living in a provisional shelter."

His offer was undeniably generous considering his miserliness, but upon deliberation I realized that he wished me out of his house and out of the city as soon as possible. Yet to begin cultivating fifteen jugera I would be compelled to seek Roman citizenship, and that I wanted to avoid.

Finally I said, "I accept your gift lest I shame your generosity, noble Tertius Valerius. I shall be happy to have the farm as a memento of Arsinoe, though I hardly think I myself will cultivate it, for I prefer to continue to live in the city. Presumably I can earn my living by teaching Greek to children or prophesying from the hand or appearing as a dancer in the sacred performances at the circus."

Arsinoe's head moved violently and Tertius Valerius felt ashamed for me. Touching her hand reassuringly he said to me, "Dear Turnus, I am happy that you are not ashamed to admit your humble origin but are content to be what you are without aspiring to citizenship. I think that Suburra is just the right place for you, for I heard earlier that you had enjoyed life there with your own kind although I didn't mention it while you were my guest."

Arsinoe flushed and exclaimed, "At last you have betrayed yourself, Turms! That is your place, among the disreputable women, and I cannot say that I miss you. But drag yourself in the mud if you will, I cannot watch out for you all my life. I must think of my own future and that of my unborn son. Go to your sluts, the sooner the better! I will not have such a notorious man in this house."

"Now, now," said Tertius Valerius soothingly. But I was warmed by the knowledge that Arsinoe still was jealous of me even though she had chosen the better life. Finally she burst into tears once more, covered her eyes with her hands and fled from the room.

Everything happened according to plan and soon I was inspecting my weed-covered fifteen jugera far beyond the hill of Janiculum near the Etruscan border. The gray and toothless slave couple feared me greatly and tremblingly showed me a sow in the sty and a few goats and heifers. As his greatest treasure the old man brought out an ox hide that he himself had tanned and hidden from the Volscians, for he had had sufficient wit to slaughter the ox and skin it before the Volscians' arrival.

I would, of course, have had the right to kill the old couple, incapable of work as they were, using as a pretext the wretched condition into which they had allowed the farm to lapse. That was what the Romans did to their decrepit slaves, as mercifully as they killed old beasts of burden. But my heart did not permit it so, instead, I sold my gold ring and jeweled band for a pair of oxen, and to help the old slaves hired a shepherd boy whose parents had been killed by the Volscians. Later I built a small summer house and decorated its gables with painted clay ornaments in the Etruscan manner.

In Suburra, where I rented a room, and at the market place it was easy for me to obtain the truth about Arsinoe's incomparable heroism during the Volscian siege, truth which made it apparent that she had deliberately sent me away so that she might be free to win a place for herself among the women of Rome.

When the Volscians had besieged the city the people had emphatically refused to fight beside the patricians. Disturbances increased in the Forum and the Senate did not even dare to appoint a dictator as it had during previous emergencies. Arsinoe had found her opportunity by joining the sewing circle in which the Roman women regardless of rank wove warm shirts for those unselfish citizens who placed the fatherland above class conflicts and shivered atop the wall during the cold autumn days and nights.

Side by side with the patrician women Arsinoe had carried hot soup and warm bread to the wall from Tertius Valerius' kitchen. Among the patriotic women who thus distinguished themselves were Coriolanus' spirited mother Veturia and his Etruscan-born wife Volumnia, whom he had married only for her dowry and for whom he cared little although she had given him two sons. Both the women, the old mother and the humiliated wife, sought to prove by their actions that their sympathies were entirely with Rome.

When the people had compelled the Senate to send emissaries to Coriolanus' camp to offer peace and the priest of Regia had in vain attempted to persuade him, Arsinoe had suggested that the Roman women send their own delegation to Coriolanus. Surely he could not resist the tears of his old mother, the reproachful look of his wife and the sight of his young sons.

Although the women had been afraid of the Volscians, Arsinoe's enthusiasm and fearlessness had been contagious and some twenty patrician women had followed her as she herself led the swaying Veturia and the weeping Volumnia and her sons. The soldiers, remembering Arsinoe's hot soup and friendly visits, had opened the gates before the Senate had had time to forbid such a foolhardy venture.

The shivering and hungry Volscians had been so amazed by the arrival of the women that they had gladly accepted the meat and bread in the women's baskets, and led them in a festive procession to the camp and Coriolanus' tent. There the women had gathered about a fire to warm themselves, for it was night before Coriolanus consented to see his mother and sons. There by the fire Arsinoe had told the women in confidence about her goddess and assured them that as a final resort she herself, with the aid of the goddess, would persuade Coriolanus.

Finally Coriolanus had admitted the women into his tent. His mother had tearfully cursed her son and declared that she would have strangled him in his crib with her own hands had she known that she had given birth to a traitor. Volumnia for her part had thrust forward her sons and demanded whether he intended to destroy his own sons' fatherland.

Coriolanus, who was a handsome man and a head taller than the other Romans, had listened patiently while glancing with curiosity at Arsinoe, who stood with shyly bowed head. But if I knew her she surely made certain that Coriolanus saw her red-gold curls and white neck and probably she had even allowed her robe to slip open.

At length Coriolanus had spoken a few sharp words to his mother and wife and declared that unless the women had more sensible things to say he would send them back to the city. At that point the women had pushed forward a modest Arsinoe and urged her to call upon her goddess. Arsinoe had explained that to do that she had to be alone with Coriolanus in his tent. And so he had dismissed the women and his guards.

More than that was not known about the conversation between Arsinoe and Coriolanus, but she had remained in his tent until dawn. When she finally appeared, exhausted from her efforts to persuade Coriolanus, she had urged the women to praise the goddess Venus and her power, and had fallen unconscious into their arms. Coriolanus had not appeared at all but had courteously sent guards to escort the women to the city. That same day he had given the order to lift the siege.

Whether the ending of the siege was due to Arsinoe and her goddess I dare not say. On the basis of what I heard I concluded that the Volscian army was incapable of storming the Roman wall and did not even wish to try. Also, autumn was far advanced and no nation of Latium could endure a winter war. Coriolanus was an able commander and even without the intervention of the women would surely have dispersed his army before winter.

With or without reason Veturia and Volumnia achieved fame as a result of the event and willingly shared their glory with Arsinoe. They received the public thanks of the Senate as the saviors of the city and from that moment Arsinoe was a famous woman in Rome, and her goddess and secret knowledge were respected.

I did not see Arsinoe for many months and did not even walk by Tertius Valerius' house, for due to her condition Arsinoe secluded herself. She gave birth in the hottest time of the summer. A slave whom I had bribed brought me word of it and the long hours seemed unbearable to me because I could not be with her. Despite all she had done to me I loved her and nothing could quench my devotion to her.

But during our separation my love had matured and I no longer thought of her so much as a woman to whom desire had bound me but as a person who had become near to me. I remembered how she had made me laugh in my moments of depression and how I had sat for hours watching her as she had skillfully cared for her beauty, chattering gaily the while about people and things. I did not wish harm to come to her no matter what she did because I understood her, her lies and her need for security.

Her delivery was difficult and lasted through a day and a night, for the boy weighed ten pounds. When he finally came into the world a hailstorm broke in the midst of the heat and lightning flashed wildly. But it was not my doing even though my heart was in an upheaval because of Arsinoe.

When he heard the howls of the male child who had been born to life's pain, when he felt the weight in his lap, Tertius Valerius became delirious with joy and sacrificed bulls, sheep and pigs in various temples as though a state event had occurred. Some of the meat he distributed to the people, some he sent to his farms, and gave the slaves a holiday since they could hardly have worked in the fields anyway because of the storm.

Arsinoe, as an exemplary Roman mother, nursed her child herself and did not appear in public until her appearance and beauty had been restored. But when autumn came I saw her sitting in the place of honor at the circus immediately behind the vestals and near the ivory seat of Manius Valerius. I could see her only from a distance since I myself was seated on the opposite side among the aliens and the artisans of foreign origin, but she was still as beautiful as the goddess and I watched her more than the events in the arena.

But I did not seek her out to speak to her for I had no wish to disturb her peace. Time passed and the boy was already a year old when I again saw Arsinoe.

2.

It was late summer and the city was quiet, for the people worked busily in the fields and those who had remained in the city sought the shade and moved about only after nightfall. The stench of filth, rotten fruit and tanned hides filled the narrow streets of Suburra. And Fortune continued to smile on Rome, for the Volsci, having allied themselves with the Aequi against Rome, had fallen out with them and waged a bitter war, thus exhausting their own strength and that of the Aequi so that Rome had nothing to fear from either.

I was teaching a young dancer from the circus the movements of the Etruscans' holy wreath dance when Arsinoe unexpectedly appeared in my room in Suburra. It was not my fault that the girl had nothing on, for the day was hot and besides it is best for a dancer to be naked when practicing in order to know her own body. Nevertheless I wanted to sink into the ground when I saw how Arsinoe looked first at me and then at the poor girl who did not realize that she was doing anything wrong. In her innocence the girl did not even have the wit to cover herself with a robe but remained standing with bent knee and upraised palms in the position I was attempting to teach her.

Arsinoe was her old self but riper and more beautiful than before. Sarcastically she said, "Forgive me, Turms. I don't wish to disturb your pleasure but I must talk with you and today was my only opportunity."

With trembling hands I picked up the girl's cheap clothes, thrust them into her arms, pushed her out and closed the squeaking wooden door. Arsinoe seated herself on my unadorned seat without permission, looked around, sighed deeply and shook her head.

"I am sorry for you, Turms," she lamented. "Although I heard that you had fallen into bad company I did not believe it all but tried to think well of you. But now I must believe my own eyes and I am grieved."

Bitterness choked my throat as I watched her sitting as calmly before me as though nothing had happened. "I have lived a bad life and fallen into bad company," I admitted. "I was teaching Greek to some stupid boys and happened to teach them Hipponax's verse: 'A man has two fortunate days in his life, one when he is married and the other when he lays his wife in her tomb.' Hipponax lived in Ephesus, which is why those lines have remained in my memory. But the parents did not appreciate such teaching and I lost my pupils."

Arsinoe pretended not to listen but sighed lightly and remarked, "Her thighs and hips are too heavy. She is too short as well."

"But she has talent," I insisted in defense of my pupil. "That is why I am helping her."

"Alas, Turms, I thought you were a little more exacting in the matter of women. He who has tasted the exalted grape is no longer content with turnips. But you have always been different. I have marveled at your poor taste in the past."

Absently she bared her head and my heart leaped as I noticed that her hair had just been arranged by a Greek hairdresser. She had painted her face carefully and I could only marvel at her skill in draping the Roman women's simple mantle so temptingly.

"How hot your room is!" she exclaimed and allowed the mantle to slip off her white shoulders and bare arms. Her eyes were grave and dark and her lips parted. But I had no intention of succumbing to her charms.

"Don't," I said. "Instead, tell me how you dared come to meet me, especially here in Suburra. Aren't you afraid of your reputation? Surely you remember that you are a senator's wife."

"Ah, yes," she agreed and looked at me accusingly. "But who is to blame? Didn't you yourself leave me to the mercy of Tertius Valerius for years at a time? You were tired of me and that is why you pushed me into the lap of a lustful old man."

"Arsinoe," I demanded in horror, "how can you distort everything in such a terrible way! Are you shameless enough to accuse me to my face of what you yourself so shrewdly planned and accomplished?"

She managed to summon tears to her eyes and looked at me mistily. "How bitter and unjust you are toward me, always ready to pick a quarrel although we have not met in such a long time. I should know you by now, but I always make the mistake of thinking well of you." She sobbed and peered at me through her dark blue lashes.

I breathed violently, clenched my fist but said nothing.

Arsinoe pressed her palms together beseechingly. "Why don't you say something, Turms? Why are you so harsh?"

I almost confessed that my whole being rejoiced in radiance at the mere sight of her but it was better for me not to surrender myself once more to her power. And so, when my knees failed, I sat on the edge of the bed and asked, "What do you want of me, Arsinoe?"

She laughed gaily, dropped all pretense, stretched herself and extended her legs for me to see.

"Of course I want something of you, Turms. Otherwise I would not have come. But I am happy to see you and my heart leaps strangely in my breast when I look at your broad mocking mouth and oval eyes."

"Don't," I pleaded humbly and looked about for a knife with which to cut off a finger if it should attempt to caress her skin against my will. That I would in truth have done, for if I had touched her I would have been lost. But fortunately my will was stronger than my hands.

"You yourself know best how deeply I loved you," said Arsinoe weakly. "Even now my heart secretly yearns for you, though I am hurting Tertius Valerius and my son. But let us control our emotions and remain merely friends. It is best that way. When a woman has reached my age and her beauty begins to fade she needs security. I was tired of sacrificing everything because of your whims. Now you have your freedom, Turms, and I have an understanding husband who doesn't make too many demands on me."

When I said nothing she felt her waist and said ruefully, "I have aged greatly, my arms are heavy and my hips become broader no matter what I do. The last delivery tore my muscles so that my loins and thighs have white scars which have ruined my beauty for all time. Do you want to see them?"

She began to lift the hem of her tunic but I hastened to cover my eyes. "I must be terribly ugly," she said with a sigh, "since you don't even want to look at me. Of course, the girl's youth is in her favor and a smooth fruit is fresh to the taste, but believe me, my friend, there is not much joy in foolish youth. You will only have trouble, for you yourself are no longer in your prime. The bad life has etched furrows around your mouth and there are wrinkles under your eyes."

"They are only laughing wrinkles," I said bitterly. "I have had so much reason to laugh. But tell me quickly what you want of me. I would not want you to endanger your reputation by remaining in a disreputable house and in my bad company."

She rose, left her mantle on the seat and went to the door. Drawing the wooden bolt she remarked, "I suppose you will permit me to lock the door so that we may talk in peace." She walked past me and stared out of the narrow window opening, so that I might admire her also from the side and rear. But when she realized that I remained firm she sat down again and laid her hand on my knee.

"You have always been a selfish man, Turms, but surely you realize that you have certain responsibilities toward Misme. The girl is almost seven years old and it is high time that she left Tertius Valerius' house. As kind a man as Tertius is, he is irritated by her constant flying about. Besides, Misme reminds me unpleasantly of unhappy events in the past."

"Ah, yes," I said. "I didn't know that you were born in Rome of a patrician family."

"I suppose I didn't tell you enough about my sad childhood," Arsinoe said brazenly. "But in Rome Misme is considered an illegitimate child and that doesn't suit my new position. If I had thought to make her father a patrician I might have been able to arrange for her to be one of the vestal virgins and that would have secured her future. But it is impossible to think of everything at once. I had enough to do in trying to prove my own birth, as you can imagine. Now the boy fills our house and Tertius Valerius is able to think only of him. For the sake of my reputation think of your responsibilities toward me this once, remove your daughter and take care of her."

"My daughter?"

Arsinoe became annoyed. "Of course Misme is your daughter in a way, or at least the daughter of your best friend. If you won't think of me, think of Mikon. Surely you won't permit his daughter to be abandoned."

"It is not a question of that," I said. "Of course I'll be happy to take Misme and not only to help you, for I like the girl and have missed her.

But speaking of your son, forgive my human curiosity. Judging from what I have heard and computed, I presume he is Coriolanus' son."

Arsinoe pressed her palm to her mouth and glanced about in panic. But we were alone and she grew calm again and smiled.

"I can't hide anything from you, Turms. You of all people know me best. Anyway, the boy has the noblest patrician blood in him and his father is the most gallant of Roman men. I felt that I owed that to Tertius Valerius. No, he doesn't have to be ashamed of his son although the boy's father is stupidly vain and thus is compelled to live in exile the rest of his life. But perhaps that is best for the sake of my own peace."

Her frank confession broke the ice within me and we began to talk as animatedly as we had in earlier days. She made me laugh and once again I realized why I had loved her and why I still loved her, for there was no other woman like her in the world. She did her best to amuse me and in doing so enjoyed herself, for I was the only person who understood her and in whom she could trust. But I did not touch her. The time passed and suddenly, realizing that the room had darkened, she wrapped the mantle around her and covered her head in the manner of a respectable Roman woman.

"I must leave," she said. "In a few days I will have Misme brought to you and I trust that you will care for her as though she were your own daughter."

I felt that Arsinoe cared little whether Misme would be brought up in Suburra or not but was disappointed because the girl had inherited Mikon's round cheeks and stocky figure, was clumsy in her actions and did not know how to please her mother.

But I could not bear the thought that Misme would grow up in the midst of the immoral elements and the people of the circus. I took her to my little farm and left her in the care of the old slave couple, and thus I myself came to spend more time there than I had formerly. I wanted to teach Misme to read and to write and to help her to develop into a free and self-reliant girl, but I could not afford to engage a teacher for her nor was that the custom in Rome. In Rome girls were so despised that a female infant could be abandoned, and the only education a girl received was in spinning, weaving, cooking the simple Roman food and performing heavy household tasks. Even the daughters of senators had to be content with that.

Arsinoe erred in despising her daughter, for Misme had good powers of comprehension. Having left behind the gloomy house and the ceaseless scoldings, she began to develop quickly in the freedom of country life. She loved animals, willingly took care of the cattle and even dared to climb onto a horse and gallop down the pastures. I kept a few of the Senate's cavalry horses on my farm to augment my income, for at that time the Senate still provided the cavalry horses and during the winter quartered them in nearby farms. On certain days the horses had to be brought into Rome when the patrician youths gathered in the pastures of the wolf god for cavalry exercises. But in that way I could ride to Rome and back whereas I could not have afforded to keep horses myself. Fifteen jugera did not suffice for such luxury.

In a few years Misme's skin turned rosy and smooth, her limbs became slender and she no longer moved clumsily although she still was scraggy as a calf. Because of my journeys I had to leave her with the slave couple for long periods, but each time upon my return I felt increasing joy at the glow of happiness in her dark eyes. She ran to fling her arms around my neck and to kiss me, and I could not bear to tell her that I was not her real father. As she grew she seemed beautiful in my eyes, her brows were slender and whimsical and her lips like rose petals. But by the time she had become a maiden the expression in her eyes reminded me increasingly of Mikon's restless eyes and she learned to laugh mockingly at others and herself. Into such a girl did Misme grow.

3.

I will not describe Rome's disputes with its neighbors or its perpetual raids. The problem of land distribution came up in the Senate but Tertius Valerius had long ago, because of Arsinoe, given up his favorite plan. Now that he had an heir he clung to his land tooth and nail and thus regained the confidence of his patrician brothers. He was no longer considered a simpleton but was pushed to the fore as necessity dictated to calm the people, who believed in him because of his former opinions. In that manner Tertius Valerius gained political influence and the patricians, the senators and even his own relatives began to admire Arsinoe more and more for having such a beneficial influence on the old man.

Nor was he a stupid person. True, he granted Arsinoe the luxuries demanded by the new times and patiently endured her extravagance, but he himself retained his simple habits. Thus he remained healthy and strong and his head no longer wobbled when he made a speech in the Senate. That weakness he permitted himself only at home.

I learned all this by observing life in Tertius Valerius' house from the sidelines and was greatly amused, upon occasionally seeing Arsinoe, to notice the sour expression usually on her face, as though Tertius Valerius' surprising vitality had plunged her into the pit that she herself had dug.

From sheer vexation and boredom Arsinoe seemed to have aged much more than had tenacious Tertius.

News of the death of King Darius carried as far as Rome. Truly the whole world was shaken by it. The Greeks rejoiced and held festivals of thanks at Herakles' altar, for they felt the danger which had threatened the mainland of Greece had receded, and that the revolts and disturbances which inevitably accompany a ruler's death in such a large country as Persia would give the heir other things to think about than Greece. But Darius had built such a strong kingdom from the nations that he ruled that nothing happened. On the contrary, his son Xerxes, himself no longer a young man, was said immediately to have dispatched emissaries to Athens and other Greek cities with a demand for earth and water as symbols of submission. Several cities acceded, thinking that such a slight indication of sympathy carried no obligations.

All this happened far away, but as ripples from a cast stone spread slowly and break only on the shores of a pond, so were the effects of world events felt even in Rome. After all, the Persian empire comprised the Eastern world from the Scythians' steppes to the streams of Egypt and India, so that the Great King rightly considered the entire world his play pond. He felt it his personal responsibility to be the bringer of peace and security to all lands, thus ending wars for all time. Thinking of that, it seemed to me that the quarrels of Rome and its steady expansion at the expense of its neighbors were as insignificant as shepherds' quarrelings over pastures.

I met my friend Xenodotos immediately after his arrival in Rome as he was stepping out of the temple of Mercury where he had been offering a sacrifice for a successfully completed voyage. He had abandoned his Persian attire and was dressed in the latest Ionian fashion; his hair was fragrant and on his feet he wore shoes trimmed with silver. He had even shaved his curly beard. But I recognized him immediately and hastened to greet him.

When he recognized me he embraced me warmly and exclaimed, "Luck is with me, for I would immediately have sought you out, Turms of Ephesus. I need your advice in this strange city and have many matters to discuss with you once we are alone."

I was in the habit of loitering with the others in front of the temple of Mercury whenever I was not practicing in the circus arena or teaching some chance pupil or trading cattle or passing my time in prophesying for the Suburran girls. There I caught a breath of strange cities and the expanding world of Rome, I could learn about a profitable trade, and because of my knowledge of languages could guide and otherwise be of use to wealthy foreigners. But I did not tell Xenodotos this, preferring to let him think that our meeting was a miracle arranged by the gods.

I found lodgings for him and his servants in the Etruscan inn which was the largest and best in Rome. Thereafter I showed Xenodotos what there was to show in Rome, but as one who had just arrived from Carthage he was not impressed by the wooden temples of Rome and the clay images painted by Etruscan artists. His interest was aroused more by the Roman constitution which effectively prevented the return of autocracy and also protected the rights of the people against the aristocracy. He also admired the order and discipline of the Roman army when I explained it to him. He considered it amazing that the state did not have to pay wages to the soldiers, who not only equipped themselves except for the cavalry horses but considered it the privilege and duty of a citizen to go to war for his native city without always sharing in the spoils. Any booty was sold for the benefit of the state treasury and so greatly did the Romans fear the return of autocracy that the commander-consul who distributed spoils to the army as gifts was immediately suspected as aspiring to become an autocrat.

Since I did not wish to show Xenodotos my room in Suburra I told him that I lived in modest circumstances in my little house outside Rome. He for his part did not wish to discuss matters at the inn, although we ate and drank there. Thus the following day we walked together along the bridge to the other bank of the Tiber, looked at the scenery and the cattle and finally reached my summer house. He said politely that the walk did him good and that the country air was fresh to breathe, but he perspired as he walked and it was apparent that he had not used his legs much in the past. He had also grown stouter and his former eager curiosity had sharpened to a tendency to cold-blooded criticism.

He admitted having attained an important position in Susa as an adviser on Western affairs, and having won the personal favor of the new king, Xerxes, even before the death of Darius. Now, in the necessary reorganization he, despite his comparative youth, had been entrusted with the observation of Western affairs outside the King's sphere of influence.

"In Carthage we of course have our Persian House and our ambassador," he said. "I have come from there and the interests of the King and Carthage are not in conflict but rather in agreement. The Carthaginian council knows that trade would be impossible if the King were to forbid Carthage the ports of the eastern sea. So, although the merchants of Carthage are so arrogant as to refuse to send earth and water to the King, they have agreed to an immeasurably more important matter. And because of that I have personally left Susa on this long and dangerous journey."

As we walked he mentioned in passing that in Susa he had a house cared for by a hundred slaves and in Persepolis a modest summer building for whose gardens and fountains fifty slaves sufficed. But he did not keep any wives because he wished to avoid the unpleasantness caused by women, a decision which he said King Xerxes considered praiseworthy. From that I judged how and why Xenodotos had won the new king's favor although he himself was too sensitive to boast about it.

For my part I did not wish to appear wealthier than I was. I had an attractive spring surrounded by shade trees that I myself had planted and I had had the convivial couches brought to the edge of the spring and had hung holy ribbons on the bushes. The water of the spring was our cooling vessel and Misme served us such simple country food as bread, cheese, cooked vegetables and a roasted pig which I had that morning sacrificed to Hecate. My serving dishes were heavy Etruscan clay ware, but the shallow drinking cups were from Athens and decorated by a skilled artist, for I did not want to flaunt my silver goblets.

Our walk had given Xenodotos a good appetite. He ate heartily and the old slave woman, who had feared the simplicity of her meal, wept with joy when Xenodotos summoned her before him and thanked her for an incomparable meal. When I saw how gracefully that man of the world behaved and how he won the hearts of simple people I began to understand the high position he had achieved and to respect Persian manners.

"Don't consider this mere pretense, my friend Turms," he said. "The simple food tasted good in my spice-cloyed mouth, and the country wine still has the flavor of the earth. Also the pig flavored with rosemary was delicious."

I told him that it was an Etruscan dish for which I had brought back instructions from Fiesole. Before I realized it I was drawing a map on the ground with a stick, showing the location of the large Etruscan cities and describing their wealth and naval forces and the iron smelters of Populonia and Vetulonia. Xenodotos listened attentively, time passed, and Misme exchanged our violet wreaths for rose ones.

As the heavy fragrance of country roses wafted over us, Xenodotos looked around warily, grew serious and said, "We are friends, Turms, and I don't want to tempt or bribe you. If you will just tell me whether you are for or against the Greeks I will know whether to remain silent or to speak frankly. There is much that I would tell you, knowing that I can trust you."

I had found refuge in Ephesus, Herakleitos had reared me and I had even fought for Ionia for three years. I had followed Dorieus, had shed blood and received scars for Greece. But when I honestly studied my heart I knew that I no longer cared for the Greeks and their customs. The better I had come to know the Etruscans and the more I had traveled in their cities the more I had begun to shun the Greeks. I was not a Roman and had grown away from that which was Greek in me. I was a stranger on earth who did not even know his own origin.

I explained, "The Greeks are admirable in many respects but in my heart I am tired of them and in this country they are intruders who are elbowing room for themselves. The Greeks and the Greek spirit are rotting everything surrounding them, ruining everything which is there."

Nor do I understand the reason for my extreme bitterness, but once I became aware of it, it poisoned my mind and turned my belly sour. Perhaps the humiliations of my youth in Ephesus were to blame. Perhaps I had been bound too long to Dorieus to be able to appreciate the Greek in him. Mikon also had betrayed me. Even the Scythians declared that the Greeks were better suited to be slaves and servants than free men.

Xenodotos nodded and said, "I myself am an Ionian, but, speaking honestly, I miss my Persian attire and Persian truth. A Persian is a man of his word and does not betray his companions, but we Greeks are accustomed to deceiving even our gods with ambiguous promises. It is true that nothing black in the world is absolutely black, nor is anything white pure white, but in serving the Persian king's cause I believe that I am also serving my own people best."

Realizing that I was not as captivated by the idea as he, he quickly picked up a stick and began to draw a map in the sand to show me how advanced the preparations were for a military expedition. "The King will vanquish Greece by land," he explained. "For that reason he has secured bases in Trachia. The combined fleets of Phoenicia and Ionia will accompany an army the like of which has not been seen before, to assure its maintenance and communications. A bridge of ships as hard as earth is being built across the Bosphorus, and in the event of storms canals have been dug across Trachian peninsulas so that the ships will not have to sail around them. For nine years these preparations have been under way. When the army begins marching from Asia to Europe every step will have been planned. True, Athens is agitating violently throughout the Greek world and has dedicated the output of its silver mines to the construction of new triremes. But actually Athens is filled with despair and a spirit of defeat although it tries to appear bold." Xenodotos smiled his narrow smile and added, "Even the oracle at Delphi is uncertain and gives ambiguous responses."

He pressed his fingertips together and remarked, "That is why I have come to Rome, from where it is easy to observe what is going on in the Etruscan cities. I myself cannot and must not participate visibly in the conferences. Outwardly it is a question only of the Carthaginians' and the Etruscans' own interests in resisting Greek pressure. The Etruscans will not even have to know that the Persian king is financing the arming of Carthage. But it is most important for the Etruscans that their leaders realize in advance the propitiousness of the moment for crushing the Greeks in the West. The goddess of victory will hardly offer them another opportunity like this."

I took the crock of wine from the spring and filled our cups. The hilltops were turning red and dusk settled on their slopes. The odor of the wine and the roses seemed stronger as the evening cooled.

"Xenodotos," I said, "be honest. Such thorough preparations and such an enormous army cannot be intended merely for the conquest of the Greek mainland. One does not need a smith's hammer to kill a mosquito."

He laughed nervously, sought my eye in the dusk and admitted, "Once Greece belongs to Persia the next step, of course, will be to send armies to the Italian mainland. But the King will remember his allies. You surely know that from friendly cities he demands no more than earth and water. The removal of a single stone from the wall will suffice as token recognition of Persian power."

It was strange that I, who as a youth had so ardently joined in the Ionian revolt and fought the Persians, should now without hesitation have chosen the supremacy of Persia. But that decision had ripened in my heart and I made the choice with open eyes, once again committed by earthly reason to struggle against the blind forces of Fate.

I said to Xenodotos, "I have made friends in the Etruscan cities and will be glad to talk to them before their leaders meet to drive another yearly nail in the wooden pillar at the temple of Volsinii. I have learned to admire the Etruscans and to respect them and their gods. For their own security, if they wish to remain the masters of their sea, they must support the Carthaginian expedition."

"You will not regret your decision, Turms!" cried Xenodotos. "And don't fear for yourself. I inquired about you in Ephesus. The King does not bear a grudge against you for burning the temple of Cybele. On the contrary, your crime agrees with his policy perfectly by obligating him to an unexpiated war against Athens. As far as you are concerned it is forgotten and wiped away."

But I said morosely, "My crime is a matter between me and the gods. I do not seek forgiveness of humans."

Understanding my pride he easily turned the conversation to other important matters. "You understand the conditions better than I and know what to do. If you need Persian gold you will have it. Later you will be rewarded personally for every Tyrrhenian warship and every Etruscan soldier who joins the Carthaginian expedition to conquer Himera, regardless of the outcome."

"I have no desire for Persian gold," I told him. "I have enough for my needs. It is wiser not to circulate Persian gold in these lands, for the Etruscans are suspicious and easily hurt. It is better merely to convince them that the future of their seafaring cities depends on it."

Xenodotos shook his head in disbelief. "You are stupid and politically unenlightened, Turms. Warfare requires gold first, last and always. Everything else follows logically. But do as you please. Perhaps the King's favor will some day mean more to you than gold."

"I don't aspire to be in the good graces of the King," I said stubbornly. "I don't agree with you otherwise, either. Gold does not decide wars, but rather the discipline of the men and training in the use of weapons. One who is hungry and lean will defeat one who is wealthy and fat."

Xenodotos burst into laughter. "Undoubtedly I have grown stouter and walking makes me perspire, but my knowledge has increased and I believe that I have become cleverer than I would have by running in the Siccanian forest and sleeping on the bare ground. I can always hire disciplined soldiers to protect me from the lean Greeks. Whosoever grasps a sword himself is mad. The wise man makes others fight and himself watches the outcome of the battle from a secure place."

His cynical words made me decide firmly to accompany the Etruscans to Himera and to fight at their side even though bloodshed had become repugnant to me. I felt that I owed it to them if I succeeded in inducing them to participate in a distant war. But I did not tell Xenodotos of my decision, for he would have considered it laughable.

Still smiling, he took from his neck a heavy gold chain, hung it around my neck and asked, "At least take this as a memento of me and my friendship. All the pieces are of the same size and they do not bear the Persian stamp. You can remove them one at a time according to need."

The chain weighed around my neck like a fetter but I could not return it without hurting him. Something in me warned me that I was committing myself to something that did not concern me, but I had spent a purposeless life for so long a time that I yearned for significant deeds.

4.

Xenodotos remained in Rome while I journeyed to Tarquinia to meet Lars Arnth Velthuru. Despite his youth he immediately understood the importance of the matter and the opportunities that it offered for reviving waning Etruscan sea power and crushing Greek competition.

He said, "The inland cities have young and ambitious men who are dissatisfied with the old. There are also hardy shepherds and farmers who dare place their lives at stake to win more with one blow in a war than they could hope to obtain by a lifetime of serving others. Although our large islands can hardly release their vessels, which are needed to guard the mines, the iron families of Populonia and Vetulonia will realize what is for their own good, and Tarquinia will provide us with at least ten warships."

He took me to see his father, Aruns Velthuru, who respected tradition to such a degree that he did not permit himself to be called a Lucumo but had Tarquinia ruled by a council instead. A more august man I had never met. Despite his position he received me courteously and understandingly once I had reached his presence. With the aid of a map I explained the plan for the Persian king's military expedition and repeated Xenodotos' contention that a more opportune moment for vanquishing the Greeks would hardly arrive.

He listened carefully, his face slender and ageless, and said finally, "I do not believe that it is the gods' intention that only one man or one nation rule the entire world. Nations keep one another in balance. They grow and progress as the result of mutual competition. All nations are equal and human suffering is the same, no matter whether the person be Etruscan, Greek, or black. Nations rise and recede in cycles and each nation's growth, blossoming and fading has been measured. Etruscan cities are no better or more important than Greek cities, although we perhaps know more about the gods than the other peoples. A human can redeem ten additional years from the gods and a nation or city one hundred years, but by more than that none can prolong existence."

His words of wisdom made a deep impression on me, but Lars Arnth became impatient and said, "My father, you are old and do not understand the new times as well as we who are younger. The question of Greek influence on land and sea is for us a matter of life and death. If Carthage feels that it is compelled to go to war, we must support Car-

317

thage. And if we support Carthage we must do so with all our resources."

His father sighed and said, "You are still very young, my son Arnth. Whosoever clutches the sword dies by the sword. We no longer offer human sacrifices to the gods."

Arnth clenched his slender fingers and gritted his teeth, but bowed his proud head before his father who then smiled the beautiful, sad smile of an old Etruscan.

"This is a political matter and as such must be decided by the council. If you consider it so important, you yourself may journey to Volsinii in my stead in September. Why should I become involved in something that I cannot prevent?"

Thus did Lars Aruns elevate his son to the regency of Tarquinia. After all, his tomb was completed and decorated with the eternal paintings of the artist Aruns, and he had no wish to redeem from the gods an additional ten years of life, which for a ruler can prove more burdensome than joyous.

After the conversation had had such unexpected results, Lars Aruns rose, placed his hands lightly on my shoulders and said, "I am happy to have seen you, Turms. Remember me when you enter into your kingdom."

His words surprised Lars Arnth as much as me, although Lars Alsir had once used the same words in Himera, but I considered them merely an old greeting which was used as a special indication of friendship. Only later did I realize that old Lars Aruns Velthuru knew and recognized me and considered me a herald of the gods in that matter. Thus it was that he relinquished his power to his son rather than become involved in a matter which was distasteful to him.

No longer did I have to struggle on Xenodotos' behalf, for Lars Arnth took the matter as his own and journeyed himself and sent his friends to the distant Etruscan cities to prepare the ground. I, however, decided not to go to the holy cities but remained in Tarquinia to await the decision of the league.

At the sacred celebration twelve days were devoted to the gods, seven days to internal political matters and three days to problems of foreign policy. The decision was that each city could decide for itself whether it wished to aid Carthage or not, and whether to do so in the name of the city or merely by enlisting volunteers. The holy Lucumones of both Volterra and Volsinii announced immediately that their cities would not permit even the raising of voluntary recruits. But they were inland cities, and in such a matter the decision of the coastal cities was of greater importance.

After the assembly the Carthaginian emissaries approached the delegates and rulers of the various cities and sought their promises of aid. Veii promised two thousand heavily armored men, Tarquinia its cavalry and twenty warships, Populonia and Vetulonia each ten warships, and the inland cities each at least five hundred men complete with equipment. Everything indicated that it would be the Etruscans' most extensive sea expedition since their fleet had destroyed the vastly larger Phoenician fleet off the shore of Sardinia a lifetime ago.

When I returned to Rome I had only good news for Xenodotos and felt certain that the Etruscans would support Carthage as decisively as possible despite their old doubts. From Arnth I had received a copy of the secret list of commitments. Xenodotos was highly pleased to see it and declared that it exceeded his highest hopes.

"And all this you bring as a gift to me!" he exclaimed. "Now what shall I do with the golden bull's-heads that I have transported with me with such effort?"

He had brought with him some bull's-heads molded in the ancient Cretan manner which weighed a talent and were used as currency in Carthage. They had been hidden at the mouth of the river lest the Senate's suspicions be roused by such immense wealth, and I laughingly urged him to take them back with him and said proudly that this was the Etruscans' own war and that no one was bribing or compelling them to participate in it.

But Xenodotos declared that he would be suspect and his information considered worthless if he were to return the bull's-heads. "This wealth is a sheer burden to me now that I have accomplished my task," he lamented. "It is troublesome to transport and might even subject me to robbery. I could not have believed that everything would proceed so smoothly."

Realizing that no benefit would be derived from awkwardly transporting the gold back to Susa, I suggested that we purchase a few shiploads of iron from Populonia, have it made into weapons, and hire someone to smuggle them to the Siccani. True, Hiuls was but a half-grown boy and I had heard nothing about him during all these years, but the iron would strengthen his position among the Siccani and as the son of Dorieus he would know best how to use it. The Siccani might either serve the Carthaginian army as guides or tie up the Greeks by attacking Agrigentum. I suggested that Xenodotos might also send a few bull's-heads to Lars Arnth, who was an intelligent youth and could use the money to build several modern warships.

That was our decision, but he insisted that I accept one talent of gold as a present, if only to provide for unexpected expenses. So, after a night of drinking to the Etruscans and the Persian king, we parted as friends.

The council of Carthage had chosen Hamilcar as its military leader and bestowed upon him the powers of an autocrat for the period of the war. The son of that famous seafarer Hanno under whose direction expeditions had explored the ocean beyond the Pillars of Herakles, Hamilcar was an ambitious man. He also possessed the ability to plan, and during the winter he had recruited forces from the backwoods of all the Carthaginian colonies and even from Iberia, so that many lands and skin colors were represented in his army. Further, each nation was accustomed to fighting in its own manner and with its own weapons, and this, together with the various languages and eating habits, caused great confusion.

The Greeks' equipment, on the other hand, was uniform, they were trained to fight in an open field as a moving front, and their heavily-armored soldiers had metal cuirasses and metal shields. And all during the winter Gelon and Theron vied with each other in building new triremes. We heard that Syracuse alone had almost one hundred triremes at sea that spring on maneuvers.

The worst surprise, however, was that the Roman Senate unexpectedly broke its agreement with Veii and had a bloody spear thrown into Veian territory. The Roman emissaries mentioned certain border violations, but that was merely a pretext, for agreement could have been reached just as it was every spring in the litigations between shepherds. Rome's attack on Veii and its threatening movements near Caere and Tarquinia were the greatest misfortunes that could have befallen the Etruscan cause, for it made it necessary to cut the Sicilian expedition to an insignificant size. We sailed for Sicily only when we realized that in one way or another the Greeks had succeeded in inciting Rome to war against the Etruscans and that the Romans were deliberately engaged in raids to tie up Veian troops. We were forty light warships, two triremes and a number of cargo vessels with several thousand men, most of them heavily armored and trained to use a sword, shield and spear in the Greek manner. But we had no cavalry whatsoever and Lars Arnth was unable to accompany us. Tarquinia needed its cavalry to guard its borders against Rome.

It was late summer when we sighted the Sicilian shore but the Carthaginian fleet which we had joined at sea managed so well that we made directly for Himera without being bothered by the Greeks and softly pulled our vessels ashore. Hamilcar had seized the harbor and the mouth of the river and laid siege to the city, thus sparing his disgruntled mercenaries an exhausting march through the land of Eryx to Himera by way of the Siccanian mountains and forest. There were more than thirty thousand Carthaginian mercenaries and their encampment stretched around Himera as far as the eye could see.

Off from the others, in the woods, were a thousand Siccanians and, leaving the Etruscan chiefs to confer with Hamilcar, I hastened to their camp. My heart melted at my first sight of the black-, red- and white-striped faces and arms. The Siccanians were greatly surprised when I spoke to them in their own language and brought me quickly to their sacred rock. Around it were gathered the chiefs of the various tribes with their wooden masks. Among them I saw a stalwart boy carrying my own shield and, recognizing him immediately despite his mask, I ran to embrace him.

Hiuls was not yet thirteen, and his youth made him suspicious. He retreated before me and the Siccanian chiefs shouted angrily at me for so disrespectfully daring to lay hands on their Erkle. But when he realized who I was Hiuls took off his mask, asked to have meat and fat brought for me, and thanked me for the weapons that I had sent him.

He explained, "Hamilcar of Carthage is a mighty warrior and with him are powerful Baal and many other gods. We Siccanians are leaving our forest as an organized army for the first time to support him against the Greeks. But we worship only our own gods and are not bound to the Carthaginian or Elymian gods. The battles will benefit my people by teaching them how to fight in a real war, and we shall grow wealthy from the booty. But after the war we will return to our forests and mountains and have nothing to do with the Carthaginians or Elymians."

"You are Erkle," I said. "You must decide for your people. Whatsoever happens, think only of the good of your people. I will not thrust my advice upon you, for you are the king, not I."

Seeing that I did not attempt to advise him or demand gifts for the weapons I had sent, Hiuls relented and seated himself cross-legged on his shield. He sent his men running by with their weapons, ten at a time, and contentedly observed how accurately they could toss their spears.

Meeting the Siccani warmed my heart. I even drank a drop of the poisonous potion with their chiefs and was once again able to see through tree trunks and rocks. I spent the night with them on the bare ground, but my body had grown flabby and accustomed to the comforts of life, with the result that I caught a bad cold. Thereafter I thought it best to spend the night on an Etruscan vessel.

We had to conquer Himera first and thereafter decide whether we should turn upon the Greeks in terrain of our choice or fortify ourselves in Himera and wait for them to attack. The only disturbing factor was that the Carthaginian vessels at the mouth of the strait had not yet made contact with the Syracusan fleet. The Greek triremes had disappeared from the sea and Hamilcar feared that they would attempt to cut his supply line. He declared that he dreaded that more than a battle with the small Greek land forces.

Although he respected the Etruscans' fame as soldiers so highly that he asked us to form the center of his front, he reproached us for being so few that we broke the Etruscans' promise concerning the number of troops they would send. And he had reason to censure us, for our forces no doubt were more troublesome than helpful. But what had happened had happened and could not be changed. For our part we asked the Etruscan chiefs to express our amazement at Hamilcar's purple tent, ivory couches, gold and silver dishes, images of deities and great number of slaves, all of which had taken up most of the space on several cargo vessels. I myself said that the Carthaginians appeared to have devoted more time and effort to making their lives comfortable than to fortifying the camp.

Hamilcar called on Baal and other gods, shouted that his Negroes and Libyans were not accustomed to digging pits in the ground, and said it was far better for his troops to trust to the Carthaginian gods with full bellies and happy minds.

When I explained that the Romans were in the habit of digging trenches as soon as they had made camp, Hamilcar said stiffly, "My way of waging war is the Carthaginian way. I think that I understand my own troops better than you, stranger."

In talking to the brutal and belligerent mercenaries who were tired of their inactivity I realized that they were completely ready to storm Himera. They burned with desire for loot and were prepared to risk their lives for the chance to plunder and rape as much as they pleased in a Greek city. Slowly I began to suspect that Hamilcar had a political reason for hesitating outside Himera's wall.

This reason became apparent at a banquet the Carthaginian arrranged for us. Suddenly the purple drapes at the rear of the tent parted and in stepped Kydippe, leading her two small sons while the two older boys clung to her robe with grave eyes.

As a matured woman Kydippe was more beautiful than she had ever been as a maiden. Gold dust was sprinkled in her Aphrodite hairdress, and her neck, arms and ankles were weighted with heavy jeweled ornaments. Her lips still smiled temptingly and although she had given birth to four sons her waist was still slender and she wore her Phoenician robe tightly belted. We cried out in amazement upon sight of her and leaped from our couches to drink to her honor.

Hamilcar greatly enjoyed our surprise and said with a smile, "Our hostage, Kydippe, has accompanied us from Carthage with her children to guard the interests of Himera. We left Terillos in Carthage since he is politically incompetent. Indeed it might be best to leave Himera to Anaxilaos until one of the boys becomes old enough to rule the city."

Even as he spoke I saw that Hamilcar's face and expression betrayed his obvious infatuation for Kydippe. Who would not have become enchanted with that beautiful and ambitious woman who even as a young girl knew cold-bloodedly how to take advantage of men's senses to gain her own ends? With a bright voice she urged us to continue our banquet and began moving slowly from one couch to another, addressing the Carthaginian leaders by name. We forgot our conversation and followed her with our eyes.

Finally she sat on the edge of my couch and began to talk to the Etruscan leaders. "I speak your language poorly, you incomparable warriors, but as civilized men you undoubtedly speak Greek. I was born and reared in Himera and in this river I swam as a maiden. That is why I am horrified by the thought that its houses will go up in smoke and its wealth will be destroyed. It has suffered enough already at the hands of the Syracusan soldiers. If you overcome the Greeks, Himera will drop into your lap without resistance."

Hamilcar confirmed her words. "Anaxilaos of Rhegion asked for our assistance and left his wife and sons as hostages, binding himself to fight for Carthage and his own cause to the last man. We will benefit nothing if we destroy Himera but will only lose a prosperous trading center."

I rose onto my elbow and said vehemently, "I also pity Himera and its residents, but the laws of war are merciless. The commander who deliberately places himself between two fires is mad. If we wage an open battle with the Greeks here, the Himeran garrison will attack our rear at the decisive moment."

Kydippe raised her white hand to her mouth, turned to look at me, pretended to recognize me only then and exclaimed joyously, "You,

Turms! How I rejoice to see your face once more. Let us drink a cup of wine together and not talk nonsense."

She pressed the edge of her golden goblet to my lips and poured strong wine down my throat. As I coughed and swallowed she explained to the others, "Don't be offended, but this fair man was my first love and I think I even kissed him once when I was a thoughtless girl. That is why I still feel a certain weakness toward him and all my girlhood memories return when I drink wine with him."

When I still tried to say something she made her sons hug me and kiss my cheeks and placed her own hand on my neck so cleverly that a tremor passed through my body.

Hamilcar did not like it. His face darkened and he bit his lip. "Let us bar the gates of Himera with branches and logs and if need be set fire to them to prevent the garrison from attacking us. I have made preparations for all eventualities and the gods of Carthage still offer me favorable omens. The power of decision is mine and I will endure no criticism of my decision."

Since Hamilcar was interested only in talk that pleased him, I ceased speaking and was content to watch Kydippe. She fingered my braid and whispered, "Truly, Turms, I still remember vividly how your mouth kissed mine and your hand caressed my body. I was certainly not indifferent although I pretended to be. At my age and as the mother of four boys I confess that I have never been able to forget you. Once on a moonlit night you even appeared beside my bed and I awakened with a start, but it was only a dream."

As I held Kydippe's hand and drank from her goblet, Hamilcar could no longer control himself but leaped from the couch of honor and declared in a trembling voice that Kydippe had already said enough for a hostage and a woman and bade her return to the protection of the eunuchs. I alone knew that Kydippe had deliberately encouraged his jealousy to demonstrate to herself her influence over him, for as she led her sons away, she glanced around the tent in triumph.

5.

I was filled with a deep foreboding and life at Hamilcar's encampment did not please me. The Etruscan commanders spent their days training the soldiers to fight breast to breast in a closed column, and although the mercenaries at first gathered around us to laugh and jeer at our efforts, their commanders soon became ambitious and ordered their own troops into training. We saw Libyans who linked their man-high shields to one another to form a wall of shields, and other troops who had iron bands around their waists by which they were fettered to one another to prevent a break in the line.

Then one day Hamilcar's scouts galloped into camp with lathered horses and shouted that the Greeks were but a day's march away, their numbers were countless and their shields and armor flashed dazzlingly in the sunlight as they rolled over the inland hills like the waves of the sea. The news created such a panic in the camp that many ran to the shore and fought their way onto the cargo vessels. Indeed, some were crushed to death and a number were drowned before Hamilcar managed to subdue them with whip and truncheon.

From the Siccanians we learned the exact size of the combined Syracusan and Agrigentian forces as well as the number of their heavily armored troops, their stone-slingers and their cavalrymen, for the Siccani could move through the forest on horny soles faster than the cavalry. It was not the number of the Greeks that was alarming but rather their order and the uniformity of their weapons. In fact, it became apparent that Hamilcar's forces numbered at least three times those of the Greeks. He was certain of victory, had giant bonfires lighted before the images of the gods that had been erected in various parts of the camp, and circulated among his troops, encouraging them and sacrificing rams to the gods.

The paucity of the Greeks was, however, compensated for by their strategy. A half day's march from Himera they paused to scout our camp and to establish contact with the Himeran garrison by means of Egyptian doves. Now Hamilcar thought they hesitated because of his overwhelming superiority and planned to send his troops against them. But it became apparent why they waited when the combined fleets of Syracuse and Agrigentum, totaling over two hundred modern triremes, rowed out of the morning haze, filling the entire sea. Moreover, the fleet arrived from the west, from the direction of Panormos and not from the strait to the east where Hamilcar had stationed half his fleet. Thus we could not believe our eyes at first and thought that the vessels were Carthaginian until we recognized them as triremes and distinguished the Greek emblems.

When the warships had closed the sea we learned that the Greek land forces had begun to move and were quick-marching toward Himera. Without hesitation Hamilcar took the necessary action and sent numerous warnings to his fleet at the strait by both sea and land. But only two Siccanians were able to get through and Hamilcar's commanders at first refused to believe them, thinking it a Greek stratagem. Only when the fishermen on the shore confirmed the incredible fact that the Greek fleet had circled Sicily did the commanders obey the order. But by then it was too late.

For on the following morning the Greek forces spread themselves in battle formation before Himera, supporting their flank on one side with the river, on the other with the forest and slopes. Contrary to custom, they had placed their cavalry in the center to try to break through Hamilcar's front and establish contact with Himera during the battle. The mournful drums of the Siccani began to sound in the forest and for once our camp was afoot in the gray of dawn as the troops marched in good order to their indicated positions.

Immediately he saw the position of the Greek cavalry Hamilcar changed his battle plan at the last moment and withdrew forces from both wings to support the center. These consisted of the heavily armored Iberians and the Libyans who were linked together, for Hamilcar did not intend to permit his foe to break through his center. His lack of confidence in us Etruscans angered us, nor were we pleased by the fact that fettered barbarians would drive us ahead once the battle started and thus isolate us from our ships. But the ceaseless clatter of the Carthaginians' rattles and the sound of their long horns prevented any further thinking. Nor did the Greeks pause to await our attack but sent their cavalry forward and resolutely advanced toward us.

When he saw that the battle was beginning Hamilcar gave the order to set fire to the logs piled before the gates of Himera to prevent an attack by the garrison. Also at the last moment we managed to strike sharp piles and stakes into the ground before us while the war machines catapulted boulders into the cavalry. But otherwise we remained in the path of the hoofs.

During the first attack more than half the Etruscans died or were incapacitated. Thus we had no alternative but to fall back, allow the cavalry to penetrate our front and close our thinned ranks again behind it.

The cavalry was followed by the columns of heavily armored men. Now the battle was more equal and the biting swords of the Etruscans began to have their effect. But still the force of the attack thrust us backward and those of us who survived did so not so much by our own efforts as through a miracle.

Behind us the wall of Himera was hidden by black smoke and from a distance the entire city seemed to be in flames. After they had broken through our center the remnants of the Greek cavalry galloped toward the city and the Greek heavily armored troops began to roll toward both our flanks, cutting Hamilcar's army in two. The battle would have been decided then and there had not the Greeks' left wing, which had pushed into the edge of the forest, suddenly been disorganized by a Siccanian thrust. Swiftly the Siccanians struck and retreated again into the forest leaving the Segestan forces to shout in triumph and attack the Greek flank, dispersing it and sending the Agrigentian lightly armored troops fleeing to the protection of the slopes.

Thereafter it was impossible to obtain a clear picture of the battle, for it raged violently from early morning until late night. I myself had been thrust with the remaining Etruscans to the right flank near the edge of the forest, where we paused for breath as the rested troops of Eryx pushed by us in a counterattack. In a manner worthy of him, Hamilcar, in the midst of the dreadful chaos of the attack, sent a runner to withdraw us from the battle. Swaying from exhaustion, bloody from head to toe, our shields dented and our swords dull, we stumbled back to the rear to rest.

Hamilcar had erected a high altar on the hill of the encampment and from that point followed the battle. With glowing eyes he raised his arms in greeting, thanked us for a heroic effort and had his slaves toss golden chains to us. But so bitterly did we mourn our fallen comrades that not one of us troubled to pick them from the ground.

With the aid of the counterattacks by the reserve troops and by drawing back his left wing as far as the encampment, Hamilcar managed to close his ranks again, but the Greeks who had broken through forced their way to the wall of Himera, scattered the flaming logs before the south gate and escaped through the opened gate into the city. But the remnants of their cavalry made a final surprise attack on Hamilcar's camp, actually throwing glowing firebrands into the tents before they retreated into the city.

When we had quenched our thirst, bound up our wounds and stolen food from the camp peddlers, we went to our vessels in the hope of meeting the surviving Etruscans. Brother called to brother, friend to friend, commander to helmsman and rower to benchmate, but no one replied to the calls. We noticed then that there were barely enough of us to man two warships and even that would have availed us nothing since the Greek triremes closed the sea. Our fearful losses proved that we at least had maintained the Etruscans' reputation as warriors at the battle of Himera.

As the sun began to sink in the west in the midst of the smoke and the chaos, we saw the Greeks force the left wing of the Carthaginian army into the river and the sea and the Himeran garrison, having torn down its burned gate, fall on the rear of Hamilcar's victorious right wing. In the camp, plunderers fell upon the executioners and floggers and killed them, after which they cold-bloodedly began to loot. That in my opinion was the surest indication of defeat. In vain Hamilcar attempted to rally his forces, but by now the barbarians were rushing into their own camp and killing their commanders. Others of them fled to the shore and boarded the vessels in the hope of escaping by sea, only to be rammed and sunk by a Greek trireme.

We consulted among ourselves and the Etruscans decided to remain near their vessels to await the coming of darkness when they could perhaps slip out to sea. For my part I suggested that they accompany me and seek shelter among the Siccani, but as seafaring people they could not bring themselves to relinquish their vessels. Thus I was alone as I made my way across the encampment and behind the city to the Siccanian forest. Surely the gods protected me in the midst of the horrifying confusion as the Greeks and the barbarians fought for loot.

Conceding defeat, Hamilcar covered his head and descended from his hill. His Greek mercenaries cleared the way for him to his tent, where he smashed the image of Baal and threw the pieces into the sacrificial fire lest his god fall under the influence of the enemy. His eyes wild and his lips frothing as though he had taken poison, he screamed for the guards to bring forth Kydippe and her sons and to kill them. But then the mercenaries, most of whom were from Rhegion, turned against him and began plundering the camp. A few of them did, however, go into the tent, but they did not have to drag Kydippe out by force, for she ran out ahead of them, plunged a knife into Hamilcar's throat and pushed his corpse into the fire. The guards surrounded Kydippe, protected her and her sons with their shields, and began to call to their Greek kinsmen to aid Kydippe's surrender to Gelon. So clear a sense of political reality did Kydippe have and so swiftly did she make her decision.

But the Siccanians' Erkle, despite his youth, was equally realistic. Seeing that Hamilcar's center was hopelessly broken and his left wing collapsing, Erkle quickly dispatched his Greek teacher, a green branch in his hand, to tyrant Theron of Agrigentum, and sent his troops to attack the Elymians from the rear as they were victoriously pursuing the Agrigentians. Through all the succeeding days they killed and robbed the retreating Carthaginian forces and Theron was so grateful for the assistance that he sent Hiuls a golden shield, a golden chain and the golden eagle of Agrigentum to fasten on his shield. But Hiuls, though he accepted the remainder, rejected the eagle since he did not wish to bind the Siccani to Theron.

Undoubtedly, as I myself had said to Hiuls, a talented politician must consider only his own people and forget the laws of honesty and honor that prevail among ordinary men. But in his actions I recognized all too well the shade of Dorieus who, having gained the dog crown, was ready to desert Dionysius and his men.

When I saw what had happened I no longer wished to find a haven among the Siccani but returned to the shore to share the fate of the Etruscans. We decided not to surrender our arms, for the fate of a slave did not please us, but instead to sell our lives dearly. In the darkness we manned the two fastest vessels, thrust them out to sea and, regardless of rank, seized the oars.

Noticing the two ships making for the sea, Tyrant Gelon began to roar so loudly that we heard his curses above the crackle of the burning vessels on the shore. Then we said to one another, "Tonight Etruscan lives are cheap and the gods do not watch over us at sea. Let us avenge the death of our comrades by sinking a Greek trireme as a sign that the sea still belongs to the Tyrrhenians."

Our determination saved us, for the Syracusan triremes were not expecting an attack and were preparing to sink us as we sought to flee. As they backed water and flashed signal lights to one another we increased our speed to the utmost and almost simultaneously both our rams struck the side of one of the triremes with a crash of oaken planks. Immediately the mighty vessel tilted and its Greeks fell into the sea. Our attack was so unexpected that they did not at first even know what had happened, for we heard the commander shout that he had hit a reef. Quickly we rowed free of the sinking vessel, bumped into another trireme and slid into the protective darkness of the sea without ourselves realizing how it had all happened.

We rowed through the night and towards morning a wind rose and storm clouds pursued us and drove our vessels toward the Italian coast. Finally we had to put ashore at Cumae to repair the damage and obtain provisions. Here Tyrant Demadotos welcomed us in a friendly manner, but when he heard about the battle of Himera and the crushing defeat of Carthage, he said, "Legally and by testament I am the heir of Tarquinius, the last ruler of Rome, although I still have not received compensation for his property. I have never been ill-disposed toward the Etruscans, but I must think of my responsibilities toward my city and my family. Therefore, I greatly fear that I must hold both vessels as security until King Tarquinius' legacy has been clarified."

While we were in Cumae, more as prisoners than as guests, disturbing news came from Poseidonia. There a noisy crowd had robbed the shops of the Carthaginian merchants and the Tyrrhenian storehouses, but instead of punishing the criminals the city's autocrat had imprisoned the Carthaginians and Etruscans, ostensibly for their own security.

But even more alarming news awaited us. Over the sea, on the wings of the goddess of victory, came news that the Athenians had completely destroyed the Persian fleet in the straits of Salamis near Athens. The Great King himself had had to flee back to Asia by land lest the Greeks destroy his bridge of ships across the Bosphorus and cut off his escape. True, the mighty Persian army had plundered and burned Athens and overturned the images of the gods, but it had suffered heavy losses at Thermopylae and its wintering in Greece would be difficult with Athenian ships controlling the seas to Asia. Nor could the Persian army, weakened by hunger and cold, be expected to vanquish the Spartan-led Greek land forces the following spring, when only three hundred Spartans had been able to hold them at Thermopylae until the Athenians had had time to transport their people to the safety of the islands.

Although I knew the Greek habit of exaggerating success, the same news came from so many directions that I had to believe it. Thus the Etruscan expedition to Himera became purposeless, for I had tried to console myself by thinking that the Etruscans' blood had not been shed in vain since even in dying they had prevented the Greek cities in the west from giving aid to their mother country.

Upon hearing of our plight Lars Arnth Velthuru sent Demadotos a message in which he threatened to withdraw all Tarquinian merchants from Cumae and confiscate all Cumaean supplies in Tarquinia unless both warships and their men were immediately released. Gelon for his part sent a herald from Syracuse to declare that he would consider it a hostile act if Demadotos were to free warships which had interfered in Sicily's internal affairs.

Demadotos sighed and groaned, clutched his head and lamented, "What misfortune sent your vessels to our harbor? My weak heart cannot endure such conflict."

We replied that the traditional friendship between Cumae and the Etruscan seaports had prompted us to seek refuge in his harbor.

"Yes, yes, undoubtedly," he said. "But Gelon of Syracuse is a powerful and ugly man. If he takes offense I will be lost and so will Cumaean trade."

He pondered the matter and finally found a solution. "We have our famous oracle, Hierofila, who inherited her position from antiquity even before there was a city at Cumae. The gods speak through her mouth and I doubt whether even Gelon dare question her decision."

He himself did not wish to go to the sibyl's cave, pleading that it was a trying journey and the cave's unpleasant vapors made his head ache. Instead he sent his adviser with the three of us who had been chosen by lots, and said to him, "Take my gift to the hag and demand that she for once say yes or no without babbling nonsense."

The sibyl's cave was in a gorge high on a mountaintop and the goat path leading to it was worn smooth from centuries of suppliants' steps. The temple itself was simple and faded by rain and wind but we were told that vast treasures were hidden in caves beneath, although from the priests' appearance it was difficult to believe. They had simple woolen bands around their heads and a coarse brown robe on their shoulders.

The sulphuric vapors of the cave were stifling. Our eyes smarted and we coughed so that we saw the interior of the cave and Hierofila on her pedestal through a veil of tears. The cave was unbearably hot because she kept a perpetual fire in the hearth. She had long ago lost her hair but vanity prompted her to wear a peaked cap. A wan girl with unkempt hair served her, and in the girl's eyes I recognized the wild eyes of the Delphic pythia and guessed that Hierofila was training her to be her successor. Hierofila's own eyes were like gray stone. She must have been completely blind.

Upon our arrival the girl began to run restlessly to and fro and thrust her face to each of ours in turn. Then she burst into wild laughter and began to shout, scream and leap like a madwoman until Hierofila commanded her to be silent in an oddly hollow and metallic voice which I would not have expected to issue from the lips of an old woman. Then Demadotos' emissary bowed his head before her and began to explain our mission.

But Hierofila ordered him also to be silent. "Why are you chattering? I know of these men and foresaw their arrival in Cumae when the ravens disappeared from the mountain and flew in flocks over the sea from whence these men came. Nor will I permit the spirits of the dead with their swollen tongues and gaping eyes to force their way into my dwelling with these men. Go your way and take the deceased with you."

She began to pant and to make forbidding gestures. After consulting among ourselves the two Etruscans left, summoning the spirits of the deceased.

The sibyl grew calm. "Now there is room to breathe again. But whence came that brightness that surrounds me and the roar of an invisible storm?"

331

The girl, who had been busy in a corner of the cave, stepped forth. She touched Hierofila's hand and placed on my head a wreath of dry bay leaves.

Hierofila began to titter. Staring at me with blind eyes she said, "You favorite of the gods, I see the blue of the moon at your temples but the sun shines from your face. I myself would tie a wreath of myrtle and willow for you, but content yourself with bay since we have nothing else."

Demadotos' emissary thought that she was raving and impatiently began to explain our mission once more. But again Hierofila interrupted him. "What do two vessels mean when a thousand vessels will clash on the sea near Cumae? Let Demadotos permit these men to go in peace and release their vessels. Emblems, not ships, determine wars."

Her voice swelled as though she were shouting through a metal trumpet. "Demadotos does not need ships but emblems. The god has spoken." When she had regained her breath she said more calmly, "Go your way, you stupid man, and leave me alone with the messenger of the gods."

Demadotos' adviser entered the prophecy in a wax tablet and tried to draw me out of the cave with him, but the girl fell upon him, scratching his face with her long nails. Then she wound her arms around my neck. She was not clean, but such a powerful smell of bay leaves and strong herbs exuded from her skin and clothes that she did not seem repulsive. I said that I would remain in the cave for a moment since that was apparently intended, and Demadotos' emissary left alone, holding the corner of his mantle to his mouth. Then only did Hierofila descend from her pedestal and open a wooden shutter in the wall, letting in fresh air that immediately swept away the poisonous vapors. Through a cleft in the mountain I saw the sky and the blue of the sea.

The sibyl stepped before me, felt me with her hands, touched my cheeks and hair with her fingertips, and said with feeling, "Son of your father, I recognize you. Why do you not kiss your mother?"

I stooped, touched the floor of the cave and kissed my palm to indicate that I acknowledged the earth as my mother. My whole being seemed suddenly to have broadened and brightness shone within me. The girl approached me, felt my knees and shoulders and rubbed her body against my loins. My strength seemed to ebb away and my armpits perspired so that beads of sweat ran down my sides. But Hierofila boxed the girl's ears and pushed her away.

"You recognize your mother," she said. "Why don't you greet your father?"

I shook my head in bewilderment. "I have never known my father or my origin."

Hierofila began to speak in a godlike voice. "My son, you will know yourself when you lay your hand on the round summit of your father's tombstone. I see your lake, I see your mountain, I see your city. Seek and you will find. Knock and it will be opened unto you. And when you return from the sealed gate remember me."

Suddenly she exclaimed, "Look behind you!"

I did so but saw nothing, although the flames which blazed brightly in the draft illumined every corner of the cave. I shook my head.

In apparent amazement Hierofila placed her palm on my forehead and urged, "Look again. Do you not see the goddess? Taller and fairer than mortals, she is looking at you and extending her arms. A mural crown is on her head. She is the moon goddess and also the goddess of the fountain. She is the goddess of foam and deer, cypress and myrtle."

I looked again but saw no goddess with a mural crown. Instead, another form began to take shape before my eyes—a stiff form, bent forward like a vessel's prow, grew from the stone wall of the cave. It was tightly robed in white and its face was sheathed in bandages. Silent, motionless, the shape leaned forward stiffly. Its position was expectant and indicative.

Hierofila took her hand from my forehead and asked tremblingly, "What do you see?"

"He is motionless," I said. "His face is wrapped in linen bands and he is indicating the north."

At that moment the roar in my ears became supernal, whiteness dazzled my eyes and I fell unconscious to the ground. When I awakened I seemed to be flying through space with the starry sky above and the earth below, the roar still echoing in my ears. Only when I opened my eyes did I realize that I was lying on the stone floor of the cave while Hierofila knelt beside me chafing my hands and the girl was wiping my forehead and temples with a cloth dipped in wine.

Hierofila said in her quavering old woman's voice, "Your arrival has been predicted and you have been recognized. But don't tie your heart to the earth. Search only for yourself that you may acknowledge yourself, you immortal."

I ate bread and drank wine with her as she told me about her visions. Then when I finally stepped out of the cave a ray of sunlight struck a tiny pebble on the ground before me. It was a dull white transparent pebble with an oval shape and as I placed it among the other stones of my life in the pouch around my neck for the first time I comprehended that the picking up of the pebble signified the end of one era in my life and the beginning of another.

Making my way from the cave in a daze, I rejoined my comrades and together we returned to the city where Demadotos interpreted the oracle's prophecy in his own way. He allowed us to sail from Cumae, but first he removed the emblems from our vessels and carefully put them in his treasure vault without sending them to Gelon. Nor did we care about the emblems; nothing made any difference so long as we could leave that unfriendly city.

6.

In the harbor of Tarquinia we handed our leaking vessels over to the guards. When we went on shore, however, the people did not greet us but turned their backs and covered their heads. The alleys emptied before us. Such sorrow did we bring to the land of the Etruscans. And so we parted silently from one another in the harbor.

I myself accompanied the ten or so Tarquinian survivors to the city, where Lars Arnth received us with deep concern but without a word of reproach. He merely listened to our story and gave us gifts. When the others had left he asked me to remain.

"It is useless for even the bravest man to struggle against Fate, which not even the gods control. I mean the gods whose number and holy names we know and to whom we sacrifice. The veiled gods, whom we don't know, are above everything, perhaps even above Fate."

"Blame me, abuse me, strike me," I begged. "I would feel better."

Lars Arnth smiled his sadly beautiful smile and said, "You are not to blame, Turms. You were merely the messenger. But I am in a difficult position. The leaders of our four hundred families are divided, with those who are friendly toward the Greeks censuring me bitterly for having needlessly antagonized them. Imported goods have become more expensive and the Attic vases that we are accustomed to placing in our rulers' tombs are obtainable only at usurious prices. Who could have foretold the Greeks' success against the Persian king? But I believe they are only using our expedition to Sicily as a pretext to destroy our trade."

He laid his hands on my shoulders and continued: "Far too many of our people already admire Greek culture and adopt the spirit of skepticism and derision that everywhere accompanies the Greeks. Only the inland cities are still sacred, for our seaports are unholy and poisoned. Don't remain in Tarquinia, Turms, for soon you may be stoned as a stranger who interfered in Etruscan affairs."

334

I opened my robe and showed him the barely healed wound in my side and the blisters in my palms. "At least I have risked my life for the Etruscan cause," I said bitterly. "It is not my fault that I was lucky and returned alive."

Lars Arnth looked uncomfortable, avoided my eyes and said, "To me you are not a stranger, Turms. I know better and recognize you just as my father immediately recognized you. But for political reasons I must avoid trouble. Not even for your own sake would I wish an unknowing people to stone you."

He banished me from his city with assurances of friendship although as a wealthy man he did not realize that I had been impoverished. I had long since used the gold chain that Xenodotos had given me, for in Cumae we survivors had shared everything. I had to sell my notched sword and dented shield in Tarquinia and as the wintery winds blew down from the mountains I wandered on foot to Rome by way of Caere, for I was too thin and feverish to work my passage on a cargo vessel.

When I finally stood at the top of Janiculum and looked down on the yellow river, the bridge, the wall and the temples beyond, I saw that the destruction had extended as far as Rome. But in the midst of the wasteland I found my own summer house unharmed, and Misme ran toward me on brown legs, her eyes shining with happiness.

"We have lived through alarming times," she explained. "We didn't even have time to flee to Rome as you suggested. But the men of Veii thrust holy stakes in our yard and thereafter no one disturbed us or even stole our cattle. We have had a good harvest and hidden it. Now we will become wealthy, for the price of grain has risen in Rome. Surely, now that we have taken such good care of everything, you will buy me a new garment and shoes for my feet."

I realized that my house had been spared through the thoughtfulness of Lars Arnth. But in meaning well he did me only harm, for as soon as I stepped on the bridge to Rome I was arrested, turned over to a lictor, and placed in a dungeon in the Mamertine prison. On cold nights the water on the floor of the cell froze, rotting straw was my bed, and I had to fight with the rats for the food which I myself had to supply. My fever increased, I had hallucinations, and when I rarely regained my senses I thought I was dying.

Because of my illness I could not be tried and condemned. In truth, the officials considered me an insignificant person and my arrest was merely a political move to provide the people with a scapegoat in the unsuccessful war. Little attention was paid me and the consuls were unconcerned about my fate.

335

But I did not die. My fever diminished and one morning I awakened with a clear head but so weak that I could hardly raise a hand. When the guard saw that I had recovered he permitted Misme to see me. Day after day she had walked the long distance to the city and back again after waiting in vain at the prison gate. But the food that she had brought me saved my life, for the guard said that I had eaten and drunk during my lucid moments although I did not remember it.

Upon seeing me Misme burst into tears, sank onto the dirty straw and fed me with her own hands, forcing down every mouthful and compelling me to drink a little wine. When I had regained my senses I warned her against coming to the prison since the officials might arrest her also, child though she was.

Misme stared at me with frightened eyes. "I don't think I am a child any more. I understand much that I didn't understand before."

My pride forbade me to inform Arsinoe of my plight nor did I wish to create difficulties for her. Although Misme did not tell me I knew that I would be charged with treason, the strongest evidence against me being my house which stood while others around it had been destroyed. Why would the Veian soldiers have spared my small farm unless I had done them some service? My position would become even worse when the hearing would reveal that I had participated in a military expedition to Sicily with the Etruscans. Indeed, had I been a Roman citizen I would probably have been flogged and beheaded despite my illness. But I had never applied for citizenship. On the contrary, I had joined the guild of teachers, which the Romans despised, solely to avoid citizenship.

I feared for Misme more than for myself. My land and cattle would undoubtedly be confiscated by the state and I myself at best banished from Rome. True, I still had the golden bull's-head—a fortune in itself—hidden in the ground, but if I tried to bribe some official he would keep the gold and its possession would be considered even stronger evidence against me.

After long consideration I said, "Dear Misme, don't return any more to the farm but seek refuge in your mother's house. You are her daughter and she can protect you. But say nothing of me. Explain only that I have disappeared and that because of it you are in need."

"I will never seek Arsinoe's protection!" cried Misme. "I don't even want to call her my mother. I would rather become a shepherdess or sell myself as a slave."

I had not realized that she felt such bitterness toward Arsinoe. "After all, she is your own mother and gave birth to you," I said.

336

Tears of anger rose to Misme's eyes and she shouted, "She is a bad and cruel mother! Throughout my childhood she shunned me because I didn't know how to please her. But I could forgive even that if she hadn't taken away Hanna, who was gentler to me than my mother and was my only friend."

I was shocked to remember how Arsinoe had treated Hanna. Every detail of the past came back to torment me and I realized that there was more to Hanna's fate than I had thought. I asked whether Misme had ever noticed anything suspicious about Hanna and her behavior.

"I was still a child when that terrible thing happened," said Misme, "but I would surely have known if she had wantonly slept with men. After all, we shared the same bed and were always together. It was she who warned me about my mother and told me that you were not my real father, so you don't have to conceal it from me any longer. She told me how Arsinoe taunted my real father until he took his life in the swamp. He was a Greek physician and your friend, wasn't he? But you, Turms, you were the only man whom Hanna ever loved. Because of her I also love you, although you don't deserve it.

"No, I shouldn't say that," she interrupted herself. "You have been good to me and better than a real father. But how could you desert Hanna after she had become pregnant by you?"

"In the name of the gods," I cried, "what are you saying, you unfortunate girl!" Sweat leaped to my brow and I did not need Misme's accusing glance to know that she spoke the truth. After all, I had had no other proof of my sterility than Arsinoe's scornful words.

Misme demanded sarcastically, "Do you think she became pregnant by the gods? You certainly were the only man who ever laid hands on her. That she swore to me when she began to be afraid, but I was only a child and didn't understand everything. Now I do understand and realize that Arsinoe must have known. That is why she sold Hanna to the worst place she could imagine."

She looked at my expression in disbelief. "Didn't you really know? I thought that you despised Hanna and wanted to escape your responsibility. All men are cowards. That at least my mother taught me, if nothing else. She didn't tell me where she sold Hanna, but I learned it from the stable slave before Arsinoe sent him away. A Phoenician slave merchant was in Rome at the time buying Volscian girls at the cattle market for brothels in Tyre. It was to him that Arsinoe sold Hanna. He assured her that if Hanna's child were a boy he would be castrated and sent to Persia, while a girl would be trained from the beginning for her mother's profession. I was so bitter and shed so many tears for

Hanna that in my heart I could not forgive you for years because I thought that you knew."

Tears began to stream down her cheeks, she touched my hand and pleaded, "Oh, foster father, dear Turms, forgive me for thinking so harshly of you! Why didn't I keep the matter to myself? I am glad, though, that you didn't hurt Hanna deliberately, for I loved her so much that I would have been happy if you had taken her to be my mother and I would have had my own little brother or sister."

I could bear no more. My horror became raging anger, I called upon the gods of the underworld and cursed Arsinoe living and dead for the terrible crime she had committed toward me and innocent Hanna. My curses were so dreadful that Misme covered her ears. Then my anger became anguish as I realized that Hanna had surely died and my child had disappeared for all time. It was useless to search for him. The brothels of Phoenicia kept their secrets and once in them nothing could save one. That Arsinoe knew well.

At length I became calm and said to Misme, "Perhaps it is best that you don't go to that woman's house. Any other fate would be preferable to being dependent on her."

Because I was unable to protect Misme I had to trust to her intelligence and resourcefulness. I told her of the golden bull's-head and explained where it was buried. I warned her not to try to sell it in Rome but to chip off pieces and sell them in some Etruscan city if she were in need.

Then I kissed and embraced her and said, "I have my guardian spirit and hope that you have yours, you good and dear girl. Don't worry about me. Just take care of yourself."

That night I had a clear dream. In it a stoop-shouldered woman, her head covered by a fold of her brown mantle, came to my stone cell. In my dream I knew her and trusted her but upon awakening I could not think who she might be. Nevertheless a feeling of confidence came over me.

Finally I was allowed to wash and put on clean clothing and was taken to the house of justice. I was questioned as to why the Veian robbers had spared my house and I said that I knew nothing about it since I had been with the Etruscans in Sicily. But I mentioned that my ties of friendship in the various Etruscan cities might account for it.

The morning was cold and the consul and quaestor had braziers under their seats. They spread their togas and lifted their feet from the stone floor, and hardly troubled to conceal their yawns. They considered me guilty of treason in time of war on the basis of my own admission and the only question in their minds was whether they had the juridical right to condemn me to death since I was not a Roman citizen. On this point they conveniently concluded that in the eyes of the law I could be compared to a citizen, since I owned fifteen jugera within the borders of Rome and thus could have attained citizenship had I bothered to apply for it. But they could not throw me off a precipice and drag me into the river because I was not actually a citizen. Hence they condemned me to be flogged and beheaded although as a traitor I did not deserve such a respectable death.

Certain death awaited me, for Roman law knew no pardon once judgment was passed nor could I appeal to the people since I was not a citizen. But I was not afraid and did not think that I would die. Indeed, my calmness and confidence so amazed the guard that he became friendly and on many occasions remained to talk with me.

Arsinoe heard about me after my sentence and had made the matter public. Also Misme broke her promise and went to talk to her mother when she heard that any day I would be publicly executed in the market place. As a result Arsinoe appeared in the prison with a basket in her hand to distribute alms to the criminals and prisoners.

When the guard had opened my door she pretended not to see me but said to the senator's wife who accompanied her, "This man seems to be a Greek. You go ahead and I will feed him, for with his fettered wrists he cannot eat."

In a clay crock she had the same soup made of ox, pig and lamb meat that had made her famous during the Volscian siege. Dropping to her knees beside me on the dirty straw she began to feed me, holding her face close to mine.

"Oh, Turms," she whispered, "what have you done to yourself and why did you betray Rome, at whose hands you have met only with kindness? I don't know how I can aid you or save your life. Nor can Tertius Valerius help, for he is in bed and can no longer talk. He had another stroke yesterday."

Misunderstanding my expression, she put her hand on my bare chest, stroked it lightly as she had in the past and continued to chatter. "How dirty you are and as thin as a stray dog! I can feel your every rib with my fingers. I have asked advice of a jurist and he has said that if only you were a Roman citizen you could appeal to the people. But one who has been found guilty of treason cannot apply for citizenship. Oh, Turms, you are as impossible as ever! You should at least have thought of Misme. Now because of you she is poor and homeless. Who do you think will marry the daughter of a man who is executed for treason?"

When I was finally able to speak I said, "Arsinoe, take your hand

339

away or I will kill you, fettered though I am. With death before my eyes I implore you to speak the truth for once. Did you know that Hanna was pregnant by me when you so mercilessly had her flogged and then sold her as a slave?"

Arsinoe thrust the ladle into the crock in annoyance and pleaded, "Why speak of old and unpleasant matters when we can still look upon each other with living eyes? You caused me quite enough grief with that disagreeable girl. If you insist, of course you could not deceive me. After all, I am a woman. With the first glance I realized what had happened that night in Panormos when I left you to yourself. And afterward I had only to look at the girl's dog's-eyes when she thought that no one noticed. At first it amused me but you can imagine my feelings when I realized that she was pregnant by you. I am enough of a woman not to want your bastard in my house." Even after nine years her face reddened with anger and she raised her voice. "I could strangle you with my own hands for so hatefully betraying me and my love for you!"

Nor was her anger mere pretense. No, she firmly believed that I and not she was responsible for Hanna's fate. Most deeply she was wounded by the fact that, by a quirk of fate or her own goddess, she herself had not become pregnant by me. For my part I was only grateful and realized that it was by design of the gods. I expected nothing good of Arsinoe's offspring. I did not even fully trust Misme.

Arsinoe sobbed in anger; then she began to stroke my knee and confessed, "At this stage I have sometimes regretted my deed and I fear greatly that Hanna and her then unborn child will haunt me as lemures in my old age. Such matters are unimportant, of course, and it was not the first time that a master has gotten a slave with child. But I loved you so blindly then, Turms. I was jealous and my pride was hurt. I forgive you now, though."

She bent over me. I smelled the fragrance of narcissus on her face and noticed that she had reddened her lips and shadowed her eyelids. Her voice was low as she whispered, "Oh, Turms, how I have longed for you, and how often you have come to me in my dreams! But I had to think of my future. All I had was my beauty. Such a commodity must be sold in time for the best price."

Nor could I help myself as I looked at her glowing eyes and her beautiful mouth, nose and cheeks. "Arsinoe," I said, "you are still beautiful and in my eyes the loveliest woman on earth."

She opened her mantle, lifted her face and touched her chin. "How beautifully you lie, Turms! I am an old woman, and it will not be many years before I will be fifty. To be honest, since that is what you wish,

340

I must be almost ten years older than you, although the goddess has helped me seem years younger than I truly am."

"Arsinoe," I assured her, "your beauty will never fade. It is as eternal as your goddess."

She warmed to me then, but as she smiled I saw the gleam of gold in the gums of her front teeth. "I haven't even my own teeth," she lamented. "When I gave birth to Julius I lost many of them. But an Etruscan tooth-maker made these of gold and ivory and fastened them so cleverly that they are stronger than my own were."

I admitted that they were incomparably better than those of Tanakil. Then I asked, "How can your son's name be Julius? Aren't the Juliuses one of the oldest Latin patrician families?"

Arsinoe moved uncomfortably. "I myself am of a collateral branch of the Julius family," she claimed. "That I proved at the time Tertius Valerius married me so that our son would be born a patrician. The Juliuses are few and they are poor, but they are descended from Ascanius, son of Aeneas of Troy who founded Alba Longa. You see, both my other children were unsuccessful. Hiuls is only a barbarian king and Misme will presumably be nothing. But certain omens lead me to hope for much from Julius. That is why, when poor Tertius is dead, I will not, after all, marry Manius Valerius. Besides, his wife is still alive and appears very healthy. But there is a poor but pleasing Julius who has become our family friend. When I have married him I shall forget the Valerius family completely and my son will be a Julius. The oldest vestal, who remembers the days of the kings and who best knows the old families, has advised me."

But as she talked about her son I suddenly remembered Hanna. Arsinoe noticed it and became alarmed.

"Of course I did wrong in selling Hanna but I wanted her as far away from Rome as possible. A Phoenician merchant bought her." She looked at me with bright eyes. "In the name of the goddess and in Hiuls' and Misme's names and by my own hair, the vessel sank with its slaves and cargo in a fearful storm off Cumae. Not a single person was saved, so you don't have to worry about Hanna and her unborn child. Don't hate me because of them."

I knew that she was lying. But finally I said, "Be it as you wish, Arsinoe. So Hanna drowned. The guilt is mine, not yours. You don't have to fear the evil lemures. I forgive you and ask that you forgive me for not being the man you wished. For the sake of our love, always remain as beautiful and glowing as you now are. Always and eternally, Arsinoe."

Her face brightened, her hair began to gleam golden and the goddess's light radiated from her as though the sun shone in the dark cell. I smelled the fragrance of roses and crocuses. Trembling and melting I recognized the goddess in her and rejoiced that in her heart she was not evil. Cruel, capricious, selfish and even false, she was the earthly reflection of the foam-born. A wave of desire, tenderness and love rushed from her to me, scorching my body as I looked at her. But I did not extend my hand to touch her. That time was past and I was free of her.

She raised her hand to her breast and exclaimed, "What did you say, what did you do to me, Turms? I am hot, my heart is pounding and the blood of youth flows through me. I myself feel how young and radiant I am. The goddess has returned to me!"

A thought came to her. "Roman law and justice cannot help you, but because of the goddess I know how I can save your life. Thus neither of us will owe the other anything, although we may never meet again."

She stooped to touch her mouth to mine. Her lips were cool but her cheeks were as flushed as those of a young girl. It was the last time I caressed her, nor did we ever meet again. But my heart glows in being able to remember her like that.

Our meeting made me take an assenting attitude toward death and each morning I expected to hear the crowd shouting in the market place and the steps of the lictors. I paid little attention to Arsinoe's promise. But a few days later the door was opened and in stepped the brown-robed woman whom I had seen in my dream. Only when the guard had bolted the door again did she reveal her withered face so that I recognized her as the oldest of the vestals. I had seen her many times at the circus in the vestal virgins' seat of honor.

"You are the man I seek," she said. "I recognize you by your face."

I saw her but dimly and then in a moment of clarity the cell walls dissolved and I saw her sitting on a pedestal under a parasol. I knelt before her and bowed my head.

She smiled the thin smile of an old woman and touched my dirty hair. "Don't you remember me, Turms? You met me on your first day in Rome nine years ago when you yourself found your way to the sacred cave, sprinkled water on your face and of the wreaths chose the ivy. That was sufficient proof for me. But already I had recognized your face. The gods have given me my task. The Romans must not dishonor and kill you, Turms, for it would bring disaster upon the city. For the sake of Rome you must be freed. And for your own sake as well, since Rome is also your city."

I said, "I have not had much joy of Rome. Life has become bitter, so that I do not fear death."

She shook her head. "My dear son, you who had to come, your wandering has not yet ended. You cannot rest and forget yet." Her black eyes stared at me. "Blessed, blessed is oblivion," she conceded. "But you were not born a human being merely for your own sake. You have wandered freely but now you have reached the ordained age. You must go north. That is a command. Obey your omens."

"I must go under the axe," I said mockingly. "What can you do about that, old woman?"

She straightened and lifted her head. "Your god is a strange god to the Romans, Turms, but he has given sufficient warning omens on your behalf. Hail has never hurt your fields. Your cattle have not been ill. Your ewes have borne twins. The Romans respect their laws but even more they fear strange gods. The wife of a noble senator came to talk to me about you. At first I did not know whom she meant and I suspected her. But her goddess took care of me when I was deaf and blind. Quickly I looked into the matter. The High Bridge Builder found your name in his book and the Senate had to yield, for the oldest families know well what is meant. Your sentence is revoked, Turms, and you will not even be flogged. But you must leave Rome. Go north, where you are expected. Your lake is awaiting you, your mountain is awaiting you."

She rapped sharply on the door and the guard opened it immediately and carried in a bucket of water. Soon a smith came and removed my fetters. The old vestal bade me take off my dirty clothes; then she washed me with her own hands, and anointed and braided my hair. When she had finished, the guard extended a basket from which she took a shirt of the finest wool and slipped it over me. But on my shoulders she placed a coarse brown mantle similar to her own. Finally she placed a wreath of oak leaves and acorns on my head.

"You are ready to leave," she said. "But remember, everything must happen secretly and without the knowledge of the people. Go, therefore. Hasten, holy deer. The field brothers are waiting to escort you to the city border and they will protect you should someone recognize you. You see, for the first time during the republic the consul has revoked a sentence. But the people do not know that."

Taking me by the hand she led me up from the damp cell and a guard opened the gate for us. As we stepped into the market place I saw that a heavy fog had covered the market place so that the field brothers who awaited us in their gray mantles and wreaths of wheatears seemed like ghosts in the mist.

The vestal said, "You can see for yourself—the gods have descended upon the city as mist to shield your departure."

She thrust me forward and I did not turn to bid her farewell, for something told me that a woman such as she was expected no farewell or thanks. The holy mist deadened the sound of footsteps and cartwheels as the field brothers who surrounded me steadied my faltering steps, for I was still weak after my illness.

On the bridge the guards turned their backs to us and for the last time I crossed the Roman bridge, smelled the stench of cattle manure and heard the creak of the worn planks under my feet. But the fog was so thick that I could not distinguish the water of the Tiber, although I heard it splash gently against the pillars as though bidding me farewell.

At the northern boundary the brothers wrapped their mantles about them and sat in a circle around me on the fog-dampened ground. The wind began to blow and the mists to disperse as solemnly they broke a barley loaf and each, from the eldest to youngest, took a piece and ate. The eldest poured red wine into a clay vessel which passed from hand to hand. But they did not offer any to me.

A strengthening north wind tore the mist into shreds and swept the sky clean. As the sun began to shine they rose as one man, hung a leather knapsack on my back, and pushed me across the border into the land of the Etruscans. In my heart I knew that what they did was right. The north wind blew triumphantly in my face, the blood began to flow warmly in my veins, but I did not recognize the earth that my feet trod.

7.

The north was my fate and I wandered freer than ever before, for I had discarded my old life as I would a tattered garment. After my illness I felt as light and airy as though my feet had wings and did not even touch the earth's dust. The sunshine was intoxicating, the green of the budding meadows soothed my eyes, and I smiled as I wandered. Spring wandered with me with twittering birds, swelling streams, gentle days.

I did not hurry but rested often in the homes of shepherds and the round huts of poor farmers. The water tasted fresh in my mouth. The bread was delectable. I regained my strength and felt my body was cleansed of life's deadening poisons and the oppression of deeds, thoughts and tormenting reason. I was free, I was happy, I was blissfully alone as I wandered.

Then came the hills with shadows of clouds gliding over them. And at last, after weeks of wandering, I saw fertile fields, sloping vineyards, silver-gray olive groves and ancient fig trees. Atop its mountain rose a city with its grassy wall, archways and colorful buildings. But I did not turn toward it. Profound yearning compelled me instead to leave the road and climb through thickets straight to the peak of the next mountain. Birds startled into flight flew ahead of me to the mountain and a fox lying at the mouth of its den flashed ahead of me up the mountainside. A proud deer rose from a clump of bushes, lifted its antlers and also ran lightly before me. Stones under my feet rolled down the slope, my mantle was torn and my breath quickened from the effort, but as I struggled upward I felt the approach of holiness. Moment by moment it became stronger until I no longer was merely myself. I was one with earth and sky, air and mountain. I was more than myself.

I saw the entrances to the tombs, the holy pillars before them, the shelters of the stonecutters and painters. I saw the holy stairs but still I did not pause. I rose above the tombs to the highest peak of the mountain.

Suddenly a storm broke. The sky arched above me cloudlessly but the wind blew as it will blow when, in a new human body, I will ascend the steps of my tomb holding in my hand the stones of this life. Although my writing may disappear and my memory fail, I shall read the events of this life pebble by pebble and a storm will again blow from a clear sky over my mountaintop.

To the north I saw a lake. In the distance, surrounded by hazy mountains, it gleamed bluely and I knew it was my lake, my beautiful lake. I felt as though I could hear the rustle of reeds in my ears, smell the shores and taste the fresh water. As the storm roared I turned my glance westward over the tombs to where the goddess's mountain rose in a bluish cone. This too I recognized. Only then did I let my glance wander down the steps lined with painted pillars and follow the holy road across the plain and up the slope on the other side of the fields. And there I recognized my city. This rolling land with its hazy, beautiful slopes was my land and my father's land. In my feet and in my heart I had recognized it already upon crossing the border and as the shadows of clouds had leaped toward me from peak to peak.

Overcome with a glorious intoxication, I dropped to my knees and kissed the land that had given me birth. I kissed the earth, my mother, in gratitude for having finally found my home after my long wandering.

As I descended the slope, shapeless beings of light darted across the sky. I looked into the black darkness of the sacrificial well and stepped before the tombs. I did not hesitate but laid my hand on the round summit of a pillar decorated with graceful startled deer, and whispered brokenly, "My father, my father, your son has returned!"

I sank to the warm ground before my father's tomb and an inexpressible feeling of peace and security swept over me. The sun set behind the graceful cone of the goddess's mountain, coloring the hills and the painted images on the temple roofs beyond the valley. It grew dark and I slept.

In the middle of the night I awakened to the rumble of thunder. The wind roared, the clouds loosed warm rain, and thunderbolts flashed around me. Suddenly the earth beneath me trembled as lightning struck the peak before me and the smell of the cleft stone filled my nostrils. My limbs began to move as the ancient dance came upon me. In the warm rain I joyously raised my arms and danced the lightning dance as I once had danced the storm dance on the road to Delphi.

When I awakened, stiff with cold, the sun was shining brightly. I sat up to rub my limbs and saw that the stonecutters and painters had paused on their way to work and were staring at me with frightened eyes. When I moved they stepped back and the guard of the tombs raised his holy staff. Then along a winding path came the lightning priest dressed in his robe of authority and wearing a wreath on his head.

The guard hastened toward him, raising his voice, shouted, "Lo, when I arrived I found a brown-clad stranger before the royal tomb of Lars Porsenna. Upon my arrival a doe sprang to her feet and fled, but a flock of white doves swooped across the valley from the goddess's mountain and surrounded the sleeper. Then the workers came and awakened him."

The priest said, "I saw bright flashes of lightning in the middle of the night and came to see what had happened on the sacred mountain." He stepped before me and looked at me sharply. Suddenly he covered his eyes with his left hand and raised his right arm in greeting as though I were a god.

"I recognize your face," he said and began to tremble. "I recognize you by your statues and the paintings of you. Who are you and what do you want?"

"I have sought and found," I said. "In my heart I knocked until the door was opened. I, Turms, have returned home. I am my father's son."

An old weather-beaten stonecutter flung down his tools, dropped to the ground and began to weep. "It is he, I recognize him! Our king has returned to us alive, as fair as he was in the best days of his manhood."

He would have embraced my knees but I forbade it, protesting, "No, no, you are mistaken. I am not a king."

Some of the workers ran to the city to spread the news of my arrival. The priest said, "I saw the thunderbolts. Your arrival has been discussed among the consecrated for nine years. Many feared that you would never find your way home, but no one dared interfere in divine matters and guide you. Our augur greeted you upon your first arrival in Rome, read you the omens and spread the news among the consecrated. From the high priest of lightning on the island we heard that you were coming and that the thunderbolt struck a full circle for you in elation. Tell me, are you a true Lucumo?"

"I do not know," I said. "I know only that I have returned home."

"Yes," he admitted, "at least you are Lars Porsenna's son. You have slept by your father's tomb. One cannot mistake your face. Even if you are not a Lucumo you are of noble blood."

I saw the plowers in the valley leave their plows and oxen and the hoers drop their hoes. One after another they stepped onto the holy road and began to climb toward us.

"I ask for nothing," I said, "only my native land and a place in which to live my life. I demand no inheritance, I aspire to no power. I am the humblest of the humble now that I have reached my home. I knew the hills, I knew the mountain, the lake and my father's tomb. That is enough for me. Tell me of my father."

"Your city is Clusium," he said evasively. "It is the city of black vases and eternal human faces. For so long as we can remember, our potters and sculptors have made eternal human faces of clay, soft stone and alabaster. That is why you were so easily recognized. Soon you will see your father's likeness, for down in his tomb he rests eternally on his sarcophagus with a sacrificial cup in his hand. There are also many likenesses of him in the city."

"Tell me of my father," I pleaded again. "Until now I have known nothing about my birth."

He said, "Lars Porsenna was the bravest of the inland rulers but he did not acknowledge himself to be a Lucumo, and we called him King only after his death. He even conquered Rome although he did not compel the Romans to reinstate their exiled ruler. Instead he taught the Romans the same form of government that we have followed in our city ever since his death. We have two leaders, a council of two hundred, and officials who are elected yearly. We also listen to the voice of the people. Ambitious men who followed Porsenna have all failed in their

347

attempts to seize power. Unless we find a true Lucumo, we decided, we will not be ruled by any man.

"Your father was adventuresome and restless in his youth," the lightning priest related. "He took part in a military expedition into Cumae and when we were defeated he asked, 'What do the Greeks have that we lack?' And so he traveled to the Greek cities to learn their customs."

In the distance a white crowd began to swarm out of the city gate. The first farmers reached us and paused at a respectful distance to look at me, their hardened hands hanging at their sides. "The Lucumo," they whispered to one another. "The Lucumo has come."

The priest turned toward them and explained, "It is but Lars Porsenna's son who has returned from strange lands. He does not even know what 'Lucumo' means. Do not disturb him with your foolish whispers."

But the farmers mumbled and from lip to lip passed the words, "He brought a good rain with him. He arrived with the waxing moon on the day of the blessing of the fields."

They bent leafy branches from the trees, waved them in greeting and shouted jubilantly, "Lucumo, Lucumo!"

The lightning priest was disturbed. "You are making the people restless. That is not good. If you are in truth a Lucumo you must first be examined and recognized. That can happen only in the autumn at the holy meeting of the cities by the lake at Volsinii. Until then it would be best if you were not to reveal yourself."

But the first arrivals from the city, hastily dressed in their best, were already arriving, breathless from the climb. The babble rose to a roar as the people described what had happened. I even heard it said that I had dropped from the sky on a thunderbolt, while others claimed that I had arrived on the back of a doe. Ever more triumphantly rose the cry, "Lucumo, Lucumo!"

Then came the augurs with their curved staves and the sacrificial priests each with a bronze or clay model of a sheep's liver marked with the names and regions of the various gods. The crowd made way for them and they stepped before me, studying me shrewdly. The sun went behind a cloud and a shadow fell on us although the goddess's mountain still gleamed in brilliant sunlight across the valley.

The priests were in a predicament, as I realized later. True, the oldest among them were consecrated and knew of my coming, but even they disputed whether I was a true Lucumo or merely Lars Porsenna's son, which in itself pleased the people. Mere omens and prophesies were not sufficient to prove me a Lucumo until such time as I acknowledged myself and was acknowledged. That could be done only by a true

348

Lucumo and there were but two still living in all the land. The new times had made many people, especially in the seaports, suspect the reality of Lucumones. That was the Greek influence. The hot wind of doubt swept over sea and land from Ionia.

The priests would probably have preferred to take me aside and talk to me, but the crowd was first. Joyous, laughing people sped the divine litter to the holy mountain from the temple where youths and maidens had seized it and wreathed their heads in myrtle, violet and ivy. Musicians blew on their double pipes and sacred dancers waved their rattles as the people fearlessly pushed their way to me and forced me to seat myself on the double cushion of the god.

As they began to lift the litter to their shoulders I rose angrily to my feet, pushing them from me. The music ceased and the youths stared at me in alarm and rubbed their arms as though they had been injured although I had merely pushed them aside. On my own feet I walked to the sacred stairs and descended them. At that moment the sun burst forth between the clouds, shining directly on me and the stairs. As the rays glinted in my hair the crowd behind me chanted solemnly, "Lucumo, Lucumo!" They were no longer gay and joyous but deeply respectful.

The priests followed me and behind them came the people, quietly and no longer shoving one another. Thus, on my own feet, I crossed the valley and ascended the winding road, on my own feet stepped through the archway into my city. The sun shone brightly all the while and a warm breeze caressed my face.

I spent the beautiful summer quietly in a house which the city fathers provided for me. Silent servants took care of my needs and I studied myself and listened to myself. Consecrated priests told me that which I had to know but added, "The knowledge is in yourself if you are a Lucumo, not in us."

That hot summer was the happiest in my life as I groped to open the secret doors of my innermost self. It was a fruitful and beautiful summer for all Clusium, with sunshine, warm winds and sufficient rain. The harvest was better than it had been within the memory of man, and the wine was sweet and good. The cattle thrived, there was not a single act of violence within the city, and neighbors solved their old differences peacefully. Good fortune had accompanied me to Clusium after many difficult and discordant years.

The consecrated told me about my birth and how I had been born with my face covered by a membrane. There had been other omens as well which had prompted the old men to predict to my father that I would develop into a Lucumo for my people.

But he had replied, "I have not acknowledged myself to be a Lucumo though men have tempted me, for I am not a Lucumo. Intelligence, courage and integrity suffice for a man. Pity the suffering, support the weak, slap the insolent across the mouth, tear the pouch of the greedy, concede the plowman his plowed land, protect the people from robbers and usurpers. A ruler needs no other guide and does not have to be a Lucumo to follow it. If my son is a true Lucumo he must be able to find himself and his city as the Lucumones did in former times. No one is a true Lucumo merely because of birth. Only at the age of forty can a Lucumo acknowledge himself and be acknowledged. That is why I must give up my son."

So when I was seven my father had taken me to Sybaris, the most civilized Greek city in Italy, and entrusted my care to a friend from whom he extracted a promise not to tell me of my birth. It must have been hard for him to do that for I was his only son. My mother had died when I was three and he had not wished to marry again. But he considered it his duty to his people to sacrifice me because he did not wish me to be a false Lucumo.

It was probably his intention to follow my development from afar, but the war with Croton broke out suddenly and Sybaris was destroyed more thoroughly than any city previously had been. Of the four hundred families of Sybaris only the women and children were sent by sea to the safety of Ionia and Miletus. Not even in the moment of greatest danger did my father's friend break his oath and reveal my birth to those who took me to Ionia with them. And after the destruction of Sybaris had been mourned for a time the wretched refugees had been forgotten and pushed from place to place.

My father was killed unexpectedly by a wild boar before he had even reached fifty, and after his death many considered that he had, after all, been a Lucumo who had chosen to conceal the fact. Others again claimed that he was not since he had gone to war, and these considered his death a punishment for having interfered in Roman politics. After all, the wild boar was the sacred animal of the Latins, even older and more sacred than the Romans' wolf.

My father's sisters came to meet me but they did not embrace me and their children stared at me with wide eyes. They declared that they would gladly share my father's inheritance with me even without proof of my birth, but when I told them that I had not come in search of an inheritance they left relieved. It would have been difficult for them to have persuaded their husbands to agree to a division of the legacy although among Etruscans the wife controls her own property and inherits on equal terms with a man. Hence a man who is proud of his family always mentions his mother's name together with that of his father. My real name was thus Lars Turms Larkhna Porsenna, for my mother was of the ancient Larkhna family.

During the summer the youths of the city practiced zealously for the holy game to be held that autumn. From among them would be chosen the strongest and fairest to represent Clusium in the traditional combat which yearly determined the leading city. He would be crowned with a wreath and receive the city's sacred round shield and the sacred sword so that he might become accustomed to them. But the consecrated explained that the outcome of the combat had not had political significance for centuries. Now the winner merely won the maiden whom he had freed, and the city gained a place of honor at the conference for a year.

I did not listen carefully to the tales about traditions for I had enough to do in learning to know myself, no longer as a mere human but as something more than a human. Sometimes dazzling perception filled my mind and I was happy. Then again I felt the weight of my body and my limbs.

But it was nevertheless the happiest summer of my life as I groped to find my true self. Then, as autumn approached, I became so melancholy that I could no longer rejoice. In the dark of the moon I journeyed to the shore of the sacred lake at Volsinii with the delegates from my city. But I was not permitted to walk on my own feet or ride on the back of a horse or a donkey. Instead I was drawn in a closed cart by white oxen. Red tassels ornamented the forehead of the oxen and heavy curtains concealed me from the eyes of the people.

In the same cart, hidden from human eyes in the same manner, both white stone cones have just been brought to my city from the temple of the mutable. Once again I shall recline on the couch of the gods and partake of the feast of the gods as beads of death glisten on my brow. For that reason I, Turms, am hastening my writing to conclude all that I would not forget.

BOOK TEN

The Feast of the Gods

I.

THE brightest and bluest of all the lakes I have ever seen was our people's sacred lake surrounded by its high mountains. The darkness of autumn had settled on its calm surface when I first saw it and the temples, the sacred circle of stones, the plowed furrow from which Tages had sprung to speak his wisdom, and the spring of the nymph Begoe. Perhaps Tages and Begoe had appeared elsewhere as well, but tradition had hallowed those places in the land of Volsinii.

Most sacred to me was the temple of the mutable, Voltumna's stone-pillared building in which the center chamber was empty. It was guarded by a beautiful bronze Chimera—a lion, a snake and an eagle in the same body—combining in itself the earth, the sky and the underworld as a symbol of the mutable. Invincibly it guarded the empty chamber of Voltumna. The Greeks claimed that their hero, riding on a winged horse, had vanquished and killed the Chimera, and in my youth in Corinth I had even been shown the fountain of Pegasus. But among my people Chimera still lives as the sacred symbol of the mutable, so the Greeks have not yet succeeded in killing him.

Crowds gathered from all the cities for the autumn festival although only the delegates with their escorts were permitted to enter the sacred area and to live in the sacred huts. The powerful and wealthy city of Volsinii rose from its mountain half a day's journey away. It was famous for its crafts and articles of trade, and benefited by the autumn festival.

On the first morning I was led with covered head to the conference house where the twelve delegates from the twelve cities were gathered. Among them were the two true Lucumones, five others who but used the title of Lucumo, one who had been chosen king by his people, and four who were but delegates chosen by their city councils. Clusium's delegate was one of these latter. Some of the twelve were old, but others, such as Lars Arnth Velthuru of Tarquinia who came as his father's regent, were young. But all wore the sacred mantles of their cities and looked with equal curiosity at me.

I bared my head and knew that this was the first and simplest test. As my glance went from man to man each tried to give me a sign, some with a gesture, some by blinking, some by smiling, some by growing serious. They had turned their mantles inside out so that I could not guess their identity by their emblems, yet I knew and immediately recognized both true Lucumones. I cannot explain how I knew, but absolute certainty came over me and I smiled at the childishness of the game.

I bowed my head first before the old man of Volsinii and then greeted the dark-faced Lucumo of eternally cold Volterra, a sturdy man not yet fifty. Perhaps I recognized them by their eyes, perhaps by the smiling wrinkles at the corners of the mouth. I greeted the others merely with a nod.

Both Lucumones looked at each other and stepped forward. The old man said, "I recognize you, Lars Turms."

Immediately the other delegates began to argue among themselves as though I were not there, with several of them declaring that this was not real evidence, since the appearance of the two Lucumones might have been described to me or the delegate from Clusium might have secretly signaled their identity to me.

But the old Lucumo placed his hand on my shoulder and inexpressible goodness, gentleness and mercy radiated from him as he said with a smile, "Go freely where and when you wish during these days, in holy or unholy places. Follow the sacrifices if you wish. Watch the games. No door will be closed to you. No door will you be compelled to open."

The Volterran Lucumo touched my arm. A feeling of strength and security flowed from his hand. "Prepare yourself if you wish, Lars Turms," he said. "No one compels you to do so. Why should a true Lucumo prepare himself? But by preparing yourself you will become responsive to receive and experience that which you have not previously experienced."

"How must I prepare myself, my father? How must I prepare myself, my brothers?" I asked.

The old man laughed and said, "Exactly as you wish, Turms. Some seek the solitude of the mountains, others seek themselves in noisy crowds. There are many paths, but they all lead to the same goal. You

353

may remain awake and fast during these days. That often enables a man to see that which he otherwise would not see. Or you may drink wine until you are in a daze and your knees fail, and drink still more when you have awakened and vomited the old. You may make love to woman and gratify your senses to the point of exhaustion. That also produces the right dreams and visions. At my age I regret that I did not try that path as well. Now it is too late. I am almost seventy, my son, and I have no desire to redeem time from the gods to endure this ailing body of mine yet another ten years."

The man of Volterra said, "Senses caress a person to glorious exhaustion. They help us to endure this life, even to praise it. But remember also, Turms, that hunger, thirst and abstinence likewise become pleasures if they are continued to the point of visions, though I don't claim that they are nobler pleasures than intoxication or satiety. Each follows his own path. I cannot advise you which to take; I can only tell you of my own path."

The old man pointed to him with a hazel switch and said, "He was born a shepherd and saw his visions in the solitude of the mountains. My body was born into an old family. And yet, as a Lucumo, he may be older than I."

More advice than that they did not give me, but I saw and felt that in their hearts they had recognized me. As Lucumones and men who had acknowledged themselves they needed no other test than that I, Turms, was I. But because of tradition they had to test me to enable me to find and acknowledge myself. That is the most agonizing test for a Lucumo.

On that day I watched them drive a new copper nail into the time-worn gray wooden pillar in the temple of Fate. It was studded with nails, head beside head, the oldest clumsily made and green with age, but there was still room for many more. The gods were still measuring time for the Etruscan peoples and cities.

For three days the delegates conferred on matters of foreign policy and the Veian war against Rome, until Caere and Tarquinia promised to support Veii with arms and troops. They also discussed the Greeks, and Lars Arnth maintained that war against Greece was inevitable. But he received no support. Neither Lucumo participated in the discussions since a Lucumo does not recognize war save in defense of his own city. Even then he loses his power.

But as the others argued the old man of Volsinii whispered in my ear, "Let them war against Rome. They cannot conquer it anyway. You probably know that Rome is your father's city and that the most secret omens bind it to your city. If Rome were destroyed, Clusium also would be destroyed."

I shook my head. "There are many things that I do not know and the consecrated in Clusium said nothing about that."

He laid his hand on my shoulder. "How strong and fair you are, Turms! I rejoice that I could see you with living eyes. But I warn you, do not believe the consecrated, for they know only what they have learned by rote. Perhaps I should not yet reveal such secret matters as this to you, but I may forget to do so later. Your father conquered Rome and lived there for several years. He would have restored it to Lars Tarkhon or his son had not the Romans convinced him that they preferred to rule themselves. The Romans even tried to murder him. Then in the holy cave of Egeria he met the oldest vestal and she read and interpreted the omens for him. Your father believed her and voluntarily relinquished Rome. But because of the omens he bound its fate to that of Clusium. If danger threatens Clusium, Rome must come to her defense. So it is written in the sacred books and confirmed by a feast of the gods."

"This you must know," he continued. "Clusium can never embark upon a war against Rome, and Clusium must speak in its defense if its neighbors wish to destroy it. And should complete destruction threaten it at the hands of the Etruscans, Clusium must, for the sake of its own future, fight for Rome rather than against it. So binding and holy an agreement is it that the very gods themselves descended to earth to confirm it. And yet the only outward indication of it is the fact that no public sale can be made in Rome without the declaration, 'This is Porsenna's land,' or 'This is Porsenna's house,' or 'These are Porsenna's goods.'"

I remembered having marked the peculiar way in which Roman auctioneers had made their sales legal. I realized also why my feet had been irresistibly drawn to the holy cave; why I had recognized it and sprinkled its water on my face. I had but followed in my father's footsteps. And the oldest of the vestals also had immediately recognized me as my father's son.

For seven days the delegates discussed internal matters and resolved border disputes. Then the sacrifices and traditional games began. The sacrifices took place in the temples but the sacred combats were held within a circle of stones. The Lucumones and the delegates sat on twelve rocks covered with cushions and all who were admitted to the sacred area stood behind them while the ordinary people watched from the mountain slopes and the roofs of houses. No noise or shouts of approval were permitted and the combats were waged in deep silence.

On the day of the god Turms I had to choose a ewe to be sacrificed in my name on the altar. The ewe did not resist when the priest's stone knife slit its throat, and after the blood had flowed into the sacrificial cups the priest cut open its belly and dug out the liver. The color was right and the liver flawless but twice as large as usual. The haruspex did not interpret the omens further, but he and his comrades looked at me thereafter with new eyes, bowed their heads before me and greeted me as the gods are greeted.

On the following day the old Lucumo of Volsinii summoned me to his house on some pretext. As I entered between the eight pillars I saw a man sitting tensely on a hard seat, staring straight ahead with glassy eyes.

Hearing my steps he asked anxiously, "Is it you, giver of gifts? Put your hand on my eyes, healer."

I declared that I was not a healer but merely a chance visitor. But he did not believe me and so insistent was he that finally, in sheer pity, I placed my hand over his eyes. Immediately something seemed to burst within me and I felt myself growing weaker moment by moment until my head swam. Finally I withdrew my hand. His eyes still closed, he sighed deeply and thanked me.

In the Lucumo's room lay a pale young girl, almost a child, extending her hands toward a brazier to warm them. She looked at me disconsolately and suspiciously. When I asked for the Lucumo she said that he would soon return and bade me sit on the edge of her couch meanwhile.

"Are you ill?" I asked.

She pushed aside the cover and showed me her legs. The muscles were so withered that they were like sticks although she was otherwise a beautiful girl. She told me that a bull had gored and trampled her when she was seven and that though the wounds and bruises had healed she had been unable to walk since then.

A moment later she whispered timidly, "You are good and fair, giver of gifts. Rub my legs. They began to ache badly when you entered the room."

I was not a skilled massager although in my youth I had of course learned the proper ways of rubbing my muscles after exercise. Also after a battle one comrade helped another by rubbing his stiff muscles. But no matter how carefully I rubbed the girl's legs she moaned in pain. When I asked whether I should cease she said, "No, no, it doesn't hurt."

Finally the old Lucumo entered and demanded, "What are you doing, Turms? Why are you torturing the poor girl?"

356

"She herself asked for it," I answered defensively.

"Will you then help every suppliant?" he snapped. "Will you give to whomsoever asks? There are good and evil suppliants, guilty and innocent sufferers. Don't you realize that you must distinguish between them?"

I thought for a moment. "It is not this poor girl's fault that she suffers. But if I see someone who suffers I probably will not distinguish between the good and the evil, the guilty and the guiltless, but help each if I can. After all, the sun shines with equal warmth on the evil and the good. I do not imagine that I have greater understanding than the sun."

He nodded impatiently as though he would have protested. Then he sat down, struck a bronze shield and called for wine. "You are very pale," he said. "Do you feel weak?"

My head swam and my limbs trembled with weakness but I tried to assure him that all was well. It was a great honor to be summoned before him in his own house and I did not wish to destroy the pleasure by complaining. We drank the wine and I felt better. But all the while he stared at the girl lying on the couch and she returned his gaze expectantly.

Soon the dark-faced Lucumo of Volterra entered and greeted us. The old man poured him some wine and as he raised the cup to his lips the Volsinian pointed suddenly to the girl.

"Arise, child, and walk."

To my inexpressible amazement the girl's face brightened, she began to move her legs and carefully placed them on the floor. Slowly, holding onto the couch, she rose to her feet. I tried to hasten to her lest she fall, but the old man restrained me without a word. The three of us stared at the girl. She swayed badly but took one step and then another, holding onto the painted wall.

Weeping and laughing she cried, "I can walk, I can walk!" Extending her arms toward me she staggered across the floor, fell before me and kissed my knees. "Lucumo," she whispered devoutly. "Lucumo."

I was as surprised by her sudden recovery as the girl herself. Trying her withered muscles, I shook my head and declared, "This is a miracle!"

The old Lucumo laughed benevolently. "You performed it. The strength came from you, Lucumo."

I raised my hands in protest. "No, no. Do not mock me."

The old man nodded to the Volterran Lucumo, who went to the door. "Come and show us your eyes, you who believe."

The man who sat in the entrance hall came in, his hands over his eyes. Time and again he lowered his hands, looked around and again covered his eyes. "I can see," he said finally. Humbly he bowed his head before me and raised his arm in a divine greeting. "It is you who have done this, Lucumo!" he exclaimed. "I can see. I can see you and the radiance around your head."

The old Lucumo explained, "This man has been blind for four years. He was defending his vessel against pirates when it seemed as though a gigantic bearded creature struck him a fearful blow on the head. Since then he has seen nothing."

The man nodded eagerly. "Yes, the vessel was saved, but since then I have seen nothing until you touched my eyes, Lucumo."

I looked around in bewilderment, thinking surely I was intoxicated from the wine. "You mock me," I said accusingly. "I have done nothing."

Both Lucumones spoke at once. "The power and the strength are in you and of you if you but will it. Admit to yourself that you were born a Lucumo. We do not doubt it."

Still I could not realize it. I looked at the young girl's admiring face, at the eyes which but shortly before had been blind. "No," I said again, "I do not ask for such power. I do not want such strength. I am only a human, and I am afraid."

The old Lucumo spoke to the two who had been healed. "Go and offer thanks to the gods. Whatsoever you do unto others will happen unto you." Absently he extended his hand in a blessing as they left, the girl tottering on her own feet and the seeing one supporting her steps.

When they were gone the Lucumo turned to me. "You were born into a human body," he explained, "and that is why you are a human. But you are also a Lucumo if you will but admit it to yourself. The moment has arrived. Fear no more and do not flee from yourself."

The younger Lucumo said, "Wounds are healed and blood ceases to flow when you touch the wound, you returned who are yet to return. Acknowledge yourself to yourself."

The old man declared, "A Lucumo can even arouse the dead for a moment or a day if he believes in himself and feels his power. But such an act shortens his own life and oppresses the deceased by compelling the spirit to return to a body smelling of death. Do it only when you must. You may summon spirits if you wish and give them form so that they may speak and reply to you. But that torments the spirits. Do it also only when you must."

Realizing that I swayed between certainty and doubt, the old Lucumo said, "Do you not know what I mean?" He took a piece of wood, held it before my eyes and urged, "Watch." Then he tossed the wood onto the floor and said, "Behold, it is a frog!"

Before my eyes the piece of wood changed into a frog which gave a few frightened leaps and then paused to blink at me with round protruding eyes.

"Take it in your hand and feel it," the old Lucumo urged with a laugh when he noticed how suspiciously I looked at the living thing he had created. Ashamed of my doubt, I nevertheless took the frog in my hand and felt its coldness and sliminess. It was a live frog that struggled in my hand.

"Release it," the old man said, and I allowed the frog to leap from my hand. As it touched the floor it again changed into a dry piece of wood before my very eyes.

The Volterran Lucumo picked it up in turn, showed it to me and said, "I summon not an underground creature but an earthly one. Behold how a calf becomes a bull!"

He tossed the piece of wood onto the floor and before my eyes it became a new-born calf which, still wet, rose on tottering legs. Then it began to swell. Tapering horns appeared on its head and its size increased until it finally filled the entire room and could not have squeezed through the narrow doorway. I smelled the bull and saw the bluish flash of its eyes. It was a terrifying bull.

The Lucumo snapped his fingers as though tired of the play. The bull disappeared and on the stone floor was again just a gray piece of wood.

"You also can do that if you wish," said the old Lucumo. "Be brave. Take it in your hand. Say what you wish to have born and it will be born."

As in a dream I stooped to pick up the piece of wood and turned it in my fingers. "I summon neither the earthly nor the underworld but the heavenly, and the dove is my bird," I said slowly, looking intently at the piece of wood. At that very moment I felt the feathers, the downy warmth and rapid heartbeat of a bird in my hand. A snow-white dove took wing, circled the room and returned to my hand as lightly as air, flapping its wings so that I felt the caressing touch of its claws.

The Volterran Lucumo extended a hand to stroke the dove's feathers. "What a beautiful bird you have created. It is the goddess's bird. Snow-white."

The old man asked, "Now do you believe, Turms?" The bird disappeared and in my hand was again a piece of gray wood.

Undoubtedly I must have looked astonished, for they both laughed and the old man said, "Now do you understand why it is better for a Lucumo to find and acknowledge himself only at the age of forty? If you were a boy and discovered your ability you would be tempted to play and create innumerable forms, would alarm the people around you and would perhaps begin to compete with the mutable herself in creating shapes that have not previously existed. That is tempting the gods. If you are alone and depressed, you may create a pet animal to lie at the foot of your bed or warm you with its body. But do it only when you are alone and don't show it to others. It will return when you summon it."

Power radiated from me. "What of a human?" I demanded. "Can I create a human for a companion?"

They looked at each and then at me, shook their heads and said, "No, Turms, you cannot create a human. You can make only a vanishing shape and for a moment conjure into it a spirit that will reply to your questions. But there are both evil and good spirits and the evil may arrive to deceive you. You are not omniscient, Turms. Remember always that you were born into a human body which restricts you and determines the bounds of your knowledge. Learn to know the walls of your prison, for only death will tear them down. Then you will be free until you must be born again to another time, another place. But in between your rest will be blissful."

They did not tire me further that day but allowed me to ponder in peace on what I had learned. The following morning, however, they again summoned me before them, showed me a garment stiff with blood and suggested, "Feel this garment, close your eyes and tell us what you see."

I closed my eyes as I gripped the garment and a horrible oppression came over me. Mistily as in a dream I saw everything happen, and related: "This is an old man's garment. He is returning home from somewhere and although he is dusty and sweaty, he is cheerful and is walking briskly. A frenzied shepherd leaps from the bushes and hits him with a rock. The old man falls to his knees, raises his arms and pleads for mercy, but the shepherd strikes again. He robs the body while glancing around apprehensively. Then there is only mist."

Sweat flowed from my body as I opened my eyes and dropped the fearful garment.

"Would you recognize the shepherd?" they asked.

I thought of what I had seen. "It was a hot day," I said hesitantly. "He wore only a loincloth and his skin was burned a blackish brown. He had a morose face and a large scar on his calf."

They nodded and said, "Do not trouble your mind any more. The judges could not find sufficient evidence against the shepherd. We indicated the place where he had hidden the loot and he was pushed into a spring with a willow basket over his head for not having mercy on a helpless man. But we are glad that you confirmed his guilt. We do not willingly do this, for the possibility of error is too great. But sometimes we must. An undetected murder encourages new murders."

To help me forget my oppression they placed in each of my hands an identical black cup decorated with identical reliefs. Without even closing my eyes, I immediately raised the cup in my left hand and said, "This is a holy cup. The other is unholy."

They declared, "Turms, you are a Lucumo. Are you not ready to admit and believe it?"

But I was still perplexed. The old Lucumo explained, "You can read the past from objects. The less you think at a time like that the clearer will be your vision. Again because of this it is better that a Lucumo has reached the age of forty before recognizing himself, otherwise he would constantly be tempted to hold objects and develop this talent which actually is of little significance. Many ordinary people possess that same ability."

"You may leave your body if you wish and see that which happens elsewhere," they said, "but don't do it. It is dangerous and your effect on events would only be seeming. Everything happens as it must happen. After all, we have our signs and our omens. Lightning, birds and sheep's livers indicate quite enough of what we should know."

They raised their arms to greet me like a god and said, "So it is, Turms; you are a Lucumo. Much is possible to you but not all of it is beneficial. Learn to choose, learn to discriminate, learn to restrict. Do not trouble yourself unnecessarily or torment the gods. For your people and your city it is enough that you exist. It is enough that an immortal is born as a human in their midst."

The words made me tremble. Once again I raised my hands in protest and cried, "No, no! Can I, Turms, be an immortal?"

With deep earnestness they assured me, "It is so, Lucumo Turms. You are immortal if you but dare admit it. Tear the veil finally from before your eyes and admit your true identity.

"In every man there is the seed of immortality," they went on. "But most men are content with the earth and the seed never germinates. Such a one is pitiable, but let him have the lot with which he is content."

They said further, "Our knowledge is limited because we were born into a human body. We believe that the seed of immortality distinguishes a human from an animal, but we are not certain. Everything living is in the guise of her, the mutable. Nor do we even distinguish the living from the lifeless. In a moment of splendor you may feel how a hard stone radiates beneath your hand. No, our knowledge is imperfect, although we were born Lucumones."

Then they uttered a warning: "When you have acknowledged yourself to be a Lucumo you will no longer live for yourself but for the good of your people and city. You are a giver of gifts. But the grainfields will not billow and the earth will not bear fruit because of you and your power. Everything merely happens through you. Don't permit yourself to be annoyed. Do nothing merely to please people but only to benefit them. Don't fetter yourself to trivialities. Laws and customs, judges, governors, priests and diviners exist to take care of them. Make your prison as pleasant as you can without hurting your people and aggravating others. Although you are the high priest, the highest legislator, the supreme judge, the less you are appealed to the better. Nations and cities must learn to live without Lucumones. Evil times are coming. You will return, but your people will never return once their allotted time has ended."

They were compassionate in their teaching because they knew from their own experience what a crushing burden they were laying upon me. The old Lucumo of Volsinii placed a protective arm around my neck.

"Doubt will be your greatest torment," he said. "In our moments of weakness we are all tormented. Everything occurs in cycles. There are days when your power is at its peak and you radiate joy and confidence. Those are blessed days. But the cycle turns and your power ebbs and everything around you grows dark. At such times remain silent, be submissive and meek. When your weakness is the greatest, temptation is the strongest."

The Volterran Lucumo said, "Your power may increase and decrease with the phases of the moon. Or it may vary with the seasons. Or the weather. We all differ in that respect. Perhaps the weather rules us rather than we it, even though we can summon the wind and raise a storm. When my weakness began to oppress me I climbed to a precipice. Temptation whispered in my ear, 'If you are a true Lucumo, jump off the precipice into the valley. The air will bear you lightly to the ground and you will not be injured. If you are not a true Lucumo, it matters little if you crush your head.' That is what temptation will whisper."

I looked at his brooding eyes and became curious. "Did you jump off the precipice?" I asked. "Tell me."

The old Lucumo began to titter merrily. "Glance at the scars on his knees. Not many of his bones remained whole when the people of Volterra removed him from the foot of the precipice. He had fallen

362

onto a bush growing out of a crevice and that slowed his fall. Then he was hurled into a pine tree and fell from branch to branch, his bones snapping together with the branches. If he were not a Lucumo, he would hardly be able to walk. Even so his back is stiff although he cannot be called a cripple. A Lucumo is never so seriously injured as to remain maimed, but he is occasionally reminded of mortality lest he forget that he was born into a human body."

That also was true. I had experienced the dangers of war and the terrors of the sea, but at no time had I been seriously wounded or injured. It was as though unseen wings had protected me.

The Volterran Lucumo lowered his glance and confessed in shame, "I felt not the slightest pain as I fell. Only when the people lifted me from the ground and I regained consciousness did the pain begin. Truly I have tasted bitterly of human mortality, but it served me right and was a good lesson."

His tale brought me so near the point of collapse that I felt my weakness as though the bones in my body had melted.

"Release me from this burden," I begged. "I am only Turms. Must I acknowledge myself as a Lucumo and believe in myself if I would not?"

They said, "You are Turms, an immortal and a true Lucumo. You must admit it to yourself for you can no longer deny yourself." But they added consolingly, "We understand you, for we ourselves have experienced man's most dreadful suffering—doubt and the pangs of one's own imperfection. But on the night of the twelfth day you may share with us the feast of the gods just as we shared it upon finding and acknowledging ourselves. There are still three of us to share it, but on the day of your earthly death, Turms, you must meet the gods alone."

2.

On the twelfth day occurred the traditional sacred combat that determined the leader among the cities. It was a bright autumn day and the sun shone with warm rays upon the holy lake and the blue mountains. The Lucumones and delegates from the twelve cities sat on the twelve sacred stones of the ring. I myself stood among the others in the crowd behind the delegate from Clusium, for I had not yet been publicly acknowledged as a Lucumo nor had the holy mantle been placed on my shoulders. For that reason everyone pretended not to pay any attention to me although space had been left around me and no one touched or brushed past me.

First to enter was the eldest of the augurs, a worn staff in his hand. He was followed by the twelve youths representing the different cities.

363

They were naked save for the purple band around their heads, and each carried his city's round shield and sacred sword. Their order had been determined by lot, for no Etruscan city was better than the next, but once within the circle of stones each placed himself before his city's delegate.

The augur fetched a maiden from a curtained litter and led her to a sacred bed of stones in the center of the ring. She, too, was naked, but tightly wound around her eyes was a sacred woolen band. She was a well-formed untouched young girl, and as the augur opened the knot at her neck and revealed her face, she looked around with a flushed, startled face and instinctively attempted to shield her nakedness with her hands. The youths straightened themselves as they looked at her and their eyes began to glow with eagerness for combat. But with a shock that touched the roots of my heart I recognized the girl as Misme.

True, I knew that the Etruscans' most beautiful and noble maiden was chosen each year as an offering and that selection was considered to be the greatest honor that could befall a girl. Where they had found Misme, and why she in particular had been chosen, I could not understand. But the alarmed expression on her face made me suspect that she had not voluntarily submitted to the sacrifice.

Deep silence prevailed, as custom decreed, and I watched the rapid rise and fall of the youths' chests. But a reluctant offering is worthless. Hence the augur reassured Misme until she lifted her head proudly, acknowledged her own youth and the beauty of her body, suffered the glances of the youths and permitted the augur to bind her hands with a woolen band.

I could endure no more. Despair came over me and I waved my arms violently. Both Lucumones looked at me searchingly and I saw that the other delegates were watching me as curiously as they were Misme. Abruptly I realized that this was also my test. They believed Misme to be my daughter and wished to see whether I was ready to sacrifice her in accordance with the sacred Etruscan customs to prove that I was a true Lucumo.

I was not certain what would happen but I knew that the bed of stones in the center of the ring was a sacrificial altar before which the youths had to fight one another with sword and shield. Only he who, wounded, stepped outside the ring, saved his life, although the augur might spare a badly wounded combatant from the mortal thrust if the youth collapsed without relinquishing his sword.

I remained silent and suddenly I met Misme's glance. She smiled at me and there was something so irresistibly impudent and enchanting

364

in her glance that I recognized a flash of Arsinoe in her. She was not so beautiful as Arsinoe and her body was still girlish and undeveloped. But her breasts were like little wild pears, her legs slender, her hips well rounded, and she was no longer at all shy. On the contrary, I could see by the provocative glint of her eye that she was well aware of the feelings which the sight of her aroused in those twelve youths.

No, I need not fear for Misme. She was her mother's daughter and knew into what game she had entered. I calmed myself with the knowledge that no matter how the Etruscans had got hold of her, she had voluntarily consented to be the sacrifice. Seeing how beautiful she had grown, I knew that I was proud of her. Then as I looked around, I suddenly met the glance of Lars Arnth as he sat on the holy rock of Tarquinia. He had been staring at Misme with as great fascination as the youths. Now he looked at me and narrowed his eyes questioningly. Instinctively I nodded my consent.

Lars Arnth rose imperiously, doffed his robe and tossed it onto the shoulders of the Tarquinian youth who stood in the circle with sword and shield. Then he drew off his shirt, unfastened his armbands and the chain around his neck, dropped them onto the ground and finally pulled the gold ring off his thumb. As though the matter were self-evident, he took his city's sacred shield and sword from the youth, stepped into his place and indicated that he should sit on the holy rock. So great was the honor that the youth's disappointment was assuaged.

The augur looked around as though inquiring whether anyone opposed the change in combatants. Then he touched Lars Arnth with his staff as an indication of acceptance. Lars Arnth was slenderer than the other youths and his skin gleamed white as a woman's as he stood there naked and, with expectant, parted lips, gazed at Misme while she for her part looked straight into his eyes. It was obvious that the girl's vanity was flattered by the readiness of the regent of the most powerful of Etruscan cities to risk his life to win her.

But I had to smile with inexpressible relief on realizing that it was all a jest of the gods intended to indicate to me how blind even the most clear-sighted man can be and how useless it is to consider anything on earth important. I read Lars Arnth's thoughts as from an open scroll. Certainly the sight of Misme had enchanted him, but at the same moment he had perceived how much he would win if he were to emerge the victor in the holy combat. He had suffered a defeat in the foreign policy negotiations and his authority in Tarquinia had suffered as a result of the unsuccessful military expedition to Himera. Old Aruns still lived and his authority was unshakeable, but it was not at all certain that

Arnth would succeed him as ruler of Tarquinia even though he had been raised to the regency. Lars Arnth's decisive policy was farsighted and dictated by the times but it did not please the old people or those who were pro-Greek.

But should he emerge the victor in the holy combat, he would personally secure a position of honor for Tarquinia among the Etruscan cities. True, in ancient times the rulers themselves had stepped into the sacred circle to fight among themselves for supremacy, but it was unprecedented for a young regent in these times to risk his life for his city. Should he win, Tarquinia's supremacy would be no mere formality and honor but the victory would be considered a divine sign. And at the same time he would win for himself the daughter of a living Lucumo who was also the great Lars Porsenna's granddaughter.

The gods smiled and I smiled with them, for everything was a lie. Misme was merely believed to be my daughter. And yet, in comprehending that, I realized at the same time that there is little difference between truth and falsehood in the mortal world. Everything depends on what a person believes to be true. The gods are above truth and falsehood, right and wrong. In my heart I decided to acknowledge Misme as my daughter and to forbid her ever to tell anyone that I was not her real father. It was enough that we both knew; it did not concern others. And with all my heart I wished Lars Arnth victory, for a nobler husband Misme could not find, although to be truthful I did not know whether Arsinoe's daughter could bring happiness to any man or to the Etruscans as a whole. But why should I care, if in my heart I acknowledged Misme as my daughter? In that case only the best among the Etruscans was good enough for her. Mockingly I thought how badly Arsinoe had been mistaken about Misme.

The augur laid the traditional black leather collar on Misme's bare shoulders and forced her to sit on the edge of the bed of stones, her bound wrists before her. Then he gave a sign with his staff and the combatants rushed together so violently that the first clash blurred before our eyes into flashing confusion. Sooner than the eye could comprehend, two youths lay bleeding on the ground.

The other contestants would have been wise, I think, if they had all united to force Lars Arnth outside the circle since they dared not kill him because of his noble birth. They were fighting only formally for honor and a beautiful sacrifice. He fought for his entire future, for the kingship of Tarquinia, even for the salvation of the Etruscan peoples, since he believed that only his own policy could free the Etruscan cities from fatal Greek pressure. But how could his rivals have known that?

No, in the traditional manner they rushed six against six in the first skirmish, paused for the period of a breath to appraise the situation; then five plunged against five, swords flashed and shield crashed against shield. We heard groans of pain and only four youths drew back, gasping for breath. One had toppled outside the ring, two crawled out leaving bloodstains behind, one's sword had been struck from his hand, severing his fingers, one lay on his back with the air bubbling from his gashed throat, and one was shielded by the augur's staff as he still tried to wield his sword although on his knees.

Without a glance at those who had dropped out, the four measured one another. Lars Arnth was one of the four and I crossed my hands tightly, hoping that he would last and at least save his life. For a moment they stood there with their backs to the sacred circle, then the most impatient lost his nerve and rushed with upraised shield at his nearest opponent. This youth struck it in the air with his own shield and plunged his sword through the other's body. Instantly the third rival recognized his opportunity and leaped to thrust his sword into the defender's back, not to kill but merely to render him incapable of combat.

Everything had occurred with incredible speed and ten of the bravest and fairest Etruscan youths were already out of the game. I thought sadly of their hopes and how they had toughened their bodies and improved their skills with ceaseless practice. In a few fleeting moments all was over and hope gone. Now only Lars Arnth and the Veian youth remained, and the real battle could begin. Chance and good fortune no longer determined the outcome but only swordsmanship, endurance and nerves.

Haste availed nothing. That they both must have realized as they warily crept along the edge of the ring, for each took a moment to glance at Misme who stared at them with shining eyes. Later I heard that the Veian youth had been among those who had fetched Misme and that he had held her in his arms on horseback. Then and there he had decided to die rather than surrender. But despite his youth Lars Arnth had attended the bitter school of political life and well knew the power of patience and perseverance to overcome a rival's endurance. Cold-bloodedly he waited, even dropping his shield and stretching his limbs.

The youth from Veii could bear no more but plunged ahead, the shields clanging against each other and the swords striking bright sparks as they clashed. But the youths were of the same size and equally skilled, and neither succeeded in thrusting the other backward. After exchanging

367

some ten rapid strokes they leaped apart to regain their breath. Blood streamed down Lars Arnth's thigh, but he shook his head sharply as the augur prepared to raise his staff. The Veian youth forgot and looked at him and at that moment Lars Arnth charged at him with bowed head and thrust his sword under his foe's shield. The youth dropped to one knee but kept his shield up and lashed out so violently with his sword that Lars Arnth had to retreat. The Veian had received a bad wound in his groin and could not rise, but with knee to the ground he slashed aside the augur's staff and glared at Lars Arnth.

Lars Arnth was compelled to continue, willingly or not. He seemed to sense that the Veian had more endurance than he, and that thus he had to bring the combat to a quick conclusion. Holding his shield as low as possible, he attacked. But the Veian warded off the blow and with the speed of light dropped his sword, scooped up a handful of sand and threw it at Lars Arnth's eyes. Then he snatched the sword again and plunged it at Lars Arnth's unprotected chest with such force that he toppled off his knee and fell on his face to the ground as, more by instinct than skill, Lars Arnth thrust the blade aside blindly so that he suffered only a harmless cut. He could have struck the Veian youth on the neck with the edge of his shield or cut off the fingers grasping the sword. But Lars Arnth was content to step on his hand and press the youth's face to the ground with his shield without hurting him. It was nobly done.

The Veian youth was fearless and tried once more to wrench himself free. Only then did he accept his defeat and a sob of disappointment rose from his throat. He released his sword and Lars Arnth, stooping to snatch it from the ground, threw it outside the ring. Magnanimously he extended his hand to his opponent and helped him to rise although his own eyes were still blinded by the sand and his own blood.

Then Lars Arnth did something the like of which had surely never happened before. Still panting from his exertion he glanced around searchingly, then stepped to the augur and pulled off the loose augur's cloak so that the old man stood clad only in a shirt, his thin legs bare. With the cloak over his arm Lars Arnth stepped to Misme, cut the holy woolen band that bound her wrists, bent reverently to touch her mouth with his and, dropping onto the stone bed, took Misme in his arms and covered them both with the augur's cloak.

This was so amazing that not even the most sacred tradition could stifle the laughter. At sight of the augur's helpless air and thin legs we laughed still more, and when Misme extended a bare foot from the cloak and wiggled her toes at us even the Lucumones laughed so that tears rolled from their eyes.

With such relief did we laugh at Lars Arnth's unexpected thoughtfulness, nor was anyone opposed to it. On the contrary, everyone admitted later that such a noble youth as Lars Arnth and the granddaughter of Lars Porsenna could not have performed the traditional sacrifice before the stares of the people. Probably Misme and Arnth also laughed as they embraced each other under the augur's cloak and left the sacrifice to a more propitious time.

When the laughter finally began to die down, Lars Arnth tossed off the cloak. They rose, holding each other's hand and looking into each other's eyes as though they had forgotten the rest of the world. They were a beautiful pair. The angry augur snatched back his cloak, flung it over his shoulder, rapped them both on the head with his staff harder than was necessary, and pronounced them man and wife and Tarquinia the supreme Etruscan city. Now Lars Arnth took the black collar from Misme's neck and reversed it so that the white side was on top to indicate, in accordance with the ancient tradition, that life had conquered death. Hand in hand they stepped outside the circle, a wedding cloak was thrown over Misme's nakedness and a myrtle wreath placed on her head. Lars Arnth took his own mantle, pulled on his shirt, and I hastened to embrace Misme as my daughter.

"How could you frighten me so?" I scolded her.

But Misme tossed her head capriciously and laughed aloud. "Now do you believe that I am able to take care of myself, Turms?"

Glancing at Lars Arnth, I whispered in her ear that from now on she must address me as her father, show the proper respect and remember that she was the granddaughter of the great Etruscan hero Lars Porsenna. She in turn told me that the field brothers had attempted to protect both her and my farm but that the enraged Romans had burned the buildings, stolen the cattle and trampled the fields when they had learned of my escape from the Mamertine prison. She and the old slaves had hidden themselves and that same night she had dug up the gold bull's-head, chipped off the horns and given one to the old slave couple and the other to the shepherd youth who had become the keeper of my farm so that he might, in Misme's name, obtain staffs of emancipation for the couple.

Then hardly had she returned the bull's-head to its place of concealment than Veian patrols, aroused by the fire, had ridden across the border and abducted her. But they had treated her respectfully although the youth who had just fought had crushed her to him as they rode.

"It was not quite new to me and I wasn't afraid," Misme assured me.

"After all, our keeper always tried to touch and kiss me so that I learned to depend on myself and no longer wondered whether I was ugly. I could never have consented to him, but now with the gold horn he can obtain a suitable wife for himself and purchase land. He also promised to care for the old slaves whom I freed."

She looked at me accusingly. "But why have you never told me how beautiful and refined life among the Etruscans is? I would have learned their difficult language long before this. I have known only goodness both in Veii and here, although I first feared that I was a prisoner and would be sold as a slave. But their beautiful women taught me how to bathe and care for my skin and curl my hair, called me beautiful and made me understand what an incomparable honor it was to be chosen as the maiden for the sacred combat. I thought it was for my own sake and because they considered me beautiful, but they probably chose me because of you, my father. I have heard many things about you."

Lars Arnth hastened to swear by the names of the smiling gods that she was the fairest girl he had ever met and that he had risked his life because he had realized at first glance that life would be nothing without her. Probably he believed what he said, but I knew that his ecstatic dazzlement, as the goddess blinded him with her golden mist, was but one of his reasons for entering the combat.

Nevertheless I rejoiced for Misme and also for Lars Arnth, since I knew him and he was deserving of all human happiness, if Arsinoe's daughter could bring a man more happiness than trouble. However, Misme swore that she was wiser than her mother and that she would remain faithful to her husband because in all the land there could not be a fairer man or one more to her liking. Still I could not trust her completely since she felt it necessary to swear such an oath. It seemed to indicate that she herself had begun to suspect that she was her mother's daughter. Looking into her eyes I realized that Lars Arnth's life with Misme would not be monotonous.

3.

Everything was calm. As the sunset began to redden the dark surface of the lake and the hazy mountain peaks behind it, the priests erected the holy tent of the gods. Before it women were turning grindstones in order to bake the gods' cakes of new flour. Nets had been thrown into the water and the gods' red-eyed fish had been caught. A bull calf, a lamb and a pig had been sacrificed and consecrated to the gods. Cooking fires were burning in the open while the priests conferred among themselves and repeated the sacred verses so that the cakes would be baked and the foods prepared in the traditional manner. A feast of the gods had not been celebrated in many years.

As the sun set I felt the coolness of the lake, the lingering warmth of the earth, the fragrance of baking cakes and herbs. Finally both the Lucumones arrived, their holy mantles tossed over their shoulders. Behind them were borne the holy dishes of the gods.

"Have you cleansed yourself?" they asked.

"I have," I assured them. "My eyes are clean. My mouth is clean. My ears are clean. My nostrils are clean. All the openings in my body are clean. My head has been washed. My feet and hands have been washed. My whole body has been scrubbed clean. For the first time I wear a shirt woven of the finest wool."

They said with a smile, "Tonight you are host at the feast, Turms. You are the giver of gifts. You may invite two gods to eat with us. Whom do you choose?"

I did not hesitate. "I owe the goddess an invitation," I said. "I invite her, the mural-crowned. Turan is her holy name."

The old Lucumo feigned amazement and said slyly, "You yourself have told us how the goddess Artemis has favored you and as Hecate taken care of your earthly well-being. You also owe much to the foamborn who is worshiped in Eryx both as Aphrodite and Ishtar, as you have told us."

"They are the same goddess," I said, "although she appears in different guises in different places to different peoples. Her real name is Turan and the moon her emblem. That I have understood. Her I choose. Her I invite."

They said, "What of your second guest? Whom do you choose?"

With a glow I said, "I choose him, the mutable himself. Voltumna. I did not understand him earlier. Now I want finally to know him. For his sake the sea horse was already sacred at the dawn of time. His likeness is Chimera."

The smile faded from their faces, they glanced at each other and cried warningly, "Do you realize what you dare?"

In the grip of a holy joy I cried, "I choose him. I invite him. Voltumna, be my guest!"

Then they drew open the sacred curtains of the tent. In the bright light of smokeless torches I saw the high couch of the gods with its numerous mattresses and on each of the double cushions the two holy white stone cones. A low couch had been prepared for each of us three and low tables stood beside them. The wine was in the mixing vessel and I saw the sheaves of grain, the fruit of the earth and the wreaths.

The Lucumones said, "Wreathe your heavenly guests."

I chose an ivy wreath and wreathed one of the white cones. "For you, Turan. You as a goddess, I as a human."

Unspeakable joy seized me. I took a roseberry wreath and wreathed the second cone. "For you, Voltumna. Any wreath is as you wish it. Take the roseberry wreath, you as a god, I as an immortal."

Thus did I finally acknowledge myself to be immortal. Why and how it happened and why I chose just the roseberry wreath I cannot say. But my doubts disappeared like a mist and the sky of my heart radiated the glory of immortality.

We reclined on the couches and heavy garlands of autumn flowers, berries and leaves were placed around our necks. The pipers began to blow wistful tunes on their double pipes, stringed instruments sounded and dancers clothed in holy garments danced the dances of the gods before the tent. Food was served to us from old black bowls and as we ate we used ancient flint knives, although we were also given two-pronged golden forks.

Gradually the sound of the pipes and strings grew wilder as the dancers performed the earth dance, the sea dance, the heavens' dance. They performed the dance of the virgin goddess and the love dance, the dogs' dance and bulls' dance and even the horses' dance. Pleasant fragrances arose in clouds around us from the high-legged censers, and the wine warmed my body and rose to my head. But the further the feast progressed, the greater my disappointment when I looked at the two motionless cones on the gods' high couch.

The old Lucumo from his couch to my right saw my glances and consoled me with a laugh. "Do not be impatient, Turms, for the night is long. Perhaps the gods are preparing for us just as we prepared to meet them. Perhaps there is hustle and bustle in the eternal halls of the gods as festive garments are carried to and fro and hair is anointed and braided. Who knows?"

"Do not mock me," I said angrily.

He extended his old hand and touched my shoulder. "This is the most exalted night of your life, Turms. But the people also must share in it. They can see the cones which you wreathed, they can watch us eating and drinking, they can see the holy dances and enjoy the music. Only then will we three be alone. Only then will the curtains be closed and the guests arrive."

Outside the tent, under a canopy of stars, thousands of silent people had gathered to look at the lighted tent. The breathing of the dense crowd could be sensed but not a sound could be heard for the people were careful of every rustle and were afraid even to move their feet.

The cooking fires were extinguished, the servants departed one after the other, the dancers disappeared, the music ceased and all became still. The white cones with their wreaths seemed to ascend to the dimness of the tent ceiling. Now the last servant set before me a covered dish, and I saw both Lucumones raise themselves and stare at me tensely. The servant removed the lid, I smelled the strong odor of herbs, and seeing the pieces of meat in the sauce, extended my fork and brought a piece to my mouth. It had no evil taste from what I could determine, yet I could not bite or swallow it but had to spit it from my mouth.

At that moment the curtains were lowered with a thud. Silently the servant hastened from the tent, leaving the open dish to steam before me on the low table. I wiped my mouth with the back of my hand, rinsed my palate with wine and spat it out.

Both Lucumones watched me expectantly. "Why don't you eat, Turms?" they asked.

I shook my head. "I cannot."

They nodded and confessed, "True. Neither can we, for it is the food of the gods."

With the golden fork I stirred the pieces of meat floating in the sauce. They did not look unpalatable, nor did the steam arising from the dish smell bad. "What is it?" I asked.

"It is hedgehog," they explained. "The hedgehog is the oldest animal. With the coming of winter it curls into a sleep and forgets time, and in the spring it awakens again. That is why it is the food of the gods."

With his fingertips the old Lucumo picked up a boiled and peeled egg which he held up for me to see. "The egg is the beginning of everything," he said. "The egg is the symbol of birth and return, the symbol of immortality."

He placed the egg in the hollow of the shallow sacrificial cup, and the younger Lucumo and I likewise peeled our eggs and placed them in our cups. Then the Volterran Lucumo rose, carefully took a sealed clay jar, opened the stopper, dug out the wax with a flint knife and poured the bitter herb wine into our sacrificial cups.

"The moment has arrived," he said. "The gods are coming. Let us drink the drink of immortality to enable our eyes to withstand their radiance."

I emptied my cup as did they and the drink burned my throat and my belly became numb. Following their example I then ate the egg that I had peeled.

The old Lucumo said in a low voice, "You have drunk the drink of immortality with us, Turms. You have eaten the egg of immortality with us. Now be silent. The gods are arriving."

As the three of us tremblingly watched, the two white stone cones began to grow before our eyes. The bright flames of the torches seemed to dim and the cones glowed more brightly than the flames. Then they disappeared and I saw her, the goddess, taking shape and resting lightly on the couch, lovelier than all earthly women. She smiled lest we fear her and her oval eyes radiated glory. But her tresses wriggled alive and on her head was the fearful mural crown.

Then he appeared, the mutable. At first he trifled with us. We felt him as a cold blast and the yellowish dull flames of the torches flickered violently. Then we felt him as water and we struggled as though drowning to breathe through the invisible water running through our nostrils and mouth to our lungs. As fire he felt our skin and limbs until we thought we would be charred alive. But not a mark remained and he cooled us until our skin grew as cold as though we had been anointed with mint ointment. His form floated in the air above us as a gigantic sea horse. Finally the goddess Turan tired of his play and extended her divine hand. Voltumna grew calm and descended as dazzling light to behave like a human in our company.

I did not have to serve them, for the hedgehog dwindled until the bowl was empty. But how they partook of the meal I cannot explain. The level of the wine in the mixing vessel likewise fell lower and lower until the final drop disappeared and the vessel was dry. They were not hungry since gods do not feel hunger and thirst like humans, but having arrived as our guests in recognizable guises they ate the holy meal and drank the holy wine as an indication of friendliness.

The earthly food appeared to please them and earthly wine to rise to their heads as happens at a feast, for the goddess smiled capriciously and looked temptingly at me with her oval eyes as she absently wound her arms around Voltumna's neck. He, the mutable, looked at me intently as though he were tempted to test my endurance.

"Alas, you Lucumones," he said suddenly, "perhaps you are immortal, but eternal you are not." His voice rang like metal and rumbled like a storm, yet it held incalculable envy.

The goddess Turan stroked his hair soothingly and forbade him to seek a quarrel. "Be not afraid of him," she said in a voice that rang like silver bells and cooed like a dove. "He, Voltumna, is a restless god. But understand him. We others appear in many guises and rest in our holy images, but he has no permanent form. Ceaseless changing, expanding

374

then contracting, warming then cooling, storm then calm, makes him restless."

Voltumna's outline began to waver and glitter, but Turan hastily placed her hands on his shoulders, kissed the corners of his mouth and eyes and said, "This guise is the most beautiful and complete in which I have ever met you. Remain so and do not make me nervous by suddenly changing into something entirely different."

Apparently Voltumna's self-esteem was flattered by the admiration of the brilliant goddess, although he well knew that in his mutability he was the supreme god since he created all that existed and lived on earth while the other gods merely affected in their own ways that which he created. Seeing that, I understood at last the vanity and rivalry of the gods and why they could be persuaded and bribed with promises and offerings.

As the thought formed in my mind I suddenly felt the warning pressure of slender fingers of fire on my shoulder. Turning, I saw to my amazement that my guardian spirit's winged being of light was sitting behind me on the edge of the couch. For the second time in my life she appeared to me and without a word I knew that now I must take more care than ever before. Seeing her I knew in my heart that I had longed for her more than for anything on earth. I felt her living nearness as though molten metal were surging through my body.

When I looked around I saw that both the other Lucumones' guardian spirits had also appeared to shield them with their radiant wings. The spirits looked at one another inquisitively as though comparing one another, and their wings quivered. But in my eyes my guardian spirit was the fairest.

Voltumna extended a beckoning hand and said accusingly, "Alas, you Lucumones, what cautious hosts you are in calling your spirits to protect you. What do you fear?"

The goddess Turan likewise said, "You insult me as a goddess and offend me by preferring to loll on the couches with your guardian spirits rather than with me. You yourselves invited me and not I you. You at least, Turms, must send away your guardian spirit immediately. Perhaps I shall descend for a moment and lay my hand on your neck."

The wings of my guardian spirit quivered with rage for she was very hot-tempered. The goddess Turan looked at her critically as a woman looks at another woman and remarked, "Undoubtedly she is fair, your winged creature, but surely she cannot compete with me. After all, I am a goddess and as eternal as the earth. She is only an immortal like you."

I was distressed, but as I looked at the radiant face of my guardian spirit I felt much closer to her than to the goddess. "I cannot send her away since she arrived uninvited," I said quickly. A sudden perception made my voice tremble. "Perhaps someone even higher than you has sent her."

I could not continue, for at that very moment a motionless being taller than mortals or gods took shape in the middle of the tent. A cold mantle of light covered him and bands of cloth circled his face so that it was invisible. He was he whom even the gods do not know—he whose names and numbers no one knows, neither humans nor earth-bound gods. When I saw his motionless form both the earth gods faded to shadows and my guardian spirit covered me with her wings as though to indicate that we were one, she and I. Then I tasted metal in my mouth as though I were already dead, a storm roared in my ears, I smelled the odor of ice in my nostrils and fire blinded my eyes.

I awakened to consciousness on my low couch. The torches had gone out, wine had splashed onto the wooden floor of the tent, grain had dropped from the sheaves, crushed fruit lay on the floor. Both the cones rose whitely from their cushions on the gods' high couch and I realized that they were lighted by the gray dawn that shone through the cracks. But the wreaths around them were faded and black as though scorched. I myself seemed as faded and scorched as though I had lost years of my life during that single night. My limbs were numb and stiff with cold.

We awakened, I think, at the same time and sat up holding our heads. Finally we looked at one another.

"Did I dream?" I asked.

The old Lucumo of Volsinii shook his head. "No. If it was a dream, we all had the same dream."

The Volterran Lucumo said, "We saw the veiled god. How can we still be alive?"

"It means the changing of an era," the old Lucumo surmised. "The former is ending and a new begins. The veiled god has never before appeared during a feast of the gods. But as Lucumones we recognized him. Perhaps we are the last Lucumones and that is why he came."

The Volterran Lucumo lifted the curtain and peered out. "The sky is cloudy," he said. "It is a raw morning."

The servants came immediately, bringing us a steaming morning drink of hot milk and honey. I drank greedily and the drink warmed my body and made me feel better. They brought us water so that we might wash our faces, hands and feet. I noticed that my shirt was smeared and that my nose had bled. My belly smarted as though I had eaten deadly poison.

376

The old Lucumo came to me. "You have shared a feast of the gods, Turms; you have drunk the wine of immortality. You are no longer your former self. Soon you will realize that nothing is the same. Now do you recognize and acknowledge yourself, Turms, the son of Porsenna, the son of Larkhna?"

"Not so," I said quietly. "The earth is my mother, the heavens my father. The sun is my brother, the moon my sister. I acknowledge myself. I was born a Lucumo among humans. I am Turms the immortal. I acknowledge that I have returned and that I shall return again. But why, I do not yet know."

"Remove your soiled shirt as you will some day remove your earthly body like a worn garment. Step out of the tent of the gods as naked as when you were born into a human body. Kiss your mother. Raise your face to your father. We greet you, you Lucumo, you immortal."

They drew aside the curtains. Beneath a gray cloudy sky I saw the silent faces of the people. A gust of wind blew in my face and the curtains fluttered as I doffed my shirt and stepped out of the tent. I knelt to kiss the ground and as I did so the clouds were rent and the sun burst upon me with warm rays. Had I still doubted I could have done so no longer. My father, the heavens, recognized me as his son. My brother, the sun, embraced me with gentle rays. A miracle had happened.

Stronger than the roar of the storm the cry burst forth from the crowd, "The Lucumo, the Lucumo has come!" The people waved their garments and shouted again and again. The other two Lucumones, my guides along the path, stepped out of the tent and spread the holy mantle of a Lucumo on my shoulders. With the mantle blessed peace and joy enfolded me and melted my heart. I was no longer empty, no longer naked, no longer cold.

4.

Nor have I anything else to relate. Pebble by pebble I have held my life in my hands and dropped the pebbles back into the simplest black vessel that stands before the image of the goddess. In them I will recognize myself, from them I will remember myself when I return and as a stranger descend the steps of the tomb and pluck the stones into my hand. Perhaps the cheap vessel will be broken. Perhaps the dust of centuries will have covered the floor of my tomb. Perhaps the sarcophagus with its beautiful sculpted images will have disappeared and my body become dust among dust. But the pebbles will remain. Who will read them?

Thus I know that I shall recognize myself as I stoop to pick the smooth pebbles from the dust of centuries. I shall ascend the narrow stairs back to the light of earth. With living eyes I shall see the lovely cone of the goddess's mountain across the valley from my tomb. I shall know and remember myself. And then the storm will rage.

So I believe, I, Turms the immortal. Although this that I have written may disappear, though the ink may fade, the papyrus decay and the languages in which I have written be no longer understood, by writing I have bound to every pebble of my life that which I wish to remember.

My hands are trembling, my breath is beginning to rattle. The ten years are ended and finally the moment of my death is near when I may be liberated from my body of clay. But my people thrive, the cattle have increased, the fields have borne harvests and mothers have given birth to healthy children. I have taught them to live correctly even after I am gone.

If they asked me for omens I said, "For that there are augurs, haruspices and lightning priests. Believe them. Disturb me not with trifling matters."

I let the council enact the laws and the people ratify them; the judges judged and the officials carried out just sentences. I merely warned them, "The law must protect the weak against the strong. The strong do not need protection."

But as I spoke I remembered Hanna, who had loved me, and my child as yet unborn whom she had taken with her. They were weak and I could not protect them. As soon as possible I had sought them from the ends of the land and even in Phoenicia. But no trace of them could be found.

I felt the ache of guilt and prayed, "You supreme being above the earth gods, you who cover your face, you immovable, only you have the power to erase my crime. You can call back time, you can raise the dead from the bottom of the sea. Make amends for my cruel deed and give me peace. Although I tire of this body's prison I promise to redeem the allotted ten years from the earth gods for the good of my people. But let nothing bad have happened to Hanna and the child because of my cowardice."

I did not make an offering. How could one sacrifice to the veiled gods whose names and numbers no one knew? I merely prayed. I, a Lucumo, through whom blessings flowed on my people, could not help myself.

And then a miracle occurred. When I had lived among my people as a Lucumo for many years, two simple wayfarers sought me. Unexpectedly, without omens, they arrived. I saw Hanna and recognized her immediately although she bowed her head humbly before me as did her husband. She had grown into a beautiful country woman in the prime of life. But her eyes were sad when she raised her face to look at me.

Her husband's face was kind and open. They had wandered far for my sake and now held hands tightly in fear.

"Lucumo Turms," they said, "we are poor people but we had to come before you to ask a great gift."

Hanna related how she had jumped into the sea one night from the Phoenician slave ship near Greek Poseidonia to escape the fate that Arsinoe had planned for her. But the waves had carried her gently to shore where she had met a friendly shepherd. He had concealed her and protected her and after the birth of my son he had cared for the boy as well. In time she had realized that she loved him.

"Good fortune came to us with the boy," said Hanna, "and we have our little house, our fields and vineyards and also cattle. But we have had no other children, so that we still have only your son, Turms."

The man looked at me pleadingly. "The boy believes me to be his father, thrives with us and loves the land. He has learned to play the pipes and to compose songs. He has not an unkind thought. But we have grieved because of him, not knowing what to do. Finally we had to come here before you. Do you demand your son or will you permit us to keep him?"

Hanna said, "You are a Lucumo. You know better than we what would give the boy happiness."

With a quivering heart I asked, "Where is he, your son?"

I followed them outside and saw a curly-haired youth playing the pipes on the edge of the market place. So beautifully did he play that people had gathered to listen. His skin was burned brown and his eyes were large and dreamy. He started when he saw me and stared suspiciously, afraid that I had harmed his parents. He was barefooted and wore only a home-loomed country garment. He was fair, so fair. They three belonged together. My prayer had been answered.

I looked at my son to implant his features in my heart for all time. Then I returned to the solitude of my house. I thanked Hanna and the man for coming, gave them gifts and acknowledged the boy to be their son. I asked them to turn to me if they should ever be in need, but they never did. And I sent them simple gifts until they moved from the path of the Greeks without leaving word where they had gone. Hanna understood. That was best, both for her and the boy.

Since then I have lived for the good of my people. For them it suffices that I live among them as a Lucumo.

I did not permit them to war, not even against the Romans. Nor would

I allow them to join in Lars Arnth's war. Only after Misme's scoldings made me weak did I permit those desirous of going to war to do so. It happened six years after Himera. But the bottom had dropped off and the vessel was broken. At sea off Cumae our fleet suffered the greatest defeat ever suffered by Tyrrhenian vessels. The sea is no longer ours. Greeks are founding colonies on the islands of our sea. Instead of ships, we have begun to build walls to defend our cities. The wealth of generations has been spent on them now that the Greeks have destroyed our trade. And every year the Romans grow bolder, more insolent and more intolerable.

When I heard of our people's defeat in the sea battles off Cumae I did not show myself to my people until I had marked the site of my tomb. As a Lucumo I had transgressed in permitting participation in the war. For ten years I have not shown myself to my people. They have been long years, but my people have done well and by writing I have made the time pass. Now the years have finally ended.

And the Etruscan people still live, the inland cities still prosper, and the Veian potters, the Tarquinian painters and my own city's sculptors still vie with one another in perpetuating humans and gods. My own image lies ready within the mountain on the lid of the alabaster sarcophagus with a sacrificial cup in its hand and a garland around its neck. I would rather rest on a stone bed surrounded by wall paintings and my people's gifts. I could not, however, hurt my sculptors because their art preserves a person as he has lived. In the work of its artists my people and city will live even after its death. I am proud of my people, proud of my city.

But I am weary of my body's prison and the new day will be the glorious day of liberation. The tent of the gods has been erected before the tombs on the holy mountain. The holy stone cones have been lifted onto the double cushions of the gods' couch. In the air is the smell of autumn, the taste of fresh flour and wine. The water birds are flocking. Women are singing as they turn the grindstones to bake the cakes of the gods of new flour.

This much yet must I endure. With my hands, arms and face painted red, with the holy mantle of the Lucumo on my shoulders and an ivy wreath on my head, I will be carried on the gods' litter to my deathbed in the tent of the gods. As the beads of death spring to my forehead, as the black hem of death flutters before my eyes, I must watch the dances of the gods and partake of the feast of the gods before my people's eyes. Only then will the curtains be closed. I will remain alone to meet the gods and to drink the wine of immortality.

For the last time I will taste life in the barley cake baked in ashes, in the wine mixed with fresh water. Then the gods may come. But more than for them I long for my guardian spirit. As a body of light, a body of fire, she will spread her wings over me and kiss the breath from my mouth. At that moment she will at last whisper her name in my ear and I will recognize her.

Because of that I know that I will die happy, as ardent as a youth upon finally enfolding her in my embrace and recognizing her. Her powerful wings will carry me to immortality. Then I will have my rest and oblivion. Blessed, blessed oblivion. For one hundred years or one thousand, I care not. Then some day I, Turms the immortal, will return.

Massilia

Fiesole Clusium

Populonia

Tarquinia Veii
Caere Rome

Kyme

Sybaris
Crotone

Panormos Himera

Rhegion

Eryx Messina
Segesta Syracuse
Akragas

Carthage